PENGUIN BOOKS

Assassin's Creed

Assassin's Creed
Renaissance

OLIVER BOWDEN

PENGUIN BOOKS

PENGUIN BOOKS

Published by the Penguin Group
Penguin Books Ltd, 80 Strand, London WC2R ORL, England
Penguin Group (USA) Inc., 375 Hudson Street, New York, New York 10014, USA
Penguin Group (Canada), 90 Eglinton Avenue East, Suite 700, Toronto, Ontario, Canada MP4 2Y3
(a division of Pearson Penguin Canada Inc.)
Penguin Ireland, 25 St Stephen's Green, Dublin 2, Ireland (a division of Penguin Books Ltd)
Penguin Group (Australia), 250 Camberwell Road, Camberwell, Victoria 3124, Australia
(a division of Pearson Australia Group Pty Ltd)
Penguin Books India Pvt Ltd, 11 Community Centre, Panchsheel Park, New Delhi – 110 017, India
Penguin Group (NZ), 67 Apollo Drive, Rosedale, North Shore 0632, New Zealand
(a division of Pearson New Zealand Ltd)
Penguin Books (South Africa) (Pty) Ltd, 24 Sturdee Avenue, Rosebank,
Johannesburg 2196, South Africa

Penguin Books Ltd, Registered Offices: 80 Strand, London WC2R ORL, England

www.penguin.com

First published 2009
18

'Sonnet of Lorenzo' translated by De' Lucchi, Lorna, 1967 (1922). *An Anthology of Italian Poems*,
New York, Biblio and Tannen.

Every effort has been made to contact copyright holders. The publishers will be glad
to correct any errors or omissions in future editions.

Set in Garamond MT 12.75/15.25pt by Palimpsest Book Production Limited,
Grangemouth, Stirlingshire
Printed in England by Clays Ltd, St Ives plc

ISBN: 978-0-141-04630-3

www.greenpenguin.co.uk

Penguin Books is committed to a sustainable future
for our business, our readers and our planet.
The book in your hands is made from paper
certified by the Forest Stewardship Council.

While I thought that I was learning how to live,
I have been learning how to die.
– Leonardo da Vinci

Renaissance Italy

N

Milan
●

**Duchy of
Milan**

Pordenone
●

Venice
●

Padua ●

R e p u b l i c   o f   V e n i c e

Rep. of Genoa

Ravenna ●
Forlì ●

● Florence

● Siena

Papal

● Ancona

Adriatic Sea

Corsica

States

● Rome

**Kingdom of
Sardinia**

Tyrrhenian Sea

Naples ●

**Kingdom
of
Naples**

**Duchy of
Modena**

**Papal
States**

Ravenna ●

● Forlì

Lucca
●

CaREGGi
● Florence

Rep. of Florence

San Gimignano ●

Volterra
●

● Monteriggioni
● Siena
● Monticiano

**Rep. of
Siena**

**Papal
States**

**Kingdom of
Sicily**

0   100 miles

0   150 km

I

Torches gleamed and flickered high on the towers of the Palazzo Vecchio and the Bargello, and just a few lanterns shimmered in the cathedral square a little way to the north. Some also illuminated the quays along the banks of the River Arno, where, late as it was for a city where most people retired indoors with the coming of night, a few sailors and stevedores could be seen through the gloom. Some of the sailors, still attending to their ships and boats, hastened to make final repairs to rigging and to coil rope neatly on the dark, scrubbed decks, while the stevedores hurried to haul or carry cargo to the safety of the nearby warehouses.

Lights also glimmered in the winehouses and the brothels, but very few people walked the streets. It had been seven years since the then twenty-year-old Lorenzo de' Medici had been elected to the leadership of the city, bringing with him at least a sense of order and calm to the intense rivalry between the leading international banking and merchant families who had made Florence one of the wealthiest cities in the world. Despite this, the city had never ceased to simmer, and occasionally boil over, as each faction strove for control, some of them shifting alliances, some remaining permanent and implacable enemies.

Florence, in the Year of Our Lord 1476, even on a jasmine-sweet evening in spring, when you could almost forget the stench from the Arno if the wind was in the right direction, wasn't the safest place to be out in the open, after the sun had gone down.

The moon had risen in a now-cobalt sky, lording it over a host of attendant stars. Its light fell on the open square where the Ponte Vecchio, its crowded shops dark and silent now, joined the north bank of the river. Its light also found out a figure clad in black, standing on the roof of the church of Santo Stefano al Ponte. A young man, only seventeen years old, but tall and proud. Surveying the neighbourhood below keenly, he put a hand to his lips and whistled, a low but penetrating sound. In response, as he watched, first one, then three, then a dozen, and at last twenty men, young like himself, most clad in black, some with blood-red, green or azure cowls or hats, all with swords and daggers at their belts, emerged from dark streets and archways into the square. The gang of dangerous-looking youths fanned out, a cocky assuredness in their movements.

The young man looked down at the eager faces, pale in the moonlight, gazing up at him. He raised his fist above his head in a defiant salute.

'We stand together!' he cried, as they too raised their

fists, some drawing their weapons and brandishing them, and cheered: 'Together!'

The young man quickly climbed, catlike, down the unfinished façade from the roof to the church's portico, and from it leapt, cloak flying, to land in a crouch, safely in their midst. They gathered round, expectantly.

'Silence, my friends!' He held up a hand to arrest a last, lone shout. He smiled grimly. 'Do you know why I called you, my closest allies, here tonight? To ask your aid. For too long I have been silent while our enemy, you know who I mean, Vieri de' Pazzi, has gone about this town slandering my family, dragging our name in the mud, and trying in his pathetic way to demean us. Normally I would not stoop to kicking such a mangy cur, but –'

He was interrupted as a large, jagged rock, hurled from the direction of the bridge, landed at his feet.

'Enough of your nonsense, *grullo*,' a voice called.

The young man turned as one with his group in the direction of the voice. Already he knew who it belonged to. Crossing the bridge from the south side another gang of young men was approaching. Its leader swaggered at its head, a red cloak, held by a clasp bearing a device of golden dolphins and crosses on a blue ground, over his dark velvet suit, his hand on the pommel of his sword. He was a passably handsome man, his looks marred by a cruel mouth and a weak chin, and though he was a little fat, there was no doubting the power in his arms and legs.

3

'*Buona sera*, Vieri,' the young man said evenly. 'We were just talking about you.' And he bowed with exaggerated courtesy, while assuming a look of surprise. 'But you must forgive me. We were not expecting you personally. I thought the Pazzi always hired others to do their dirty work.'

Vieri, coming close, drew himself up as he and his troop came to a halt a few yards away. 'Ezio Auditore! You pampered little whelp! I'd say it was rather your family of penpushers and accountants that goes running to the guards whenever there's the faintest sign of trouble. *Codardo!*' He gripped the hilt of his sword. 'Afraid to handle things yourself, I'd say.'

'Well, what can I say, Vieri, *ciccione*. Last time I saw her, your sister Viola seemed quite satisfied with the handling I gave *her*.' Ezio Auditore gave his enemy a broad grin, content to hear his companions snigger and cheer behind him.

But he knew he'd gone too far. Vieri had already turned purple with rage. 'That's quite enough from you, Ezio, you little prick! Let's see if you fight as well as you gabble!' He turned his head back to his men, raising his sword. 'Kill the bastards!' he bellowed.

At once another rock whirled through the air, but this time it wasn't thrown as a challenge. It caught Ezio a glancing blow on the forehead, breaking the skin and drawing blood. Ezio staggered back momentarily, as a hail of rocks flew from the hands of Vieri's followers.

His own men barely had time to rally before the Pazzi gang was upon them, rushing over the bridge to Ezio and his men. All at once, the fighting was so close and so fast that there was hardly time at first to draw swords or even daggers, so the two gangs just went at each other with their fists.

The battle was hard and grim – brutal kicks and punches connected with the sickening sound of crunching bone. For a while it could have gone either way, then Ezio, his vision slightly impaired by the flow of blood from his forehead, saw two of his best men stumble and go down, to be trampled on by Pazzi thugs. Vieri laughed, and, close to Ezio, swung another blow at his head, his hand grasping a heavy stone. Ezio dropped to his haunches and the blow went wide, but it had been too close for comfort, and now the Auditore faction was getting the worst of it. Ezio did manage, before he could rise to his feet, to wrestle his dagger free and slice wildly but successfully at the thigh of a heavily built Pazzi thug who was bearing down at him with sword and dagger unsheathed. Ezio's dagger tore through fabric and into muscle and sinew, and the man let loose an agonized howl and went over, dropping his weapons and clutching at his wound with both hands as the blood belched forth.

Scrambling desperately to his feet, Ezio looked round. He could see that the Pazzi had all but surrounded his own men, penning them in against one wall of the church. Feeling some of the strength returning to his legs, he made his way towards his fellows. Ducking under the scything blade of another Pazzi henchman, he managed to connect his fist to the man's stubbly jaw and had the satisfaction of seeing teeth fly and his would-be assailant fall to his knees, stunned by the blow. He yelled to his own men to encourage them, but in truth his thoughts were turning to ways of beating a retreat with as much dignity as possible, when above the noise of the fight he heard a loud, jovial and very familiar voice calling to him from behind the Pazzi mob.

'Hey, *fratellino*, what the hell are you up to?'

Ezio's heart pounded with relief, and he managed to gasp, 'Hey, Federico! What are you doing here? I thought you'd be out on the tiles as usual!'

'Nonsense! I knew you had something planned, and I thought I'd come along to see if my little brother had finally learned how to look after himself. But maybe you need another lesson or two!'

Federico Auditore, a few years Ezio's senior and the oldest of the Auditore siblings, was a big man with a big appetite – for drink, for love and for battle. He waded in even as he was speaking, knocking two Pazzi heads together and bringing his foot up to connect with the jaw of a third as he strode through the throng to stand side by side with his brother, seeming impervious to the violence that surrounded him. Around them their own men, encouraged, redoubled their efforts. The

Pazzi on the other hand were discomfited. A few of the dockyard hands had gathered at a safe distance to watch, and in the half-light the Pazzi mistook them for Auditore reinforcements. That and Federico's roars and flying fists, his actions quickly emulated by Ezio, who learnt fast, very quickly panicked them.

Vieri de' Pazzi's furious voice rose above the general tumult. 'Fall back!' he called to his men, his voice broken with exertion and anger. He caught Ezio's eye and snarled some inaudible threat before disappearing into the darkness, back across the Ponte Vecchio, followed by those of his men who could still walk, and hotly pursued by Ezio's now triumphant allies.

Ezio was about to follow suit, but his brother's meaty hand restrained him. 'Just a minute,' he said.

'What do you mean? We've got them on the run!'

'Steady on.' Federico was frowning, gently touching the wound on Ezio's brow.

'It's just a scratch.'

'It's more than that,' his brother decided, a grave expression on his face. 'We'd better get you to a doctor.'

Ezio spat. 'I haven't got time to waste running to doctors. Besides . . .' He paused ruefully. 'I haven't any money.'

'Hah! Wasted it on women and wine, I suppose.' Federico grinned, and slapped his younger brother warmly on the shoulder.

'Not wasted exactly, I'd say. And look at the example

7

you set me.' Ezio grinned but then hesitated. He suddenly became aware that his head was thumping. 'Still, it wouldn't hurt to get it checked out. I suppose you couldn't see your way to lending me a few *fiorini*?'

Federico patted his purse. It didn't jingle. 'Fact is, I'm a bit short myself just now,' he said.

Ezio grinned at his brother's sheepishness. 'And what have you wasted yours on? Masses and Indulgences, I suppose?'

Federico laughed. 'All right. I take your point.' He looked around. In the end, only three or four of their own people had been hurt badly enough to remain on the field of battle, and they were sitting up, groaning a bit, but grinning too. It had been a tough set-to, but no one had broken any bones. On the other hand, a good half-dozen Pazzi henchmen lay completely out for the count, and one or two of them at least were expensively dressed.

'Let's see if our fallen enemies have any riches to share,' Federico suggested. 'After all, our need is greater than theirs, and I'll bet you can't lighten their load without waking them up!'

'We'll see about that,' said Ezio, and set about it with some success. Before a few minutes had elapsed, he'd harvested enough gold coins to fill both their own purses. Ezio looked over to his brother triumphantly and jingled his newly claimed wealth to emphasize the point.

'Enough!' cried Federico. 'Better leave them a bit to

limp home on. After all, we're not thieves – this is just the spoils of war. And I still don't like the look of that wound. We must get it seen to double quick.'

Ezio nodded, and turned to survey the field of the Auditore victory one last time. Losing patience, Federico rested a hand on his younger brother's shoulder. 'Come on,' he said, and without more ado he set off at such a pace that the battle-weary Ezio found it hard to keep up, though when he fell too far behind, or took a wrong turn down an alley, Federico would hold up, or hurry back to put him right. 'I'm sorry, Ezio. I just want us to get to the *medico* as soon as we can.'

And indeed it wasn't far, but Ezio was tiring by the minute. Finally they reached the shadowy room, festooned with mysterious instruments and phials of brass and glass, ranged along dark oak tables and hanging from the ceiling along with clusters of dried herbs, where their family doctor had his surgery. It was all Ezio could do to remain on his feet.

Dottore Ceresa was not best pleased at being roused in the middle of the night, but his manner changed to one of concern as soon as he had brought a candle close enough to inspect Ezio's wound in detail. 'Hmmn,' he said gravely. 'You've made quite a mess of yourself this time, young man. Can't you people think of anything better to do than go around beating each other up?'

'It was a question of honour, good doctor,' put in Federico.

'I see,' said the doctor, evenly.

'It's really nothing,' said Ezio, though he felt faint.

Federico, as usual hiding concern behind humour, said, 'Do patch him up as best you can, friend. That pretty little face of his is his only asset.'

'Hey, *fottiti*!' Ezio hit back, giving his brother the finger.

The doctor ignored them, washed his hands, probed the wound gently, and poured some clear fluid from one of his many bottles on to a piece of linen. He dabbed the wound with this and it stung so much that Ezio almost sprang from his chair, his face screwed up with the pain. Then, satisfied that the wound was clean, the doctor took a needle and threaded it with fine catgut.

'Now,' he said. 'This really will hurt, a little.'

Once the stitches were in and the wound bandaged so that Ezio looked like a turbaned Turk, the doctor smiled encouragement. 'That'll be three *fiorini*, for now. I'll come to your palazzo in a few days and remove the stitches. That'll be another three *fiorini* to pay then. You'll have a terrible headache, but it'll pass. Just try to rest – if it's in your nature! And don't worry: the wound looks worse than it is, and there's even a bonus: there shouldn't be much of a scar, so you won't be disappointing the ladies too greatly in future!'

Once they were back in the street, Federico put his arm round his younger brother. He pulled out a flask and offered it to Ezio. 'Don't worry,' he said, noticing the expression on Ezio's face. 'It's our father's best grappa. Better than mother's milk for a man in your condition.'

They both drank, feeling the fiery liquid warm them. 'Quite a night,' said Federico.

'Indeed. I only wish they were all as much fun as –' but Ezio interrupted himself as he saw that his brother was beginning to grin from ear to ear. 'Oh, wait!' he corrected himself, laughing: 'They are!'

'Even so, I think a little food and drink wouldn't be a bad thing to set you up before we go home,' said Federico. 'It's late, I know, but there's a taverna nearby where they don't close until breakfast time and –'

'– you and the *oste* are *amici intimi*?'

'How did you guess?'

An hour or so later, after a meal of *ribollita* and *bistecca* washed down with a bottle of Brunello, Ezio felt as if he'd never been wounded at all. He was young and fit, and felt that all his lost energy had flowed back into him. The adrenaline of the victory over the Pazzi mob certainly contributed to the swiftness of his recovery.

'Time to go home, little brother,' said Federico. 'Father's sure to be wondering where we are, and you're the one he looks to to help him with the bank. Luckily for me, I've no head for figures, which is why I suppose he can't wait to get me into politics!'

'Politics or the circus – the way you carry on.'

'What's the difference?'

Ezio knew that Federico bore him no ill will over the fact that their father confided more of the family business in him than in his elder brother. Federico would die of boredom if confronted by a life in banking. The problem was, Ezio had a feeling that he might be the same. But for the moment, the day when he donned the black velvet suit and the gold chain of a Florentine banker was still some way off, and he was determined to enjoy his days of freedom and irresponsibility to the full. Little did he realize just how short-lived those days would be.

'We'd better hurry, too,' Federico was saying, 'if we want to avoid a bollocking.'

'He may be worried.'

'No – he knows we can take care of ourselves.' Federico was looking at Ezio speculatively. 'But we *had* better get a move on.' He paused. 'You don't feel up to a little wager at all, do you? A race perhaps?'

'Where to?'

'Let's say,' Federico looked across the moonlit city towards a tower not far away. 'The roof of Santa Trinità. If it's not going to take too much out of you – and it's not far from home. But there's just one thing more.'

'Yes?'

'We're not racing along the streets, but across the rooftops.'

Ezio took a deep breath. 'OK. Try me,' he said.

'All right, little *tartaruga* – go!'

Without another word, Federico was off, scaling a nearby roughcast wall as easily as a lizard would. He paused at the top, seeming almost to teeter among the rounded red tiles, laughed, and was off again. By the time Ezio had reached the rooftops, his brother was twenty yards ahead. He set off in pursuit, his pain forgotten in the adrenaline-fuelled excitement of the chase. Then he saw Federico take an almighty leap across a pitch-black void, to land lightly on the flat roof of a grey palazzo slightly below the level of the one he had jumped from. He ran a little way further, and waited. Ezio felt a glimmer of fear as the chasm of the street eight storeys below loomed before him, but he knew that he would die rather than hesitate in front of his brother, and so, summoning up his courage, he took a massive leap of faith, seeing, as he soared across, the hard granite cobbles in the moonlight far beneath his feet as they flailed the air. For a split second he wondered if he'd judged it right, as the hard grey wall of the palazzo seemed to rise up to meet him, but then, some-how, it sank below him and he was on the new roof, sprawling slightly it was true, but still on his feet, and elated, though breathing hard.

'Baby brother still has much to learn,' taunted Feder-ico, setting off again, a darting shadow among the chimney-stacks under the scattering of clouds. Ezio hurled himself forward, lost in the wildness of the moment. Other abysses yawned beneath him, some defining mere alleyways, others broad thoroughfares. Federico was nowhere to be seen. Suddenly the tower of Santa Trinità rose before him, rising from the red sweep of the church's gently sloping roof. But as he approached he remembered that the church stood in the centre of a square, and that the distance between its roof and those of the surrounding buildings was far greater than any he had yet leapt. He dared not hesitate or lose speed now – his only hope was that the church roof was lower than the one he would have to jump from. If he could throw himself forward with enough force, and truly launch himself into the air, gravity would do the rest. For one or two seconds he would fly like a bird. He forced any thought of the consequences of failure out of his mind.

The edge of the roof he was on approached fast, and then – nothing. He soared, listening to the air whistle in his ears, bringing tears into his eyes. The church roof seemed an infinite distance away – he would never reach it, he would never laugh or fight or hold a woman in his arms again. He couldn't breathe. He shut his eyes, and then . . .

His body bent double, he was steadying himself with his hands and feet, but they were supported again – he had made it, within inches of the edge, but he had made it on to the church roof!

But where was Federico? He clambered up to the base of the tower and turned to look back the way he had come, just in time to see his brother flying through the air himself. Federico landed firmly, but his weight sent one or two of the red clay tiles slithering out of place and he almost lost his footing as the tiles slid down the roof and off the edge, shattering a few seconds later on the hard cobbles far below. But Federico had found his balance again, and he stood up, panting for sure, but with a broad, proud smile on his face.

'Not such a *tartaruga* after all,' he said, as he came up and clapped Ezio on the shoulder. 'You went past me like greased lightning.'

'I didn't even know that I had,' said Ezio briefly, trying to catch his breath.

'Well, you won't beat me up to the top of the tower,' retorted Federico, pushing Ezio to the side, and he started to clamber up the squat tower which the city fathers were thinking of replacing with something of a more modern design. This time Federico made it first, and even had to give a hand up to his wounded brother, who was beginning to feel that bed would be no bad thing. They were both out of breath, and stood while they recovered to look out over their city, serene and silent in the oyster-light of dawn.

'It is a good life we lead, brother,' said Federico with uncharacteristic solemnity.

'The best,' Ezio agreed. 'And may it never change.'

They both paused – neither wishing to break the perfection of the moment – but after a while Federico quietly spoke. 'May it never change us either, *fratellino*. Come, we must get back. There is the roof of our palazzo. Pray God Father hasn't stayed up all night, or we really will be for it. Let's go.'

He made for the edge of the tower in order to climb back down to the roof, but stopped when he saw that Ezio had remained where he was. 'What is it?'

'Wait a minute.'

'What are you looking at?' asked Federico, rejoining him. He followed Ezio's gaze and then his face broke out into a grin. 'You sly devil! You're not thinking of going there now, are you? Let the poor girl sleep!'

'No – I think it's time Cristina woke up.'

Ezio had met Cristina Calfucci only a short time before, but already they seemed inseparable, despite the fact that their parents still deemed them too young to form a serious alliance. Ezio disagreed, but Cristina was only seventeen and her parents expected Ezio to rein in his wild habits before they would even begin to look more kindly on him. Of course, this only served to make him more impetuous.

Federico and he had been lounging in the main market after buying some trinkets for their sister's Saint's Day, watching the pretty girls of the town with their *accompagnatrice* as they flitted from stall to stall, examining lace here, ribbons and bolts of silk there. But one girl had stood out from her companions, more beautiful and graceful than anyone Ezio had ever seen before. Ezio would never forget that day, the day on which he had first set eyes on her.

'Oh,' he had gasped involuntarily. 'Look! She's so beautiful.'

'Well,' said his ever-practical brother. 'Why don't you go over and say hello?'

'What?' Ezio was shocked. 'And after I've said hello – what then?'

'Well, you could try talking to her. What you've bought, what she's bought – it doesn't matter. You see, little brother, most men are so afraid of beautiful girls that anyone who actually plucks up the courage to have a chat stands at an immediate advantage. What? You think they don't *want* to be noticed, they don't *want* to enjoy a little conversation with a man? Of course they do! Anyway, you're not bad-looking, and you *are* an Auditore. So go for it – and I'll distract the chaperone. Come to think of it, she's not so bad-looking herself.'

Ezio remembered how, left alone with Cristina, rooted to the spot, at a loss for words, drinking in the beauty of her dark eyes, her long, soft auburn hair, her tip-tilted nose . . .

She stared at him. 'What is it?' she asked.

'What d'you mean?' he blurted out.

'Why are you just standing there?'

'Oh . . . erhm . . . because I wanted to ask you something.'

'And what might that be?'

'What's your name?'

She rolled her eyes. Damn, he thought, she's heard it all before. 'Not one you'll ever need to make use of,' she said. And off she went. Ezio stared after her for a moment, then set off after her.

'Wait!' he said, catching up, more breathless than if he'd run a mile. 'I wasn't ready. I was planning on being really charming. And suave! And witty! Won't you give me a second chance?'

She looked back at him without breaking her stride, but she did give him the faintest trace of a smile. Ezio had been in despair, but Federico had been watching and called to him softly: 'Don't give up now! I saw her smile at you! She'll remember you.'

Taking heart, Ezio had followed her — discreetly, taking care she wouldn't notice. Three or four times he had to dart behind a market stall, or, after she had left the square, duck into a doorway, but he'd managed to tail her pretty successfully right up to the door of her family mansion, where a man he recognized had blocked her path. Ezio had drawn back.

Cristina looked at the man angrily. 'I've told you before, Vieri, I'm not interested in you. Now, let me pass.'

Ezio, concealed, drew in a breath. Vieri de' Pazzi! Of course!

'But *signorina*, I am interested. Very interested indeed,' said Vieri.

'Then join the queue.'

She tried to get past him, but he moved in front of her. 'I don't think so, *amore mio*. I've decided that I'm tired of waiting for you to open your legs of your own volition.' And he seized her roughly by the arm, drawing her close, putting his other arm round her as she struggled to get free.

'I'm not sure you're getting the message,' said Ezio suddenly, stepping forward and looking Vieri in the eye.

'Ah, the little Auditore whelp. *Cane rognoso!* What the hell do you have to do with this? To the devil with you.'

'And *buon' giorno* to you too, Vieri. I'm so sorry to intrude, but I have the distinct impression that you're spoiling this young lady's day.'

'Oh, you do, do you? Excuse me, my dearest, while I kick the stuffing out of this parvenu.' With that, Vieri had thrust Cristina aside and lunged at Ezio with his right fist. Ezio parried easily and stepped aside, tripping Vieri as the momentum of his attack carried him forward, sending him sprawling in the dust.

'Had enough, friend?' said Ezio mockingly. But Vieri was on his feet in an instant, and came towards him in a rage, fists flailing. He'd got one hard blow in to the side of Ezio's jaw, but Ezio warded off a left hook and got two of his own in, one to the stomach and, as Vieri bent double, another to his jaw. Ezio had turned to Cristina to check that she was all right. Winded, Vieri backed off, but his hand flew to his dagger. Cristina saw the movement and gave an involuntary cry of alarm as Vieri brought the dagger plunging down towards Ezio's back, but, warned by the cry, Ezio had turned in the nick of time and seized Vieri firmly by the wrist, wrenching the dagger away from him. It fell to the ground. The two young men stood face to face, breathing hard.

'Is that the best you can do?' Ezio said through gritted teeth.

'Shut your mouth or by God I'll kill you!'

Ezio laughed. 'I suppose I shouldn't be surprised to see you trying to force yourself on a nice girl who clearly thinks you're a complete ball of dung – given the way your pappa tries to force his banking interests on Florence!'

'You fool! It's your father who needs to be taught a lesson in humility!'

'It's time you Pazzi stopped slandering us. But then, you're all mouth and no fist.'

Vieri's lip was bleeding badly. He wiped it with his sleeve. 'You'll pay for this – you and your whole breed. I won't forget this, Auditore!' He spat at Ezio's feet, stooped to retrieve his dagger, then turned, and ran. Ezio had watched him go.

He remembered all this, standing there on the church tower and looking across at Cristina's house. He remembered the elation he'd felt as he'd turned back to Cristina and seen a new warmth in her eyes as she'd thanked him.

'Are you all right, *signorina*?' he'd said.

'I am now – thanks to you.' She'd hesitated, her voice still trembling with fear. 'You asked me my name – well, it's Cristina. Cristina Calfucci.'

Ezio bowed. 'I am honoured to meet you, Signorina Cristina. Ezio Auditore.'

'Do you know that man?'

'Vieri? Our paths have crossed now and then. But our families have no reason to like one another.'

'I never want to see him again.'

'If I can help it, you won't.'

She smiled shyly, then said, 'Ezio, you have my gratitude – and because of that, I am prepared to give you a second chance, after your bad start!' She laughed gently, then kissed him on the cheek before disappearing into her mansion.

The small crowd that had inevitably gathered had given Ezio a round of applause. He had bowed, smilingly, but as he'd turned away he'd known that he might have made a new friend, but he had also made an implacable enemy.

'Let Cristina sleep,' Federico said again, drawing Ezio back from his reverie.

'Time enough for that – later,' he replied. 'I must see her.'

'All right, if you must – I'll try to cover for you with

Father. But watch yourself – Vieri's men may still be about.' With that, Federico shinned down the tower to the roof, and bounded off that into a hay-wagon parked in the street which led home.

Ezio watched him go, then decided to emulate his brother. The hay-wain looked very far below him, but he remembered what he'd been taught, controlled his breathing, calmed himself, and concentrated.

Then he flew into the air, taking the greatest leap of his life so far. For an instant he thought he might have misjudged his aim, but he calmed his own momentary panic and landed safely in the hay. A true leap of faith! A little breathless, but exhilarated at his success, Ezio swung himself into the street.

The sun was just appearing over the eastern hills but there were still very few people about. Ezio was just about to start off in the direction of Cristina's mansion when he heard echoing footsteps and, desperately trying to conceal himself, he shrank into the shadows of the church porch and held his breath. It was none other than Vieri and two of the Pazzi guards who rounded the corner.

'We'd better give up, chief,' said the senior guard. 'They've long gone by now.'

'I know they're here somewhere,' snapped Vieri. 'I can practically smell them.' He and his men made a circuit of the church square but showed no sign of moving on. The sunlight was shrinking the shadows.

Ezio cautiously crept into the shelter of the hay again and lay there for what seemed an age, impatient to be on his way. Once, Vieri passed so close that Ezio could practically smell *him*, but at last he motioned his men with an angry gesture to move on. Ezio lay still for a while longer, then climbed down and let out a long sigh of relief. He dusted himself off, and quickly covered the short distance that separated him from Cristina, praying that no one in her household would yet be stirring.

The mansion was still silent, though Ezio guessed that servants would be preparing the kitchen fires at the back. He knew which Cristina's window was, and threw a handful of gravel up at her shutters. The noise seemed deafening and he waited, heart in mouth. Then the shutters opened and she appeared on the balcony. Her nightdress revealed the delicious contours of her body as he gazed up at her. He was at once lost in desire.

'Who is it?' she called softly.

He stood back so she could see him. 'Me!'

Cristina sighed, though in a not unfriendly way. 'Ezio! I might have known.'

'May I come up, *mia colomba*?'

She glanced over her shoulder before answering in a whisper. 'All right. But just for a minute.'

'That's all I need.'

She grinned. 'Indeed?'

He was confused. 'No – sorry – I didn't mean it quite like that! Let me show you . . .' Looking round himself to make sure the street was still deserted, he gained a foothold in one of the large iron rings set into the grey stonework of the house for tethering horses, and hoisted himself up, finding relatively easy handholds and footholds in the rusticated masonry. In two winks of an eye he had hoisted himself over the balustrade and she was in his arms.

'Oh, Ezio!' she sighed as they kissed. 'Look at your head. What have you been doing this time?'

'It's nothing. A scratch.' Ezio paused, smiling. 'Perhaps now I'm up, I could also come in?' he said gently.

'Where?'

He was all innocence. 'To your bedchamber, of course.'

'Well, perhaps – if you're sure a minute is all you need . . .'

Their arms around each other, they went through the double doors into the warm light of Cristina's room.

An hour later, they were awakened by the sunlight streaming in through the windows, the bustling noises of carts and people in the street, and – worst of all – the sound of Cristina's father's voice as he opened the bedroom door.

'Cristina,' he was saying. 'Time to get up, girl! Your tutor will be here at any – What the devil? Son of a bitch!'

Ezio kissed Cristina, quickly but hard. 'Time to go, I think,' he said, seizing his clothes and darting to the window. He shinned down the wall and was already pulling on his suit when Antonio Calfucci appeared on the balcony above. He was in a white rage.

'*Perdonate, Messere*,' Ezio offered.

'I'll give you *perdonate, Messere*,' yelled Calfucci. 'Guards! Guards! Get after that *cimice*! Bring me his head! And I want his *coglioni* as well!'

'I've said I'm sorry –' Ezio began, but already the gates of the mansion were opening and the Calfucci bodyguards came rushing out, swords drawn. Now more or less dressed, Ezio set off at a run down the street, dodging wagons and pushing past citizens on his way, wealthy businessmen in solemn black, merchants in browns and reds, humbler folk in homespun tunics and, once, a church procession which he collided with so unexpectedly that he all but tipped over the statue of the Virgin the black-cowled monks were carrying. At last, after ducking down alleys and leaping over walls, he stopped and listened. Silence. Not even the shouts and curses that had followed him from the general population could be heard any more. As for the guards, he'd shaken them off, he was sure of that.

He only hoped Signor Calfucci hadn't recognized him. Cristina wouldn't betray him, he could be sure of that. Besides, she could run rings round her father, who adored her. And even if he did find out, Ezio reflected, he wouldn't be a bad match. His father ran one of the biggest banking houses in town, and one day it might be bigger than that of the Pazzi or even – who knew? – of the Medici.

Using back streets, he made his way home. The first to meet him was Federico, who looked at him gravely and shook his head ominously. 'You're in for it now,' he said. 'Don't say I didn't warn you.'

2

The office of Giovanni Auditore was on the first floor, and overlooked the gardens behind the palazzo through two sets of double windows which opened on to one broad balcony. The room was panelled in dark, scrolled oak, whose severity was scarcely mitigated by the ornate plasterwork of the ceiling. Two desks faced each other in the room, the larger of which belonged to Giovanni, and the walls were lined with bookcases stuffed with ledgers and parchment scrolls from which heavy red seals dangled. The room was designed to say to any visitor: here you will find opulence, respectability and trust. As head of the Auditore International Bank, which specialized in loans to the kingdoms of Germania within what was notionally at least a Holy Roman Empire, Giovanni Auditore was well aware of the weighty and responsible position he held. He hoped his two older sons would make haste to come to their senses and help him shoulder the burdens he had inherited from his own father, but he could see no sign of that yet. Nevertheless . . .

He glowered across the room at his middle son from his seat at his desk. Ezio stood near the other desk, vacated by Giovanni's secretary to give father and son the privacy they required for what Ezio feared would be a very painful interview. It was now early afternoon. He'd been dreading the summons all morning, though he'd also used the time to snatch a couple of hours of necessary sleep and smarten himself up. He guessed his father had wanted to give him those opportunities before carpeting him.

'Do you think me blind and deaf, my son?' Giovanni was thundering. 'Do you think I haven't heard all about the fight with Vieri de' Pazzi and his lot down by the bridge last night? Sometimes, Ezio, I think you're not much better than he is, and the Pazzi make for dangerous enemies.' Ezio was about to speak, but his father held up a cautionary hand. 'Kindly allow me to finish!' He took a breath. 'And as if that weren't bad enough, you take it upon yourself to chase after Cristina Calfucci, the daughter of one of the most successful merchants in all Tuscany, and, not content with that, to tumble her in her own bed! It's intolerable! Don't you consider our family's reputation at all?' He paused, and Ezio was surprised to see the ghost of a twinkle in his eye. 'You do realize what all this means, don't you?' continued Giovanni. 'You do realize who you remind me of, don't you?'

Ezio bowed his head, but then he was surprised when his father got up, crossed the room to him and put an arm round his shoulder, grinning from ear to ear.

'You little devil! You remind me of myself when I was your age!' But Giovanni immediately became grave again. 'Don't think, however, that I wouldn't punish you without mercy if I didn't have sore need of you here. If I didn't, mark my words, I'd send you off to your Uncle Mario and get him to recruit you into his *condottieri* squadron. That'd knock some sense into you! But I have to count on you, and although you don't seem to have the brains to see it, we're passing through a crucial time in our city. How's your head feeling? I see you've taken the bandage off.'

'Much better, father.'

'So I assume nothing's going to interfere with the work I have lined up for you for the rest of the day?'

'I promise you, Father.'

'It's a promise you'd better keep.' Giovanni returned to his desk and, from a compartment, drew a letter bearing his own seal and passed it to his son, together with two parchment documents in a leather case. 'I want you to deliver these to Lorenzo de' Medici at his bank without any delay.'

'May I ask what it concerns, Father?'

'As for the documents, you may not. But it'd be as well for you to know that the letter brings Lorenzo up to date on our dealings with Milan. I spent all this morning preparing it. This must go no farther, but if I don't give you my trust, you'll never learn responsibility. There's a rumour of a plot against Duke Galeazzo – a

nasty piece of work, I grant you, but Florence can't –
afford to have Milan destabilized.'

'Who's involved?'

Giovanni looked at his son narrowly: 'They say the
principal conspirators are Giovanni Lampugnani, Gerolamo Olgiati and Carlo Visconti; but it looks as if our
own dear Francesco de' Pazzi is involved as well, and
above all, there's a plan afoot which seems to encom-
pass more than just the politics of two city-states. The
Gonfaloniere here has taken Francesco into custody
for the moment but the Pazzi won't like that at all.'
Giovanni stopped himself. 'There. I've already told you
far too much. Make sure this gets to Lorenzo quickly
– I've heard he's leaving for Careggi very soon to take
some country air, and while the cat's away . . .'

'I'll get it there as fast as possible.'

'Good boy. Go now!'

Ezio set off on his own, using the back streets as far
as possible, never thinking that Vieri might still be out
looking for him. But suddenly, in a quiet street within
minutes of the Medici Bank, there he stood, blocking
Ezio's path. Trying to double back, Ezio found more
of Vieri's men blocking his retreat. He turned again.
'Sorry, my little piglet,' he shouted at Vieri, 'but I simply
don't have time to give you another drubbing now.'

'It's not me that's going to get a drubbing,' Vieri
shouted back. 'You're cornered; but don't worry – I'll
send a nice wreath for your funeral.'

The Pazzi men were closing in. No doubt Vieri knew of his father's imprisonment by now. Ezio looked around desperately. The street's tall houses and walls hemmed him in. Slinging the satchel containing the precious documents securely round his body, he selected the most likely house within his reach and sprang at its wall, gripping the rough-hewn stone with both hands and feet before scaling up to the roof. Once there, he paused a moment to look down at Vieri's irate face. 'I haven't even got time to piss on you,' he said, and scampered away along the rooftop as fast as he could, dropping to the ground with new-found agility as soon as he was clear of his pursuers.

A few moments later, he was at the doors of the bank. He entered and recognized Boetio, one of Lorenzo's most trusted servants. Here was a stroke of luck. Ezio hurried up to him.

'Hey, Ezio! What brings you here in such a hurry?'

'Boetio, there is no time to waste. I have letters here from my father for Lorenzo.'

Boetio looked serious, and spread his hands. '*Ahimè*, Ezio! You're too late. He's gone to Careggi.'

'Then you must make sure he gets these as soon as possible.'

'I'm sure he hasn't gone for more than a day or so. In these times . . .'

'I'm beginning to find out about these times! Make sure he gets them, Boetio, and in confidence! As soon as possible!'

When he had returned to his own palazzo, he made his way quickly to his father's office, ignoring both the amiable backchat from Federico, who was lazing under a tree in the garden, and the attempts of his father's secretary, Giulio, to prevent him from passing the closed door of Giovanni's inner sanctum. There, he discovered his father in deep conversation with the Chief Justice of Florence, the Gonfaloniere Uberto Alberti. No surprise there, for the two men were old friends, and Ezio treated Alberti as he would an uncle. But he'd caught expressions of deep seriousness on their faces.

'Ezio, my boy!' said Uberto, genially. 'How are you? Out of breath as usual, I see.'

Ezio looked urgently at his father.

'I've been trying to calm your father down,' continued Uberto. 'There's been a lot of trouble, you know; but –' he turned to Giovanni and his tone became more earnest, '– the threat is ended.'

'Have you delivered the documents?' Giovanni asked, crisply.

'Yes, father. But Duke Lorenzo had already left.'

Giovanni frowned. 'I hadn't anticipated his leaving so soon.'

'I left them with Boetio,' said Ezio. 'He'll get them to him as soon as possible.'

'That may not be soon enough,' said Giovanni, darkly.

Uberto patted him on the back. 'Look,' he said. 'It can only mean a day or two. We have Francesco under lock and key. What could possibly happen in such a short time?'

Giovanni seemed partially reassured, but it was clear that the two men had more to discuss, and that Ezio's presence wasn't desired.

'Go and find your mother and your sister,' said Giovanni. 'You should spend time with some of the rest of the family other than Federico, you know! And rest that head of yours – I'll have need of you again later.' And with a wave of his father's hand, Ezio was dismissed.

He wandered through the house, nodding greetings to one or two of the family's servants, and to Giulio, who was hurrying back to the bank office from some-where, a sheaf of papers in his hand and looking, as usual, haunted by all the business he carried in his head. Ezio waved to his brother, still lounging in the garden, but felt no desire to join him. Besides, he'd been told to keep his mother and sister company, and he knew better than to disobey his father, especially after their discussion earlier in the day.

He found his sister sitting alone in the loggia, a neglected book of Petrarch in her hands. That figured. He knew she was in love.

'*Ciao*, Claudia,' he said.

'*Ciao*, Ezio. Where *have* you been?'

Ezio spread his hands. 'I've been running a business errand for Father.'

'That's not all, I hear,' she retorted, but her smile was faint and automatic.

'Where's Mother?'

Claudia sighed. 'She's gone to see that young painter they're all talking about. You know, the one who's just finished his apprenticeship with Verrocchio.'

'Really?'

'Don't you pay attention to anything that goes on in this house? She's commissioned some paintings from him. She believes that they'll be a good investment in time.'

'That's our mother for you!'

But Claudia didn't respond, and for the first time Ezio became fully aware of the sadness in her face. It made her look much older than her sixteen years.

'What's the matter, *sorellina*?' he asked, sitting on the stone bench beside her.

She sighed, and looked at him with a rueful smile. 'It's Duccio,' she said at last.

'What about him?'

Her eyes filled with tears. 'I've found out that he's being unfaithful to me.'

Ezio frowned. Duccio was practically engaged to Claudia, and even though there hadn't yet been any formal announcement . . .

'Who told you that?' he asked, putting an arm round her.

'The other girls.' She wiped her eyes and looked at

him. 'I thought they were my friends, but I think they enjoyed telling me.'

Ezio stood up angrily. 'Then they're little better than harpies! You're better off without them.'

'But I loved him!'

Ezio took a moment before replying. 'Are you sure? Maybe you only thought you did. How do you feel now?'

Claudia's eyes were dry. 'I'd like to see him suffer, even if only a little. He's really hurt me, Ezio.'

Ezio looked at his sister, looked at the sadness in her eyes, a sadness suffused with not a little flare of anger. His heart steeled.

'I think I'll pay him a visit.'

Duccio Dovizi wasn't at home, but the housekeeper told Ezio where to find him. Ezio made his way across the Ponte Vecchio and westward along the south bank of the Arno to the church of San Jacopo Soprano. There were some secluded gardens nearby, where lovers occasionally kept their trysts. Ezio, whose blood was boiling on behalf of his sister, yet needed more proof of Duccio's infidelity than hearsay, began to think that he was about to get it.

Sure enough, he soon caught sight of the blond young man, dressed to kill, sitting on a bench overlooking the river, his arm round a dark-haired girl he didn't recognize. He made his way forward cautiously.

'Darling, it's beautiful,' the girl was saying, holding out her hand. Ezio saw the flash of a diamond ring.

'Nothing but the best for you, *amore*,' Duccio purred, pulling her towards him for a kiss.

But the girl pulled back. 'Not so fast. You can't just buy me. We haven't been seeing each other that long, and I've heard you've been promised to Claudia Auditore.'

Duccio spat. 'It's over. Anyway, Father says I can do better than an Auditore.' He clamped her bottom in his hand. 'You, for example!'

'*Birbante!* Let's walk a bit.'

'I can think of something that'd be much more fun,' said Duccio, putting his hand between her legs.

That was enough for Ezio. 'Hey, *lurido porco*,' he snapped.

Duccio was taken completely by surprise, and spun round, releasing his hold on the girl. 'Hey, Ezio, my friend,' he cried, but there was nervousness in his voice. How much had Ezio seen? 'I don't think you've met my . . . cousin?'

Ezio, enraged at the treachery, stepped forward and punched his former friend full in the face. 'Duccio, you should be ashamed of yourself! You insult my sister, parading around with this . . . this *puttana*!'

'Who are you calling a *puttana*?' the girl snarled, but she got to her feet and backed off.

'I should have thought even a girl like you could do

better than this arsehole,' Ezio told her. 'Do you really think he's going to make you into a lady?'

'Don't you talk to her like that,' Duccio hissed. 'At least she's more generous with her favours than your tight-assed little sister. But I guess she's got a hole as dry as a nun's. Pity, I could have taught her a thing or two. But there again –'

Ezio interrupted him coldly. 'You've broken her heart, Duccio –'

'Have I? What a shame.'

'– Which is why I am going to break your arm.'

The girl screamed at this, and fled. Ezio seized the whining Duccio and forced the young gallant's right arm over the edge of the stone bench on which he'd been sitting with a hard-on only moments before. He pushed the forearm against the stone until Duccio's whining turned to tears.

'Stop it, Ezio! I beg you! I'm my father's only son!'

Ezio looked at him with contempt, and released him. Duccio fell to the ground and rolled over, nursing his bruised arm and whimpering, his fine clothes torn and besmirched.

'You're not worth the effort,' Ezio told him. 'But if you don't want me to change my mind about that arm of yours, stay away from Claudia. And stay away from me.'

After the incident, Ezio walked a long way home, wandering along the riverbank until he'd almost reached the fields. When he turned back, the shadows were lengthening, but his mind was calmer. It would never become him as a man, he told himself, to allow his anger ever fully to rule him.

Close to his house, he caught sight of his younger brother, whom he hadn't seen since the morning of the previous day. He greeted the lad warmly. '*Ciao*, Petruccio. What are you up to? Have you given your tutor the slip? And anyway, isn't it past your bedtime?'

'Don't be silly. I'm practically grown-up. In a few years' time, I'll be able to knock the stuffing out of you!' The brothers grinned at each other. Petruccio was holding a carved pearwood box close to his chest. It was open, and Ezio noticed a handful of white and brown feathers in it. 'They're eagle's feathers,' explained the boy. He pointed to the top of the tower of a nearby building. 'There's an old nest up there. The young must have fledged and gone. I can see plenty more feathers caught in the stonework.' Petruccio looked at his brother pleadingly. 'Ezio, would you mind getting a few more for me?'

'Well, what do you want them for?'

Petruccio looked down. 'It's a secret,' he said.

'If I get them for you, will you go in? It's late.'

'Yes.'

'Promise?'

'Promise.'

'All right, then.' Ezio thought, well, I've done Claudia

a favour today, no reason why I shouldn't do one for Petruccio as well.

Climbing the tower was tricky, as its stone was smooth and he had to concentrate to find grips and toeholds in the joints between its stones. Higher up, ornamental mouldings helped as well. In the end, it took him half an hour, but he managed to gather fifteen more feathers – all that he could see – and brought them back to Petruccio.

'You missed one,' said Petruccio, pointing up.

'Bed!' growled his brother.

Petruccio fled.

Ezio hoped their mother would be pleased with the gift. It didn't take much to fathom Petruccio's secrets.

He smiled as he entered the house himself.

3

The following morning Ezio woke late, but found to his relief that his father had no immediate business for him to see to. He wandered into the garden, where he found his mother overseeing work on her cherry trees, from which the blossom was just beginning to fade. She smiled when she saw him, and beckoned him over. Maria Auditore was a tall, dignified woman in her early forties, her long black hair braided under a pure white muslin cap edged with the black and gold colours of the family.

'Ezio! *Buon' giorno.*'

'*Madre.*'

'How are you? Better, I hope.' Gently, she touched the wound on his head.

'I'm fine.'

'Your father said you should rest as long as you could.'

'I have no need of rest, Mamma!'

'Well, at any rate there will be no excitement for you this morning. Your father has asked that I take care of you. I know what you've been up to.'

'I don't know what you mean.'

'Don't play games with me, Ezio. I know about your fight with Vieri.'

'He has been spreading foul stories about our family. I could not let that go unpunished.'

'Vieri's under pressure, the more so since his father was arrested.' She paused thoughtfully. 'Francesco de' Pazzi may be many things, but I never would have imagined him capable of joining a plot to murder a duke.'

'What will happen to him?'

'There'll be a trial. I imagine your father may be a key witness, when our own Duke Lorenzo returns.'

Ezio looked restless.

'Don't worry, you've nothing to fear. And I'm not going to ask you to do anything you wouldn't like – in fact, I want you to accompany me on an errand I have to run. It won't take long, and I think you may even find it enjoyable.'

'I'll be happy to help you, Mamma.'

'Come, then. It's not far.'

They left the palazzo on foot together, arm in arm, and walked in the direction of the cathedral, to the small quarter near it where many of the artists of Florence had their workshops and studios. Some, like those of Verrocchio and the rising star Alessandro di Moriano Filipepi, who'd already acquired the nickname Botticelli, were large, busy places, where assistants and apprentices were busy grinding colours and mixing pigments, others, humbler. It was at the door of one of these that Maria halted and knocked. It was opened immediately by a handsome, well-dressed young man, almost dandified but athletic-looking, with a shock of dark brown hair and a luxuriant beard. He might have been six or seven years older than Ezio.

'Madonna Auditore! Welcome! I've been expecting you.'

'Leonardo, *buon' giorno*.' The two exchanged formal kisses. This artist must be well in with my mother, thought Ezio, but already he liked the look of the man. 'This is my son, Ezio,' continued Maria.

The artist bowed. 'Leonardo da Vinci,' he said. '*Molto onorato, signore*.'

'Maestro.'

'Not quite that – yet,' smiled Leonardo. 'But what am I thinking of? Come in, come in! Wait here, I'll see if my assistant can find some wine for you while I go and get your paintings.'

The studio was not large, but the clutter in it made it look even smaller than it was. Tables were heaped with the skeletons of birds and small mammals, while jars filled with colourless fluid contained organic objects of one kind or another, though Ezio was hard put to it to recognize any of them. A broad workbench at the back held some curious structures painstakingly crafted in wood, and two easels bore unfinished paintings whose tones were darker than usual, and whose outlines were less clearly defined. Ezio and Maria made themselves comfortable, and, emerging from an inner room, a handsome youth appeared with a tray bearing wine and small cakes. He served them, smiled shyly, and withdrew.

'Leonardo's very talented.'

'If you say so, *Madre*. I know little of art.' Ezio thought that his life would consist of following in his father's footsteps, even though, deep within him, there was a rebellious and adventurous streak which he knew would sit ill in the character of a Florentine banker. In any case, like his older brother, he saw himself as a man of action, not as an artist or a connoisseur.

'You know, self-expression is a vital part of under-standing life, and enjoying it to the full.' She looked at him. 'You should find an outlet yourself, my dear.'

Ezio was piqued. 'I have plenty of outlets.'

'I meant apart from tarts,' retorted his mother matter-of-factly.

'Mother!' But Maria's only answer to that was a shrug and a pursing of her lips. 'It would be good if you could cultivate a man like Leonardo as a friend. I think he has a promising future ahead of him.'

'From the look of this place, I'm inclined to disagree with you.'

'Don't be cheeky!'

They were interrupted by Leonardo's return from his inner room, carrying two boxes. He set one down on the ground. 'Do you mind carrying that one?' he asked Ezio. 'I'd ask Agniolo, but he has to stay and guard the shop. Also, I don't think he's strong enough for this kind of work, poor dear.'

Ezio stooped to pick up the box, and was surprised at how heavy it was. He almost dropped it.

'Careful!' warned Leonardo. 'The paintings in there are delicate, and your mother's just paid me good money for them!'

'Shall we go?' said Maria. 'I can't wait to hang them. I've selected places which I hope you'll approve of,' she added to Leonardo. Ezio baulked at this a little: was a fledgling artist really worth such deference?

As they walked, Leonardo chatted amiably, and Ezio found that despite himself he was won over by the other man's charm. And yet there was something about him that he instinctively found disquieting, something he couldn't quite put his finger on. A coolness? A sense of detachment from his fellow beings? Perhaps it was just that he had his head in the clouds, like so many other artists, or so Ezio was told. But Ezio felt an instant, instinctive respect for the man.

'So, Ezio, what do you do?' Leonardo asked him.

'He works for his father,' Maria replied.

'Ah. A financier! Well, you were born in the right city for that!'

'It's a good city for artists too,' said Ezio. 'All those rich patrons.'

'There are so many of us, though,' grumbled Leonardo. 'It's hard to attract attention. That's why I am so indebted to your mother. Mind you, she has a very discerning eye!'

'Do you concentrate on painting?' asked Ezio, thinking of the diversity he'd seen in the studio.

Leonardo looked thoughtful. 'That's a hard question. To tell the truth, I'm finding it difficult to settle down to anything, now I'm on my own. I adore painting, and I know I can do it, but . . . somehow I can see the end before I get there, and that makes it hard to finish things sometimes. I have to be pushed! But that's not all. I often feel that my work lacks . . . I don't know . . . purpose. Does that make any sense?'

'You should have more faith in yourself, Leonardo,' said Maria.

'Thank you, but there are moments when I think I'd rather do more practical work, work that has a direct bearing on life. I want to understand life – how it works, how everything works.'

'Then you'd have to be one hundred men in one,' said Ezio.

'If only I could be! I know what I want to explore: architecture, anatomy, engineering even. I don't want to capture the world with my brush, I want to change it!'

He was so impassioned that Ezio was more impressed than irritated – the man clearly wasn't boasting; if anything, he seemed almost tormented by the ideas that simmered within him. Next thing, thought Ezio, is that he'll tell us he's involved with music and poetry as well!

'Do you want to put that down and rest for a moment, Ezio?' Leonardo asked. 'It might be a bit too heavy for you.'

Ezio gritted his teeth. 'No, *grazie*. Anyway, we're almost there.'

When they arrived at the Palazzo Auditore, he carried his box into the entrance hall and set it down as slowly and as carefully as his aching muscles would let him, and he was more relieved than he'd ever admit, even to himself.

'Thank you, Ezio,' said his mother. 'I think we can manage very well without you now, though of course if you wish to come and help with the hanging of the pictures –'

'Thank you, Mother – I think that's a job best left to the two of you.'

Leonardo held out his hand. 'It was very good to meet you, Ezio. I hope our paths cross again soon.'

'*Anch'io.*'

'You might just call one of the servants to give Leonardo a hand,' Maria told him.

'No,' said Leonardo. 'I prefer to take care of this myself. Imagine if someone dropped one of the boxes!' And bending his knees, he hoisted the box Ezio had put down into the crook of his arm. 'Shall we?' he said to Maria.

'This way,' said Maria. "Goodbye, Ezio, I'll see you at dinner this evening. Come, Leonardo.'

Ezio watched as they left the hall. This Leonardo was obviously one to respect.

After lunch, late in the afternoon, Giulio came hurrying (as he always did) to tell him that his father required his presence in the office. Ezio hastened to follow the secretary down the long oak-lined corridor that led to the back of the mansion.

'Ah, Ezio! Come in, my boy.' Giovanni's tone was serious and businesslike. He stood up behind his desk, on which two bulky letters lay, wrapped in vellum and sealed.

'They say Duke Lorenzo will return tomorrow or the day after at the latest,' said Ezio.

'I know. But there is no time to waste. I want you to deliver these to certain associates of mine, here in the city.' He pushed the letters across the desk.

'Yes, Father.'

'I also need you to retrieve a message which a carrier pigeon should have brought to the coop in the piazza at the end of the street. Try to make sure no one sees you fetch it.'

'I'll see to it.'

'Good. Come back here immediately you've finished. I have some important things I need to discuss with you.'

'Sir.'

'So, this time, behave. No scrapping this time.'

Ezio decided to tackle the pigeon coop first. Dusk

47

was approaching, and he knew there'd be few people out at that time – a little later the square would be thronged with Florentines making their *passeggiata*. When he reached his goal he noticed some graffiti on the wall behind and above the coop. He was puzzled: was it recent or had he just never been aware of it before? Carefully inscribed was a line he recognized from the Book of Ecclesiastes: HE THAT INCREASETH KNOWL-EDGE INCREASETH SORROW. A little below this, someone had added in a ruder script: WHERE IS THE PROPHET?

But his mind soon returned to his task. He recognized the pigeon he was after instantly – it was the only one with a note attached to its leg. He detached it quickly and gently placed the bird back on its ledge, then he hesitated. Should he read the note? It wasn't sealed. Quickly he unrolled the little scroll and found it contained nothing but a name – that of Francesco de' Pazzi. Ezio shrugged. He supposed that would mean something more to his father than it did to him. Why the name of Vieri's father and one of the possible conspirators in a plot to topple the Duke of Milan – facts already known to Giovanni – should be of further significance was beyond him. Unless it signified some kind of confirmation.

But he had to hurry on with his work. Stashing the note in his belt-pouch, he made his way to the address on the first envelope. Its location surprised him, for it was in the red-light district. He'd been there often with Federico – before he had met Cristina, that is – but he had never felt comfortable there. He placed a hand on his dagger-hilt to reassure himself as he approached the dingy alley his father had indicated. The address turned out to be a low tavern, ill-lit and serving cheap Chianti in clay beakers.

At a loss about what to do next, for there seemed to be no one about, he was surprised by a voice at his side.

'You Giovanni's boy?'

He turned to confront a rough-looking man whose breath smelled of onions. He was accompanied by a woman who might once have been pretty, but it looked as if ten years on her back had rubbed most of any loveliness away. If it was left anywhere, it was in her clear, intelligent eyes.

'No, you idiot,' she said to the man. 'He just happens to look exactly like his dad.'

'You got something for us,' said the man, ignoring her. 'Give it here.'

Ezio hesitated. He checked the address. It was the right one.

'Hand it over, friend,' said the man, leaning closer. Ezio got a full blast of his breath. Did the man live on onions and garlic?

He placed the letter in the man's open hand, which closed round it immediately and transferred it to a leather pouch at his side.

'Good boy,' he said, and then smiled. Ezio was surprised to see that the smile gave his face a certain – surprising – nobility. But not his words. 'And don't worry,' he added. 'We ain't contagious.' He paused to glance at the woman. 'At least, *I* ain't!'

The woman laughed and punched his arm. Then they were gone.

Ezio made his way out of the alley with relief. The address on the second letter directed him to a street just west of the Baptistry. A much better district, but a quiet one at this time of day. He hastened across town.

Waiting for him under an arch which spanned the street was a burly man who looked like a soldier. He was dressed in what looked like leather country clothes, but he smelled clean and fresh, and he was cleanshaven.

'Over here,' he beckoned.

'I have something for you,' said Ezio. 'From –'

'– Giovanni Auditore?' The man spoke little above a whisper.

'*Sì.*'

The man glanced around, up and down the street. Only a lamplighter was visible, some distance away. 'Were you followed?'

'No – why should I have been?'

'Never mind. Give me the letter. Quickly.'

Ezio handed it over.

'Things are hotting up,' said the man. 'Tell your father

they're making a move tonight. He should make plans to get to safety.'

Ezio was taken aback. 'What? What are you talking about?'

'I've already said too much. Hurry home.' And the man melted into the shadows.

'Wait!' Ezio called after him. 'What do you mean? Come back!'

But the man had gone.

Ezio walked quickly up the street to the lamplighter. 'What time is it?' he asked. The man screwed up his eyes and looked at the sky. 'Must be an hour since I came on duty,' he said. 'Makes it about the twentieth hour.'

Ezio made a quick calculation. He must have left his palazzo two hours earlier, and it would take him perhaps twenty minutes to reach home again. He took off at a run. Some awful premonition caught at his soul.

As soon as he came within sight of the Auditore mansion, he knew something was wrong. There were no lights anywhere, and the great front doors stood open. He quickened his pace, calling as he ran: 'Father! Federico!'

The great hall of the palazzo stood dark and empty, but there was enough light for Ezio to see tables over-turned, chairs smashed, broken crockery and glassware. Someone had torn Leonardo's paintings from the walls and slashed them with a knife. From the darkness beyond, he could hear the sound of sobbing – a woman sobbing: his mother!

He started to make his way towards the sound when a shadow moved behind him, something raised above its head. Ezio twisted round and seized a heavy silver candlestick which someone was bringing down on his head. He gave a savage wrench and his attacker let go of the candlestick with a cry of alarm. He tossed the candlestick away, out of reach, grabbed the arm of his assailant, and pulled the person towards what light there was. There was murder in his heart, and already his dagger was out.

'Oh! *Ser* Ezio! It's you! Thank God!'

Ezio recognized the voice, and now the face, of the family housekeeper, Annetta, a feisty countrywoman who'd been with the family for years.

'What has *happened*?' he asked Annetta, taking both her wrists in his hands and almost shaking her in his anguish and panic.

'They came – the city guards. They've arrested your father and Federico – they even took little Petruccio, they tore him from your mother's arms!'

'Where is my mother? Where is Claudia?'

'Here we are,' came a shaky voice from the shadows. Claudia emerged, her mother leaning on her arm. Ezio righted a chair for his mother to sit on. In the dim light, he could see that Claudia was bleeding, her clothes dirty and torn. Maria did not acknowledge him. She sat on the chair, keening and rocking. In her hands she clutched the little pearwood box of feathers Petruccio had given her not two days – a lifetime – before.

'My God, Claudia! Are you all right?' He looked at her and anger flooded through him. 'Did they – ?'

'No – I'm all right. They roughed me up a little because they thought I could tell them where you were. But Mother . . . Oh, Ezio, they've taken Father and Federico and Petruccio to the Palazzo Vecchio!'

'Your mother's in shock,' said Annetta. 'When she resisted them, they –' She broke off. '*Bastardi!*'

Ezio thought quickly. 'It's not safe here. Is there somewhere you can take them, Annetta?'

'Yes, yes . . . to my sister's. They'll be safe there.' Annetta barely managed to get the words out, the fear and anguish choking her voice.

'We must move fast. The guards will almost certainly come back for me. Claudia, Mother – there's no time to waste. Don't take anything, just go with Annetta. Now! Claudia, let Mamma lean on you.'

He escorted them out of their stricken home, still in shock himself, and helped them on their way before leaving them in the capable hands of the loyal Annetta, who had begun to regain her composure. Ezio's mind raced with all the implications, his world rocked by the terrible turn of events. Desperately, he tried to assess all that had happened, and just what he must do now, what he must do to save his father and brothers . . .

Straight away, he knew that he had to find some way of seeing his father, finding out what had brought on this attack, this outrage to his family. But the Palazzo Vecchio! They'd have put his kinsmen in the two small cells in the tower, of that he was sure. Maybe there'd be a chance . . . But the place was fortified like a castle keep; and there'd be a redoubtable guard placed on it, tonight of all nights.

Forcing himself to be calm and to think clearly, he slipped through the streets to the Piazza della Signoria, hugging its walls, and looking up. Torches burned from the battlements and from the top of the tower, illuminating the giant red fleur-de-lys that was the city's emblem, and the great clock at the tower's base. Higher up, squinting to see more clearly, Ezio thought he could discern the dim light of a taper in the small barred window near the top. There were guards posted outside the palazzo's great double doors, and more on the battlements. But there were none that Ezio could see at the top of the tower, whose battlements anyway were above the window he needed to reach.

He skirted the square away from the palazzo and found his way to the narrow street which led off the piazza, along the palazzo's north side. Fortunately, there were still a reasonable number of people about, strolling and enjoying the evening air. It seemed to Ezio that he suddenly existed in another world from theirs, that he had been cut off from the society he had swum in like a fish until only three or four short hours ago. He bristled at the thought that life could still continue in its even routine for all these people, while that of his own family had been shattered. Again, he felt his heart swell with an almost overwhelming rush of anger and fear. But then he turned his mind firmly back to the work in hand, and a look of steel crossed his face.

The wall rising above him was sheer and giddyingly high, but it was in darkness and that would be to his advantage. Moreover, the stones of which the palazzo was constructed were rough-hewn, so he would have plenty of handholds and footholds to aid him in his ascent. One problem would be any guards posted on the north-side battlements, but he'd have to deal with that when he came to it. He hoped that most would be grouped along the west-facing main façade of the building.

Taking a breath and glancing round – there was no one else in this dark street – he gave a leap, took a firm hold of the wall, gripped with his toes in their soft leather boots, and began to scale upwards.

Once he'd reached the battlements he dropped to a crouch, the tendons in his calves straining with tension. There were two guards here, but they had their backs to him, looking towards the lighted square beneath. Ezio stayed motionless for a moment, until it became clear that any sound he'd made had not alerted them to his presence. Staying low, he darted towards them and then struck, drawing them back, one hand around each of their necks, using their own weight and the element of surprise to bring them down on their backs. In barely a heartbeat, he had their helmets off and smashed their heads together violently – they were unconscious before they could register any surprise on their faces. If that hadn't worked, Ezio knew he would have cut their throats without a second's hesitation.

He paused again, breathing hard. Now for the tower. This was of more smoothly trimmed stone, and the going was hard. What's more, he had to climb round from the north to the west side of it, where the cell window was. He prayed that no one in the square or on the battlements would look up. He didn't fancy being brought down by a crossbow bolt after having got so far.

The corner where the north and west walls met was hard and unpromising, and for a moment Ezio clung there, frozen, looking for a handhold that didn't seem to exist. He looked down, and saw far beneath him one of the guards on the battlements looking up. He could see the pale face clearly. He could see the man's eyes. He pressed himself to the wall. In his dark clothing he'd be as conspicuous as a cockroach on a white tablecloth. But, inexplicably, the man lowered his gaze and continued his patrol. Had he seen him? Had he not been able to believe what he'd seen? Ezio's throat thumped with the strain. Only able to relax after a long minute had passed, he breathed once more.

After a monumental effort he arrived at his goal, grateful for the narrow ledge on which he could just perch as he peered into the narrow cell beyond the window. God is merciful, he thought, as he recognized the figure of his father, his back turned towards him, apparently reading by the thin light of a taper.

'Father!' he called softly.

Giovanni spun round. 'Ezio! In God's name, how did you –'

'Never mind, Father.' As Giovanni approached, Ezio could see that his hands were bloody and bruised, and his face pale and drawn. 'My God, Father, what have they done to you?'

'I took a bit of a beating, but I'm all right. More importantly, what of your mother and sister?'

'Safe now.'

'With Annetta?'

'Yes.'

'God be praised.'

'What happened, Father? Were you expecting this?'

'Not as quickly as this. They arrested Federico and Petruccio too – I think they're in the cell behind this one. If Lorenzo had been here things would have been different. I should have taken precautions.'

'What are you talking about?'

'There's no time for that now!' Giovanni almost

shouted. 'Now, listen to me: you must get back to our house. There's a hidden door in my office. There's a chest concealed in a chamber beyond it. Take *everything* you find inside it. Do you hear? *Everything!* Much of it will seem strange to you, but all of it is important.'

'Yes, Father.' Ezio shifted his weight slightly, still clinging for dear life to the bars that crossed the window. He didn't dare look down now, and he didn't know how much longer he could remain motionless.

'Among the contents you'll find a letter and with it some documents. You must take them without delay – tonight! – to *Messer* Alberti –'

'The Gonfalionere?'

'Exactly. Now, go!'

'But, Father . . . ' Ezio struggled to get the words out, and, wishing that he could do more than just ferry documents, he stammered, 'Are the Pazzi behind this? I read the note from the carrier pigeon. It said –'

But then Giovanni hushed him. Ezio could hear the key turning in the lock of the cell door.

'They're taking me for interrogation,' said Giovanni grimly. 'Get away before they discover you. My God, you're a brave boy. You'll be worthy of your destiny. Now, for the last time – go!'

Ezio edged himself off the ledge and clung to the wall out of sight as he heard his father being led away. He almost couldn't bear to listen. Then he steeled himself for the climb down. He knew that descents are almost always harder than ascents, but even in the last forty-eight hours he'd gained plenty of experience of scaling up and down buildings. And now he clambered down the tower, slipping once or twice, but regaining his hold, until he had reached the battlements again, where the two guardsmen still lay where he had left them. Another stroke of luck! He'd knocked their heads together as hard as he could, but if they'd chanced to regain consciousness while he was up on the tower and raised the alarm . . . well, the consequences didn't bear thinking about.

Indeed, there was no time to think of such things. He swung himself over the battlements and peered down. Time was of the essence. If he could see something down below which might break his fall, he might dare to leap. As his eyes adjusted to the gloom, he saw the awning of a deserted stall attached to the wall, far below. Should he risk it? If he succeeded, he'd gain a few precious minutes. If he failed, a broken leg would be the least of his problems. He would have to have faith in himself.

He took a deep breath and dived into the darkness.

From such a height the awning collapsed under his weight, but it had been firmly secured and gave just enough resistance to break his fall. He was winded, and he'd have a few bruised ribs in the morning, but he was down! And no alarm had been raised.

He shook himself and sped off in the direction of

what only hours ago had been his home. When he reached it, he realized that in his haste his father had neglected to tell him how to locate the secret door. Giulio would know, but where was Giulio now?

Luckily there had been no guards lurking in the vicinity of the house, and he'd been able to gain access unchallenged. He had stopped for a minute, outside the house, almost unable to propel himself in through the darkness of the doorway – it seemed that the house had changed, its sanctity defiled. Again, Ezio had to collect his thoughts, knowing that his actions were critical. His family depended on him now. He pressed on into his family home, into the dark. Shortly afterwards he stood in the centre of the office, eerily lit by a single candle, and looked about him.

The place had been turned over by the guards, who had clearly confiscated a large number of bank documents, and the general chaos of fallen bookcases, overturned chairs, drawers cast to the ground and scattered papers and books everywhere didn't make Ezio's task any easier. But he knew the office, his eyesight was keen, and he used his wits. The walls were thick, any could have a chamber concealed within them, but he made for the wall into which the large fireplace was set and started his search there, where the walls would be thickest, to contain the chimneypiece. Holding the candle close, and looking searchingly, while keeping an ear cocked for any sound of returning guards, finally, on the left-hand side of the great moulded mantel he thought he could discern the faint outline of a door set into the panelling. There had to be a means of opening it nearby. He looked carefully at the carved *colossi* which held the marble mantelpiece on their shoulders. The nose of the one on the left-hand side looked as if it had once been broken, and repaired, for there was a fine crack around its base. He touched the nose and found it to be slightly loose. Heart in mouth, he moved it gently, and the door swung inwards on silent spring-mounted hinges, revealing a stone-floored corridor which led to the left.

As he entered, his right foot encountered a flagstone which moved beneath it, and as it did so, oil-lamps set into the passageway's walls suddenly flared into life. It ran a short way, sloping slightly downwards, and terminated in a circular chamber decorated more in the style of Syria than Italy. Ezio's mind flashed on a picture which hung in his father's private study of the castle of Masyaf, once the seat of the ancient Order of Assassins. But he had no time to ponder whether or not this curious decor could be of any special significance. The room was unfurnished, and in its centre stood a large, iron-bound chest, securely sealed with two heavy locks. He looked around the room to see if a key might be anywhere, but aside from its ornamentation it was bare. Ezio was wondering if he'd have to return to the office, or make his way to his father's study, to search for one there, and if he'd have time to do so, when by chance his hand brushed against one of the locks, and at that, it sprang open. The other one opened as easily. Had his father given him some power he did not know of? Were the locks in some way programmed to respond to a certain person's touch? Mystery was piling on mystery, but there was no time to dwell on them now.

He opened the chest and saw that it contained a white hood, evidently old, and made of some perhaps woollen material which he didn't recognize. Something compelled him to put it on, and at once a strange power surged through him. He lowered the hood, but did not take it off.

The chest contained a leather bracer, a cracked dagger blade connected, instead of to a hilt, to a strange mechanism whose workings were beyond him, a sword, a page of vellum covered with symbols and letters and what looked like part of a plan, and the letter and documents his father had told him to take to Uberto Alberti. He gathered them all up, closed the chest, and retreated to his father's office, closing the secret door carefully behind him. In the office, he found a discarded document pouch of Giulio's and stashed the contents of the chest in it, slinging the pouch across his chest. He buckled on the sword. Not knowing what to make of this strange collection of objects, and not having time to reflect on why his father would keep such things in a secret chamber, he made his way cautiously back towards the main doors of the palazzo.

But, just as he entered the fore-courtyard, he saw two city guards on their way in. It was too late to hide. They had seen him.

'Halt!' one of them cried, and they both began advancing quickly towards him. There was no retreat. Ezio saw that they had already drawn their swords.

'What are you here for? To arrest me?'

'No,' said the one who had spoken first. 'Our orders are to kill you.' At that, the second guard rushed him.

Ezio drew his own sword as they closed in on him. It was a weapon he was unfamiliar with, but it felt light and capable in his hand, and it was as if he had used it all his life. He parried the first thrusts, right and left, both guards lunging at him at the same time. Sparks flew from all three swords, but Ezio felt his new blade hold firm, the edge biting and keen. Just as the second guard was bringing his sword down to sever Ezio's arm from his shoulder, Ezio feinted right, under the incoming blade. He shifted his balance from back to front foot, and lunged. The guard was caught off balance as his sword arm thudded harmlessly against Ezio's shoulder. Ezio used his own momentum to thrust his new sword up, piercing the man directly through the heart. Standing tall, Ezio rocked on the balls of his feet, raised his left foot and pushed the dead guard off his blade in time to swivel round to confront his companion. The other guard came forward with a roar, wielding a heavy sword. 'Prepare to die, *traditore!*'

'I am no traitor, nor is any member of my family.'

The guard swung at him, tearing at his left sleeve and drawing blood. Ezio winced, but only for a second. The guard pressed forward, seeing an advantage, and Ezio allowed him to lunge once more, then, stepping back, tripped him, swinging his own sword unflinchingly and very hard at the man's neck as he fell, and severing his head from his shoulders before he hit the ground.

For a moment Ezio stood trembling in the sudden silence that followed the mêlée, breathing hard. These were the first killings of his life – or were they? – for he felt another, older life within him, a life which seemed to have years of experience in death-dealing.

The sensation frightened him. This night had seen him age far beyond his years – but this new sensation seemed to be the awakening of some darker force deep within him. It was something more than simply the effects of the harrowing experiences of the last few hours. His shoulders sagged as he made his way through the darkened streets to Alberti's mansion, starting at every sound, and looking behind him frequently. At last, on the edge of exhaustion but able somehow to bear up, he arrived at the Gonfaloniere's home. He looked up at the façade, and saw a dim light in one of the front windows. He knocked hard on the door with the pommel of his sword.

Receiving no answer, nervous and impatient, he knocked again, harder and louder. Still nothing.

But, at the third time of trying, a hatch in the door opened briefly, then closed. The door swung open almost immediately thereafter, and a suspicious armed servant admitted him. He blurted out his business and was conducted to a first-floor room where Alberti sat at a desk covered with papers. Beyond him, half-turned away and sitting in a chair by a dying fire, Ezio thought he could see another man, tall and powerful, but only part of his profile was visible, and that indistinctly.

'Ezio?' Alberti stood up, surprised. 'What are you doing here at this hour?'

'I . . . I don't . . .'

Alberti approached him and put a hand on his shoulder. 'Wait, child. Take a breath. Collect your thoughts.'

Ezio nodded. Now he felt safer, he also felt more vulnerable. The events of the evening and night since he had set out to deliver Giovanni's letters were catching up with him. From the brass pedestal clock on the desk he could see that it was close to midnight. Could it really only be twelve hours since Ezio the boy had gone with his mother to collect paintings from an artist's studio? Despite himself he felt close to tears. But he collected himself, and it was Ezio the man who spoke. 'My father and brothers have been imprisoned – I do not know on whose authority – my mother and sister are in hiding and our family seat is ransacked.

My father enjoined me to deliver this letter and these papers to you . . .' Ezio drew the documents from his pouch.

'Thank you.' Alberti put on a pair of eyeglasses and took Giovanni's letter to the light of the candle burning on his desk. There was no sound in the room apart from the ticking of the clock and the occasional soft crash as the embers of the fire collapsed on themselves. If there was another presence in the room, Ezio had forgotten it.

Alberti now turned his attention to the documents. He took some time over them, and finally placed one of them discreetly inside his black doublet. The others he put carefully to one side, apart from the other papers on his desk.

'There's been a terrible misunderstanding, my dear Ezio,' he said, taking off his spectacles. 'It's true that allegations were laid – serious allegations – and that a trial has been scheduled for tomorrow morning. But it seems that someone may have been, perhaps for reasons of their own, overly zealous. But don't worry. I'll clear everything up.'

Ezio hardly dared to believe him. 'How?'

'The documents you've given me contain evidence of a conspiracy against your father and against the city. I'll present these papers at the hearing in the morning, and Giovanni and your brothers will be released. I guarantee it.'

Relief flooded through the young man. He clasped the Gonfaloniere's hand. 'How can I thank you?'

'The administration of justice is my job, Ezio. I take it very seriously, and –' for a fraction of a second he hesitated, '– your father is one of my dearest friends.' Alberti smiled. 'But where are my manners? I haven't even offered you a glass of wine.' He paused. 'And where will you spend the night? I still have some urgent business to attend to, but my servants will see that you have food and drink and a warm bed.'

At the time, Ezio didn't know why he refused so kind an offer.

It was well after midnight by the time he left the Gonfaloniere's mansion. Pulling up his hood again, he prowled through the streets trying to arrange his thoughts. Presently, he knew where his feet were taking him.

Once there, he climbed to the balcony with greater ease than he'd imagined possible – perhaps urgency lent strength to his muscles – and knocked gently on her shutters, calling quietly, 'Cristina! *Amore!* Wake up! It's me.' He waited, silent as a cat, and listened. He could hear her stirring, rising. And then her voice, scared, on the other side of the shutters.

'Who is it?'

'Ezio.'

She opened the shutters swiftly. 'What is it? What's wrong?'

'Let me come in. Please.'

Sitting on her bed, he told her the whole story.

'I knew something was amiss,' she said. 'My father seemed troubled this evening. But it does sound as if all will be well.'

'I need you to let me stay here tonight – don't worry, I'll be gone long before dawn – and I need to leave something with you for safekeeping.' He unslung his pouch and placed it between them. 'I must trust you.'

'Oh, Ezio, of course you can.'

He fell into a troubled sleep, in her arms.

4

It was a grey and overcast morning – and the city felt oppressed with the muggy heat that was trapped by the overhanging cloud. Ezio arrived at the Piazza della Signoria and saw, to his intense surprise, that a dense crowd had gathered already. A platform had been erected, and on it was placed a table covered with a heavy brocade cloth bearing the arms of the city. Standing behind it were Uberto Alberti and a tall, powerfully built man with a beaky nose and careful, calculating eyes, dressed in robes of rich crimson – a stranger to Ezio, at least. But his attention was caught by the sight of the other occupants of the platform – his father, and his brothers, all in chains; and just beyond them stood a tall construction with a heavy crossbeam from which three nooses were suspended.

Ezio had arrived at the piazza in a mood of anxious optimism – had not the Gonfaloniere told him that all would be resolved this day? Now his feelings changed. Something was wrong – badly wrong. He tried to push his way forward, but could not press through the mob – he felt the claustrophobia threaten to overwhelm him. Desperately trying to calm down, to rationalise his actions, he paused, drew his hood close over his head, and adjusted the sword at his belt. Surely Alberti would not let him down? And all the time he noticed that the tall man, a Spaniard by his dress, his face and his complexion, was ranging the mass of people with those piercing eyes. Who was he? Why did he stir something in Ezio's memory? Had he seen him somewhere before?

The Gonfaloniere, resplendent in his robes of office, raised his arms to quieten the people, and instantly a hush fell over them.

'Giovanni Auditore,' said Alberti in a commanding tone which failed, to Ezio's acute ear, to conceal a note of fear. 'You and your accomplices stand accused of the crime of treason. Have you any evidence to counter this charge?'

Giovanni looked at once surprised and uneasy. 'Yes, you have it all in the documents that were delivered to you last night.'

But Alberti said, 'I know of no such documents, Auditore.'

Ezio saw at once that this was a show-trial, but he couldn't understand what looked like deep treachery on Alberti's part. He shouted, 'It's a lie!' But his voice was drowned by the roar of the crowd. He struggled to get closer, shoving angry citizens aside, but there were too many of them, and he was trapped in their midst.

Alberti was speaking again: 'The evidence against you has been amassed and examined. It is irrefutable. In the absence of any proof to the contrary, I am bound by my office to pronounce you and your accomplices, Federico and Petruccio, and – *in absentia* – your son Ezio – *guilty* of the crime you stand accused of.' He paused as the crowd once more fell silent. 'I hereby sentence you all to death, the sentence to be carried out immediately!'

The crowd roared again. At a signal from Alberti, the hangman prepared the nooses, while two of his assistants took first little Petruccio, who was fighting back tears, to the gallows. The rope was placed round his neck as he prayed rapidly and the attendant priest shook Holy Water on to his head. Then the executioner pulled a lever set into the scaffold, and the boy dangled, kicking the air until he was still. 'No!' mouthed Ezio, barely able to believe what he was seeing. 'No, God, please no!' But his words were choked in his throat, his loss overcoming all.

Federico was next, bellowing his innocence and that of his family, struggling in vain to break loose from the guards who wrestled him towards the gallows. Ezio, now beside himself, striving desperately forward again, saw a solitary tear roll down his father's ashen cheek. Aghast, Ezio watched as his older brother and greatest friend jolted at the rope's end – it took longer for him to leave the world than it had taken Petruccio, but at last he, too, was still, swaying from the gallows – you could hear the wooden crossbeam creak in the silence. Ezio fought with the disbelief within him – could this really be happening?

The crowd began to murmur, but then a firm voice stilled it. Giovanni Auditore was speaking. 'It is you who are the traitor, Uberto. You, one of my closest associates and friends, in whom I entrusted my life! And I am a fool. I did not see that you are one of *them*!' Here he raised his voice to a great cry of anguish and of rage. 'You may take our lives this day, but mark this – we will have *yours* in return!'

He bowed his head and fell silent. A deep silence, interrupted only by the murmured prayers of the priest, followed as Giovanni Auditore walked with dignity to the gallows and commended his soul to the last great adventure it would travel on.

Ezio was too shocked to feel grief at first. It was as if a great iron fist had slammed into him. But as the trap opened below Giovanni, he couldn't help himself. '*Father!*' he cried, his voice cracking.

Instantly the Spaniard's eyes were on him. Was there something supernatural about the man's vision, to pick him out in such a throng? As if in slow motion, Ezio saw the Spaniard lean towards Alberti, whisper something, and point.

'Guards!' shouted Alberti, pointing as well. 'There! That's another one of them! Seize him!'

Before the crowd could react and restrain him, Ezio muscled through it to its edge, smashing his fists into anyone who stood barring his way. A guard was already waiting for him. He snatched at Ezio, pulling back his hood. Acting now on some instinctive drive within him, Ezio wrenched free and drew his sword with one hand, grabbing the guard by the throat with the other. Ezio's reaction had been far faster than the guard had anticipated, and before he could bring his arms up to defend himself Ezio tightened his grip on both throat and sword, and in one swift punching movement ran the guard through, slicing the sword in the body as he drew it out so that the man's intestines spilled from under his tunic on to the cobblestones. He threw the body aside and turned to the rostrum, fixing Alberti with his eye. 'I will kill you for this!' he screamed, his voice straining with hatred and rage.

But other guards were closing in. Ezio, his instinct for survival taking over, sped away from them, towards the comparative safety of the narrow streets beyond the square. To his dismay, he saw two more guards, swift of foot, rushing to cut him off.

They confronted each other at the edge of the square. The two guards faced him, blocking his retreat, the others closing in behind. Ezio fought them both frantically. Then an unlucky parry from one of them knocked his sword out of his hand. Fearing that this was the end, Ezio turned to flee from his attackers – but before he could find his feet, something astonishing happened. From the narrow street he was making for, and was within a few feet of, a roughly dressed man appeared. With lightning speed he came up on the two guards from behind, and, with a long dagger, cut deep under the pits of their sword arms, tearing through tendons and rendering them useless. He moved so fast that Ezio could scarcely follow his movements as he retrieved the young man's fallen sword and threw it to him. Ezio suddenly recognized him, and smelled once more the stench of onions and garlic. At that moment, damask roses couldn't have smelled sweeter.

'Get out of here,' said the man; and then he, too, was gone. Ezio plunged down the street, and ducked off it down alleys and lanes he knew intimately from his nightly forays with Federico. The hue and cry behind him faded. He made his way down to the river, and found refuge in a disused watchman's shack behind one of the warehouses belonging to Cristina's father.

In that hour Ezio ceased to be a boy and became a man. The weight of the responsibility he now felt he carried to avenge and correct this hideous wrong fell on his shoulders like a heavy cloak.

Slumping down on a pile of discarded sacks, he felt his whole body begin to shake. His world had just been torn apart. His father . . . Federico . . . and, God, no, little Petruccio . . . all gone, all dead, all murdered. Holding his head in his hands, he broke down – unable to control the pouring out of sorrow, fear and hatred. Only after several hours was he able to uncover his face – his eyes bloodshot and run through with an unbending vengeance. At that moment, Ezio knew his former life was over – Ezio the boy was gone for ever. From now, his life was forged for one purpose and one purpose alone – revenge.

Much later in the day, knowing full well that the watch would still be out looking for him relentlessly, he made his way via back alleys to Cristina's family mansion. He didn't want to put her in any danger, but he needed to collect his pouch with its precious contents. He waited in a dark alcove that stank of urine, not moving even when rats scuttled at his feet, until a light in her window told him that she had retired for the night.

'Ezio!' she cried as she saw him on her balcony. 'Thank God you're alive.' Her face flooded with relief – but that was short-lived, grief taking over. 'Your father, and brothers . . .' She couldn't finish the sentence, and her head bowed.

Ezio took her in his arms, and for several minutes they just stood holding each other.

Finally, she broke away. 'You're mad! What are you still doing in Florence?'

'I still have matters to attend to,' he said grimly. 'But I cannot stay here long, it's too big a risk for your family. If they thought you were harbouring me –'

Cristina was silent.

'Give me my satchel and I'll be gone.'

She fetched it for him, but before she gave it to him said, 'What about your family?'

'That is my first duty. To bury my dead. I can't see them thrown into a lime-pit like common criminals.'

'I know where they have taken them.'

'How?'

'The town's been talking all day. But no one will be there now. They're down near the Porta San Niccolò, with the bodies of paupers. There's a pit prepared, and they're waiting for the lime-carts to come in the morning. Oh, Ezio – !'

Ezio spoke calmly but grimly. 'I must see to it that my father and my brothers have a fitting departure from this earth. I cannot offer them a Requiem Mass, but I can spare their bodies indignity.'

'I'll come with you!'

'No! Do you realize what it would mean if you were caught with me?'

Cristina lowered her eyes.

'I must see that my mother and sister are safe too, and I owe my family one more death.' He hesitated. 'Then I will leave. Perhaps for ever. The question is – will you come with me?'

She drew back, and he could see a host of conflicting emotions in her eyes. Love was there, deep and lasting, but he had grown so much older than she since they had first held each other in their arms. She was still a girl. How could he expect her to make such a sacrifice? 'I want to, Ezio, you don't know how much – but my family – it would kill my parents –'

Ezio looked at her gently. Though they were the same age, his recent experience had made him suddenly far more mature than she was. He had no family to depend on any more, just responsibility and duty, and it was hard. 'I was wrong to ask. And who knows, perhaps, some day, when all this is behind us –' He put his hands to his neck and from the folds of his collar withdrew a heavy silver pendant on a fine chain of gold. He took it off. The pendant bore a simple design – just the initial letter 'A' of his family name. 'I want you to have this. Take it, please.'

With trembling hands she accepted it, crying softly. She looked down at it, then up at him, to thank him, to make some further excuse.

But he was gone.

On the south bank of the Arno, near the Porta San Niccolò, Ezio found the bleak place where the bodies were arranged next to a huge gaping pit. Two sorry-looking guards, raw recruits by the look of them, patrolled nearby, dragging their halberds as much as carrying them. The sight of their uniforms aroused Ezio's anger, and his first instinct was to kill them, but he had seen enough of death that day, and these were just country boys who'd stumbled into uniforms for want of anything better. It caught at his heart when he saw his father's and his brothers' bodies lying near the edge of the pit, still with their nooses round their scorched necks, but he could see that, once the guards fell asleep, as they surely soon would, he could carry the corpses to the river's edge, where he had prepared an open boat which he'd loaded with brushwood.

It was about the third hour, and the first faint light of dawn was already bleaching the eastern sky by the time he had completed his task. He stood alone on the riverbank, watching as the boat bearing his kinsmen's bodies, all aflame, drifted slowly with the current towards the sea. He watched until the light of the fire flickered away into the distance . . .

He made his way back to the city. A hard resolve had overcome his grief. There was still much to do. But first, he must rest. He returned to the watchman's shack, and made himself as comfortable as he could. Some little sleep would not be denied; but even as he slept, Cristina would not leave his thoughts, or dreams.

He knew the approximate whereabouts of the house of Annetta's sister, though he had never been there, or indeed met Paola; but Annetta had been his wet-nurse, and he knew that if he could trust no one else, he could trust her. He wondered if she knew, as she must, of the fate that had befallen his father and brothers, and if so, whether she had told his mother and sister.

He approached the house with great care, using an indirect route, and covering the distance where he could by running at a crouch over rooftops in order to avoid the busy streets where, he was sure, Uberto Alberti would have his men searching. Ezio could not rid himself of the thought of Alberti's treachery. What faction had his father referred to on the gallows? What could induce Alberti to bring about the death of one of his closest allies?

Paola's house lay in a street just north of the cathedral, Ezio knew. But when he got there, he didn't know which it was. There were few signs hanging from the fronts of the buildings here to identify them, and he could not afford to loiter in case he was recognized. He was about to depart when he saw Annetta herself, coming from the direction of the Piazza San Lorenzo.

Pulling his hood down so that his face was shadowed, he made his way to meet her, making himself walk at a normal pace, trying as best he could to blend in with his fellow citizens as they went about their business. He passed Annetta herself, and was gratified that she did not give any sign that she had noticed him. A few yards on, he doubled back and fell into step just behind her.

'Annetta –'

She had the wit not to turn round. 'Ezio. You're safe.'

'I wouldn't say that. Are my mother and sister . . . ?'

'They are protected. Oh, Ezio, your poor father. And Federico. And –' she stifled a sob, '– little Petruccio. I have just come from San Lorenzo. I lit a candle to San Antonio for them. They say the Duke will be here soon. Perhaps –'

'Do my mother and Maria know what has happened?'

'We thought it best to keep that knowledge from them.'

Ezio thought for a moment. 'It is best so. I will tell them when the time is right.' He paused. 'Will you take me to them? I couldn't identify your sister's house.'

'I am on my way there now. Stay close and follow me.'

He fell back a little, but kept her in sight.

The establishment she entered had the grim, fortress-like façade of so many of the grander Florentine buildings, but once inside, Ezio was taken aback. This was not quite what he had expected.

He found himself in a richly decorated parlour of great size, and high-ceilinged. It was dark, and the air was close. Velvet hangings in dark reds and deep browns covered the walls, interspersed with oriental tapestries depicting scenes of unequivocal luxury and sexual pleasure. The room was illuminated by candlelight, and a smell of incense hung in the air. The furniture mainly consisted of deep-seated daybeds covered with cushions of the costly brocade, and low tables on which there were trays bearing wine in silver carafes, Venetian glasses, and golden bowls of sweetmeats. But what was most surprising were the people in the room. A dozen beautiful girls, wearing silks and satins in green and yellow, cut in the Florentine fashion but with skirts slit to the top of the thigh, and plunging necklines that left nothing to the imagination except the promise of where it should not venture. Around three walls of the room, beneath the hangings and tapestries, a number of doors could be seen.

Ezio looked round, in a sense not knowing *where* to look. 'Are you sure this is the right place?' he asked Annetta.

'*Ma certo!* And here is my sister to greet us.'

An elegant woman who must have been in her late thirties but looked ten years younger, as beautiful as any *principessa* and better dressed than most, was coming towards them from the centre of the room. There was a veiled sadness in her eyes which somehow increased the sexual charge she transmitted, and Ezio, for all else that was on his mind, found himself stirred.

She extended her long-fingered, bejewelled hand to him. 'It is a pleasure to make your acquaintance, *Messer* Auditore.' She looked at him appraisingly. 'Annetta speaks quite highly of you. And now I can see why.'

Ezio, blushing despite himself, replied, 'I appreciate the kind words, Madonna –'

'Please, call me Paola.'

Ezio bowed. 'I cannot sufficiently express my gratitude to you for extending your protection to my mother and sister, Mado – I mean, Paola.'

'It was the least I could do.'

'Are they here? May I see them?'

'They are not here – this would be no place for them,

and some of my clients are highly placed in the city's governance.'

'Is this place then, forgive me, but is it what I think it is?'

Paola laughed. 'Of course! But I hope it is rather different from those stews down by the docks! It is really too early for business, but we like to be ready – there's always the chance of the occasional caller on his way to the office. Your timing is perfect.'

'Where is my mother? Where is Claudia?'

'They are safe, Ezio; but it's too risky to take you to see them now, and we mustn't compromise their security.' She drew him to a sofa and sat down with him. Annetta, meanwhile, disappeared into the bowels of the house on some business of her own.

'I think it will be best,' Paola continued, 'for you to leave Florence with them at the earliest opportunity. But you must rest first. You must gather your strength, for you have a long and arduous road ahead of you. Perhaps you'd like –'

'You are kind, Paola,' he interrupted her gently, 'and you are right in what you suggest. But just now, I cannot stay.'

'Why? Where are you going?'

During their conversation Ezio had been growing ever calmer, as all his racing thoughts came crashing together. At last he found himself able to shrug off his shock and his fear, for he had come to a decision and found a purpose, both of which he knew were irrevocable. 'I am going to kill Uberto Alberti,' he said.

Paola looked worried. 'I understand your desire for vengeance, but the Gonfaloniere is a powerful man, and you're not a natural killer, Ezio –'

Fate is making me one, he thought, but he said, as politely as he could, 'Spare me the lecture,' for he was bent on his mission.

Paola ignore him and completed her sentence: '– but I can make you one.'

Ezio fought down suspicion. 'And why would you want to teach me how to kill?'

She shook her head, 'In order to teach you how to survive.'

'I'm not sure that I need any training from you.'

She smiled. 'I know how you feel, but please allow me to hone the skills I am sure you have naturally. Think of my teaching as an extra weapon in your armoury.'

She started his training that very day, recruiting those girls who were off-duty, and trusted house-servants, to help her. In the high-walled garden behind the house she organized twenty of her people into five groups of four. They then started to mill around the garden, crisscrossing each other, talking and laughing, some of the girls casting bold looks on Ezio, and smiling. Ezio, who still carried his precious pouch at his side, was immune to their charms.

'Now,' Paola told him, 'discretion is paramount in my profession. We must be able to walk the streets freely – seen, but unseen. You too must learn properly how to blend in like us, and become one with the city's crowds.' Ezio was about to protest but she held up her hand. 'I know! Annetta tells me you do not acquit yourself badly, but you have more to learn than you know. I want you to pick a group and try to blend in with them. I don't want to be able to pick you out. Remember what almost happened to you at the execution.'

These harsh words stung Ezio, but the task didn't appear to him that difficult, provided he used his discretion. Still, under her unforgiving eye he found it harder than he'd expected. He would jostle clumsily against someone, or trip up, sometimes causing the girls or the male servants in his selected group to scatter from him, leaving him exposed. The garden was a pleasant place, sunlit and lush, and birds chirruped in the ornamental trees, but in Ezio's mind it became a labyrinth of unfriendly city streets, a potential enemy in every passerby. And always he was nettled by Paola's unremitting criticism. 'Careful!' she would say. 'You can't go charging in like that!' 'Show my girls some respect! Tread carefully when you're near them!' 'How do you plan to blend in with people if you're busy knocking them around?' 'Oh, Ezio! I expected better from you!'

But at last, on the third day, the biting comments grew fewer, and on the morning of the fourth he was able to pass right under Paola's nose without her batting an eyelid. Indeed, after fifteen minutes without saying a word, Paola called out: 'All right, Ezio, I give up! Where are you?'

Pleased with himself, he emerged from a group of girls, himself the very model of one of the young male house-servants. Paola smiled and clapped her hands, and the others joined in the applause.

But the work didn't end there.

'Now that you have learned to blend into a crowd,' Paola told him on the morning of the following day, 'I am going to show you how to use your new-found skill – in order to steal.'

Ezio baulked at this but Paola explained, 'It is an essential survival skill which you may need on your journey. A man is nothing without money, and you may not always be in a position to earn it honestly. I know you would never take anything from anyone who could not afford to lose it, or from a friend. Think of it as a blade in a penknife, which you seldom use, though it's good to know it's there.'

Learning how to pick pockets was a lot harder. He would sidle up to a girl successfully enough, but as soon as his hand closed on the purse at her girdle, she would scream '*Al ladro!*' and flee from him. When he first managed to draw some coins out successfully, he stayed where he was for a moment, triumphant, then felt a heavy hand on his shoulder. '*Ti arresto!*' said the manservant who was playing the role of a city watchman, grinning; but Paola did not smile. 'Once you've stolen from someone, Ezio,' she said, 'you mustn't linger.'

He was learning faster now, though, and was beginning to appreciate the need to acquire the skills he was being taught as necessary for the successful accomplishment of his mission. Once he had successfully fleeced ten girls, the last five without even Paola noticing, she announced that the tutorial was at an end.

'Back to work, girls,' she said. 'Playtime's over.'

'Do we have to?' the girls murmured reluctantly as they took their leave of Ezio. 'He's so cute, so innocent . . .' But Paola was adamant.

She walked with him alone in the garden. As always, he kept one hand on his pouch. 'Now that you've learned how to approach the enemy,' she said, 'we need to find you a suitable weapon – something far more subtle than a sword.'

'Well, but what would you have me use?'

'Why, you already have the answer!' And she produced the broken blade and bracer which Ezio had taken from his father's strongbox, and which even now he believed to be safely stowed in his pouch. Shocked, he opened it and rummaged. They were indeed gone.

'Paola! How the devil – ?'

Paola laughed. 'Did I get them? By using the same skills I've just taught you. But there's another little lesson for you. Now you know how to pick a pocket successfully, you must also learn to be on guard against people with the same skill!'

Ezio looked gloomily at the broken blade, which she'd returned to him with the bracer. 'There's some kind of mechanism that goes with them. None of this is exactly in working condition,' he said.

'Ah,' she said. 'True. But I think you already know *Messer* Leonardo?'

'Da Vinci? Yes, I met him just before —' He broke off, forcing himself not to dwell on the painful memory. 'But how can a painter be of any help to me with this?'

'He's a lot more than just a painter. Take him the pieces. You'll see.'

Ezio, seeing the sense of what she was telling him, nodded his agreement, then said, 'Before I go, may I ask you one last question?'

'Of course.'

'Why have you given your aid so readily to me — a stranger?'

Paola gave him a sad smile. By way of an answer, she drew up one of the sleeves of her robe, revealing a pale, delicate forearm — whose beauty was marred by the ugly, long dark scars which criss-crossed it. Ezio looked and knew. At some time in her life this lady had been tortured.

'I, too, have known betrayal,' Paola said.

And Ezio recognized without hesitation that he had met a kindred spirit.

5

It was not far from Paola's luxurious House of Pleasure to the busy back streets where Leonardo's workshop was, but Ezio did have to cross the spacious and busy Piazza del Duomo, and here he found his newly acquired skills of merging into the crowd especially useful. It was a good ten days since the executions, and it was likely that Alberti would imagine that Ezio would have left Florence long since, but Ezio was taking no chances, and nor, by the look of the number of guards posted in and around the square, was Alberti. There would be plain-clothes agents in place as well. Ezio kept his head well down, especially when passing between the cathedral and the Baptistry, where the square was busiest. He passed by Giotto's campanile, which had dominated the city for almost one hundred and fifty years, and the great red mass of Brunelleschi's cathedral dome, completed only fifteen years earlier, without seeing them, though he was aware of groups of French and Spanish tourists gazing up in unfeigned amazement and admiration, and a little burst of pride in his city tugged at his heart. But was it his city, really, any more?

Suppressing any gloomy thoughts, he quickly made

his way from the south side of the piazza to Leonardo's workshop. The Master was at home, he was told, in the yard at the back. The studio was, if anything, in a greater state of chaos than ever, though there did seem to be some rough method in the madness. The artefacts Ezio had noticed on his earlier visit had been added to, and from the ceiling hung a strange contraption in wood, though it looked like a scaled-up skeleton of a bat. On one of the easels a large parchment pinned to a board carried a massive and impossibly intricate knot-design, and in a corner of it some indecipherable scribbling in Leonardo's hand. Agniolo had been joined by another assistant, Innocento, and the two were trying to impose some order on the studio, cataloguing the stuff in order to keep track of it.

'He's in the back yard,' Agniolo told Ezio. 'Just go through. He won't mind.'

Ezio found Leonardo engaged in a curious activity. Everywhere in Florence you could buy caged song-birds. People hung them in their windows for pleasure, and when they died, simply replaced them. Leonardo was surrounded by a dozen such cages and, as Ezio watched, he selected one, opened the little wicker door, held the cage up, and watched as the linnet (in this case) found the entrance, pushed its way through, and flew free. Leonardo watched its departure keenly, and was turning to pick up another cage when he noticed Ezio standing there.

He smiled winningly and warmly at the sight of him, and embraced him. Then his face grew grave. 'Ezio! My friend. I hardly expected to see you here, after what you've been through. But welcome, welcome. Just bear with me one minute. This won't take long.'

Ezio watched as he released one after another of the various thrushes, bullfinches, larks and far more expensive nightingales into the air, watching each one very carefully.

'What are you doing?' asked Ezio, wonderingly.

'All life is precious,' Leonardo replied simply. 'I cannot bear to see my fellow creatures imprisoned like this, just because they have fine voices.'

'Is that the only reason you release them?' Ezio suspected an ulterior motive.

Leonardo grinned, but gave no direct answer. 'I won't eat meat any more either. Why should some poor animal die just because it tastes good to us?'

'There'd be no work for farmers else.'

'They could all grow corn.'

'Imagine how boring that'd be. Anyway, there'd be a glut.'

'Ah, I was forgetting that you're a *finanziatore*. And I am forgetting my manners. What brings you here?'

'I need a favour, Leonardo.'

'How can I be of service?'

'There's something I . . . inherited from my father that I'd like you to repair, if you can.'

Leonardo's eyes lit up. 'Of course. Come this way. We'll use my inner chamber – those boys are cluttering everything up in the studio as usual. I sometimes wonder why I bother to employ them at all!'

Ezio smiled. He was beginning to see why, but at the same time sensed that Leonardo's first love was, and would always be, his work.

'Come this way.'

Leonardo's smaller, inner room was even more untidy than the studio, but among the masses of books and specimens, and papers covered with that indecipherable scrawl, the artist, as always (and incongruously) impeccably dressed and scented, carefully piled some stuff on other stuff until a space was cleared on a large drafting table.

'Forgive the confusion,' he said. 'But at last we have an oasis! Let's see what you've got for me. Unless you'd like a glass of wine first?'

'No, no.'

'Good,' said Leonardo eagerly. 'Let's see it, then!'

Ezio carefully extracted the blade, bracer and mechanism, which he had previously wrapped in the mysterious vellum page that had accompanied them. Leonardo tried in vain to put the pieces of machinery back together but failed, and seemed for a moment to despair.

'I don't know, Ezio,' he said. 'This mechanism is old – very old – but it's very sophisticated as well, and its construction is ahead I would say even of our time. Fascinating.' He looked up. 'I've certainly never seen anything like it. But I'm afraid there's little I can do without the original plans.'

Then he turned his attention to the vellum page, which he had picked up in order to wrap Ezio's pieces back up again. 'Wait a second!' he cried, poring over it. Then he placed the broken blade and bracer to one side, spread out the sheet, and, referring to it, began to rummage among a row of old books and manuscripts on a nearby shelf. Finding the two he wanted, he placed them on the table and began carefully to leaf through them.

'What are you doing?' asked Ezio, slightly impatiently.

'This is very interesting,' said Leonardo. 'This looks very like a page from a Codex.'

'A what?'

'It's a page from an ancient book. This isn't printed, it's in manuscript. It's very old indeed. Have you any more of them?'

'No.'

'Pity. People shouldn't tear the pages out of books like this.' Leonardo paused. 'Unless, perhaps, the whole thing together –'

'What?'

'Nothing. Look, the contents of this page are encrypted; but if my theory is correct . . . based on these sketches it may very well be that . . .'

Ezio waited, but Leonardo was lost in a world of his own. He took a seat and waited patiently while Leonardo rummaged through and pored over a number of books and scrolls, making cross-references and notes, all in that curious left-handed mirror-writing he used. Ezio wasn't the only one, he supposed, to live his life with one eye looking behind him. From the little he'd seen of what was going on in the studio, if the Church got wind of some of the things Leonardo was up to, he didn't doubt that his friend would be for the high jump.

At last Leonardo looked up. But by that time Ezio was beginning to doze. 'Remarkable,' muttered Leonardo to himself, and then in a louder voice, 'Remarkable! If we transpose the letters and then select every third . . .'

He set to work, drawing the blade, bracer and mechanism towards him. He dug out a toolbox from under the table, set up a vice, and quietly became absorbed in his work. An hour passed, two . . . Ezio by now was sleeping peacefully, lulled by the warm fug of the room and the gentle sounds of tapping and scraping as Leonardo worked on. And at last –

'Ezio! Wake up!'

'Eh?'

'Look!' And Leonardo pointed to the tabletop. The dagger blade, fully restored, had been fitted into the strange mechanism, which in turn was fixed to the bracer. Everything was polished and looked as if it had just been made, but nothing shone. 'A matt finish, I decided,' said Leonardo. 'Like Roman armour. Anything which shines glints in the sun, and that's a dead giveaway.'

Ezio picked up the weapon and hefted it in his hands. It was light, but the strong blade was perfectly balanced on it. Ezio had never seen anything like it. A spring-loaded dagger that he could conceal above his wrist. All he had to do was flex his hand and the blade would spring out, ready to slash or stab as its user desired.

'I thought you were a man of peace,' said Ezio, remembering the birds.

'Ideas take precedence,' said Leonardo with decision. 'Whatever they are. Now,' he added, producing a hammer and chisel from his toolbox. 'You're right-handed, aren't you? Good. Then kindly place your right ring finger on this block.'

'What are you doing?'

'I'm sorry, but this is how it must be done. The blade is designed to ensure the total commitment of whoever wields it.'

'What do you mean?'

'It'll only work if we have that finger off.'

Ezio blinked. His mind flashed on a number of images: he remembered Alberti's supposed friendliness to his father, how Alberti had later reassured him after

94

his father's arrest, the executions, his own pursuit. He clamped his jaw. 'Do it.'

'Maybe I should use a cleaver. Cleaner cut that way.' Leonardo produced one from a drawer in the table. 'Now – just place your finger – *così.*'

Ezio steeled himself as Leonardo raised the cleaver. He closed his eyes as he heard it brought down – *schunk!* – into the wood of the block. But he'd felt no pain. He opened his eyes. The cleaver was stuck in the block, inches from his hand, which was intact.

'You bastard!' Ezio was shocked, and furious at this tasteless practical joke.

Leonardo raised his hands. 'Calm yourself! It was just a bit of fun! Cruel, I admit, but I simply couldn't resist. I wanted to see how determined you were. You see, the use of this machine originally *did* require such a sacrifice. Something to do with an ancient initiation ceremony, I think. But I've made one or two adjustments. So you can keep your finger. Look! The blade comes out well clear of them, and I've added a hilt that flips out when the blade's extended. All you have to do is remember to keep them splayed *as* it's coming out! So you can keep your finger. But you might like to wear gloves when you use it – the blade is keen.'

Ezio was too fascinated – and grateful – to be angry for long. 'This is extraordinary,' he said, opening and closing the dagger several times until he could time its use perfectly. 'Incredible.'

'Isn't it?' agreed Leonardo. 'Are you sure you don't have any more pages like this one?'

'I'm sorry.'

'Well, listen, if you do happen across any more, please bring them to me.'

'You have my word. And how much do I owe you for – ?'

'A pleasure. Most instructive. There is no –'

They were interrupted by a hammering at the outer door of the studio. Leonardo hurried through to the front of the building as Agniolo and Innocento looked up fearfully. The person on the other side of the door had started to bellow, 'Open up, by order of the Florentine Guard!'

'Just a moment!' Leonardo shouted back, but in a lower voice he said to Ezio, 'Stay back there.'

Then he opened the door, and stood in it, blocking the guardsman's way.

'You Leonardo da Vinci?' asked the guard in one of those loud, bullying, official voices.

'What can I do for you?' said Leonardo, moving out into the street, obliging the guard to step back.

'I am empowered to ask you certain questions.' Leonardo had by now so manoeuvred himself that the guard had his back to the doorway of the studio.

'What seems to be the trouble?'

'We've had a report that you were seen just now consorting with a known enemy of the city.'

'What, me? Consorting? Preposterous!'

'When was the last time you either saw or spoke to Ezio Auditore?'

'Who?'

'Don't play silly buggers with me. We know you were close to the family. Sold the mother a couple of your daubs. Maybe I need to refresh your memory a bit?' And the guard hit Leonardo in the stomach with the butt of his halberd. With a sharp cry of pain, Leonardo doubled up and fell to the ground, where the guard kicked him. 'Ready to chat now, are we? I don't like artists. Load of poofs.'

But this had given Ezio enough time to step quietly through the doorway and position himself behind the guard. The street was deserted. The nape of the man's sweaty neck was exposed. It was as good a time as any to give his new toy a trial run. He raised his hand, triggered the release mechanism, and the silent blade shot out. With a deft movement of his now open right hand, Ezio stabbed once into the side of the guard's neck. The recently honed edge of the blade was viciously sharp, and eased through the man's jugular without the slightest resistance. The guard fell, dead before he hit the ground.

Ezio helped Leonardo up.

'Thank you,' said the shaken artist.

'I'm sorry – I didn't mean to kill him – there was no time –'

'Sometimes we don't have an alternative. But I should be used to this by now.'

'What do you mean?'

'I was involved in the Saltarelli case.'

Ezio remembered then. A young artist's model, Jacopo Saltarelli, had been anonymously denounced a few weeks earlier for practising prostitution, and Leonardo, along with three others, had been accused of patronizing him. The case had fallen apart for lack of evidence, but some of the mud had stuck. 'But we don't prosecute homosexual men here,' he said. 'Why, I seem to remember that the Germans have a nickname for them – they call them *Florenzer.*'

'It's still officially against the law,' said Leonardo drily. 'You can still get fined. And with men like Alberti in charge –'

'What about the body?'

'Oh,' said Leonardo. 'It's quite a windfall. Help me drag it inside before anyone sees us. I'll put it with the others.'

'Windfall? Others?'

'The cellar's quite cold. They keep for a week. I get one or two cadavers that no one else wants from the hospital now and then. All unofficial, of course. But I cut them open, and dig about a bit – it helps me with my research.'

Ezio looked at his friend more than curiously. 'What?'

'I think I told you – I like to find out how things work.'

They dragged the body out of sight, and Leonardo's two assistants manhandled it through a door down some stone steps, out of sight.

'But what if they send someone after him – to find out what happened to him?'

Leonardo shrugged. 'I'll deny all knowledge.' He winked. 'I'm not without powerful friends here, Ezio.'

Ezio was nonplussed. He said, 'Well, you seem confident enough . . .'

'Just don't mention this incident to anyone else.'

'I won't – and thank you, Leonardo, for everything.'

'A pleasure. And don't forget –' a hungry look had crept into his eyes, '– if you find any more pages from this Codex, bring them to me. Who knows what other new designs they might contain.'

'I promise!'

Ezio made his way back to Paola's house in triumphant mood, though he did not forget to lose himself in the anonymity of the crowd as he passed back north through the town.

Paola greeted him with some relief. 'You were gone longer than I'd expected.'

'Leonardo likes to talk.'

'But that's not all he did, I hope?'

'Oh no. Look!' And he showed her the wrist-dagger,

extending it from his sleeve with an extravagant flourish, and a boyish grin.

'Impressive.'

'Yes.' Ezio looked at it admiringly. 'I'll need a bit of practice with it. I want to keep all my own fingers.'

Paola looked serious. 'Well, Ezio, it looks as if you're all set. I've given you the skills you need, Leonardo has repaired your weapon.' She took a breath. 'All that's needed now is for you to do the deed.'

'Yes,' said Ezio quietly, his expression darkening again. 'The question is, how best to gain access to *Messer* Alberti.'

Paola looked thoughtful. 'Duke Lorenzo is back with us. He isn't happy about the executions Alberti authorized in his absence, but he doesn't have the power to challenge the Gonfaloniere. Nevertheless, there's to be a vernissage for Maestro Verrocchio's latest work at the cloister of Santa Croce tomorrow night. All Florentine society will be there, including Alberti.' She looked at him. 'I think you should be, too.'

Ezio found out that the piece of sculpture to be unveiled was a bronze statue of David, the biblical hero with whom Florence associated itself, poised as the city was between the twin Goliaths of Rome to the south and the land-hungry kings of France to the north. It had been commissioned by the Medici family and was destined to be installed in the Palazzo Vecchio. The Maestro had started work on it three or four years earlier, and a rumour had been going round that the head was modelled on one of Verrocchio's handsomer young apprentices of the time – a certain Leonardo da Vinci. At any rate, there was great excitement, and people were already dithering about what to wear for the occasion.

Ezio had other matters to ponder.

'Watch over my mother and sister while I'm gone,' he asked Paola.

'As if they were my own.'

'And if anything should happen to me –'

'Have faith, and it won't.'

Ezio made his way to Santa Croce in good time the following evening. He had spent the previous hours preparing himself, and honing his skills with his new weapon, until he was satisfied that he was fully proficient in its use. His thoughts dwelt on the deaths of his father and brothers, and the cruel tones of Alberti's voice as he passed sentence rang all too clearly in his mind.

As he approached, he saw two figures whom he recognized walking ahead of him, slightly apart from a small squad of bodyguards whose uniform displayed a badge of five red balls on a yellow ground. They appeared to be arguing, and he hurried forward to bring himself within earshot of them. They paused in front of the portico of the church, and he hovered nearby, out of sight, to listen. The men addressed each other in tight-lipped tones. One was Uberto Alberti; the other, a slim young man in his mid to late twenties, with a prominent nose and a determined face, was richly dressed in a red cap and cloak, over which he wore a silver-grey tunic. Duke Lorenzo – *Il Magnifico*, as his subjects called him, to the disgust of the Pazzi and their faction.

'You cannot tax me with this,' Alberti was saying. 'I acted on information received and irrefutable evidence – I acted within the law and within the bounds of my office!'

'No! You overstepped your bounds, Gonfaloniere, and you took advantage of my absence from Florence to do so. I am more than displeased.'

'Who are you to speak of bounds? You have seized power over this city, made yourself duke of it, without the formal consent of the Signoria or anyone else!'

'I have done no such thing!'

Alberti permitted himself a sardonic laugh. 'Of course you'd say that! Ever the innocent! How convenient for you. You surround yourself at Careggi with men most of the rest of us consider dangerous freethinkers – Ficino, Mirandola, and that creep Poliziano! But at least now we have had a chance to see how far your reach really extends – which is to say, nowhere at all, in any practical terms. That has proved a valuable lesson for my allies and me.'

'Yes. Your allies the Pazzi. That's what this is really all about, isn't it?'

Alberti studied his fingernails elaborately before replying. 'I'd be careful what you say, Duce. You might attract the wrong sort of attention.' But he didn't sound completely sure of himself.

'You are the one who should watch his mouth, Gonfaloniere. And I suggest you pass that advice on to your associates – take it as a friendly warning.' With that, Lorenzo swept away with his bodyguard in the direction of the cloister. After a moment, muttering some oath under his breath, Alberti followed. It almost sounded to Ezio as if the man were cursing himself.

The cloisters themselves had been draped with cloth-of-gold for the occasion, which dazzlingly reflected the light from hundreds of candles. On a rostrum near the fountain in the centre, a group of musicians played, and on another stood the bronze statue, a half life-size figure of exquisite beauty. As Ezio entered, using columns and shadows to conceal himself, he could see Lorenzo complimenting the artist. Ezio also recognized the mysterious cowled figure who'd been on the execution platform with Alberti.

Some distance away, Alberti himself stood surrounded by admiring members of the local nobility. From what he could hear, Ezio understood that they were congratulating the Gonfaloniere on ridding the city of the canker of the Auditore family. He had not thought that his father had so many enemies, as well as friends, in the city, but realized that they had only dared move against him when his principal ally, Lorenzo, had been absent. Ezio smiled as one noblewoman told Alberti that she hoped the Duke appreciated his integrity. It was clear that Alberti didn't like that suggestion one bit. Then he overheard more.

'What of the other son?' a nobleman was asking. 'Ezio, wasn't it? Has he escaped for good?'

Alberti managed a smile. 'The boy poses no danger whatsoever. Soft hands and an even softer head. He'll be caught and executed before the week is out.'

The company around him laughed.

'So – what's next for you, Uberto?' asked another man. 'The Chair of the Signoria, perhaps?'

Alberti spread his hands. 'It is as God wills. My only interest is to continue to serve Florence, faithfully and diligently.'

'Well, whatever you choose, know that you have our support.'

'That is most gratifying. We'll see what the future brings.' Alberti beamed, but modestly. 'And now, my friends, I suggest that we put politics aside and give ourselves over to the enjoyment of this sublime work of art, so generously donated by the noble Medici.'

Ezio waited until Alberti's companions wandered away in the direction of the *David*. For his part, Alberti took a goblet of wine and surveyed the scene, a mixture of satisfaction and wariness in his eyes. Ezio knew that this was his opportunity. All other eyes were on the statue, near which Verrocchio was stumbling through a short speech. Ezio slipped up to Alberti's side.

'It must have stuck in your craw to pay that last compliment,' Ezio hissed. 'But it's appropriate that you should be insincere to the end.'

Recognizing him, Alberti's eyes bulged in terror. 'You!'

'Yes, Gonfaloniere. It's Ezio. Here to avenge the murder of my father – your friend – and my innocent brothers.'

Alberti heard the dull click of a spring, a metallic sound, and saw the blade poised at his throat.

'Goodbye, Gonfaloniere,' said Ezio, coldly.

'Stop,' gasped Alberti. 'In my position, you would have done the same – to protect the ones you loved. Forgive me, Ezio – I had no choice.'

Ezio leant close, ignoring his plea. He knew the man had had a choice – an honourable one – and had been too supine to make it. 'Do you not think I am not protecting the ones *I* love? What mercy would you show my mother or my sister, if you could lay your hands on them? Now: where are the documents I gave you from my father? You must have them somewhere safe.'

'You'll never get them. I always carry them on my person!' Alberti tried to push Ezio away, and drew in a breath to call for the guards, but Ezio plunged the dagger into his throat and dragged its blade through the man's jugular artery. Unable now even to gurgle, Alberti sank to his knees, his hands instinctively clutching at his neck in a vain attempt to staunch the blood that cascaded down on to the grass. As he fell on his side, Ezio stooped swiftly and cut the man's wallet free of his belt. He glanced inside. Alberti in his final hubris had been telling the truth. The documents were indeed there.

But now there was silence. Verrocchio's speech had ground to a halt as the guests began to turn and stare, not yet comprehending what had happened. Ezio stood and faced them.

'Yes! What you see is real! What you see is vengeance! The Auditore family still lives. I am still here! Ezio Auditore!'

He caught his breath at the same moment as a woman's voice rang out, '*Assassino!*'

Now chaos reigned. Lorenzo's bodyguard quickly formed up round him, swords drawn. The guests ran hither and yon, some trying to escape, the braver ones going through the motions at least of trying to seize Ezio, though none quite dared make a real attempt. Ezio noticed the cowled figure slipping away into the shadows. Verrocchio stood protectively by his statue. Women screamed, men shouted, and city guards streamed into the cloisters, unsure of whom to pursue. Ezio took advantage of this, climbing up to the roof of the cloister colonnade and vaulting over it into a courtyard beyond, whose open gate led into the square in front of the church, where a curious crowd was already gathering, attracted by the sound of the commotion within.

'What's happening?' someone asked Ezio.

'Justice has been done,' Ezio replied, before racing north-west across town to the safety of Paola's mansion.

He paused on the way to verify the contents of Alberti's wallet. At least the man's last words had been truthful. Everything was there. And there was something else. An undelivered letter in Alberti's hand. Perhaps fresh knowledge for Ezio, who broke the seal and tore the parchment open.

But it was a personal note from Alberti to his wife. As he read it, Ezio could at least understand what kind of forces might be brought to bear to break a man's integrity.

My love

I put these thoughts to paper in the hope that I might one day have the courage to share them with you. In time, you'll no doubt learn that I betrayed Giovanni Auditore, labelled him a traitor and sentenced him to die. History will likely judge this act to have been a matter of politics and greed. But you must understand that it was not fate that forced my hand, but fear.

When the Medici robbed our family of all we owned, I found myself afraid. For you. For our son. For the future. What hope is there in this world for a man without proper means? As for the others, they offered me money, land and title in exchange for my collaboration.

And this is how I came to betray my closest friend.
However unspeakable the act, it seemed necessary at the time.
And even now, looking back, I can see no other way . . .

Ezio folded the letter carefully and replaced it in his wallet. He would reseal it, and see that it was delivered. He was determined not to stoop to mean-spiritedness, ever.

6

'It's done,' he told Paola, simply.

She embraced him briefly, then stood back. 'I know. I am glad to see you safe.'

'I think it's time for me to leave Florence.'

'Where will you go?'

'My father's brother Mario has an estate near Monteriggioni. We'll go there.'

'There's a huge hunt on for you already, Ezio. They are putting up "wanted" posters everywhere with your picture on them. And the public orators are beginning to speak against you.' She paused, thoughtfully. 'I'll get some of my people to go out and tear down as many posters as they can, and the orators can be bribed to speak of other things.' Another thought struck her. 'And I'd better have travel papers drawn up for the three of you.'

Ezio shook his head, thinking of Alberti. 'What is this world we live in, where belief can so easily be manipulated?'

'Alberti was placed in what he saw as an impossible position, but he should have held firm against it.' She sighed. 'Truth is traded every day. It's something you'll have to get used to, Ezio.'

He took her hands in his. 'Thank you.'

'Florence will be a better place now, especially if Duke Lorenzo can get one of his own men elected Gonfaloniere. But now there is no time to waste. Your mother and sister are here.' She turned and clapped her hands. 'Annetta!'

Annetta emerged from the back of the house, bringing Maria and Claudia with her. It was an emotional reunion. Ezio saw that his mother was not much recovered, and still clasped Petruccio's little box of feathers in her hand. She returned his embrace, though absently, while Paola looked on with a sad smile.

Claudia, on the other hand, clung to him. 'Ezio! Where have you been? Paola and Annetta have been so kind, but they won't let us go home. And Mother hasn't spoken a word since –' She broke off, fighting her own tears. 'Well,' she said, recovering, 'perhaps now Father will be able to sort things out for us. It must all have been a dreadful misunderstanding, no?'

Paola looked at him. 'This might be the time,' she said softly. 'They will have to know the truth soon.'

Claudia's gaze shifted from Ezio to Paola and back again. Maria had seated herself next to Annetta, who had her arm round her. Maria stared into space, smiling faintly, caressing the pearwood box.

'What is it, Ezio?' asked Claudia, fear in her voice.

'Something's happened.'

'What do you mean?'

Ezio was silent, at a loss for words, but his expression told her everything.

'Oh, God, no!'

'Claudia —'

'Tell me it's not true!'

Ezio hung his head.

'No, no, no, no, no!' cried Claudia.

'Shhh.' He tried to calm her. 'I did everything I could, *piccina*.'

Claudia buried her head in his chest and cried, long, harsh sobs, while Ezio did his best to comfort her. He looked over her head at his mother, but she didn't appear to have heard. Perhaps, in her own way, she already knew. After all the turmoil that had descended upon Ezio's life, having to witness his sister and his mother thrown into the depths of despair was almost enough to break him. He stood, holding his sister in his arms, for what seemed an eternity — feeling the responsibility of the world on his shoulders. It was up to him to protect his family now — the Auditore name was his to honour. Ezio the boy was no more . . . He collected his thoughts.

'Listen,' he said to Claudia, once she had quietened a little. 'What matters now is that we get away from here. Somewhere safe, where you and Mamma can remain in security. But if we are to do that I need you to be brave. You must be strong for me, and look after our mother. Do you understand?'

She listened, cleared her throat, pulled away from him a little, and looked up at him. 'Yes.'

'Then we must make our preparations now. Go and pack what you need, but bring little with you – we must leave on foot – a carriage would be too dangerous to organize. Wear your simplest clothes – we must not draw attention to ourselves. And hurry!'

Claudia left with their mother and Annetta.

'You should bathe and change,' said Paola to him. 'You'll feel better.'

Two hours later their travel papers were ready and they could leave. Ezio checked the contents of his satchel carefully one last time. Perhaps his uncle could explain the contents of the documents he had taken from Alberti, which had clearly been of such vital importance to him. His new dagger was strapped to his right forearm, out of sight. He tightened his belt. Claudia led Maria into the garden and stood by the door in the wall by which they were to leave, with Annetta, who was trying not to cry.

Ezio turned to Paola. 'Goodbye. And thank you again, for everything.'

She put her arms round him and kissed him close to his mouth. 'Stay safe, Ezio, and stay vigilant. I suspect the road ahead of you is yet long.'

He bowed gravely, then drew up his hood and joined his mother and sister, picking up the bag they had packed. They kissed Annetta goodbye, and moments later they were in the street, walking north, Claudia with her arm linked through her mother's. For a while they were silent, and Ezio pondered the great responsibility he had now been obliged to shoulder. He prayed that he would be able to rise to the occasion, but it was hard. He would have to remain strong, but he would manage it for the sake of Claudia and his poor mother, who seemed to have retreated completely into herself.

They had reached the centre of the city when Claudia started to speak – and she was full of questions. He noticed with gratification, though, that her voice was firm.

'How could this have happened to us?' she said.

'I don't know.'

'Do you think we'll ever be able to come back?'

'I don't know, Claudia.'

'What will happen to our house?'

He shook his head. There had been no time to make any arrangements, and if there had been, with whom could he have made them? Perhaps Duke Lorenzo would be able to close it up, have it guarded, but that was a faint hope.

'Were they . . . Were they given a proper funeral?'

'Yes. I . . . arranged it myself.' They were crossing the Arno and Ezio allowed himself a glance downriver.

At last they were approaching the southern city gates, and Ezio was grateful that they had got this far undetected, but it was a dangerous moment, for the gates were heavily policed. Thankfully the documents in false names which Paola had provided them with passed muster, and the guards were on the lookout for a desperate young man on his own, not a modestly dressed little family.

They travelled south steadily all that day, pausing only when they were well clear of the city to buy bread, cheese and wine at a farmhouse and to rest for an hour under the shade of an oak tree at the edge of a cornfield. Ezio had to rein in his impatience, for it was almost thirty miles to Monteriggioni and they had to travel at his mother's pace. She was a strong woman at the beginning of her forties, but the massive shock she had sustained had aged her. He prayed that once they reached Uncle Mario's she would recover, though he could see that any recovery would be a slow one. He hoped that, barring any setback, they would reach Mario's estate by the afternoon of the following day.

That night they spent in a deserted barn, where at least there was clean, warm hay. They dined on the remains of their lunch, and made Maria as comfortable as possible. She made no complaint, indeed she seemed completely unaware of her surroundings; but when Claudia tried to take Petruccio's box from her when getting her ready for bed, she protested violently and pushed her daughter away, swearing at her like a fishwife. Brother and sister were shocked at that.

But she slept peacefully, and seemed refreshed the next morning. They washed themselves in a brook, drank some of its clear water in lieu of breakfast, and continued on their way. It was a bright day, pleasantly warm but with a cooling breeze, and they made good progress, passing only a handful of wagons on the road and seeing no one except the odd group of labourers in the fields and orchards they walked by. Ezio was able to buy some fruit, enough at least for Claudia and his mother, but he wasn't hungry anyway – he was too nervous to eat.

At last, in mid-afternoon, he was heartened to see the little walled town of Monteriggioni bathed in sunshine on its hill in the distance. Mario effectively ruled the district. Another mile or two, and they would be within his territory. Heartened, the little group quickened their pace.

'Nearly there,' he told Claudia, with a smile.

'*Grazie a Dio,*' she replied, returning it.

They'd just started to relax when, at a turn in the road, a familiar figure, accompanied by a dozen men in blue-and-gold liveries, blocked their way. One of the guards carried a standard bearing the hated, familiar emblem of golden dolphins and crosses on a blue ground.

'Ezio!' the figure greeted him. '*Buon' giorno*! And your

family – or at least, what's left of it! What a pleasant surprise!' He nodded to his men, who fanned out across the road, halberds at the ready.

'Vieri!'

'The same. As soon as they released my father from custody, he was more than happy to finance this little hunting party for me. I was hurt. After all, how could you think of leaving Florence without saying a proper goodbye?'

Ezio advanced a pace, ushering Claudia and his mother behind him.

'What do you want, Vieri? I should have thought you'd be satisfied with what the Pazzi have managed to achieve.'

Vieri spread his hands. 'What do I want? Well, it's hard to know where to begin. So many things! Let's see . . . I'd like a larger palazzo, a prettier wife, much more money and – what else? – Oh, yes! Your head!' He drew his sword, motioning his guards to stay ready, and advanced on Ezio himself.

'I'm surprised, Vieri – are you really going to take me on all alone? But of course your bully boys are right behind you!'

'I don't think you're worthy of my sword,' retorted Vieri, sheathing it again. 'I think I'll just finish you off with my fists. Sorry if this distresses you, *tesora*,' he added to Claudia, 'but don't worry – it won't take long, then I'll see what I can do to comfort you – and who knows, maybe your little mamma as well!'

Ezio stepped forward fast and connected his fist to Vieri's jaw so that his enemy staggered, taken off guard. But, regaining his feet, Vieri waved his men back and hurled himself on to Ezio with a furious roar, piling on blow after blow. Such was the ferocity of Vieri's attack that while Ezio parried with skill, he was unable to land a meaningful blow of his own. Both men were locked together, wrestling for control, occasionally staggering back only to fling themselves at each other with renewed vigour. Eventually Ezio was able to use Vieri's anger to work against him – no one ever fought effectively in a rage. Vieri wound up to throw a huge haymaker with his right; Ezio stepped forward and the blow glanced uselessly off his shoulder, Vieri's momentum carrying his weight forward uncontrolled. Ezio tripped up his opponent's heels and sent him rolling in the dust. Bleeding and bested, Vieri scrambled to safety behind his men, and stood up, dusting himself down with his grazed hands.

'I tire of this,' he said, and shouted to the guards. 'Finish him off, and the women too. I can do better than that scrawny little tadpole and her *carcassa* of a mother!'

'*Coniglio*!' yelled Ezio, panting for breath, drawing his sword, but the guards had formed a circle round them and extended their halberds. He knew he'd have a hard time closing with them.

The circle tightened. Ezio kept swinging round, trying to keep his womenfolk behind him, but things looked black, and Vieri's unpleasant laugh was one of triumph.

Suddenly there was a sharp, almost ethereal whistling noise and two of the guards to Ezio's left crumpled to their knees and fell forward, dropping their weapons as they did so. From each of their backs projected a throwing-knife, buried to the hilt and clearly aimed with deadly accuracy. Blood billowed out from their shirts, like crimson flowers.

The others drew back in alarm, but not before one more of their number had fallen to the ground, a knife in his back.

'What sorcery is this?' yelped Vieri, terror cutting his voice, drawing his sword and looking round wildly.

He was answered by a deep-throated, booming laugh. 'Nothing to do with sorcery, boy – everything to do with skill!' The voice was coming from a nearby coppice.

'Show yourself!'

A large bearded man wearing high boots and a light breastplate emerged from the little wood. Behind him several others, similarly attired, appeared. 'As you wish,' he said, sardonically.

'Mercenaries!' snarled Vieri, then turned to his own guards. 'What are you waiting for? Kill them! Kill them all!'

But the large man stepped forward, wrested Vieri's sword from him with unbelievable grace, and snapped the blade over his knee as easily as if it had been a twig.

'I don't think that's a very good idea, little Pazzi, though I must say you live up to your family name.'

Vieri didn't answer, but urged his men on. Not very willingly, they closed with the strangers, while Vieri, picking up the halberd of one of his dead guards, rounded on Ezio, knocking his sword out of his hand and out of reach just as he was drawing it.

'Here, Ezio, use this!' said the large man, throwing him another sword, which flew through the air to land on its point, quivering in the ground at his feet. In a flash he'd picked it up. It was a heavy weapon and he had to use both hands to wield it, but he was able to sever the shaft of Vieri's halberd. Vieri himself, seeing that his men were being easily bested by the *condottieri*, and that two more were already down, called off the attack and fled, hurling imprecations as he went. The large man approached Ezio and the women, grinning broadly.

'I'm glad I came out to meet you,' he said. 'Looks as if I arrived just in time.'

'You have my thanks, whoever you are.'

The man laughed again, and there was something familiar about his voice.

'Do I know you?' asked Ezio.

'It's been a long time. But still I'm surprised you don't recognize your own uncle!'

'Uncle Mario?'

'The same!'

He gave Ezio a bear-hug, and then approached Maria and Claudia. Distress clouded his face when he saw the condition Maria was in. 'Listen, child –' he said to Claudia. 'I'm going to take Ezio back to the *castello* now, but I'm leaving my men to guard you, and they will give you something to eat and drink. I'll send a rider ahead and he'll return with a carriage to bring you the rest of the way. You've done enough walking for one day and I can see that my poor sister-in-law is . . .' he paused before adding delicately, 'tired out.'

'Thank you, Uncle Mario.'

'It's settled then. We'll see you very soon.' He turned and issued orders to his men, then put an arm round Ezio and guided him in the direction of his castle, which dominated the little town.

'How did you know I was on my way?' asked Ezio.

Mario looked a little evasive. 'Oh – a friend in Florence sent a messenger on horseback ahead of you. But I already knew what had happened. I haven't the strength to march on Florence but now Lorenzo's back let us pray he can keep the Pazzi in check. You'd better fill me in on my brother's fate – and that of my nephews.'

Ezio paused. The memory of his kinsmen's death still haunted the darkest part of his memories.

'They . . . They were all executed for treason . . .' He paused. 'I escaped by the purest chance.'

'My God,' mouthed Mario, his face contorted with pain. 'Do you know why this happened?'

'No – but it is something I hope you may be able to help me find answers to.' And Ezio went on to tell his uncle about the hidden chest in the family palazzo and its contents, and of his revenge on Alberti and the documents he had taken from him. 'The most important-looking is a list of names,' he added, then broke off in grief. 'I cannot believe this has befallen us!'

Mario patted his arm. 'I know something of your father's business,' he said, and it occurred to Ezio that Mario hadn't shown much surprise when he'd told him of the hidden chest in the secret chamber. 'We'll make sense of this. But we must also make sure your mother and sister are properly provided for. My castle is not much of a place for women of any quality, and soldiers like me never really settle down; but there is a convent about a mile away where they will be completely safe and well cared for. If you agree, we will send them there. For you and I have much to do.'

Ezio nodded. He would see them settled and persuade Claudia that it was the best temporary solution, for he could not see her wanting to remain long in such seclusion.

They were approaching the little town.

'I thought Monteriggioni was an enemy of Florence,' Ezio said.

'No so much of Florence as of the Pazzi,' his uncle told him. 'But you are old enough to know about alliances between city-states, whether they are big ones or small ones. One year there is a friendship, the next, enmity; and the following year there is friendship again. And so it seems to go on for ever, like a mad game of chess. But you'll like it here. The people are honest and hard-working, and the goods we produce are solid and hard-wearing. The priest is a good man, doesn't drink too much, and minds his own business. And I mind mine, around him – but I've never been a very devoted son of the Church myself. Best of all is the wine – the best Chianti you will ever taste comes from my own vineyards. Come, just a little further, and we'll be there.'

Mario's castle was the ancient seat of the Auditori and had been built in the 1250s, though the site had originally been occupied by a much more ancient construction. Mario had refined and added to the building, which nowadays had more of the appearance of an opulent villa, though its walls were high, many feet in thickness, and well fortified. Before it and in place of a garden was a large practice-field, where Ezio could see a couple of dozen young armed men engaged in various exercises to improve their fighting technique.

'*Casa, dolce casa*,' said Mario. 'You haven't been here since you were a little boy. Been some changes since then. What do you think?'

'It's most impressive, Uncle.'

The rest of the day was filled with activity. Mario

showed Ezio around the castle, organized his accommodation, and made sure that Claudia and Maria had been safely housed in the nearby convent, whose abbess was an old and dear friend (and, it was rumoured, long ago a mistress) of Mario. But the following morning he was summoned early to his uncle's workroom, a large, high-ceilinged place, whose walls were festooned with maps, armour and weapons, and furnished with a heavy oak table and chairs.

'You'd better get into the town quickly,' Mario said one day soon afterwards in a businesslike voice. Get yourself properly kitted out. I'll send one of my men with you. Come back here when you've finished and we'll begin.'

'Begin what, Uncle?'

Mario looked surprised. 'I thought you'd come here to train.'

'No, Uncle – that was not my intention. This was the first place of safety I could think of once we had to flee Florence. But my intention is to take my mother and sister further still.'

Mario looked grave. 'But what about your father? Don't you think he'd want you to finish his work?'

'What – as a banker? The family business is over – the House of Auditore is no more, unless Duke Lorenzo has managed to keep it out of Pazzi hands.'

'I wasn't thinking of that,' began Mario, and then interrupted himself. 'Do you mean to say Giovanni never told you?'

'I am sorry, Uncle, but I have no idea what you are talking about.'

Mario shook his head. 'I don't know what your father must have been thinking of. Perhaps he judged the time not to be right. But events have overtaken any such consideration now.' He looked hard at Ezio. 'We must talk, long and hard. Leave me the documents you have in your pouch. I must study them while *you* go into the town and get yourself equipped. Here's a list of what you'll need, and money to pay for it.'

In a confused mood, Ezio set off for the town in the company of one of Mario's sergeants, a grizzled veteran called Orazio, and under his guidance acquired from the armourer there a battle-dagger, light body-armour, and – from the local doctor – bandages and a basic medical kit. He returned to the castle to find Mario waiting impatiently for him.

'*Salute*,' said Ezio. 'I have done as you requested.'

'And quickly too. *Ben fatto!* And now, we must teach you properly how to fight.'

'Uncle, forgive me, but as I told you, I have no intention of staying.'

Mario bit his lip. 'Listen, Ezio, you were barely able to hold your own against Vieri. If I hadn't arrived when I did . . .' He broke off. 'Well, leave if you must, but at least first learn the skills and knowledge you'll need to defend yourself, or you won't last a week on the road.'

Ezio was silent.

'If not for me, do it for the sake of your mother and sister,' Mario pressed him.

Ezio considered his options, but he had to admit that his uncle had a point. 'Well, then,' he said. 'Since you've been kind enough to see me kitted out.'

Mario beamed and clapped him on the shoulder. 'Good man! You'll live to thank me!'

In the following weeks the most intensive instruction in the use of arms followed, but while he was learning new battle skills, Ezio was also finding out more about his family background, and the secrets his father had not had time to divulge to him. And, as Mario let him have the run of his library, he gradually became troubled by the fact that he might be on the verge of a far more important destiny than he had believed possible.

'You say my father was more than just a banker?' he asked his uncle.

'Far more,' replied Mario gravely. 'You father was a highly trained killer.'

'That cannot be – my father was always a financier, a businessman . . . how could he have possibly been a killer?'

'No, Ezio, he was much more than that. He was born and bred to kill. He was a senior member of the Order of Assassins.' Mario hesitated. 'I know you must have found out something more about all this in the library. We must discuss the documents that were entrusted to

you, and which you – thank God! – had the wit to
retrieve from Alberti. That list of names – it isn't a
catalogue of debtors, you know. It carries the names of
all those responsible for your father's murder – and they
are men who form part of a still greater conspiracy.'

Ezio struggled to take it all in – everything he
thought he knew about his father, his family, it all now
seemed to be a half-truth. How could his father have
kept this from him? It was all so inconceivable, so
alien. Ezio chose his words with care – his father must
have had a reason for this secrecy. 'I accept that there
was more to my father than I ever knew, and forgive
me for doubting your word, but why is the need for
secrecy so great?'

Mario paused before replying. 'Are you familiar with
the Order of the Knights Templar?'

'I have heard of them.'

'They were founded many centuries ago, soon after
the First of the Crusades, and became an elite fighting
force of warriors for God – effectively they were monks
in armour. They took a pledge of abstinence and a vow
of poverty. But the years rolled by, and their status
changed. In time, they became involved in international
finance, and very successful they were at it, too. Other
Orders of Knights – the Hospitallers and the Teutonic
Knights – looked on them askance, and their power
began to be a cause for concern, even to kings. They
established a base in southern France, and planned to

form their own state. They paid no taxes, supported their own private army, and began to lord it over everyone. At last, nearly two hundred years ago, King Philip the Fair of France moved against them. There was a terrible purge, the Templars were arrested and driven away, massacred, and at last excommunicated by the Pope. But they could not all be rooted out – they had fifteen thousand chapters throughout Europe. Nevertheless, with their estates and properties annexed, the Templars seemed to disappear, their power apparently broken.'

'What happened to them?'

Mario shook his head. 'Of course, it was a ruse to ensure their own survival. They went underground, hoarding the riches they had salvaged, maintaining their organization, and bent more than ever now on their true goal.'

'And what was that?'

'What *is* that, you mean!' Mario's eyes blazed. 'Their intention is nothing less than world domination. And only one organization is devoted to thwarting them. The Order of the Assassins, to which your father – and I – have the honour to belong.'

Ezio needed a moment to take this in. 'And was Alberti one of the Templars?'

Mario nodded solemnly. 'Yes. As are all the others on your father's list.'

'And – Vieri?'

'He is one as well, and his father Francesco, and all the Pazzi clan.'

Ezio pondered this. 'That explains much . . .' he said. 'There is something I haven't shown you yet –'

He rolled up his sleeve to reveal his secret dagger.

'Ah,' said Mario. 'You were wise not to reveal that until you were sure you could trust even me completely. I was wondering what had become of it. And I see that you have had it repaired. It was your father's, given to him by our father, and to him by his. It was broken in . . . a confrontation your father was involved in many years ago, but he could never find a craftsman skilled or trustworthy enough to restore it. You have done well, my boy.'

'Even so,' said Ezio. 'All this talk of Assassins and Templars sounds like something from an ancient tale – it reeks of the fantastic.'

Mario smiled. 'Like something from an old parchment covered in arcane writing, perhaps?'

'You know of the Codex page?'

Mario shrugged. 'Had you forgotten? It was with the papers you handed over to me.'

'Can you tell me what it is?' Ezio was somehow reluctant to involve his friend Leonardo in this unless it became strictly necessary.

'Well, whoever repaired your blade must have been able to read at least some of it,' said Mario, but he raised his hand as Ezio was about to open his mouth. 'But I will ask you no questions. I can see that you wish to protect someone, and I will respect that. But there is more to the page than the working instructions for your weapon. The pages of the Codex are scattered now throughout Italy. It is a guide to the inner workings of the Assassins' Order, its origin, purpose and techniques. It is, if you will, our Creed. Your father believed that the Codex contained a powerful secret. Something that would change the world.' He paused for thought. 'Perhaps that is why they came for him.'

Ezio was overwhelmed at this information – it was a huge amount to take in all at once. 'Assassins, Templars, this strange Codex –'

'I will be your guide, Ezio. But you must first learn to open your mind, and always remember this: nothing is true. Everything is permitted.'

Mario would tell him nothing more then, though Ezio pressed him. Instead, his uncle continued to put him through the most rigorous process of military training, and from dawn to dusk he found himself exercising with the young *condottieri* on the practice-ground, falling into bed each night too exhausted to think of anything but sleep. And then, one day . . .

'Well done, nephew!' his uncle told him. 'I think you are ready.'

Ezio was pleased. 'Thank you, Uncle, for all you've given me.'

Mario's answer was to give the boy a bear-hug. 'You are family! Such is my duty and desire!'

'I'm glad you persuaded me to stay.'

Mario looked at him keenly. 'So – have you reconsidered your decision to leave?'

Ezio returned his gaze. 'I am sorry, Uncle, but my mind is made up. For the safety of Mamma and Claudia – I still intend to make for the coast and take ship for Spain.'

Mario did not hide his displeasure. 'Forgive me, nephew, but I have not taught you the skills you now have either for my own amusement or your exclusive benefit. I have taught you so that you may be better prepared to strike against our enemies.'

'And, if they find me, so I will.'

'So,' Mario said bitterly. 'You want to leave? To throw away everything your father fought and died for? To deny your very heritage? Well! I cannot pretend to you that I am not disappointed – highly disappointed. But so be it. Orazio will take you to the convent when you judge the moment to be right for your mother to travel, and he will see you on your way. I wish you *buona fortuna*.'

With that, Mario turned his back on his nephew and stalked away.

More time passed, as Ezio found he had to allow his mother enough peace and quiet to pave the way to her recovery. He himself made his preparations for leaving with a heavy heart. At last he set out to pay what he imagined might be his last visit to the convent to visit his mother and sister before taking them away, and found them better than he'd dared to hope. Claudia had made friends with some of the younger nuns, and it was clear to Ezio, to his surprise and not greatly to his pleasure, that she was beginning to be attracted to the life. Meanwhile his mother was making a steady but slow recovery, and the abbess, on hearing of his plans, demurred, advising him that rest was what she still badly needed, and that she should not be moved again just yet.

When he returned to Mario's castle, therefore, he was full of misgivings, and he was aware that these misgivings had grown with time.

At that period, some kind of military preparations had been going on in Monteriggioni, and now they seemed to be coming to a head. The sight of them distracted him. His uncle was nowhere to be seen, but he managed to track Orazio down to the map-room.

'What's going on?' he asked. 'Where's my uncle?'

'He's preparing for battle.'

'What? With whom?'

'Oh, I expect he'd have told you if he'd thought you were staying. But we all know that that is not your intention.'

'Well . . .'

'Listen, your old friend Vieri de' Pazzi has set himself up at San Gimignano. He's tripling the garrison there and has let it be known that as soon as he's ready, he's coming to raze Monteriggioni to the ground. So we're going there first, to crush the little snake and teach the Pazzi a lesson they won't forget in a hurry.'

Ezio took a deep breath. Surely this changed everything. And perhaps it was Fate – the very stimulus he'd unconsciously been seeking. 'Where is my uncle?'

'In the stables.'

Ezio was already halfway out of the room.

'Hey! Where are you off to?'

'To the stables! There must be a horse for me, too!'

Orazio smiled as he watched him go.

7

Mario, with Ezio riding at his side, led his forces to within sight of San Gimignano in the middle of a spring night in 1477. It was to be the beginning of a tough confrontation.

'Tell me again what made you change your mind,' said Mario, still much pleased by his nephew's change of heart.

'You just like to hear it.'

'What if I do? Anyway, I knew it'd take Maria a good while to recover, and they are safe enough where they are, as you well know.'

Ezio smiled. 'As I've already told you, I wanted to take responsibility. As I've already told you, Vieri troubles *you* because of *me*.'

'And as I've told you, young man, you certainly have a healthy sense of your own importance. The truth is, Vieri troubles us because he is a Templar and we are Assassins.'

As he spoke, Mario was scanning the tall towers, built close together, of San Gimignano. The square-built structures seemed almost to scrape the sky, and Ezio had a strange sense of having seen such a view before, but it must have been either in a dream or in another life, for he had no precise memory of the occasion.

The tops of the towers were each aflame with torchlight, and there were many other torches visible on the battlements of the town walls, and at its gates.

'He's well garrisoned,' said Mario. 'And to judge by the torches it looks as if Vieri may well be expecting us. It's a pity, but I'm not surprised. After all, he has his spies just as I have mine.' He paused. 'I can see archers on the ramparts, and the gates are heavily guarded.' He continued to scan the city. 'But even so, it looks as if he hasn't got enough men to cover every gate sufficiently. The one on the south side looks less well defended – it must be the place he expects an attack to be least likely. So that is where we'll strike.'

He raised an arm and kicked his horse's flanks. His force moved forward behind him. Ezio rode beside him. 'This is what we'll do,' said Mario, his voice urgent. 'My men and I will engage the guards at the gate, while you must find a way over the wall and get the gate opened from the inside. We must be silent and swift.'

He unslung a bandolier of throwing-knives and handed it to Ezio. 'Take these. Use them to dispatch the archers.'

As soon as they were close enough, they dismounted. Mario led a group of his best soldiers towards the cohort of guards posted at the southern entrance to the town. Ezio left them, and hurried the last hundred yards on foot, using the cover of bushes and shrubs to conceal his progress, until he found himself at the foot of the wall. He had his hood up, and by the light of the torches at the gate he could see that the shadow cast by his hood on the wall bore a strange resemblance to an eagle's head. He looked up. The wall rose sheer above him, fifty feet or more. He couldn't see if anyone was on the battlements above. Slinging his bandolier securely, he began to climb. It was hard, as the walls were of dressed stone and gave few opportunities for footholds, but embrasures near the top allowed him to gain a firm place to lodge himself while he peered warily over the battlements' edge. Along the rampart to his left, two archers, their backs to him, were leaning over the wall, bows drawn. They had seen Mario's attack begin, and were preparing to fire down on the Assassin *condottieri*. Ezio did not hesitate. It was their lives or those of his friends, and now he appreciated the new skills his uncle had insisted on teaching him. Quickly, concentrating his mind and his eye in the flickering semi-darkness, he drew two knives and threw them, one after the other, with deadly accuracy. The first struck an archer in the nape of the neck – the blow fatal in an instant. The man slumped over the crenellations without a whisper. The next knife flew a little lower, catching the second man full in the back with such force that, with a hollow cry, he pitched forward into the blackness beneath.

Below him, at the foot of a narrow stone stairway, lay the gate, but now he appreciated that Vieri's force was not enough to guard the city with absolute efficiency, for there were no soldiers posted on its interior side. He bounded down the steps three at a time, seeming almost to fly, and soon located the lever that operated the heavy iron bolts which locked the solid, ten-foot-high oak doors. He pulled it, needing all his strength to do so, for it was not designed to yield to the force of just one man, but at last the job was done, and he hauled on one of the massive rings which were set into the doors at shoulder height. It gave, and the gate began to swing open, revealing as it did so that Mario and his men were just completing their bloody task. Two Assassin men lay dead, but twenty of Vieri's force had been sent to their Maker.

'Well done, Ezio!' Mario cried softly. So far, no alarm seemed to have been raised, but it would only be a matter of time.

'Come on!' said Mario. 'Silently, now!' He turned to one of his sergeants and said, 'Go back and bring the main force up.'

Then he led the way carefully through the silent streets – Vieri must have imposed some kind of curfew, for there was no one to be seen. Once, they almost fell foul of a Pazzi patrol. Shrinking back into the shadows, they let it pass, before rushing up from the rear to attack the men and bring them down with clinical efficiency.

'What next?' Ezio asked his uncle.

'We need to locate the captain of the guard here. His name's Roberto. He'll know where Vieri is.' Mario was showing more stress than usual. 'This is taking too long. It'll be better if we split up. Look, I know Roberto. At this time of night, he'll either be drunk in his favourite taverna or he'll be already sleeping it off in the citadel. You take the citadel. Take Orazio and a dozen good men with you.' He looked at the sky, which was just beginning to lighten, and tasted the air, which already carried the coolness of a new day in it. 'Meet me by the cathedral before cock-crow to report. And don't forget – I leave you in command of this gang of hooligans!' He smiled affectionately at his men, took his own force, and disappeared along a street that led uphill.

'The citadel's in the north-west of the town – sir,' said Orazio. He grinned, as did the others. Ezio sensed both their obedience to Mario, and their misgivings at having been entrusted to the command of such an untried officer.

'Then let's go,' Ezio replied firmly. 'Follow me. At my signal.'

The citadel formed one side of the town's main square, not far from the cathedral and near the top of the small hill on which the town was built. They reached it without difficulty, but before they entered it Ezio noticed a number of Pazzi guards posted at its entrance. Motioning his men to stay back, he approached them, keeping to the shadows and silent as a fox, until he was close enough to overhear the conversation which was going on between two of them. It was clear that they were unhappy with Vieri's leadership, and the more vehement of the two was in full flow.

'I tell you, Tebaldo,' the former was saying, 'I'm not happy with that young puppy Vieri. I don't think he could aim his piss into a bucket, let alone defend a town against a determined force. As for Capitano Roberto, he drinks so much he's like a bottle of Chianti dressed in a uniform!'

'You talk too much, Zohane,' cautioned Tebaldo. 'Remember what happened to Bernardo when he dared to open his mouth.'

The other checked himself, and nodded soberly. 'You are right . . . I heard Vieri had him blinded.'

'Well, I'd like to keep my eyesight, thank you very much, so we should end this talk. We don't know how many of our comrades feel like us, and Vieri has spies everywhere.'

Satisfied, Ezio made his way back to his own troop. An unhappy garrison is rarely an efficient one; but there was no guarantee that Vieri did not command a strong loyal core of Pazzi adherents. As for the rest of Vieri's men, Ezio had learned for himself how strong a commander fear itself can be. But the task now was to gain access to the citadel. Ezio scanned the square. Apart from the small force of Pazzi guards, it was dark and empty.

'Orazio?'

'Yessir?'

'Will you engage these men and finish them off? Quickly and silently. I'm going to try to get up on the roof and see whether they've got any more people posted in the courtyard.'

'It's what we came here to do, sir.'

Leaving Orazio and his soldiers to take on the guards, Ezio, checking that he still had sufficient throwing-knives in his bandolier, ran a little way into a side street adjacent to the citadel, climbed to a nearby roof, and from it leapt to the roof of the citadel, which was built round its own interior courtyard. He thanked God that Vieri had evidently neglected to post men in the high towers of the houses of the dominant local families, which punctuated the town, since from that vantage point they could have surveyed everything that was going on. But he also knew that gaining control of those towers would be the first objective of Mario's main force. From the roof of the citadel, he could see that the courtyard was deserted, leapt down to the top of its colonnade, and from there dropped to the ground. It was an easy manoeuvre to open the gates, and to position his men, who had dragged the bodies of the defeated Pazzi patrol out of sight, in the shadows of the colonnade. To avoid suspicion, they had reclosed the citadel gates behind them.

The citadel seemed, to all intents and purposes,

deserted. But soon afterwards there came the sound of voices from the square beyond, and another group of Vieri's men appeared, opening the gates and entering the courtyard, supporting among them a thickset man, running to fat, who was clearly drunk.

'Where've the gate guards buggered off to?' the man wanted to know. 'Don't say Vieri's countermanded me and sent them off on another one of his bloody patrols!'

'*Ser* Roberto,' one of the men supporting him pleaded. 'Isn't it time you got some rest?'

'Whaddyew mean? Made it back here just fine, didn't I? Anyway, night's still young!'

The new arrivals managed to seat their chief on the edge of the fountain in the middle of the courtyard and gathered round, uncertain what to do next.

'Anyone would think I'm not a good captain!' said Roberto, self-pityingly.

'Nonsense, sir!' said the man closest to him.

'Vieri thinks I'm not,' said Roberto, 'You should hear the way he talks to me!' He paused, looking round and trying to focus before continuing in a maudlin tone: 'It's only a matter of time before I'm replaced – or worse!' He stopped again, snuffling. 'Where's that bloody bottle? Give it here!' He drank a deep draught, looked at the bottle to assure himself that it was empty, and flung it away. 'It's Mario's fault! I couldn't believe it when our spies reported that he'd taken his nephew in – rescued the little bugger from Vieri himself! Now

Vieri can scarcely think straight for rage, and I have to face my old *compagno*!' He looked around blearily. 'Dear old Mario! We were brothers-in-arms once, did you know that? But he refused to come over to the Pazzi with me, even though it was better money, better quarters, better equipment – the lot! I wish he were here now. For two pins, I'd –'

'Excuse me,' Ezio interrupted, stepping forward.

'Wha– ?' said Roberto. 'Who're you?'

'Allow me to introduce myself. I'm Mario's nephew.'

'What?' Roberto roared, struggling to his feet and grabbing unsuccessfully for his sword. 'Arrest the little tyke!' He leant close, so that Ezio could smell the sour wine on his breath. Onions, too. 'You know what, Ezio,' he smiled. 'I should be grateful to you. Now that I've got you, there's nothing Vieri wouldn't give me. Maybe I'll retire. A nice little villa on the coast, perhaps –'

'Don't count your chickens, *Capitano*,' said Ezio. Roberto spun round to see what his men had already discovered: that they were surrounded by Assassin mercenaries, all armed to the teeth.

'Ah,' said Roberto, sinking down again. All the fight seemed to have gone out of him.

Once the Pazzi guards had been manacled and taken to the citadel's dungeon, Roberto, provided with a fresh bottle, sat with Ezio at a table in a room off the court-yard, and talked. At last Roberto was convinced.

'You want Vieri? I'll tell you where he is. It's all up

with me anyway. Go to the Palazzo of the Dolphin in the square near the northern gate. There's a meeting being held there . . .'

'Who is he meeting? Do you know?'

Roberto shrugged. 'More of his people from Florence, I think. Supposed to be bringing reinforcements with them.'

They were interrupted by Orazio, looking worried. 'Ezio! Quickly! There's a battle going on over by the cathedral. We'd better get going!'

'All right! Let's go!'

'What about him?'

Ezio looked at Roberto. 'Leave him. I think he may have chosen the right side at last.'

As soon as he was out in the square, Ezio could hear the noise of fighting coming from the open space in front of the cathedral. Drawing nearer, he saw that his uncle's men, their backs to him, were being forced to retreat by a large brigade of Pazzi troops. Using his throwing-knives to clear a path, he fought his way to his uncle's side and told him what he'd learned.

'Good for Roberto!' said Mario, barely missing a beat, as he cut and sliced at his attackers. 'I always regretted his going over to the Pazzi, but he's turned up trumps at last. Go! Find out what Vieri's up to.'

'But what about you? Will you be able to hold them off?'

Mario looked grim. 'For a while at least, but our main

force should have secured most of the towers by now, and then they'll be here to join us. So make haste, Ezio! Don't let Vieri escape!'

The palazzo lay in the extreme north of the city, far from the fighting, though the Pazzi guards here were numerous – probably the reinforcements of whom Roberto had spoken – and Ezio had to pick his way carefully to avoid them.

He arrived just in time: the meeting appeared to be over, and he could see a group of four robed men making their way to a group of tethered horses. Ezio recognized Jacopo de' Pazzi, his nephew, Francesco, Vieri himself, and – he let out a gasp of surprise – the tall Spaniard who had been present at his father's execution. To his further surprise, Ezio noticed the arms of a cardinal embroidered on the shoulder of the man's cloak. The men drew to a halt by the horses, and Ezio managed to reach the cover of a nearby tree to see if he could catch anything of their conversation. He had to strain, and the words came in snatches, but he overheard enough to intrigue him.

'Then it's settled,' the Spaniard was saying. 'Vieri, you will remain here and re-establish our position as soon as possible. Francesco will organize our forces in Florence for the moment when the right time comes to strike, and you, Jacopo, must be prepared to calm the populace once we have seized control. Do not hurry things: the better planned our action is, the greater the likelihood of success.'

'But, *Ser* Rodrigo,' put in Vieri, 'what am I to do with that *ubriacone*, Mario?'

'Get rid of him! There is no way that he must learn of our intentions.' The man they called Rodrigo swung himself up into the saddle. Ezio saw his face clearly for a moment, the cold eyes, the aquiline nose, and guessed him to be in his mid-forties.

'He's always been trouble,' snarled Francesco. 'Just like that *bastardo* of a brother of his.'

'Don't worry, *padre*,' said Vieri. 'I will soon reunite them – in death!'

'Come,' said the man they called Rodrigo. 'We have stayed too long.' Jacopo and Francesco mounted their steeds beside him, and they turned towards the northern gate, which the Pazzi guards were already opening. 'May the Father of Understanding guide us all!'

They rode out and the gates closed again behind them. Ezio was wondering whether now would be a good opportunity to try to cut Vieri down, but he was too well guarded, and besides, it might be better to take him alive and question him. But he carefully made a mental note of the names of the men he had overheard, intending to add them to his father's list of enemies, for clearly a conspiracy was afoot in which they were all involved.

As it was, he was interrupted by the arrival of a further squad of Pazzi guards, the leader of which approached Vieri at a run.

'What is it?' snapped Vieri.

'*Commandante*, I bring bad news. Mario Auditore's men have broken through our last defences.'

Vieri sneered. 'That's what he thinks. But see,' he waved at the strong force of men around him, 'more men have arrived from Florence. We will sweep him out of San Gimignano before the day is done like the vermin he is!' He raised his voice to the assembled soldiers. 'Hurry to meet the enemy!' he cried. 'Crush them like the scum they are!'

Raising a harsh battle-cry, the Pazzi militia formed up under their officers and moved away from the north gate southwards through the city to encounter Mario's *condottieri*. Ezio prayed that his uncle would not be taken unawares, for now he would be severely outnumbered. But Vieri had remained behind, and, alone now except for his personal bodyguard, was making his way back into the safety of the palazzo. No doubt he still had some business pertaining to the meeting to conclude there. Or perhaps he was returning to strap on his armour for the fray. Either way, soon, the sun would be up. It was now or never. Ezio stepped out of the darkness, pulling back the cowl from over his head.

'Good morning, *Messer* de' Pazzi,' he said. 'Had a busy night?'

Vieri rounded on him – a combination of shock and terror flickering across his face for an instant. He regained his composure, and blustered, 'I might have known you'd turn up again. Make your peace with God, Ezio – I've more important things than you to deal with now. You're just a pawn to be swept off the board.'

His guards rushed Ezio, but he was ready for them. He brought down the first of them with his last throwing-knife – the small blade scything through the air with a devilish zinging sound. Then he drew his sword and battle-dagger and closed with the rest of the guards. He cut and thrust like a madman in a swirl of blood, his movement economical and lethal, until the last, badly wounded, limped away to safety. But now Vieri was on him, wielding a cruel-looking battleaxe he'd seized from the saddle of his horse, which still stood where the others had been tethered. Ezio swerved to avoid his deadly aim, but the blow, though it glanced off his body-armour, still sent him reeling and he fell, letting his sword drop. In a moment, Vieri stood over him, kicking the sword out of reach, the axe raised above his head. Summoning his remaining strength, Ezio aimed a kick at his opponent's groin, but Vieri saw it coming and jumped back. As Ezio took the chance to regain his feet, Vieri threw his axe at his left wrist, knocking the battle-dagger out of it and cutting a deep wound in the back of his left hand. Vieri drew his own sword and dagger.

'If you want a job doing well, do it yourself,' Vieri said. 'Sometimes I wonder what I pay these so-called body-guards for. Goodbye, Ezio!' And he closed on his enemy.

The heat of pain had seared through the young man's

body as the axe had slashed his hand, making his head swim and his vision white-out. But now he remembered all that he had been taught, instinct taking over. He shook himself, and in the moment when Vieri poised himself to deliver the fatal blow on his supposedly unarmed opponent, Ezio flexed his right hand, spreading his fingers up and open. Instantaneously, the mechanism of his father's concealed dagger clicked, the blade shooting out from under his fingers, extending to its full and lethal length, the dull metal belying the vicious edge. Vieri's arm was raised. His flank was open. Ezio plunged the dagger into his side – the blade slipping in without the least resistance.

Vieri stood for a moment transfixed, then, dropping his weapons, fell to his knees. Blood flowed like a waterfall from between his ribs. Ezio caught him as he sank to the ground.

'You don't have much time, Vieri,' he said urgently. 'Now it is *your* chance to make your peace with God. Tell me, what were you discussing? What are your plans?'

Vieri answered him with a slow smile. 'You will never defeat us,' he said. 'You will never conquer the Pazzi and you will certainly never conquer Rodrigo Borgia.'

Ezio knew he had only moments before he'd be talking to a corpse. He persisted with even greater urgency. 'Tell me, Vieri! Had my father discovered your plans? Is that why your people had him killed?'

But Vieri's face was ashen. He grasped Ezio's arm tightly. A trickle of blood spilled from the corner of his mouth and his eyes were beginning to glaze. Still, he managed an ironic smile. 'Ezio, what are you hoping for – a full confession? I'm sorry, but I just don't have . . . the time . . .' He gasped for breath and more blood flowed from his mouth. 'A pity, really. In another world, we might even have been . . . friends.'

Ezio felt the grip on his arm relax.

But then the pain of his wound welled up again, together with the stark memory of the death of his kinsmen, and he was riven with a cold fury. 'Friends?' he said to the corpse. 'Friends! You piece of shit! Your body should be left on the side of a road to rot like a dead crow! Nobody will miss you! I only wish you'd suffered more! I –'

'Ezio,' said a strong, gentle voice behind him. 'Enough! Show the man some respect.'

Ezio stood and whirled round to confront his uncle. 'Respect? After all that's happened? Do you think, if he'd won, he wouldn't have hanged us from the nearest tree?'

Mario was battered, covered with dust and blood, but he stood firm.

'But he didn't win, Ezio. And you are not like him. Do not become a man like he was.' He knelt by the body, and with a gloved hand reached down and closed its eyes. 'May death provide the peace your poor, angry soul sought,' he said. '*Requiescat in pace*.'

Ezio watched in silence. When his uncle stood up, he said, 'Is it over?'

'No,' replied Mario. 'There is still fierce fighting. But the tide is turning in our favour, Roberto has brought some of his men over to our side, and it is only a matter of time.' He paused. 'You will I am sure be grieved to know that Orazio is dead.'

'Orazio – !'

'He told me what a brave man you were before he died. Live up to that praise, Ezio.'

'I will try.' Ezio bit his lip. Though he did not acknowledge it consciously, this was another lesson learned.

'I must rejoin my men. But I have something for you – something that will teach you a little more about your enemy. It's a letter we took from one of the priests here. It was intended for Vieri's father, but Francesco, evidently, is no longer here to receive it.' He handed over a paper, the seal broken open. 'This same priest will oversee the funeral rites. I'll get one of my sergeants to make the arrangements.'

'I have things to tell you –'

Mario raised his hand. 'Later, when our business here is finished. After this setback, our enemies won't be able to move as fast as they'd hoped, and Lorenzo in Florence will be very much on his guard. For the moment, we have the advantage of them.' He stopped. 'But I must get back. Read the letter, Ezio, and reflect on what it says. And see to your hand.'

He was gone. Ezio moved away from Vieri's body and sat beneath the tree he had hidden behind earlier. Flies were already hovering round Vieri's face. Ezio opened the letter and read:

Messer *Francesco:*
I have done as you requested and spoken with your son. I agree with your assessment, though only in part. Yes, Vieri is brash, and prone to act without forethought; and he has a habit of treating his men like playthings, like chesspieces for whose lives he shows no more concern than if they were made of ivory or wood. And his punishments are indeed cruel: I have received reports of at least three men being disfigured as a result.

But I do not think him, as you put it, beyond repair. Rather, I believe the solution to be a simple matter. He seeks your approval. Your attention. These outbursts of his are a result of insecurities borne of a sense of inadequacy. He speaks of you fondly and often, and expresses a desire to be closer to you. So, if he is loud and foul and angry, I believe it is simply because he wants to be noticed. He wants to be loved.

Act as you see fit on the information I've given you here, but now I must ask that we end this correspondence. Were he to discover the nature of our discourse, I candidly fear what might become of me.

Yours in confidence,
Father Giocondo

Ezio sat for a long while after having read the letter, thinking. He looked at Vieri's body. There was a wallet at his belt he had not noticed before. He walked over and took it, returning to his tree to examine its contents. There was a miniature picture of a woman, some florins in a pouch, a little notebook that had not been used, and, carefully rolled, a piece of vellum. With trembling hands, Ezio opened it, and immediately recognized what it was. A page of the Codex . . .

The sun rose higher, and a group of monks appeared with a wooden stretcher on which they laid Vieri's body, and carried it away.

As spring turned to summer again, and the mimosa and azaleas had given way to lilies and roses, an uneasy peace returned to Tuscany. Ezio was content to see that his mother continued in her recovery, though her nerves had been so shattered by the tragedy that had struck her that now it seemed to him she might never leave the peaceful calm of the convent. Claudia was considering taking the first vows that would lead to her novitiate, a prospect that pleased him less, but he knew that she had been born with as stubborn a streak as his own, and that to try to thwart her would merely strengthen her resolve.

Mario had spent the time ensuring that San Gimignano, now under the sober and reformed control of his old comrade, Roberto, and its territory, no longer posed a threat, and that the last pockets of Pazzi resistance had been weeded out. Monteriggioni was safe, and after the victory celebrations had been concluded, Mario's *condottieri* were allowed a well-earned furlough, using it according to their tastes by spending time with their families, or drinking, or whoring, but never neglecting their training; and their squires kept their weapons sharp and their armour free from rust, as the masons and carpenters ensured that the fortifications of both town and castle were well maintained. To the north, the external threat that might have been posed by France was in abeyance, since King Louis was busy getting rid of the last of the English invaders, and facing up to the problems the Duke of Burgundy was causing him; while to the south, Pope Sixtus IV, a potential ally of the Pazzi, was too busy promoting his relatives and supervising the construction of a magnificent new chapel in the Vatican to give much thought to interference in Tuscany.

Mario and Ezio had had many and long conversations, however, regarding the threat that they knew had not disappeared.

'I must tell you more of Rodrigo Borgia,' Mario told his nephew. 'He was born in Valencia, but studied law in Bologna and has never returned to Spain, since he is better placed to pursue his ambitions here. At the moment, he is a prominent member of the Curia in Rome, but his sights are always set higher. He is one of the most powerful men in all Europe, but he is more than a cunning politician within the Church.' He lowered his voice. 'Rodrigo is the leader of the Order of the Templars.'

Ezio felt his heart turn over in his body. 'That explains his presence at the murder of my poor father and my brothers. He was behind it.'

'Yes, and he won't have forgotten you, especially as it was largely thanks to you that he lost his power-base in Tuscany. And he knows the stock you come from, and the danger you continue to pose him. Be fully aware, Ezio, that he will have you killed as soon as he gets the chance.'

'Then I must stand against him if I wish ever to be free.'

'He must remain in our sights, but we have other business nearer home first, and we have stayed our hand long enough. Come to my study.'

They made their way from the garden where they had been walking into an inner room of the castle, at the end of a corridor that led from the map-room. It was a quiet place, dark without being gloomy, book-lined and more like the room of an *accademico* than a military commander. Its shelves also contained artefacts that looked as if they might have come from Turkey or Syria, and volumes that Ezio could see from the writing on their spines were written in Arabic. He had asked his uncle about them, but received only the vaguest of replies.

Once there, Mario unlocked a chest and from it drew a leather document wallet from which he took a sheaf of papers. Among them were some Ezio recognized immediately. 'Here is your father's list, my boy – though I should not call you that any more, for you are a man now, and a full-blooded warrior – and to it I have added the names you told me of in San Gimignano.' He looked at his nephew, and handed him the document. 'It is time for you to begin your work.'

'Every Templar on it shall fall to my blade,' said Ezio, evenly. His eye lit on the name of Francesco de' Pazzi. 'Here, with him, I will start. He is the worst of the clan and fanatical in his hatred of our allies, the Medici.'

'You are right to say so,' Mario agreed. 'So, you will make your preparations for Florence?'

'That is my resolve.'

'Good. But there is more you must learn if you are to be fully equipped. Come.' Mario turned to a bookcase and touched a hidden button set into its side. On silent hinges it swung out and open to reveal a stone wall beyond, on which a number of square slots had been marked out. Five were filled. The rest were empty.

Ezio's eyes gleamed as he saw it. The five filled spaces were occupied with pages of the Codex!

'I see you recognize what this is,' said Mario. 'And I am not surprised. After all, there is the page your father left you, which your clever friend in Florence managed to decode, and these, which Giovanni managed to find and translate before he died.'

'And the one I took from Vieri's body,' added Ezio. 'But its contents are still a mystery.'

'Alas, you are right. I am not the scholar your father was, though with every page that is added, and with the help of the books in my study, I am getting closer to unravelling the mystery. Look! Do you see the way the words cross from one page to the next, and how the symbols join?'

Ezio looked hard, an eerie feeling of remembrance flooding his brain, as though a hereditary instinct was reawakening – and with this the scrawls on the pages of the Codex seemed to come alive, their intentions untwisting in front of his eyes. 'Yes! And there seems to be part of a picture of some sort underneath it – look, it's like a map!'

'Giovanni – and now I – managed to make out what appears to be a kind of prophecy written across these pages, but what it refers to I have yet to learn. Something about "*a piece of Eden*". It was written long ago, by an Assassin like us, whose name appears to have been Altair. And there is more. He goes on to write of "*something hidden beneath the earth, something as powerful as it is old*" – but we have yet to discover what.'

'Here is Vieri's page,' said Ezio. 'Add it to the wall.'

'Not yet! I will copy it before you go, but take the original to your friend in Florence with the brilliant mind. He need not know the full picture, at least, what there is of it so far, and indeed it may be dangerous for him to have such knowledge. Later, Vieri's parchment will join the others on this wall, and we will be a little closer to deciphering the mystery.'

'What of the other pages?'

'They are yet to be rediscovered,' said Mario. 'Do not concern yourself. For you must concentrate on the undertaking you have immediately before you.'

8

Ezio had preparations to make before he left Monterig-gioni. He had much more to learn, at his uncle's side, of the Assassin's Creed, the better to equip himself for the task that faced him. There was also the need to ensure that it would be at least relatively safe for him in Florence, and there was the question of where he might lodge, since Mario's spies within the town had reported that his family palazzo had been closed and boarded up, though it remained under the protection and guard of the Medici family and so had been left unmolested. Several delays and setbacks made Ezio increasingly impatient, until, one morning in March, his uncle told him to pack his bags.

'It's been a long winter –' Mario said.

'Too long,' put in Ezio.

'– but now all is settled,' continued his uncle. 'And I would remind you that meticulous preparation accounts for most victories. Now, pay attention! I have a friend in Florence who has arranged a secure lodging for you not far from her own house.'

'Who is she, Uncle?'

Mario looked furtive. 'Her name is of no consequence to you, but you have my word that you can trust her as much as you would trust me. In any case she is presently away from the town. If you have need of help, get in touch with your old housekeeper, Annetta, whose address has not changed and who now works for the Medici, but it would be best if as few people as possible in Florence knew of your presence there. There is, however, one person you *must* contact, though he isn't easy to reach. I've written his name down here. You must ask around for him discreetly. Try asking your scientific friend while you're showing him the Codex page, but don't let him know too much, for his own good! And here, by the way, is the address of your lodgings.' He handed Ezio two slips of paper and a bulging leather pouch. 'And one hundred florins to get you started, and your travelling papers, which you will find in order. The best news of all is that you may set off tomorrow!'

Ezio used the short time left to ride to the convent to take his leave of his mother and sister, to pack all his essential clothing and equipment, and to say goodbye to his uncle and the men and women of the town who had been his companions and allies for so long. But it was with a joyful and determined heart that he saddled his horse and rode forth from the castle gates at dawn the following morning. It was a long but uneventful day's ride, and by dinner-time he was settled in his new quarters and ready to re-acquaint himself with the city which had been his home all his life, but which he had not seen for so long. But this wasn't a sentimental return, and once he had found his feet again, and permitted himself one sad walk past the façade of his old family home, he made his way straight to Leonardo da Vinci's workshop, not forgetting to take Vieri de' Pazzi's page of the Codex with him.

Leonardo had expanded into the property to the left of his own since Ezio had gone away, a vast warehouse with ample room for the physical results of the artist's imaginings to take shape. Two long trestle tables ran from one end of the place to the other, lit by oil-lamps and by windows set high in the walls – Leonardo had no need of prying eyes. On the tables, hanging from the walls, and scattered, partly assembled, in the middle of the room, were a confusing number of devices, machines and bits of engineering equipment, and pinned to the walls were hundreds of drawings and sketches. Among this pandemonium of creativity, half a dozen assistants busied and scuttled, overseen by the slightly older, but no less attractive, Agniolo and Innocento. Here, there was a model of a wagon, except that it was round, bristled with weapons, and was covered with an armoured canopy in the shape of a raised cooking pot lid, at the top of which was a hole through which a man might stick his head to ascertain what direction the machine was going in. There, the drawing of a boat in the shape of a shark but with an odd tower on its back. More oddly still, it looked from the drawing as if the boat were sailing underwater. Maps, anatomical sketches showing everything from the working of the eye, to coitus, to the embryo in the womb – and many others which it was beyond Ezio's imagination to decipher – crowded all available wall-space, and the samples and clutter piled on the tables reminded Ezio of the organized chaos he remembered from his last visit here, but multiplied one hundredfold. There were precisely figured images of animals, from the familiar to the supernatural, and designs for everything from water-pumps to defensive walls.

But what caught Ezio's eye most was hanging low from the ceiling. He had seen a version of it before, he remembered, as a smallish model, but this looked like a half-scale mock-up of what might one day be a real machine. It still looked like the skeleton of a bat, and some kind of durable animal skin had been stretched tightly over the frames of two wooden projections. Nearby was an easel with some paperwork attached to it. Among the notes and calculations, Ezio read:

... spring of horn or of steel fastened upon wood of willow encased in reed.

The impetus maintains the birds in their flying course during such time as the wings do not press the air, and they even rise upwards.

If a man weigh two hundred pounds and is at point *n*, and raises the wing with his block, which is one hundred and fifty pounds, with power amounting to three hundred pounds he would raise himself with two wings ...

It was all Greek to Ezio, but at least he could read it – Agniolo must have transcribed it from Leonardo's impenetrable scrawl. In that moment he saw Agniolo looking at him, and hastily turned his attention elsewhere. He knew how secretive Leonardo liked to be.

Presently Leonardo himself arrived from the direction of the old studio and bustled up to Ezio, embracing him warmly. 'My dear Ezio! You're back! I am so glad to see you. After all that's happened, we thought . . . ' But he let the sentence hang there, and looked troubled.

Ezio tried to lighten his mood again. 'Look at this place! Of course I can't make head or tail of any of it, but I suppose you know what you're doing! Have you given up painting?'

'No,' said Leonardo. 'Just following up . . . on other things . . . that've caught my attention.'

'So I see. And you've expanded. You must be prospering. The past two years have been good to you.'

But Leonardo could see both the underlying sadness and the severity that had settled in Ezio's face now. 'Perhaps,' said Leonardo. 'They leave me alone. I imagine they think I'll be useful to whoever wins absolute control one day . . . Not that I imagine anyone ever will.' He changed. 'But what of you, my friend?'

Ezio looked at him. 'There will be time, I hope, one day to sit down and talk over all that has happened since we last met. But now, I need your help again.'

Leonardo spread his hands. 'Anything for you!'

'I have something to show you which I think will interest you.'

'Then you had better come to my studio – it is less busy there.'

Once back in Leonardo's old quarters, Ezio produced the Codex page from his wallet and spread it on the table before them.

Leonardo's eyes widened with excitement.

'You remember the first one?' asked Ezio.

'How could I forget?' The artist gazed at the page. 'This is most exciting! May I?'

'Of course.'

Leonardo studied the page carefully, running his fingers over the parchment. Then, drawing paper and pens towards him, he began to copy the words and symbols down. Almost immediately, he was darting to and fro, consulting books and manuscripts, absorbed. Ezio watched him work with gratitude and patience.

'This is interesting,' said Leonardo. 'Some quite unknown languages here, at least to me, but they do yield a kind of pattern. Hmmn. Yes, there's a gloss here in Aramaic which makes things a bit clearer.' He looked up. 'You know, taking this with the other page, you'd almost think they were part of a guide – on one level, at least – a guide to various forms of assassination. But of course there's far more to it than that, though I have no idea what. I just know that we're only scratching the surface of what this may have to reveal. We'd need to have the whole thing complete, but you've no idea where the other pages are?'

'None.'

'Or how many in the complete volume?'

'It is possible that . . . that that may be known.'

'Aha,' said Leonardo. 'Secrets! Well, I must respect them.' But then his attention was caught by something else. 'But look at this!'

Ezio looked over his shoulder but could see nothing but a succession of closely grouped, wedge-shaped symbols. 'What is it?'

'I can't quite make it out, but if I'm right this section contains a formula for a metal or an alloy that we know nothing of – and that, logically, shouldn't *possibly* exist!'

'Is there anything else?'

'Yes – the easiest bit to decipher. It's basically the blueprint for another weapon, and it seems to complement the one you already have. But this one we'll have to make from scratch.'

'What kind of weapon?'

'Fairly simple, really. It's a metal plate encased in a leather bracer. You'd wear it on your left forearm – or your right if you were left-handed, like me – and use it to ward off blows from swords or even axes. The extraordinary thing is that although it's evidently very strong, the metal we're going to have to cast is also incredibly light. And it incorporates a double-bladed dagger, spring-loaded like the first.'

'Do you think you can make it?'

'Yes, though it will take a little time.'

'I haven't much of that.'

Leonardo pondered. 'I think I have all I need here, and my men are skilled enough to forge this.' He thought for a moment, his lips moving as he made calculations. 'It will take two days,' he decided. 'Come back then and we'll see if it works!'

Ezio bowed. 'Leonardo, I am most grateful. And I can pay you.'

'I am grateful to *you*. This Codex of yours expands my knowledge – I fancied myself an innovator, but I find much in these ancient pages to intrigue me.' He smiled, and murmured almost to himself. 'And you, Ezio, cannot guess how indebted I am to you for showing them to me. Let me see any more that you may find – where they come from is your business. I am only interested in what they contain, and that no one else outside your inner circle, apart from me, should know about them. That is all the recompense I require.'

'That is indeed a promise.'

'*Grazie!* Until Friday, then – at sunset?'

'Until Friday.'

Leonardo and his assistants discharged their commission well. The new weapon, though it was defensive in application, was extraordinarily useful. Leonardo's younger assistants mock-attacked Ezio, but using real weapons, including double-handed swords and battle-axes, and the wristplate, light as it was and easy to wield, easily deflected the heaviest blows.

'This is an amazing armament, Leonardo.'

'Indeed.'

'And it may well save my life.'

'Let's hope you get no more scars like the one across the back of your left hand,' said Leonardo.

'That is a last souvenir from an old . . . friend,' said Ezio. 'But now I need one more piece of advice from you.'

Leonardo shrugged. 'If I can help you, I will.'

Ezio glanced over at Leonardo's assistants. 'Perhaps in private?'

'Follow me.'

Back in the studio, Ezio unwrapped the slip of paper Mario had given him and handed it to Leonardo. 'This is the person my uncle told me to meet. He told me it'd be no good to try to find him directly –'

But Leonardo was staring at the name on the paper. When he looked up, his face was filled with anxiety. 'Do you know who this is?'

'I read the name – *La Volpe*. I guess it's a nickname.'

'The Fox! Yes! But do not speak it aloud, or in public. He is a man whose eyes are everywhere, but who himself is never seen.'

'Where might I find him?'

'It is impossible to say, but if you wanted to make a start – and be very careful – you should try the district of the Mercato Vecchio –'

'But every thief who isn't either in gaol or on the gallows hangs out there.'

'I told you you'd need to be careful.' Leonardo looked round as if he were being overheard. 'I . . . might be able to get word to him . . . Go and look for him tomorrow after Vespers . . . Perhaps you will be fortunate . . . perhaps not.'

Despite his uncle's warning, there was one person in Florence whom Ezio was determined to see again. In all the time of his absence, she had never been far from his heart, and now the pangs of love had increased with the knowledge that she was not far away. He could not take too many risks in the city. His face had changed, become more angular, as he had grown both in experience and years, but he was still recognizable as Ezio. His hood helped, allowing him to 'disappear' in a crowd, and he wore it low; but he knew that, although the Medici now held sway, the Pazzi had not had all their teeth drawn. They were biding their time, and they would remain vigilant: of those two things he was certain, just as he was certain that if they caught him unawares, they would kill him, Medici or no Medici. Nevertheless, the following morning he could no more prevent his feet taking the way to the Calfucci mansion than he could have flown to the moon.

The main street doors stood open, revealing the sunlit courtyard beyond, and there she was, slimmer, possibly taller, her hair up, no longer a girl but a woman. He called her name.

When she saw him she turned so pale he thought she was going to faint, but she rallied, said something to her attendant to make her go away, and came out to him, her hands outstretched. He drew her quickly out of the street into the secluded shelter of an archway nearby, whose yellow stones were festooned with ivy. He stroked her neck, and noticed that the thin chain to which his pendant was attached was still around her neck, though the pendant itself was hidden in her bosom.

'Ezio!' she cried.

'Cristina!'

'What are you doing here?'

'I am here on my father's business.'

'Where have you *been*? I have had no word of you for two *years*.'

'I have been . . . away. Also on my father's business.'

'They said you must be dead – and your mother and sister.'

'Fate dealt with us differently.' He paused. 'I could not write, but you have never left my thoughts.'

Her eyes, which had been dancing, suddenly clouded and looked troubled.

'What is it, *carissima*?' he asked.

'Nothing.' She tried to break free. He would not let her.

'Clearly it's something. Tell me!'

She met his eyes, and her own filled with tears. 'Oh, Ezio! I'm engaged to be married!'

Ezio was too taken aback to answer. He let go of her arms, realizing that he was holding her too tightly, hurting her. He saw the lonely furrow he had to plough, stretching ahead of him.

'It was my father,' she said. 'He kept on and on at me to choose. You were gone. I thought you were dead. Then my parents began to entertain visits from Manfredo d'Arzenta – you know, the son of the bullion people. They moved here from Lucca soon after you left Florence. Oh, God, Ezio, they kept asking me not to let the family down, to make a good match while I still could. I thought I'd never see you again. And now –'

She was interrupted by a girl's voice, crying out in panic at the end of the street, where there was a little square.

Cristina became instantly tense. 'That's Gianetta – do you remember her?'

They could hear more screams and yells now, and Gianetta called out a name – 'Manfredo!'

'We'd better see what's going on,' said Ezio, making his way down the street in the direction of the fracas. In the square, they found Cristina's friend Gianetta, another girl whom Ezio did not recognize, and an elderly man who, he remembered, had worked as Cristina's father's head clerk.

'What's going on?' said Ezio.

'It's Manfredo!' cried Gianetta. 'Gambling debts again! This time, they're going to kill him for sure!'

'What?' cried Cristina.

'I am so sorry, *signorina*,' said the clerk. 'Two men to whom he owes money. They've dragged him off to the foot of the New Bridge. They said they were going to beat the debt out of him. I am so sorry, *signorina* . I could do nothing.'

'That's all right, Sandeo. Go and call the house guards. I'd better go and –'

'Wait a minute,' put in Ezio. 'Who the devil is Manfredo?'

Cristina looked at him as if from the inner side of prison bars. 'My *fidanzato*,' she said.

'Let me see what I can do,' said Ezio, and rushed away down the street that led in the direction of the bridge. A minute later, he stood at the top of the embankment looking down at the narrow strip of land near the first arch of the bridge, close to the heavy, slow-moving, yellow waters of the Arno. There, a young man clad in elegant black and silver was on his knees. Two more young men were sweating and grunting as they kicked him hard, or bent down to pummel him with their fists.

'I'll pay it back, I swear!' groaned the young man in black and silver.

'We've had enough of your excuses,' said one of his tormentors. 'You've made us look very foolish. So now we're going to make an example of you.' And he raised his boot to the young man's neck, pushing him face down in the mud, while his companion kicked him in the ribs.

The first attacker was about to stamp on the young man's kidneys when he felt himself grabbed by the scruff of the neck and his coat-tails. Someone was lifting him high up – and the next thing he knew, he was flying through the air, landing seconds later in the water among the sewage and debris that had washed up around the foot of the first pier of the bridge. He was too busy choking on the disgusting water that had poured into his mouth to notice that his companion had by now suffered the same fate.

Ezio reached a hand down to the mud-spattered young man and hauled him to his feet.

'*Grazie, signore.* I think they really would have killed me this time. But they'd have been fools if they had. I could have paid them – honestly!'

'Aren't you afraid they'll come after you again?'

'Not now they think I've got a bodyguard like you.'

'I haven't introduced myself: Ezio – de Castronovo.'

'Manfredo d'Arzenta, at your service.'

'I'm not your bodyguard, Manfredo.'

'It doesn't matter. You got those clowns off my back, and I'm grateful. You don't know how much. In fact, you must let me reward you. But first, let me get cleaned up and take you for a drink. There's a little gaming-house just off the Via Fiordaliso –'

'Now, just a minute,' said Ezio, aware that Cristina and her companions were approaching.

'What is it?'

'Do you do a lot of gambling?'

'Why not? It's the best way I know of passing the time.'

'Do you love her?' Ezio cut in.

'What do you mean?'

'Your *fidanzata* – Cristina – *do you love her*?'

Manfredo looked alarmed at his rescuer's sudden vehemence. 'Of course I do – if it's any of your business. Kill me here and I'd die still loving her.'

Ezio hesitated. It sounded as though the man was telling the truth. 'Then listen: you are never going to gamble again. Do you hear?'

'Yes!' Manfredo was frightened.

'Swear!'

'I do!'

'You do not know how lucky a man you are. I want you to promise me to be a good husband to her. If I hear that you are not, I will hunt you down and kill you myself.'

Manfredo could see that his rescuer meant every

word he had said. He looked into the cold grey eyes, and something in his memory stirred. 'Do I not know you?' he said. 'There's something about you. You seem familiar.'

'We have never met before,' said Ezio. 'And we need never meet again, unless . . .' he broke off. Cristina was waiting at the end of the bridge, looking down. 'Go to her, and keep your promise.'

'I will.' Manfredo hesitated. 'I really do love her, you know. Perhaps I really have learned something today. And I will do everything in my power to make her happy. I need no threat to my life to make me promise that.'

'I hope so. Now, go!'

Ezio watched Manfredo climb the embankment for a moment, feeling his eyes irresistibly drawn to Cristina's. Their gaze met for a moment and he half-raised a hand in farewell. Then he turned and walked away. Not since the deaths of his kinsmen had his heart been so heavy.

Saturday evening found him still cast in deep gloom. At the darkest moments it seemed to him that he had lost everything – father, brothers, home, status, career – and now, wife! But then he reminded himself of the kindness and protection Mario had afforded him, and of his mother and sister, whom he had been able to save and protect. As for future and career – he still had both, except that they were running in a very different direction from that in which he had hitherto imagined they would run. He had a job to do, and no pining over Cristina would help him finish it. It would be impossible for him ever to cut her out of his heart, but he would have to accept the lonely destiny Fate had accorded him. Perhaps that was the way of the Assassin? Perhaps that was what adherence to the Creed involved?

He made his way to the Mercato Vecchio in a sombre mood. The district was shunned by most people he knew, and he himself had only once visited it before. The old market square was dingy and neglected, as were the buildings and streets that surrounded it. A number of people were passing to and fro, but this was no *passeggiata*. These people walked with a purpose, wasting no time, and kept their heads down. Ezio had taken care to dress simply, and had not worn a sword, though he had buckled on his new wristplate and his original spring-blade dagger too, in case of need. Still, he knew that he must stand out from the crowd around him, and he was on the alert.

He was wondering what course to take next, and was thinking of going into a low alehouse on the corner of the square to see if he could find out obliquely by what means he could make contact with the Fox, when a slim young man suddenly appeared from nowhere and jostled him.

'*Scusi, signore,*' said the young man politely, smiling, and moved swiftly past him. Instinctively, Ezio's hand went to his belt. His precious belongings he had left safely stowed at his lodgings, but he had brought a few florins with him in his belt-purse, and now it was gone. He spun round to see the young man heading towards one of the narrow streets that led off the square, and gave chase. Seeing him, the thief doubled his pace, but Ezio managed to keep him in sight and ran after him, catching up with him at last and collaring him as he was about to enter a tall, nondescript tenement on Via Sant' Angelo.

'Give it back,' he snarled.

'I don't know what you mean,' retorted the thief, but his eyes were scared.

Ezio, who had been on the point of releasing his dagger, reined in his anger. The man, it suddenly occurred to him, might be able to give him the information he sought. 'I have no interest in hurting you, friend,' he said. 'Just give me back my purse and we'll say no more.'

After hesitating, 'You win,' said the young man, ruefully, reaching for the satchel at his side.

'There's just one thing,' Ezio said.

The man was instantly wary. 'What?'

'Do you know where I might find a man who calls himself *La Volpe*?'

Now the man looked seriously frightened. 'Never heard of him. Here, take your money, *signore*, and let me go!'

'Not until you've told me.'

'Just a minute,' said a deep, throaty voice behind him. 'I may be able to help you.'

Ezio turned to see a broad-shouldered man of similar height to his own but perhaps ten or fifteen years older than he was. Over his head he wore a hood not unlike Ezio's, which partly obscured his face, but under it Ezio could make out two piercing violet eyes which shone with a strange power, boring into him.

'Please let my colleague go,' said the man. 'I'll answer for him.' To the young thief he said, 'Give the gentleman his money, Corradin, and make yourself scarce. We'll talk of this later.' He spoke with such authority that Ezio released his grasp. In a second Corradin had placed Ezio's purse in his hand and vanished into the building.

'Who are you?' Ezio asked.

The man smiled slowly. 'My name is Gilberto, but they call me many things: murderer, for example, and *tagliagole*; but to my friends I am simply known as the Fox.' He bowed slightly, still holding Ezio with those penetrating eyes of his. 'And I am at your service, *Messer* Auditore. Indeed, I have been expecting you.'

'How – how do you know my name?'

'It is my business to know everything in this city. And I know, I think, why you believe I can help you.'

'My uncle gave me your name –'

The Fox smiled again, but said nothing.

'I need to find someone – to be one step ahead of him as well, if I can.'

'Who is it you seek?'

'Francesco de' Pazzi.'

'Big game, I see.' The Fox looked serious. 'It may be that I *can* help you.' He paused, considering. 'I have had word that some people from Rome recently disembarked at the docks. They are here to attend a meeting which no one else is supposed to know about, but they do not know about me, still less that I am the eyes and ears of this city. The host of this meeting is the man you want.'

'When is it to take place?'

'Tonight!' The Fox smiled again. 'Don't worry, Ezio – it isn't Fate. I would have sent someone to fetch you to me if you hadn't found me yourself, but it amused me to test you. Very few who seek me succeed.'

'You mean, you set me up with Corradin?'

'Forgive me my sense of the theatrical; but I also had to be sure *you* were not followed. He's a young man, and it was also a kind of test for him. You see, I may have set you up with him, but he had no real idea of the service he was doing me. He just thought I'd singled out a victim for him!' His tone became harder, more practical. 'Now, you must find a way to spy on this meeting, but it won't be easy.' He looked at the sky. 'It is sunset. We must hurry, and the quickest way is over the rooftops. Follow me!'

Without another word he turned and scaled the wall behind him at such a speed that Ezio was hard put to keep up. They raced over the red-tiled roofs, leaping the chasms of the streets in the last afterglow of the sun, silent as cats, soft-footed as running foxes, heading north-west across the city, until they arrived in sight of the façade of the great church of Santa Maria Novella. Here the Fox came to a halt. Ezio had caught him up in seconds, but he noticed that he was more breathless than the older man.

'You've had a good teacher,' said the Fox; but Ezio had the distinct impression that if he had so chosen, his new friend could have outrun him with ease; and that increased his determination to hone his skills further. But now wasn't the time for contests or games.

'That is where *Messer* Francesco is holding his meeting,' said the Fox, pointing downwards.

'In the church?'

'Under it. Come on!'

At that hour, the piazza in front of the church was all but deserted. The Fox leapt down from the roof they were on, landing gracefully in a crouch, and Ezio followed suit. They skirted the square and the side of the church until they came to a postern-gate set into its wall. The Fox ushered Ezio through it and they found themselves in the Rucellai Chapel. Near the bronze tomb at its centre, the Fox paused. 'There is a network of catacombs which crisscross the city far and wide.

I find them very useful in my line of work, but unfortunately they are not exclusive to me. Not many know about them, however, or how to find their way about in them, but Francesco de' Pazzi is one. It is down there that he is holding his meeting with the people from Rome. This is the closest entrance to where they will be, but you will have to make your own way to them. There's a chapel, part of an abandoned crypt, fifty yards to your right once you have descended, and be very careful, for sound travels very acutely down there. It will be dark, too, so allow your vision to become accustomed to the gloom – soon you will be guided by the lights in the chapel.'

He placed his hand over a stone boss on the pedestal that supported the tomb, and pressed it. At his feet, an apparently solid flagstone swung down on invisible hinges to reveal a flight of stone steps. He stood aside. '*Buona fortuna*, Ezio.'

'You are not coming?'

'It is not necessary. And even with all my skills, two people make more noise than one. I will wait for you here. *Va*, go!'

Once below ground, Ezio groped his way along the damp stone corridor that ran away to his right. He was able to feel his way along, for the walls were close enough here for him to touch either side with each hand, and he was relieved that his feet made no sound on the wet earthen floor. Occasionally, other tunnels branched off and he could feel them rather than see them as his guiding hands touched nothing but a black void. Getting lost down here would be a nightmare, for one would never find one's way out again. Little sounds startled him at first, until he realized that they were nothing but the scuttling of rats, though once, when one ran over his feet, he could barely stifle a cry. In niches carved into the walls, he caught glimpses of the corpses from timeworn burials, their skulls shrouded in cobwebs – there was something primordial and terrifying about the catacombs, and Ezio had to bite back a rising sense of panic.

At last he saw a dim light ahead, and, moving more slowly now, advanced towards it. He stayed in the shadows as he came within earshot of the five men he could see ahead, silhouetted in the lamplight of a cramped, and very ancient, chapel.

He recognized Francesco immediately – a small, wiry, intense creature who, as Ezio arrived, was bowed before two tonsured priests he did not recognize. The older of the two was giving the blessing in a clear, nasal voice: '*Et benedictio Dei Omnipotentis, Patris et Filii et Spiritu Sancti descendat super vos et maneat semper . . .*' As his face caught the light, Ezio recognized him; he was Stefano da Bagnone, secretary to Francesco's uncle Jacopo. Jacopo himself stood near him.

'Thank you, *padre*,' said Francesco when the blessing was concluded. He straightened himself and addressed a fourth man, who was standing beside the priests. 'Bernardo, give us your report.'

'Everything is in readiness. We have a full armoury of swords, staves, axes, bows and crossbows.'

'A simple dagger would be best for the job,' put in the younger of the two priests.

'It depends on the circumstances, Antonio,' said Francesco.

'Or poison,' continued the younger priest. 'But it doesn't matter, as long as he dies. I will not easily forgive him for bringing down Volterra, my birthplace and my only true home.'

'Calm yourself,' said the man called Bernardo. 'We all have motive enough. Now, thanks to Pope Sixtus, we also have the means.'

'Indeed, *Messer* Baroncelli,' replied Antonio. 'But do we have his blessing?'

A voice came from the deep shadows beyond the lamplight at the rear of the chapel, 'He gives his blessing to our operation, "provided that nobody is killed".'

The owner of the voice emerged into the lamplight and Ezio drew in his breath as he recognized the cowled figure in crimson, though all of his face but the sneer on his lips was covered by the shadow of his hood. So this was the principal visitor from Rome: Rodrigo Borgia, *il Spagnolo*!

The conspirators all shared his knowing smile. They

all knew where the Pope's loyalty lay, and that it was the cardinal who stood before them who controlled him. But naturally, the Supreme Pontiff could not openly condone the spilling of blood.

'It's good that the job can be done at last,' said Francesco. 'We've had enough setbacks. As it is, killing them in the cathedral will draw heavy criticism on us.'

'It is our last and only option,' said Rodrigo, with authority. 'And as we are doing God's work in ridding Florence of such scum, the setting is appropriate. Besides, once we control the city, let the people murmur against us – if they dare!'

'Still, they keep changing their plans,' said Bernardo Baroncelli. 'I'm even going to have to have someone call on his younger brother Giuliano to make sure he's up in time for High Mass.'

All the men laughed at that, except Jacopo and the Spaniard, who had noticed his sober expression.

'What is it, Jacopo?' Rodrigo asked the older Pazzi. 'Do you think they suspect something?'

Before Jacopo could speak, his nephew waded in impatiently. 'It's impossible! The Medici are too arrogant or too stupid even to notice!'

'Do not underestimate our enemies,' Jacopo chided him. 'Don't you see that it was Medici money that funded the campaign against us at San Gimignano?'

'There will be no such problems this time,' snarled his nephew, bridling at having been corrected in front of his peers, and with the memory of his son Vieri's death still green in his mind.

In the silence that followed, Bernardo turned to Stefano de Bagnone. 'I'll need to borrow a set of your priestly robes for tomorrow morning, *padre*. The more they think they're surrounded by clerics, the safer they'll feel.'

'Who will strike?' asked Rodrigo.

'I!' said Francesco.

'And I!' chimed in Stefano, Antonio and Bernardo.

'Good.' Rodrigo paused. 'I think on the whole daggers *would* be best. So much easier to conceal, and very handy when close work is involved. But it's still good to have the Pope's armoury as well – I don't doubt but there'll be a few loose ends to clear up once the Medici brothers are no more.' He raised his hand and made the sign of the cross over his fellow conspirators. '*Dominus vobiscum*, gentlemen,' he said. 'And may the Father of Understanding guide us.' He looked around. 'Well, I think that concludes our business. You must forgive me if I take my leave of you now. There are several things I need to do before I return to Rome, and I must be on my way before dawn. It wouldn't do at all for me to be seen in Florence on the day the House of Medici crumbled to dust.'

Ezio waited, pressed against a wall in the shadows, until the six men had departed, leaving him in darkness. Only when he was quite sure that he was fully alone did he produce his own lamp and strike a tinder to its wick.

He made his way back the way he had come. The Fox was waiting in the shadowy Rucellai chapel. Ezio, with a full heart, told him what he had heard.

'. . . To murder Lorenzo and Giuliano de' Medici in the cathedral at High Mass tomorrow morning?' said the Fox when Ezio had finished, and Ezio could see that for once the man was almost at a loss for words. 'It is sacrilege! And it is worse than that – if Florence should fall to the Pazzi, then God help us all.'

Ezio was lost in thought. 'Can you get me a seat in the cathedral tomorrow?' he asked. 'Close to the altar. Near the Medici?'

The Fox looked grave. 'Hard, but perhaps not impossible.' He looked at the young man. 'I know what you're thinking, Ezio, but this is something you cannot possibly pull off alone.'

'I can try, and I have the element of surprise. And more than one stranger's face among the *aristocrazia* near the front might arouse the Pazzis' suspicions. But you must get me in there, Gilberto.'

'Call me the Fox,' Gilberto answered him, then grinning, 'Only foxes can match me for cunning.' He paused. 'Meet me in front of the Duomo half an hour before High Mass.' He looked Ezio in the eye with new respect. 'I will help if I can, *Messer* Ezio. Your father would have been proud of you.'

9

Ezio arose before dawn the following day, Sunday 26 April, and made his way to the cathedral. Very few people were about, though a handful of monks and nuns were making their way to perform the rite of Lauds. Aware that he should avoid notice, he climbed arduously to the very top of the campanile and watched the sun rise over the city. Gradually, beneath him, the square began to fill with citizens of every description, families and couples, merchants and nobles, eager to attend the main service of the day, graced as it would be by the presence of the Duke and his younger brother and co-ruler. Ezio surveyed the people keenly, and when he saw the Fox arrive on the cathedral steps, he made his way to the side of the tower least in view and clambered down, agile as a monkey, to join him, remembering to keep his head low and to blend in as far as was possible with the crowd, using his fellow-citizens as cover. He had put on his best clothes for the occasion, and wore no weapon openly, though many of his male fellow citizens, of the wealthy merchant and banking class, had ceremonial swords at their waistbands. He could not resist keeping an eye out for Cristina, but he did not see her.

'Here you are,' said the Fox, as Ezio joined him. 'All the arrangements have been made, and a place reserved for you on the aisle in the third row.' As he spoke, the crowd on the steps parted, and a row of heralds raised trumpets to their lips and blew a fanfare. 'They're coming,' he added.

Entering the square from the Baptistry side, Lorenzo de' Medici appeared first with his wife Clarice at his side. She held little Lucrezia, their oldest, by the hand, and five-year-old Piero marched proudly on his father's right. Behind them, accompanied by her nurse, came three-year-old Maddalena, while baby Leo, swaddled in white satin, was carried by his. They were followed by Giuliano and his heavily pregnant mistress, Fioretta. The mass of people in the square bowed low as they passed, to be met at the entrance to the Duomo by two of the attendant priests, whom Ezio recognized with a thrill of horror – Stefano da Bagnone and the one from Volterra, whose full name, as the Fox told him, was Antonio Maffei.

The Medici family entered the cathedral, followed by the priests, and they were followed by the citizens of Florence, in order of rank. The Fox nudged Ezio and pointed. Among the throng he had spotted Francesco de' Pazzi and his fellow conspirator, Bernardo Baroncelli, disguised as a deacon. 'Go now,' he hissed urgently to Ezio. 'Keep close to them.'

More and more people crowded into the cathedral until it could hold no more, so that those who had hoped for a place had to be content to remain outside. Ten thousand people had gathered in all, and the Fox had never seen such a great assembly in Florence in all his life. He prayed silently for Ezio's success.

Inside, the crowd settled in the stifling heat. Ezio had not been able to get as close to Francesco and the others as he had wished, but kept them under close eye, calculating what he would have to do to reach them as soon as they started their attack. The Bishop of Florence, meanwhile, had taken his place before the high altar, and the Mass began.

It was at the point when the Bishop was blessing the bread and wine that Ezio noticed Francesco and Bernardo exchange glances. The Medici family was seated just in front of them. At the same moment, the priests Bagnone and Maffei, on the lower steps of the altar, and closest to Lorenzo and Giuliano, looked round surreptitiously. The bishop turned to face the congregation, raised aloft the golden goblet, and started to speak.

'The Blood of Christ . . .'

Then everything happened at once. Baroncelli sprang to his feet with a cry of '*Creapa, traditore!*' and plunged a dagger into Giuliano's neck from behind. A fountain of blood spewed from the wound, showering Fioretta, who fell screaming to her knees.

'Let me finish the bastard!' yelled Francesco, elbowing Baroncelli aside and throwing Giuliano, who was trying to staunch his wound with his hands, to the floor.

Francesco knelt astride him and plunged his dagger over and over again into his victim's body, in such a frenzy that once, without seeming to notice, he drove his weapon into his own thigh. Giuliano was long dead before Francesco had struck him the nineteenth, and last, blow.

Meanwhile Lorenzo, with a cry of alarm, had spun round to face his brother's attackers, while Clarice and the nurses bundled the children and Fioretta to safety. There was confusion everywhere. Lorenzo had spurned the idea of having his bodyguards close – a murderous attack in a church was a thing all but unheard of – but now they struggled to reach him through the mass of confused and panic-stricken worshippers, jostling and trampling each other in order to get away from the scene of butchery, but the situation was made far worse by the heat, and the fact that there was scarcely any room to move at all . . .

Except for the area immediately in front of the altar. The Bishop and his attendant priests stood aghast, rooted to the spot, but Bagnone and Maffei, seeing Lorenzo's back turned to them, seized their opportunity and, drawing daggers from their robes, fell on him from behind.

Priests are rarely experienced killers, and however noble they believed their cause to be, the two managed only to give Lorenzo flesh wounds before he shook them off. But in the struggle they got the better of him again, and now Francesco, limping from his self-inflicted wound but empowered by all the hatred that was boiling within him, was closing in too, roaring imprecations as he came, raising his dagger. Bagnone and Maffei, unmanned by what they had done, turned and fled in the direction of the apse; but Lorenzo was staggering, blood pouring from him, and a cut high on the right shoulder had made his sword-arm useless.

'Your day is done, Lorenzo!' Francesco screamed. 'Your entire misbegotten family dies by my sword!'

'*Infame!*' returned Lorenzo. 'I'll kill you now!'

'With that arm?' sneered Francesco, and raised his dagger to strike.

As his fist plunged down, a strong hand caught his wrist and arrested its motion, before flinging him round. Francesco found himself looking into the face of another sworn enemy.

'Ezio!' he growled. 'You! Here!'

'It's *your* day that is done, Francesco!'

The crowd was clearing, and Lorenzo's guards were pushing closer. Baroncelli had arrived at Francesco's side. 'Come, we must fly. It's over!' he shouted.

'I'll deal with these curs first,' said Francesco, but his face was drawn. His own wound was bleeding hard.

'No! We must retreat!'

Francesco looked furious, but there was agreement in his face. 'This isn't over,' he told Ezio.

'No, it isn't. Wherever you go, I will follow, Francesco, until I have cut you down.'

Glaring, Francesco turned and followed Baroncelli, who was already vanishing behind the high altar. There had to be a door out of the cathedral in the apse. Ezio prepared to follow.

'Wait!' a broken voice behind him said. 'Let them go. They won't get far. I need you here. I need your help.'

Ezio turned to see the Duke sprawled on the ground between two overturned chairs. Not far away, his family huddled and wept, Clarice, a look of horror on her face, embracing her two oldest children tightly. Fioretta was staring dully in the direction of Giuliano's twisted and mangled corpse.

Lorenzo's guards had arrived. 'Look after my family,' he told them. 'The city will be in uproar over this. Get them to the palazzo and bar the doors.'

He turned to Ezio. 'You saved my life.'

'I did my duty! Now the Pazzi must pay the full price!' Ezio helped Lorenzo up, and placed him gently on a chair. Looking up, he saw that the Bishop and the other priests were nowhere to be seen. Behind him, people were still pushing and shoving, clawing at each other, to get out of the cathedral by the main western doors. 'I must go after Francesco!' he said.

'No!' said Lorenzo. 'I can't make it to safety on my own. You must help me. Get me to San Lorenzo. I have friends there.'

Ezio was torn, but he knew how much Lorenzo had done for his own family. He could not blame him for failing to prevent the deaths of his kinsmen, for how could anyone have predicted the suddenness of that attack? And now Lorenzo himself was the victim. He was still alive, too; but he would not be for long unless Ezio could get him to the nearest place where he could be treated. The church of San Lorenzo was only a short distance north-west of the Baptistry.

He bound Lorenzo's wounds as best he could, with strips torn from his own shirt. Then he lifted him gently to his feet. 'Put your left arm round my shoulder. Good. Now, there must be a way out beyond the altar . . .'

They hobbled in the direction their assailants had taken, and soon came to a small open door with bloodstains on its threshold. This was no doubt the way Francesco had gone. Might he be lying in wait? It would be hard for Ezio to release his spring-blade dagger, still less fight, while supporting Lorenzo on his right side. But he had his metal bracer strapped to his left forearm.

They made their way into the square outside the north wall of the cathedral and were greeted with scenes of confusion and chaos. They made their way west along the side of the cathedral, after Ezio had paused to wrap his cape over Lorenzo's shoulders in a makeshift attempt to disguise him. In the piazza between the cathedral and the Baptistry, groups of men wearing the liveries of the Pazzi and the Medici were engaged in hand-to-hand combat, so engrossed that Ezio was able to slink past them, but as they reached the street that led up to the Piazza San Lorenzo they were confronted by two men wearing the dolphin-and-crosses insignia. Both carried ugly-looking falchions.

'Halt!' one of the guards said. 'Where d'you think you're going?'

'I must get this man to safety,' said Ezio.

'And who might you be?' said the second guard, unpleasantly. He came forward and peered at Lorenzo's face. Lorenzo, half-fainting, turned away, but as he did so the cape slipped, revealing the Medici crest on his doublet.

'Oho,' said the second guard, turning to his friend. 'Looks like we might have caught a very big fish here, Terzago!'

Ezio's brain raced. He couldn't let go of Lorenzo, who was still losing blood. But if he didn't, he couldn't use his weapon. He raised his left foot quickly and gave the guard a shove in the arse. He fell, sprawling. In seconds, his mate came for them, falchion raised. As the blade came down, Ezio parried, and, using his wrist-guard, deflected the blow. As he did so, he swung his left arm, forcing the sword away, cutting at the man with the double-bladed dagger attached to the wrist-guard, though he could not get enough purchase to kill the man with it. And now the second guard was on his feet again, coming to the aid of his comrade, who in turn had staggered back, surprised that he had not cut Ezio's forearm off.

Ezio stopped the second blade in the same way, but this time he managed to run the wrist-guard down the cutting edge of the sword until it hit the hilt, bringing his hand in range of the man's wrist. He seized and twisted it so rapidly and hard that the man let go of his weapon with a sharp cry of pain. Stooping quickly, Ezio grabbed the falchion almost before it had hit the ground. It was hard, working with his left hand and encumbered by Lorenzo's weight, but he slashed it round and cut halfway through the guard's neck before he could recover. The second guard was coming at him again now, bellowing with anger. Ezio parried with his falchion and he and the guard cut and thrust at each other several times. But the guard, unaware still of the concealed metal bracer on Ezio's left arm, aimed blow after useless blow at it. Ezio's arm ached and he could barely keep on his feet, but at last he saw an opportunity. The man's helmet had worked loose, but the man was unaware of this and was looking down at Ezio's forearm, preparing to aim another blow at it. Swiftly, Ezio flicked his own blade up, feinting as though he had missed, but actually he succeeded in knocking the helmet off the man's head. Then, before he could react, Ezio slammed the heavy falchion down on the man's skull and split it in two. The falchion stuck there and Ezio was unable to work it loose. The man stood stock still for a moment, his eyes still wide with surprise, before crumpling to the dust. Looking quickly around, Ezio hauled Lorenzo up the street.

'Not much farther, *Altezza*.'

They reached the church without further annoyance, but the doors were firmly shut against them. Ezio, looking back, saw at the end of the street that the bodies of the guards he'd killed had been discovered by a group of their comrades, who were now looking in their direction. He hammered on the doors, and a spyhole opened in it, revealing an eye and part of a suspicious face.

'Lorenzo's been wounded,' Ezio gasped. 'They're coming for us! Open the door!'

'I need the password,' said the man within; Ezio was at a loss, but Lorenzo had heard the sound of the man's voice and, recognizing it, he rallied.

'Angelo!' he said loudly. 'It's Lorenzo! Open the fucking door!'

'By the Thrice Greatest,' said the man within. 'We thought you must be dead!' He turned and yelled at someone unseen. 'Get this thing unbolted! And fast!'

The spyhole closed and there was a sound of bolts quickly being drawn. Meanwhile, the Pazzi guardsmen, making their way up the street, had broken into a run. Just in time, one of the heavy doors swung open to admit Ezio and Lorenzo, and as quickly slammed shut behind them, the bolts shot back into place by the keepers in charge of them. There was a terrible noise of battle outside. Ezio found himself looking into the calm green eyes of a refined man of perhaps twenty-four.

'Angelo Poliziano,' the man introduced himself. 'I

sent some of our men round the back way to intercept those Pazzi rats. They shouldn't give us any more trouble.'

'Ezio Auditore.'

'Ah – Lorenzo has spoken of you.' He interrupted himself. 'But we can talk later. Let me help you get him to a bench. We can take a look at his wounds there.'

'He's safe now,' said Ezio, handing Lorenzo over to two attendants who gently guided him to a bench set against the north wall of the church.

'We'll patch him up, staunch the blood, and as soon as he's recovered enough, we'll get him back to his palazzo. Don't worry, Ezio, he is indeed safe now, and we will not forget what you have done.'

But Ezio was already thinking of Francesco de' Pazzi. The man had had more than enough time to make good his escape. 'I must take my leave,' he said.

'Wait!' Lorenzo called. Nodding to Poliziano, Ezio went over to him, and knelt by his side.

'I am in your debt, *signore*,' Lorenzo said. 'And I do not know why you helped me, or how you could have known what was afoot, when even my own spies could not.' He paused, his eyes wrinkling in pain as one of the attendants cleaned his shoulder wound. 'Who are you?' he continued when he had recovered a little.

'He's Ezio Auditore,' said Poliziano, coming up and placing a hand on Ezio's shoulder.

'Ezio!' Lorenzo gazed at him, deeply moved. 'Your

... a good friend. He was one
... understood honour, loyalty,
... own interests before those of
... paused again and smiled faintly, 'I
... ...berti died. Was it you?'

'... a fitting and swift revenge. As you see, I
have n... been so successful. But now, through their
overweening ambition, the Pazzi have at last cut their
own throats. I pray that . . .'

One of the men from the Medici patrol that had been
sent out to deal with Ezio's Pazzi pursuers came hurrying up, his face streaked with blood and sweat.

'What is it?' asked Poliziano.

'Bad news, sir. The Pazzi have rallied and they are
storming the Palazzo Vecchio. We can't hold them off
much longer.'

Poliziano grew pale. 'This is bad news indeed. If
they gain control of it, they'll kill all the supporters
we have that they can lay their hands on, and if they
seize power –'

'If they seize power,' Lorenzo said, 'my survival will
mean nothing. We will all be dead men.' He tried to get
up, but fell back, groaning in pain. 'Angelo! You must
take what troops we have here and –'

'No! My place is with you. We must get you to the
Palazzo Medici as soon as possible. From there we may
be able to reorganize and hit back.'

'I will go,' said Ezio. 'I have unfinished business with *Messer* Francesco as it is.'

Lorenzo looked at him. 'You have done enough.'

'Not until this job is finished, *Altezza*. And Angelo is right – he has a more important task to perform – getting you to the safety of your palazzo.'

'*Signori*,' the Medici messenger put in. 'I have more news. I saw Francesco de' Pazzi leading a troop to the rear of the Palazzo Vecchio. He's seeking a way in on the Signoria's blind side.'

Poliziano looked at Ezio. 'Go. Arm yourself and take a detachment from here, and hurry. This man will go with you and be your guide. He will show you where it is safest to leave this church. From there, it will take you ten minutes to reach the Palazzo Vecchio.'

Ezio bowed, and turned to leave.

'Florence will never forget what you are doing for her,' said Lorenzo. 'Go with God.'

Outside, the bells of most of the churches were ringing, adding to the cacophony of clashing steel, and of human cries and groans. The city was in turmoil, wagons set afire blazed in the streets, pockets of soldiery from both sides ran hither and yon, or faced each other in pitched mêlées. The dead were scattered everywhere, in the squares and along the roadways, but there was too much tumult for the crows to dare to fly in for the feast they regarded with their harsh black eyes from the rooftops.

The western doors of the Palazzo Vecchio stood open, and the noise of fighting came from the courtyard within. Ezio brought his little troop to a halt and accosted a Medici officer who was running towards the palazzo in charge of another squad.

'Do you know what's going on?'

'The Pazzi broke in from the rear and opened the doors from within. But our men inside the palazzo are keeping them off. They haven't got beyond the courtyard. With luck we'll be able to hem them in!'

'Is there news of Francesco de' Pazzi?'

'He and his men are holding the back entrance of the Palazzo. If we could gain control of that we'd have them trapped for sure.'

Ezio turned to his men. 'Let's go!' he shouted.

They rushed across the square and down the narrow street which ran along the north wall of the palazzo, where a very different Ezio had climbed to his father's cell window long ago, and, taking the first right from it, quickly encountered the Pazzi troop under Francesco guarding the rear entrance.

They were immediately on their guard, and when Francesco recognized Ezio he cried, 'You again! Why aren't you dead yet? You murdered my son!'

'He tried to murder me!'

'Kill him! Kill him now!'

The two sides engaged fiercely, hacking and cutting at each other in near-desperate fury, for the Pazzi knew full well how important it was to protect their line of retreat. Ezio, cold rage in his heart, muscled his way towards Francesco, who took a stand with his back to the palazzo door. The sword Ezio had taken from the Medici armoury was well balanced and its blade was of Toledo steel, but the weapon was unfamiliar to him and, as a consequence, his blows were a fraction less effective than he'd normally inflict. He had maimed rather than killed the men who had stood in his way. This Francesco had noticed.

'You think yourself a master swordsman now, do you, boy? You can't even make a clean kill. Let me give you a demonstration.'

They fell on each other then, sparks flying from their blades as they clashed; but Francesco had less room to manoeuvre than Ezio and, twenty years his senior, was beginning to tire, even though he had seen less action that day than his opponent.

'Guards!' he cried at last. 'To me!'

But his men had fallen back before the Medici onslaught. He and Ezio now faced each other alone. Francesco looked desperately around for a means of retreat himself, but there was none save through the palazzo itself. He threw open the door behind him and went up a stone staircase that ran up the inside wall. Ezio realized that as most of the Medici defenders would be concentrated at the front of the building where most of the fighting was, they probably didn't have enough men to cover the rear as well. Ezio raced up after him to the second floor.

The rooms here were deserted, since all the occupants of the palazzo, save for half a dozen frightened clerks who ran away as soon as they saw them, were down below, fighting to contain the Pazzi in the courtyard. Francesco and Ezio fought their way through the gilded, high-ceilinged staterooms until they reached a balcony high above the Piazza della Signoria. The noise of battle reached up to them from below, and Francesco called out hopelessly for aid, but there was no one to hear him, and his last retreat was cut off.

'Stand and fight,' said Ezio. 'It's just us now.'

'*Maledetto!*'

Ezio slashed at him, drawing blood from his left arm. 'Come on, Francesco, where's all the courage you showed when you had my father killed? When you stabbed Giuliano this morning?'

'Get the hell away from me, you spawn of the devil!' Francesco lunged, but he was tiring, and his aim went far too wide. He staggered forwards, his balance thrown, and Ezio stood deftly aside, raising his foot and bringing it firmly down on Francesco's sword blade, pulling the man down with it.

Before Francesco could recover, Ezio stamped on his hand, making him let go of the hilt, grabbed him by the shoulder and heaved him over on to his back. As he struggled to get up, Ezio kicked him brutally in the face. Francesco's eyes rolled as he struggled into unconsciousness. Ezio knelt down and proceeded to frisk the old man while he was half-awake, ripping off body-armour and his doublet, revealing the pale, wiry body beneath. But there were no documents, nothing of importance on him. Just a handful of florins in his purse.

Ezio flung aside his sword and released his spring-blade dagger. He knelt, put an arm under Francesco's neck and pulled him up so that their faces were almost touching.

Francesco's eyelids flickered open. His eyes expressed horror and fear. 'Spare me!' he managed to croak.

At that moment a great cry of victory rose from the courtyard below. Ezio listened to the voices, and caught enough to understand that the Pazzi had been routed. 'Spare you?' he said. 'I'd as soon spare a rabid wolf.'

'No!' shrieked Francesco. 'I beg you!'

'This is for my father,' said Ezio, stabbing him in the gizzard. 'And this is for Federico,' stabbing him again, 'And *this* for Petruccio; and *this* for Giuliano!'

Blood spurted and streamed from Francesco's wounds and Ezio was covered in it, but he would have gone on stabbing the dying man if Mario's words had not then come back to him: '*Do not become the man he was.*' He sank back on to his heels. Francesco's eyes still glittered, though their light was fading. He was muttering something. Ezio leaned low to listen.

'A priest . . . a priest . . . for pity's sake, fetch me a priest.'

Ezio was deeply shocked, now that the fury within him had abated, at the savagery with which he had killed. This was not in accordance with the Creed. 'There is no time,' he said. 'I will have a Mass said for your soul.'

Francesco's throat was rattling now. Then his limbs stiffened and shook as he reached his death throes, his head arching back, his mouth open wide as he fought the last impossible battle with the invincible foe whom we all have to face one day; and he sank down, an empty bag, a slight, shrunken, pallid thing.

'*Requiescat in pace*,' murmured Ezio.

Then a new roar arose from the square. Across from the south-west corner fifty or sixty men came running, led by a man Ezio recognized – Francesco's uncle, Jacopo! They bore the Pazzi banner aloft.

'*Libertà! Libertà! Popolo e libertà!*' they shouted as they came. At the same time the Medici forces streamed out of the palazzo to meet them, but they were tired and, as Ezio could see, outnumbered.

He turned back to the body. 'Well, Francesco,' he said. 'I think I have found one way in which you can repay your debt, even now.' Quickly, he reached under the corpse's shoulders, hoisted it up – it was surprisingly light – and carried it to the balcony. Here, finding a lanyard from which a banner hung, he used the length of rope to fasten around the old man's lifeless neck. He quickly attached the other end to a sturdy stone column, and, summoning up all his strength, raised it high, then tossed it over the parapet. The rope paid out, but suddenly jerked taut with a snap. Francesco's limp body hung, toes pointing listlessly at the ground far below.

Ezio hid himself behind the column. 'Jacopo!' he called in a voice of thunder. 'Jacopo de' Pazzi! Look! Your leader is dead! Your cause is finished!'

Below, he could see Jacopo look up, and falter. Behind him, his men, too, hesitated. The Medici troops had followed his gaze, and now, cheering, they were closing in. But the Pazzi had already broken ranks – and were fleeing.

In a matter of days, it was all over. The power of the Pazzi in Florence was broken. Their goods and property were seized, their coats-of-arms torn down and trampled. Despite Lorenzo's appeals for mercy, the Florentine mob hunted down and killed every Pazzi sympathizer they could find, though some of the principals had fled. Only one who was captured obtained clemency – Raffaele Riario, a nephew of the Pope, whom Lorenzo considered to be too credulous and ingenuous to have had any serious involvement, though many of the Duke's advisers thought that Lorenzo was showing more humanity than political astuteness in his decision.

Sixtus IV was furious, nevertheless, and placed Florence under an interdict, but he was powerless otherwise, and the Florentines shrugged him off.

As for Ezio, he was one of the first to be summoned to the Duke's presence. He found Lorenzo standing on a balcony overlooking the Arno, watching the water. His wounds were still bandaged but they were healing, and the pallor had left his cheeks. He stood proud and tall, and fully the man who had earned the soubriquet Florence had bestowed on him – *Il Magnifico*.

After they had greeted one another, Lorenzo gestured towards the river. 'Do you know, Ezio, when I was six years old, I fell into the Arno. I soon found myself drifting down and into darkness, certain that my life was at an end. Instead, I woke to the sound of my mother weeping. At her side stood a stranger, soaking wet and smiling. She explained to me that he had saved me. That stranger's name was Auditore. And so began a long and prosperous relationship between our two families.' He turned to look at Ezio solemnly. 'I am sorry that I could not save your kinsmen.'

Ezio found it hard to find words. The cold world of politics, where distinctions between right and wrong are too often blurred, was one he understood but rejected. 'I know you would have saved them if it had been within your power,' he said.

'Your family house, at least, is safe and under the city's protection. I have put your old housekeeper,

Annetta, in charge of it, and it is staffed and guarded at my expense. Whatever happens, it will be waiting for you whenever you wish to return to it.'

'You are gracious, *Altezza*.' Ezio paused. He was thinking of Cristina. Might it not be too late to persuade her to break her engagement, marry him, and help him bring the Auditore family back to life? But two short years had changed him beyond recognition, and he had another duty now – a duty to the Creed.

'We have won a great victory,' he said at last. 'But the war is not won. Many of our enemies have escaped.'

'But the safety of Florence is assured. Pope Sixtus wanted to persuade Naples to move against us, but I have persuaded Ferdinando not to do so; and neither will Bologna or Milan.'

Ezio could not tell the Duke of the greater battle he was engaged in, for he could not be sure if Lorenzo was privy to the secrets of the Assassins. 'For the sake of our greater security,' he said, 'I need your permission to go and seek out Jacopo de' Pazzi.'

A cloud crossed Lorenzo's face. 'That coward!' he said angrily. 'He fled before we could lay hands on him.'

'Do we have any idea where he might have gone?'

Lorenzo shook his head. 'No. They've hidden themselves well. My spies report that Baroncelli may be trying to make his way to Constantinople, but as for the others . . .'

Ezio said, 'Give me their names,' and there was

something in the firmness of his voice that told Lorenzo that here was a man it might be fatal to cross.

'How could I ever forget the names of my brother's murderers? And if you seek and find them, I shall be forever in your debt. They are the priests Antonio Maffei and Stefano da Bagnone. Bernardo Baroncelli I have mentioned. And there is another, not directly involved in the killings, but a dangerous ally of our enemies. He is the Archbishop of Pisa, Francesco Salviati – another of the Riario family, the Pope's hunting dogs. I showed his cousin clemency. I try not to be a man like they are. I wonder sometimes how wise I am in that.'

'I have a list,' said Ezio. 'Their names will be added to it.' He prepared to take his leave.

'Where will you go now?' asked Lorenzo.

'Back to my uncle Mario in Monteriggioni. That will be my base.'

'Then go with God, friend Ezio. But before you do, I have something that may interest you . . .' Lorenzo opened a leather wallet at his belt and from it extracted a sheet of vellum. Almost before he'd unrolled it, Ezio knew what it was.

'I remember years ago talking to your father about ancient documents,' said Lorenzo quietly. 'It was a shared interest that we had. I know he'd translated some. Here, take this – I found it among Francesco de' Pazzi's papers, and as he no longer needs it, I thought you might like it – as it reminded me of your father. Perhaps you might like to add it to his . . . collection?'

'I am indeed grateful for this, *Altezza.*'

'I thought you might be,' said Lorenzo, in such a way as to make Ezio wonder how much he actually knew. 'I hope you find it useful.'

Before he packed and made ready for his journey, Ezio hastened, with the fresh Codex page Lorenzo had given him, to visit his friend Leonardo da Vinci. Despite the events of the last week, the workshop was carrying on as if nothing had happened.

'I am glad to see you safe and sound, Ezio,' Leonardo greeted him.

'I see that you came through the troubles unscathed too,' replied Ezio.

'I told you – they leave me alone. They must think me either too mad, or too bad, or too dangerous to touch! But do have some wine, and there are some cakes somewhere, if they haven't gone stale – my house-keeper's useless – and tell me what's on your mind.'

'I'm leaving Florence.'

'So soon? But they tell me you're the hero of the hour! Why not sit back and enjoy it?'

'I have no time.'

'Still got enemies to pursue?'

'How do you know?'

Leonardo smiled. 'Thank you for coming to say goodbye,' he said.

'Before I go,' said Ezio, 'I have another page of the Codex for you.'

'That is indeed good news. May I see it?'

'Of course.'

Leonardo perused the new document carefully. 'I'm beginning to get the hang of this,' he said. 'I still can't quite see what the general diagram in the background is, but the writing is becoming familiar. It looks like the description of another weapon.' He rose, and brought a handful of old and fragile-looking books to the table. 'Let's see . . . I must say, whoever the inventor was who wrote all this, he must have been a very long way ahead of his time. The mechanics alone . . .' He trailed off, lost in thought. 'Aha! I see! Ezio, it's a design for another blade – one that will fit into the mechanism you attach to your arm if you need to use this one in place of the first.'

'What's the difference?'

'If I'm right, this one's quite nasty – it's hollow in the middle, see? And through the tube concealed in the blade, its user can inject poison into his victim. Death wherever you strike! This thing would make you practically invincible!'

'Can you make it?'

'On the same terms as before?'

'Of course.'

'Good! How long have I got?'

'The end of the week? I have some preparations to make, and . . . there's someone I want to try to see . . . to say goodbye. But I need to get going as soon as possible.'

'It doesn't give me long. But I still have the tools I needed for the first job, and my assistants have got their hand in, so I don't see why not.'

Ezio used the intervening time to settle his affairs in Florence, pack his bags, and arrange a courier to take a letter to Monteriggioni. He found himself putting off his final, self-imposed task again and again, but he knew he'd have to do it. At last, on his second to last evening, he walked over to the Calfucci mansion. His feet were like lead.

But when he approached the place he found it dark and closed up. Knowing he was behaving like a madman, he clambered up to Cristina's balcony, only to find her windows securely shuttered. The nasturtiums in pots on the balcony were withered and dead. As he climbed down again, wearily, he felt as if his heart had been covered in a shroud. He remained at the door in a dream, for he knew not how long, but someone must have been watching him, for finally a first-floor window opened and a woman put her head out.

'They've gone, you know. Signor Calfucci saw the trouble coming and cleared the family out to Lucca – that's where his daughter's fiancé comes from.'

'Lucca?'

'Yes. The families have got quite close, I hear.'

'When will they be back?'

'No idea.' The woman looked at him. 'Don't I know you from somewhere?'

'I don't think so,' said Ezio.

He spent that night dreaming alternately of Cristina and of Francesco's bloody end.

In the morning it was overcast, a sky to suit Ezio's mood. He made his way to Leonardo's workshop, glad that this was the day on which he would leave Florence. The new knife blade was ready, finished in dull grey steel, very hard, the edges sharp enough to sever a silk handkerchief if you just let it fall through the air on to them. The hole in the point was tiny.

'The hilt contains the poison, and you release it simply by flexing your arm muscle against this inner button. Be careful, as it's quite sensitive.'

'What poison should I use?'

'I've used a strong distillation of hemlock to get you started, but when you run out, ask any doctor.'

'Poison? From a doctor?'

'In high enough concentrations, that which cures can also kill.'

Ezio nodded sadly. 'I am in your debt once more.'

'Here is your Codex page. Must you leave so soon?'

'Florence is safe – for now. But I still have work to do.'

10

'Ezio!' beamed Mario, his beard bristlier than ever, his face burned by the Tuscan sun. 'Welcome back!'

'Uncle.'

Mario's face became more serious. 'I can see from your face that you've been through much in the months since we last met. And when you are bathed and rested, you must tell me all.' He paused. 'We have heard all the news from Florence, and I – even I – found myself praying that by some miracle you would be spared. But not only were you spared, you turned the tide against the Pazzi! The Templars will hate you for that, Ezio.'

'It is a hatred I reciprocate.'

'Rest first – then tell me all.'

That evening the two men sat down together in Mario's study. Mario listened intently as Ezio told him all he knew of the events that had passed in Florence. He returned Vieri's Codex page to his uncle, and then passed over the one he had been given by Lorenzo, describing the design it contained for the poison-blade, and showing it to him. Mario was duly impressed, but fixed his attention on the new page.

'My friend was not able to decipher more than the description of the weapon,' said Ezio.

'That is as well. Not all the pages contain such instructions, and only those that do should be of any interest to him,' said Mario, an underlying note of caution in his voice. 'In any case, only when the pages are reunited shall we be able to understand fully the meaning of the Codex. But this page, when we place it, together with Vieri's, with the others, should bring us a step further.'

He rose, walked over to the bookcase that concealed the wall on which the Codex pages hung, swung it back, and studied where the new pages might go. One of them connected with those already in place. The other touched a corner of it. 'It is interesting that Vieri and his father should have owned pages that were evidently close together,' he said. 'Now, let us see what . . .' He broke off, concentrating. 'Hmmn,' he said at last, but his voice was troubled.

'Does this bring us any further, Uncle?'

'I'm not sure. We may be just as much in the dark as ever, but there is definitely some reference to a prophet – not from the Bible, but either a living prophet, or one who is to come . . .'

'Who could it be?'

'Let's not go too fast.' Mario brooded over the pages, his lips moving, speaking a language Ezio did not understand. 'As far as I can make out, the text here roughly translates as "Only the Prophet may open it . . ." And here, there's a reference to two "Pieces of Eden", but what that means, I do not know. We must be patient, until we have more pages of the Codex.'

'I know the Codex is important, Uncle, but I have what is for me a more pressing reason to be here than to unravel its mystery. I seek the renegade, Jacopo de' Pazzi.'

'He certainly travelled south after fleeing Florence.' Mario hesitated before continuing. 'I had not meant to talk of this with you tonight, Ezio, but the matter is as urgent to me as I see it is to you, and we have to start our preparations soon. My old friend Roberto has been driven out of San Gimignano and it has become once more a stronghold of the Templars. It is too close to Florence, and to us, to remain so. I believe that Jacopo may seek refuge there.'

'I have a list of the names of the other conspirators,' said Ezio, taking it from his wallet and handing it to his uncle.

'Good. Some of these men will have far less to fall back on than Jacopo, and may be easy to root out. I'll send spies out into the countryside at dawn to see what they can discover about them, and in the meantime we must prepare to retake San Gimignano.'

'By all means make your men ready, but for me there is no time to waste if I am to bring these murderers down.'

Mario considered. 'Perhaps you are right – a man

alone can often breach walls which an army cannot. And we should bring them down while they still think they are safe.' He considered for a moment. 'So, I give you my permission. You go on ahead and see what you can discover. I know you are more than able to look after yourself these days.'

'Uncle, my thanks!'

'Not so fast, Ezio! I grant you this leave on one condition.'

'Which is?'

'That you delay your departure for a week.'

'A *week*?'

'If you are to go out into the field alone, with no back-up, you will need more than these Codex weapons to help you. You are a man now, and a brave fighter for the Assassins. But your reputation will make the Templars even hungrier for your blood, and I know that there are still skills which you lack.'

Ezio shook his head impatiently. 'No, Uncle, I am sorry, but a *week* – !'

Mario frowned, but raised his voice only slightly. It was enough. 'I have heard good things of you, Ezio, but also bad. You lost control when you killed Francesco. And you allowed sentiment over Cristina to tempt you from your path. Your whole duty now is to the Creed, for if you neglect it, there may be no world left for you to enjoy.' He drew himself up. 'I speak with your father's voice when I command your obedience.'

Ezio had watched his uncle grow in stature, even in size, as he spoke. And painful as it was to accept, he acknowledged the truth of what he had been told. Bitterly, he bowed his head.

'Good,' said Mario, more kindly. 'And you will thank me for this. Your new combat training begins in the morning. And remember, the preparation is all!'

A week later, armed and ready, Ezio rode out for San Gimignano. Mario had told him to make contact with one of the *condottieri* patrols he had posted within sight of the town to keep track of its comings and goings, and he joined one of their encampments for his first night away from Monteriggioni.

The sergeant in command, a tough, battle-scarred man of twenty-five, whose name was Gambalto, gave him a slab of bread with pecorino and a mug of heavy Vernaccia, and while he was eating and drinking told him the news.

'I think it's a shame Antonio Maffei ever left Volterra. He's got a bee in his bonnet about Lorenzo and thinks the Duke crushed his home town, whereas all he did was bring it under the wing of Florence. Now Maffei's gone mad. He's set himself up at the top of the cathedral tower, surrounded himself with Pazzi archers, and spends each day spouting scripture and arrows in equal measure. God knows what his plan is – to convert the citizens to his cause with his sermons, or kill them off with his arrows. The ordinary people of San Gimignano hate him, but as long as he continues his reign of terror, the city is powerless against him.'

'So he needs to be neutralized.'

'Well, that would certainly weaken the Pazzi power-base in the city.'

'How well defended are they?'

'Plenty of men on the watchtowers and at the gates. But they change the guard at dawn. Then, a man like you might be able to get over the walls and into the city unseen.'

Ezio mused, wondering whether this was a distraction from his own mission to hunt down Jacopo. But he reflected that he must be able to see the bigger picture – this Maffei was a Pazzi supporter and it was Ezio's wider duty as an Assassin to unseat this madman.

By sunrise the following day, any especially attentive citizen of San Gimignano might have noticed a slim, grey-eyed, hooded figure gliding like a ghost through the streets which led to the cathedral square. The market traders were already setting up their stalls, but it was the ebb of the day's cycle and the guards, bored and dispirited, leant on their halberds and dozed. The western side of the campanile was still in deep shadow, and no one saw the black-clad figure climb up it with all the quiet ease and grace of a spider.

The priest, gaunt, hollow-eyed and wild-haired, was already in position. Four tired Pazzi crossbowmen had also taken up their places, one at each corner of the tower. But, as if he did not trust the crossbowmen alone to protect him, Antonio Maffei, though clutching a Bible in his left hand, held a rondel-dagger in his right. He was already orating, and as Ezio drew close to the top of the tower, he began to catch Maffei's words.

'Citizens of San Gimignano, heed well my words! You must repent. REPENT! And seek forgiveness . . . Join me in prayer, my children, so that together we may stand against the darkness which has fallen across our beloved Tuscany! Give ear, oh Heavens, and I shall speak; and hear, oh Earth, the words of my mouth. Let my teaching drop as the rain, my speech distil as the dew, as raindrops on the tender herbs, as showers on the grass; for I proclaim the Name of the Lord! He is the Rock! His Work is perfect, for all His ways are just! Righteous and upright is He; but they who have corrupted themselves, they are not his children – a blemished, perverse and crooked generation! Citizens of San Gimignano – do you thus deal with the Lord? Oh, foolish and unwise people! Is he not your Father, who bore you? By the light of His mercy, be cleansed!'

Ezio leapt lightly over the parapet of the tower and took up a position near the trapdoor which opened on to the stairway that led below. The bowmen struggled to bring their crossbows to bear on him, but the range was short, and he had the element of surprise. He crouched and grasped the heels of one, toppling him over the parapet, howling to his death on the cobble-stones two hundred feet below. Before the others could react, he had rounded on a second, stabbing him in the arm. The man looked astonished at the small wound, but then turned grey and collapsed, the life draining from him in an instant. Ezio had strapped his new poison-blade to his arm, for there was no time for fair mortal combat now. He whirled on the third, who had dropped his crossbow and was trying to get past him to the stairs. As he reached them, Ezio kicked him in the rump and he stumbled down the wooden steps, head first, bones snapping as he crashed down the first flight. The last raised his hands and burbled something. Ezio looked down and saw that the man had pissed in his hose. He stepped aside and with an ironic bow allowed the terrified bowman to scamper down the stairs after the broken ruins of his comrade.

Then he was hit hard on the back of the neck by the heavy steel pommel of a dagger. Maffei had recovered from his shock at the attack and closed on Ezio from behind. Ezio staggered forward.

'I will put you on your knees, sinner!' screamed the priest, foam appearing at the sides of his mouth. 'Beg forgiveness!'

Why do people always waste their time in talk, thought Ezio, who had had time to recover and turn while the priest was speaking.

The two men circled each other in the narrow space.

Maffei slashed and lunged with his heavy dagger. He was clearly an unskilled fighter, but desperation and his fanaticism made him very dangerous indeed, and Ezio had to dance out of the way of the erratically swinging blade more than once, unable to land a blow himself. But at last he was able to catch the priest's wrist and pull him forwards, so that their chests were touching.

'I will send you whimpering to hell,' snarled Maffei.

'Show some respect for death, my friend,' Ezio retorted.

'I'll give you respect!'

'Give in! I'll give you time to pray.'

Maffei spat in Ezio's eyes, forcing him to let go. Then, screaming, he plunged his dagger at Ezio's left forearm, only to see the blade slide harmlessly to one side, deflected by the metal bracer in place there. 'What demon protects you?' he snapped.

'You talk too much,' Ezio said, pushing his own dagger a little way into the priest's neck, and tensing the muscles in his forearm. As the poison flowed through the blade into Maffei's jugular, the priest stiffened, opened his mouth, but nothing but foul breath came forth. Then he pushed himself away from Ezio, staggered back to the parapet, steadied himself an instant, and then fell forward into the arms of death.

Ezio stooped over Maffei's corpse. From his robes he extracted a letter, which he opened and quickly scanned.

Padrone:

It is with fear in my heart that I write this. The Prophet has arrived. I feel it. The very birds don't act as they should. They swirl aimlessly round the sky. I see them from my tower. I will not attend our meeting as you required, for I can no longer remain thus exposed in public view, for fear that the Demon may find me. Forgive me, but I must heed my inner voice.
May the Father of Understanding guide you. And guide me.
Brother A.

Gambalto was right, thought Ezio, the man had lost his mind. Sombrely, remembering his uncle's admonition, he closed the priest's eyes, saying as he did so, '*Requiescat in pace.*'

Aware that the archer to whom he'd shown mercy might have raised the alarm, he looked down over the tower's parapet at the town below, but could see no activity to worry him. The Pazzi guards still lounged at their posts, and the market had opened, doing a thin trade. No doubt the crossbowman was by now halfway across the countryside, making his way home, finding desertion preferable to a court-martial and possibly torture. He pushed his blade back into its mechanism, hidden on his forearm, taking care to touch it only with a gloved hand, and picked his way down the stairs of the tower. The sun was up, and it would make him too easily visible if he were to climb down the outside of the campanile.

When he rejoined Mario's troop of mercenaries,

Gambalto greeted him in an excited mood. 'Your presence brings us good fortune,' he said. 'Our scouts have tracked down Archbishop Salviati!'

'Where?'

'Not far from here. Do you see that mansion, on the hill, over there?'

'Yes.'

'He's there.' Gambalto remembered himself. 'But first, I must ask you, *Capitano*, how you fared in the city?'

'There will be no more sermons of hatred from that tower.'

'The people will bless you, *Capitano*.'

'I am no captain.'

'To us you are,' said Gambalto, simply. 'Take a detachment of men from here. Salviati is heavily guarded and the mansion is an old, fortified building.'

'Very well,' said Ezio. 'It is good that the eggs are close together, almost in one nest.'

'The others cannot be far away, Ezio. We will endeavour to find them during your absence.'

Ezio selected a dozen of Gambalto's best hand-to-hand combat fighters, and led them on foot across the fields that separated them from the mansion where Salviati had taken refuge. He had his men fanned out, but within calling distance of one another, and the Pazzi outposts Salviati had put into position were easily either avoided or neutralized. But Ezio lost two of his own men in the approach.

Ezio had hoped to take the mansion by surprise, before its occupants were aware of his attack, but when he came close to the solid main gates a figure appeared on the walls above them, dressed in the robes of an archbishop, gripping the battlements with claw-like hands. A vulturine face peered down, and was quickly withdrawn.

'It's Salviati,' Ezio said to himself.

There were no other guards posted outside the gates. Ezio beckoned to his men to come up close to the walls, so that archers would not have enough of an angle to fire down at them. There was no doubt that Salviati would have concentrated what remained of his body-guard inside the walls, which were high and thick enough to seem unbreachable. Ezio was wondering whether he should once again attempt climbing up and over the walls, and open the gates from the inside to admit his troops, but he knew that the Pazzi guards inside would be alerted to his presence.

Motioning to his men to stay out of sight, huddled against the walls, he crouched low and made his way back through the tall grass the short distance to where the body of one of their enemies lay. Quickly he stripped and donned the man's uniform, bundling his own clothes under his arm.

He rejoined his men, who at first bristled at the sight of a supposed Pazzi approaching, and handed his clothes over to one of them. Then he banged on the gates with the pommel of his sword.

'Open!' he cried. 'In the name of the Father of Understanding!'

A tense minute passed. Ezio stood back so that he could be seen from the walls. And then he heard the sound of heavy bolts being drawn.

As soon as the gates began to open, Ezio and his men stormed them, heaving them back and scattering the guards within. They found themselves in a court-yard, around which the mansion formed itself in three wings. Salviati himself stood at the top of a flight of stairs in the middle of the main wing. A dozen burly men, fully armed, stood between him and Ezio. More occupied the courtyard.

'Filthy treachery!' cried the archbishop. 'But you will not get out again as easily as you have got in.' He raised his voice to a commanding roar: 'Kill them! Kill them all!'

The Pazzi troops closed in, all but surrounding Ezio's men. But the Pazzi had not trained under such a man as Mario Auditore, and despite the odds against them, Ezio's *condottieri* engaged successfully with their oppon-ents in the courtyard, while Ezio sprang towards the stairs. He released his poison-blade and slashed at the men surrounding Salviati. It didn't matter where he hit; every time he struck and drew blood, be it only at a man's cheek, that man died in a heartbeat.

'You are indeed a demon – from the Fourth Ring of the Ninth Circle!' Salviati spoke in a shuddering voice as at last he and Ezio confronted one another alone.

Ezio retracted the poison-blade, but drew his battle-dagger. He grasped Salviati by the scruff of his cope and held the blade to the archbishop's neck. 'The Templars lost their Christianity when they discovered banking,' he said, evenly. 'Do you not know your own gospel? "Thou canst not serve God and Mammon!" But now is your chance to redeem yourself. Tell me – where is Jacopo?'

Salviati glared in defiance. 'You will never find him!'

Ezio drew the blade gently but firmly across the man's gizzard, drawing a little blood. 'You'll have to do better than that, *Arcivescovo*.'

'Night guards us when we meet – now, finish your business!'

'So, you skulk like the murderers you are under cover of darkness. Thank you for that. I will ask you once more. *Where?*'

'The Father of Understanding knows that what I do now is for the greater good,' said Salviati coldly, and, suddenly seizing Ezio's wrist with both his hands, he forced the dagger deep into his own throat.

'Tell me!' yelled Ezio. But the archbishop, his mouth bubbling blood, had already sunk at his feet, his gorgeous yellow-and-white robes blossoming red.

It was to be several months before Ezio had further news of the conspirators he sought. Meanwhile, he worked with Mario to plan how they might retake San Gimignano and free its citizens from the cruel yoke of the Templars, but they had learned a lesson from the last time, and maintained an iron grip on the city. Knowing that the Templars would also be searching for the still-missing pages of the Codex, Ezio roamed far and wide in quest of them himself, but to no avail. The pages already in the possession of the Assassins remained concealed, under Mario's strict guard, for without them, the secret of the Creed would never yield to the Templars.

Then, one day, a courier from Florence rode up to Monteriggioni bearing a letter from Leonardo for Ezio. Quickly, he reached for a mirror, for he knew his friend's habit, being left-handed, of writing backwards – though the spidery scrawl would have been difficult for the most talented reader, unfamiliar with it, to decipher in any circumstances. Ezio broke the seal and read eagerly, his heart lifting at every line:

Gentile *Ezio,*

Duke Lorenzo has asked me to send you news – of Bernardo Baroncelli! It seems that the man managed to take ship for Venice, and from thence secretly made his way, incognito, to the court of the Ottoman sultan at Constantinople, planning to seek refuge there. But he spent no time in Venice, and did not learn that the Venetians had recently signed a peace with the Turks – they have even sent their second-best painter,

Gentile Bellini, to make a portrait of Sultan Mehmet. So that
when he arrived, and his true identity became known, he was
arrested.

Of course then you can imagine the letters that flew
between the Sublime Porte and Venice; but the Venetians are
our allies too – at least for now – and Duke Lorenzo is
nothing if not a master diplomat. Baroncelli was sent in
chains back to Florence, and once here, he was put to the
question. But he was stubborn, or foolish, or brave, I know
not which – he withstood the rack and the white-hot tongs and
the floggings and the rats nibbling his feet, only telling us that
the conspirators used to meet by night in an old crypt under
Santa Maria Novella. Of course a search was made but
yielded nothing. So he was hanged. I have done rather a good
sketch of him hanging, which I will show you when we next
meet. I think it is, anatomically speaking, quite accurate.

Distinti saluti
Your friend
Leonardo da Vinci

'It is good that the man is dead,' commented Mario
when Ezio showed him the letter. 'He was the type who
would steal straw from his mother's kennel. But alas, it
brings us no nearer to discovering what the Templars
plan next, or even the whereabouts of Jacopo.'

Ezio had found time to visit his mother and his sister,
who continued to while away their days in the serenity

of the convent, watched over by the kindly abbess. Maria had, he saw to his sadness, made as much of a recovery as she would ever make. Her hair had turned prematurely grey, and there were fine crowsfeet lines at the corners of her eyes, but she had achieved an inner calm, and when she spoke of her dead husband and sons it was with affectionate and proud remembrance. But the sight of little Petruccio's pearwood box of eagle's plumes, which she kept on her bedside table, could still bring tears to her eyes. As for Claudia, she was now a *novizia*, but although Ezio regretted what he saw as a waste of her beauty and her spirit, he acknowledged that there was a light in her face which caused him to bow to her decision, and be happy for her. He visited them again over Christmas, and in the New Year took up his training again, though inside himself he was boiling over with impatience. To counter this, Mario had made him joint commander of his castle, and Ezio tirelessly sent out his own spies and scouts to range the country in quest of the quarry he implacably sought.

And then, at last, there was news. One morning in late spring Gambalto appeared in the doorway of the map-room where Ezio and Mario were deep in conference, his eyes ablaze.

'*Signori*! We have found Stefano da Bagnone! He has taken refuge in the Abbey Asmodeo, only a few leagues to the south. He has been right under our noses all this time!'

'They hang together like the dogs they are,' snapped Mario, his stubby workman's fingers quickly tracing a route on the map before him. He looked at Ezio. 'But he is a lead-dog. Jacopo's secretary! If we cannot beat something out of him – !'

But Ezio was already giving orders for his horse to be saddled and made ready. Swiftly, he made his way to his quarters and armed himself, strapping on the Codex weapons and choosing, this time, the original spring-blade over the poison one. He had replaced Leonardo's original hemlock distillation with henbane, on the advice of Monteriggioni's doctor, and the poison sac in its hilt was full. He had decided he would use the poison-blade with discretion, since there was always the risk of delivering himself a fatal dose. For this reason, and because his fingers were covered with small scars, he now wore supple but heavy leather gloves when using either blade.

The abbey was located near Monticiano, whose ancient castle brooded over the little hill town. It was set in the sunlit hollow of a gentle slope, packed with cypress trees. It was a new building, perhaps only one hundred years old, built of expensive imported yellow sandstone and built round a vast courtyard with a church at its centre. The gates stood wide open, and the monks of the abbey's Order, in their ochre habits, could be seen working in the fields and orchards which had been cleared around the building, and in the vineyard above it; the wine of the monastery attached to the abbey was famous, and was exported even to Paris. Part of Ezio's preparation had been to provide himself with a monk's habit of his own, and, having left his horse with an ostler at the inn where he had taken a room under the guise of a state courier, he donned his disguise before arriving at the abbey.

Soon after his arrival he spotted Stefano, deep in conversation with the abbey's *hospitarius*, a corpulent monk who looked as if he had taken on the shape of one of the wine barrels he so evidently frequently emptied. Ezio managed to manoeuvre himself close enough to listen without being noticed.

'Let us pray, brother,' said the monk.

'Pray?' said Stefano, whose black garb contrasted with all the sunny colours around him. He looked like a spider on a pancake. 'For what?' he added sardonically.

The monk looked surprised. 'For the Lord's protection!'

'If you think the Lord has any interest in our affairs, Brother Girolamo, you have another think coming! But please, by all means, continue to delude yourself, if it helps you to pass the time.'

Brother Girolamo was shocked. 'What you speak is blasphemy!'

'No. I speak truth.'

'But, to deny His most exalted Presence – !'

'– is the only rational response, when faced with the declaration that there exists some invisible madman in the sky. And believe me, if our precious Bible is anything to go by, He's completely lost His mind.'

'How can you say such things? You are yourself a priest!'

'I am an administrator. I use these clerical robes to bring me closer to the accursed Medici, so that I may chop them off at the knees, in the service of my true Master. But first, there is still the business of this Assassin, Ezio. For too long he has been a thorn in our side, and we must pluck him out.'

'There you speak truth. That unholy demon!'

'Well,' said Stefano with a crooked smile. 'At least we agree on something.'

Girolamo lowered his voice. 'They say the Devil has given him unnatural speed and strength.'

Stefano looked at him. 'The Devil? No, my friend. These are gifts he gave himself, through rigorous training over years.' He paused, his scrawny body bent at a pensive angle. 'You know, Girolamo, I find it disturbing that you are so unwilling to credit people for their own circumstances. I think you'd make victims out of the entire world if you could.'

'I forgive your lack of faith and your forked tongue,' replied Girolamo piously. 'You are still one of God's children.'

'I told you –' Stefano began with some asperity; but then spread his hands and gave it up. 'Oh, what's the use? Enough of this! It's like speaking to the wind!'

'I will pray for you.'

'As you wish. But do so quietly. I must keep watch. Until we have this Assassin dead and buried, no Templar can drop his guard for an instant.'

The monk withdrew with a bow, and Stefano was left alone in the courtyard. The bell for First and Second Qauma had sounded, and all the Community were in the abbey church. Ezio emerged from the shadows like a wraith. The sun shone with the silent heaviness of midday. Stefano, crow-like, stalked up and down by the north wall, restless, impatient, possessed.

When he saw Ezio, he showed no surprise at all.

'I am unarmed,' he said. 'I fight with the mind.'

'To use that, you must remain alive. Can you defend yourself?'

'Would you kill me in cold blood?'

'I will kill you because it is necessary that you die.'

'A good answer! But do you not think I may have secrets that would be useful to you?'

'I can see that you would not bow under any torture.'

Stefano looked at him appraisingly. 'I will take that as a compliment, though I am not so sure myself. However, it is of merely academic significance.' He paused, before continuing in his thin voice. 'You have missed your chance, Ezio. The die is cast. The Assassins' cause is lost. I know you will kill me whatever I do or say, and that I shall be dead before the midday Mass is over; but my death will profit you nothing. The Templars already have you in check, and soon it will be checkmate.'

'You cannot be sure of that.'

'I am about to meet my Maker – if He exists at all. It will be refreshing to find out. In the meantime, why should I lie?'

Ezio released his dagger.

'How clever,' commented Stefano. 'What will they think of next?'

'Redeem yourself,' said Ezio. 'Tell me what you know.'

'What do you *wish* to know? The whereabouts of my Master, Jacopo?' Stefano smiled. 'That is easy. He meets our confederates soon, at night, in the shadow of the Roman gods.' He paused. 'I hope that makes you happy, for nothing you can do will make me say more. And it is in any case of no significance, for I know in my heart that you are too late. My only regret is that I will not see your own undoing – but who knows? Perhaps there *is* an Afterlife, and I shall be able to look down on your death. But for the present – let us get this unpleasant business over with.'

The abbey bell was ringing once more. Ezio had little time. 'I think you could teach me much,' he said.

Stefano looked at him sadly. 'Not in this world,' he

said. He opened the neck of his gown. 'But do me the favour of sending me quickly into the night.'

Ezio stabbed once, deeply, and with deadly accuracy.

'There are the ruins of a Temple of Mithras to the south-west of San Gimignano,' said Mario thoughtfully when Ezio returned. 'They are the only Roman ruins of any significance for miles around, and you say he spoke of the shadow of the Roman *gods*?'

'Those were his words.'

'And the Templars are to meet there – soon?'

'Yes.'

'Then we must not delay. We must keep a vigil there from this night on.'

Ezio was despondent. 'Da Bagnone told me it was already too late to stop them.'

Mario grinned. 'Well then, it's up to us to prove him wrong.'

It was the third night of the vigil. Mario had returned to his base to continue his schemes against the Templars in San Gimignano, and left Ezio with five trusted men, Gambalto among them, to keep watch concealed in the dense woods which fringed the isolated, desolate ruins of the Temple of Mithras. This was a large set of buildings developed over centuries, whose last occupant had indeed been Mithras, the god the Roman army had adopted, but which contained more ancient chapels, once consecrated to Minerva, Venus and Mercury. There was also a theatre attached to the complex, whose stage was still solid, though faced by a broken semi-circle of terraced stone benches, the home now of scorpions and mice, backed by a crumbling wall and flanked by broken columns where owls had made their nests. Everywhere ivy climbed, and tough buddleia shouldered its way through the cracks it had made in the stained and decaying marble. Over all, the moon cast a ghastly light, and, used though they were to tackling mortal foes unafraid, one or two of the men were distinctly nervous.

Ezio had told himself that they would keep watch for a week, but he knew it would be hard for the men to keep their nerve in this place for that long, for the ghosts of the pagan past were a strong presence here. But towards midnight, as the Assassins ached in every limb from lack of activity and keeping still, they heard the faint tinkling of harness. Ezio and his men braced themselves. Soon afterwards there rode through the complex a dozen soldiers bearing torches and headed by three men. They were making for the theatre. Ezio and his *condottieri* shadowed them there.

The men dismounted and formed a protective circle round their three leaders. Watching, Ezio recognized with triumph the face of the man he had sought so long – Jacopo de' Pazzi, a harassed-looking greybeard of sixty. He was accompanied by one man he did not know and another whom he did – the beak-nosed, crimson-cowled, unmistakable figure of Rodrigo Borgia! Grimly, Ezio attached the poison-blade to the mechanism on his right wrist.

'You know why I have called this meeting,' Rodrigo began. 'I have given you more than enough time, Jacopo. But you have yet to redeem yourself.'

'I am sorry, *Commendatore*. I have done all that is within my power. The Assassins have outflanked me.'

'You have not regained Florence.'

Jacopo bowed his head.

'You have not even been able to strike off the head of Ezio Auditore, a mere cub! And with every victory over us, he gains strength, becomes more dangerous!'

'It was my nephew Francesco's fault,' babbled Jacopo. 'His impatience made him reckless! I tried to be the voice of reason –'

'More like the voice of cowardice,' put in the third man, harshly.

Jacopo turned to him with markedly less respect than he had shown Rodrigo. 'Ah, *Messer* Emilio. Perhaps we would have been better served had you sent us weaponry of quality, instead of the rubbish you Venetians call armaments! But you Barbarigi were always cheapskates.'

'Enough!' thundered Rodrigo. He turned again to Jacopo. 'We put our faith in you and your family, and how have you repaid us? With inaction and incompetence.

You retake San Gimignano! Bravo! And there you sit. You even allow them to attack you there. Brother Maffei was a valuable servant of our Cause. And you could not even save your own secretary, a man whose brain was worth ten of yours!'

'*Altezza*! Just give me the chance to make amends, and you will see –' Jacopo looked at the hardened faces surrounding him. 'I will show you –'

Rodrigo allowed his features to soften. He even sketched a smile. 'Jacopo. We know the best course to take now. You must leave it to us. Come here. Let me embrace you.'

Hesitantly, Jacopo obeyed. Rodrigo put his left arm round his shoulders, and with his right drew a stiletto from his robes and slid it firmly between Jacopo's ribs. Jacopo pushed his way back off the knife, while Rodrigo looked at him in the same way as a father might regard his errant son. Jacopo clutched his wound. Rodrigo had not penetrated any vital organ. Perhaps –

But now Emilio Barbarigo stepped up to him. Instinctively, Jacopo held up his bloodied hands to protect himself, for Emilio had drawn a wicked-looking basilard, one of its edges roughly serrated, and with a deep blood-gutter along the side of its blade.

'No,' whimpered Jacopo. 'I have done my best. I have always served the Cause loyally. All my life. Please . . . Please don't . . .'

Emilio gave a brutal laugh. 'Please don't what, you

snivelling piece of shit?' And he tore Jacopo's doublet open, immediately dragging the serrated blade of his heavy dagger across Jacopo's chest, tearing it open.

Jacopo screamed and fell first to his knees and then on to his side, writhing in blood. He looked up to see Rodrigo Borgia standing over him, a narrow sword in his hand.

'Master – have pity!' Jacopo managed to say. 'It is not too late! Give me one last chance to put matters right –' Then he choked on his own blood.

'Oh, Jacopo,' said Rodrigo, gently. 'How you have disappointed me.'

He raised his blade and thrust it through Jacopo's neck with such force that the point emerged at the nape, seeming to sever the spinal cord. He twisted it in the wound before drawing it out slowly. Jacopo raised himself, his mouth full of blood, but he was already dead and sank back, twitching, until he was, at last, still.

Rodrigo wiped his sword on the dead man's clothes, and, drawing his cloak aside, sheathed it. 'What a mess,' he murmured. Then he turned, looked directly in Ezio's direction, grinned, and shouted, 'You can come out now, Assassin! My apologies for having robbed you of your prize!'

Before he could react, Ezio found himself grabbed by two guards whose tunics bore a red cross within a yellow shield – the coat of arms of his arch-enemy. He called to Gambalto, but there was no answer from any of his men. He was dragged on to the stage of the ancient theatre.

'Greetings, Ezio!' said Rodrigo. 'I am sorry about your men, but did you really think I didn't expect to find you here? That I didn't plan for you to come? Do you think Stefano da Bagnone all but told you the exact time and place of this meeting without my knowledge and approval? Of course, we had to make it seem difficult, or you might have sensed a trap.' He laughed. 'Poor Ezio! You see, we've been at this game a lot longer than you have. I had my guards hidden in the woods here long before you even arrived. And I'm afraid your men were taken as much by surprise as you were – but I wanted to see you again alive before you leave us. Call it a whim. And now I am satisfied.' Rodrigo smiled and addressed the guards holding Ezio's arms. 'Thank you. You may kill him now.'

Together with Emilio Barbarigo, he mounted his horse and rode away, together with the guards who had accompanied him there. Ezio watched him go. He thought fast. There were the two burly men holding him – and how many others, still concealed in the woods? How many men had Borgia set in place to ambush his own troop?

'Say your prayers, boy,' one of his captors told him.

'Look,' said Ezio. 'I know you're only obeying orders. So, if you release me, I'll spare your lives. How about that?'

The guard who had spoken looked amused. 'Well! Listen to you! I don't think I've ever come across anyone able to keep their sense of humour like you at a moment like –'

But he didn't get to finish his sentence. Ezio sprang out his hidden blade and, taking advantage of their surprise, cut at the man holding him on his right. The poison did its work and the man staggered back, falling not far away. Before the other guard could react, Ezio had thrust his blade deep into his armpit, the one spot armour could not cover. Free, he leapt into the shadows at the edge of the stage and waited. He didn't have to wait long. From out of the woods the other ten guards Rodrigo had hidden there emerged, some warily scanning the fringes of the theatre, others bending over their fallen comrades. Moving with the deadly speed of a lynx, Ezio threw himself among them, slashing at them with sickle-like cuts, concentrating on any part of their bodies that was exposed. Already frightened and taken half off-guard, the Borgia troops reeled before him, and Ezio had slain five of their number before the others took to their heels and vanished, bellowing in panic, into the woods. Ezio watched them go. They wouldn't report back to Rodrigo unless they wanted to be hanged for incompetence, and it would take a while before they were missed, and Rodrigo learned that his satanic plan had misfired.

Ezio knelt over the body of Jacopo de' Pazzi. Battered

and robbed of all dignity, all that was left was the shell of a pathetic, desperate old man.

'You poor wretch,' he said. 'I was angry when I saw that Rodrigo had robbed me of my rightful prey, but now, now –'

He fell silent and reached over to close de' Pazzi's eyes. Then he realized that the eyes were looking at him. By some miracle, Jacopo was still – just – alive. He opened his mouth to speak but no sound could come. It was clear that he was in the last extremes of agony. Ezio's first thought was to leave him to a lingering death, but the eyes pleaded with him. Show mercy, he remembered, even when you yourself have been shown none. That too was part of the Creed.

'God give you peace,' he said, kissing Jacopo's forehead as he pushed his dagger firmly into his old adversary's heart.

When Ezio returned to Florence and broke the news to Duke Lorenzo of the death of the last of the Pazzi, Lorenzo was delighted, but saddened that the security of Florence and of the Medici had had to be bought at the cost of so much blood. Lorenzo preferred to find diplomatic solutions to differences, but that desire made him an exception among his peers, the rulers of the other city-states of Italy.

He rewarded Ezio with a ceremonial cape, which conferred on him the Freedom of the City of Florence.

'This is a most gracious gift, *Altezza*,' Ezio told him. 'But I fear I will have little leisure to enjoy the benefits it confers on me.'

Lorenzo was surprised. 'What? Do you intend to leave again soon? I had hoped that you would stay, reopen your family palazzo, and take up a position in the city's administration, working with me.'

Ezio bowed, but said, 'I am sorry to say that it is my belief that our troubles have not come to an end with the fall of the Pazzi. They were but one tentacle of a greater beast. My intention now is to go to Venice.'

'Venice?'

'Yes. The man who was with Rodrigo Borgia at the meeting with Francesco is a member of the Barbarigo family.'

'One of the most powerful families in La Serenissima. Are you saying this man is dangerous?'

'He is allied to Rodrigo.'

Lorenzo considered for a moment, then spread his hands. 'I let you go with the utmost regret, Ezio; but I know that I shall never be out of your debt, which means in turn that I have no power to command you. Besides, I have a feeling that the work you are engaged on will in the long run be of benefit to our city, even though I may not live to see it.'

'Don't say that, *Altezza*.'

Lorenzo smiled. 'I hope I am wrong, but living in this country at this time is like living on the rim of Vesuvius – dangerous and uncertain!'

Before leaving, Ezio brought news and gifts to Annetta, though it was painful to him to visit his former family home, and he would not enter it. He also studiously avoided the Calfucci mansion, but he did call on Paola, and found her gracious, but distracted, as if her mind were somewhere else. His last port of call was at his friend Leonardo's workshop, but when he got there he found only Agniolo and Innocento about, and the place had the look of being closed up. There was no sign of Leonardo.

Agniolo smiled and greeted him as he arrived. '*Ciao*, Ezio! It's been a long time!'

'Too long!'

Ezio looked about him, questioningly.

'You're wondering where Leonardo is.'

'Has he left?'

'Yes, but not for ever. He's taken some of his material with him, but he couldn't take it all, so Innocento and I are looking after it while he's away.'

'And where has he gone?'

'It's funny. The Maestro was in negotiations with the Sforza in Milan, but then the Conte de Pexaro invited him to spend some time in Venice – he's to complete a set of five family portraits . . .' Agniolo smiled knowingly. 'As if *that'll* ever happen; but it seems that the Council of Venice is interested in his engineering work, and they're providing him with a workshop, staff, the lot. So, dear Ezio, if you need him, that is where you'll need to go.'

'But that is exactly where I'm going,' cried Ezio. 'This is splendid news. When did he leave?'

'Two days ago. But you'll have no difficulty catching up with him. He's got a huge wagon absolutely loaded with his stuff, and a couple of oxen to draw it.'

'Any of his people with him?'

'Just the wagoners, and a couple of outriders, in case of trouble. They've taken the Ravenna road.'

Ezio took with him only what he could pack into his saddlebags, and, travelling alone, had been riding only a day and a half when, at a bend in the road, he came upon a heavy ox-drawn cart equipped with a canvas canopy beneath which any amount of machinery and models was carefully stowed.

The wagoners stood at the side of the road, scratching their heads and looking hot and bothered, while the outriders, two slightly built boys armed with crossbows and lances, kept watch from a nearby knoll. Leonardo was nearby, apparently setting up some kind of leverage system, when he looked up and saw Ezio.

'Hello, Ezio! What luck!'

'Leonardo! What's going on?'

'I seem to have run into a bit of trouble. One of the cartwheels . . .' He pointed to where one of the rear wheels had worked its way off the axle. 'The problem is that we need the wagon lifted clear so that we can refit the wheel but we just don't have the manpower to do it, and this lever I've botched together isn't going to lift it high enough. So do you think . . . ?'

'Of course.'

Ezio beckoned to the two wagoners, heavily built men who'd be more use to him than the lissom outriders, and between the three of them they were able to hoist the wagon up high enough and hold it there long enough for Leonardo to slip the wheel back on to the axle and peg it securely. While he was doing this, Ezio, straining with the others to keep the wagon up, looked in at its contents. Among them, unmistakably, was the bat-like structure he'd seen before. It looked as if it had undergone many modifications.

Once the wagon had been repaired, Leonardo took up his seat on its front bench with one of the wagoners, while the other walked at the head of the oxen. The outriders patrolled restlessly both ahead and to the rear. Ezio kept his horse at a walk, next to Leonardo, and they talked. It had been a very long time since their last meeting, and they had much to talk about. Ezio was able to bring Leonardo up to date, and Leonardo talked of his new commissions, and of his excitement at the prospect of seeing Venice.

'I am so delighted to have you as a travelling companion! Mind you, you'd get there much faster if you didn't travel at my pace.'

'It's a pleasure. And I want to make sure you get there safely.'

'I have my outriders.'

'Leonardo, don't misunderstand me, but even highwaymen still wet behind the ears could flick those two away as easily as you'd flick away a gnat.'

Leonardo looked surprised, then offended, then amused. 'Then I'm doubly glad of your company.' He looked sly. 'And I have an idea it's not just for sentimental reasons that you'd like to see me get there in one piece.'

Ezio smiled, but did not reply. Instead he said, 'I notice you're still working on that bat-contraption.'

'Eh?'

'You know what I mean.'

'Oh, that. It's nothing. Just something I've been tinkering away at. But I couldn't leave it behind.'

'What is it?'

Leonardo was reluctant. 'I don't really like to talk about things before they're ready . . .'

'Leonardo! You can trust me, surely.' Ezio lowered his voice. 'After all, I've trusted you with secrets.'

Leonardo struggled with himself, then relaxed. 'All right, but you must tell no one else.'

'*Promesso.*'

'Anyone would think you mad if you did tell them,' Leonardo continued, but his voice was excited. 'Listen. I think I have found a way to make a man fly!'

Ezio looked at him and laughed in total disbelief.

'I can see a time coming when you might want to wipe that smile off your face,' said Leonardo, good-naturedly.

He changed the subject then and started to talk about Venice, La Serenissima, aloof from the rest of Italy and often looking eastwards more than westwards, both for trade and in trepidation, for the Ottoman Turks held sway as far as halfway up the northern Adriatic coast these days. He talked of the beauty and the treachery of Venice, of the city's dedication to moneymaking, of its *richesse*, its weird construction – a city of canals rising out of fenland and built on a foundation of hundreds of thousands of huge wooden stakes – its ferocious independence, and its political power: not three hundred years earlier, the Doge of Venice had diverted an entire Crusade from the Holy Land to serve his own purposes, to destroy all commercial and military competition and opposition to his city-state, and to bring the Byzantine Empire to its knees. He talked of the secret, ink-dark backwaters, the towering, candlelit *palazzi*, the curious dialect of Italian they spoke, the silence that hovered, the gaudy splendour of their dress, their magnificent painters, of whom the prince was Giovanni Bellini, whom Leonardo was eager to meet, of their music, their masked festivals, their flashy ability to show off, their mastery of the art of poisoning. 'And all this,' he concluded, 'I know just from books. Imagine what the real thing will be like.'

It will be dirty, and human, thought Ezio coldly. Like everywhere else. But he showed his friend an agreeable smile. Leonardo was a dreamer. Dreamers should be allowed to dream.

They had entered a gorge, and their voices echoed off its rocky sides. Ezio, scanning the almost invisible crests of the cliffs that hemmed them in on both sides, was suddenly tense. The outriders had gone on ahead, but he ought to have been able, in this confined space, to hear the clatter of their horses. However, no sound came. A light mist had sprung up, together with a sudden chill, neither of which did anything to reassure him. Leonardo was oblivious, but Ezio could see that the wagoners had become tense too, and were looking warily about them.

Suddenly, a scattering of small pebbles came clattering down the rocky side of the gorge, causing Ezio's horse to shy. He looked up, squinting against the indifferent sun, high above, against which he could see an eagle soar.

Now even Leonardo was aware. 'What's wrong?' he asked.

'We're not alone,' said Ezio. 'There may be enemy archers up on the cliffs above us.'

But then he heard the thundering hooves of horses, several horses, approaching them from behind.

Ezio wheeled his horse, to see half a dozen cavalry approaching. The banner they bore was a red cross on a yellow shield.

'Borgia!' he muttered, drawing his sword as a crossbow bolt hammered into the side of the wagon. The wagoners themselves were already fleeing up the road ahead, and even the oxen were affected, for they lumbered slowly forward of their own volition.

'Take the reins and keep them going,' Ezio cried to Leonardo. 'It's me they're after, not you. Just keep going, whatever happens!'

Leonardo hastened to obey as Ezio rode back to meet the horsemen. His sword, one of Mario's, was well balanced by its pommel, and his horse was lighter and more manoeuvrable than those of his adversaries. But they were well armoured, and there would be no chance to use his Codex blades. Ezio dug his heels into the flanks of his horse, spurring it on into the thick of the enemy. Ducking low in the saddle, Ezio smashed into the group, the force of his charge causing two of their horses to rear violently. Then the swordplay began in earnest. The protective brace he wore on his left forearm deflected many blows, however, and he was able to take advantage of the surprise of a foeman when he saw that his blow did not land, to get in a meaningful blow of his own.

It was not long before he had unseated four of the men, leaving the two survivors to wheel round and gallop back the way they had come. This time, however, he knew that he must allow no one even the chance of getting back to Rodrigo. He galloped after them, cutting first one, and then the other, down off his horse as he caught up with them.

He searched the bodies swiftly, but neither yielded anything of note; then he dragged them to the roadside and covered them with rocks and stones. He remounted and rode back, pausing only to clear the road of the other corpses and give them a rudimentary burial, at least enough to conceal them, with the stones and brushwood he had at hand. There was nothing he could do about their horses, which by now had run away.

Ezio had escaped Rodrigo's vengeance once more, but he knew the Borgia cardinal would not give up until he was assured of his death. He dug his heels into his horse's flanks and rode to rejoin Leonardo. When he caught up, they looked for the wagoners and called their names in vain.

'I paid them a huge deposit on this wagon and oxen,' grumbled Leonardo. 'I don't suppose I'll ever see it again.'

'Sell them in Venice.'

'Don't they use gondolas there?'

'Plenty of farms on the mainland.'

Leonardo looked at him. 'By God, Ezio, I like a practical man!'

Their long cross-country journey continued, past the ancient town of Forlì, now a small city-state in its own right, and on to Ravenna and its port on the coast a few miles beyond. There they took ship, a coastal galley on its way from Ancona to Venice, and once he had ascertained that no one else on board presented any danger, Ezio managed to relax a little. But he was aware that, even on a relatively small ship like this, it would not be too difficult to slit someone's throat at night and cast their body into the blue-black waters, and he watched alertly the comings and goings at every little harbour they put into.

However, they arrived several days later at the Venice dockyards without incident. Only here did Ezio encounter his next setback, and that was from an unexpected source.

They had disembarked and were waiting now for the local ferry, which would take them to the island city. It duly arrived, and sailors helped Leonardo move his wagon on to the boat, which wallowed alarmingly under its weight. The ferry captain told Leonardo that some of the Conte da Pexaro's staff would be waiting on the quay to conduct him to his new quarters, and with a bow and a smile handed him on board. 'You have your pass, of course, *signore*?'

'Of course,' said Leonardo, handing the man a paper.

'And you, sir?' inquired the captain politely, turning to Ezio.

Ezio was taken aback. He had arrived without an invitation, unaware of this local law. 'But – I have no pass,' he said.

'It's all right,' put in Leonardo, speaking to the captain. 'He is with me. I can vouch for him and I am sure that the *Conte* –'

But the captain held up a hand. 'I regret, *signore*. The rules of the Council are explicit. No one may enter the city of Venice without a pass.'

Leonardo was about to remonstrate, but Ezio stopped him. 'Don't worry, Leonardo. I'll find a way round this.'

'I wish I could help you, sir,' said the captain. 'But I have my orders.' In a louder voice directed at the crowd of passengers in general, he announced: 'Attention please! Attention please! The ferry will depart at the stroke of ten!' Ezio knew that gave him a little time.

His attention was caught by an extremely well-dressed couple whom he had noticed joining the galley at the same time as he had, who had taken the best cabin, and who had kept very much to themselves. Now they were alone at the foot of one of the piers, where several private gondolas were moored, and clearly in the middle of a very acrimonious row.

'My beloved, please –' the man was saying. A weak-looking type, and twenty years older than his companion, a spirited redhead with fiery eyes.

'Girolamo – you are nothing but a fool! God knows why I ever married you but He also knows how much I've suffered as a result! You never cease to find fault, you keep me cooped up like a chicken in your horrible little provincial town, and now – now! You can't even organize a gondola to get us to Venice! And when I think your uncle's the bloody Pope, no less! You'd think you'd be able to exert some influence. But look at you – you've got about as much backbone as a slug!'

'Caterina –'

'Don't you "Caterina" me, you toad! Just get the men to deal with the luggage and for God's sake get me to Venice. I need a bath and I need wine!'

Girolamo bridled. 'I've a good mind to leave you here and go on to Pordenone without you.'

'We should have gone by land in any case.'

'It's too dangerous, travelling by road.'

'Yes! For a spineless creature like you!'

Girolamo was silent as Ezio continued to watch. Then he said cunningly, 'Why don't you step into this gondola here –' he indicated one, 'and I will find a pair of gondoliers immediately.'

'Hmmn! Talking sense at last!' she growled and allowed him to hand her into the boat. But once she was settled, Girolamo quickly cast off its painter and gave the prow a mighty shove, sending the gondola off into the lagoon.

'*Buon viaggio!*' he shouted nastily.

'*Bastardo!*' she flung back. Then, realizing her predicament, she began to shout, '*Aiuto! Aiuto!*' But Girolamo was walking back to where a knot of servants hovered uncertainly round a stack of luggage, and started giving them orders. Presently he moved off with them and the baggage to another part of the dock, where he started organizing a private ferry for himself.

Meanwhile Ezio had watched the plight of the woman Caterina, half-amused, certainly, but also half-concerned. She fixed him with her eye.

'Hey, you! Don't just stand there! I need *help!*'

Ezio unbuckled his sword, slipped off his shoes and doublet, and dived in.

Back on the quay, a smiling Caterina gave a dripping Ezio her hand. 'My hero,' she said.

'It was nothing.'

'I might have drowned! For all that *porco* cares!' She looked at Ezio appreciatively. 'But you! My goodness, you must be *strong*. I couldn't believe how you managed to swim back pulling the gondola by its rope with me in it.'

'As light as a feather,' said Ezio.

'Flatterer!'

'I mean, those boats are so well balanced –'

Caterina frowned.

'It was an honour to serve you, *signora*,' Ezio finished, lamely.

'I must return the favour some day,' she said, her eyes full of the meaning behind her words. 'What is your name?'

'Auditore, Ezio.'

'I'm Caterina.' She paused. 'Where are you bound?'

'I was going to Venice, but I have no pass, so the ferry –'

'*Basta*!' She interrupted him. 'So this little official wouldn't let you on, is that it?'

'Yes.'

'We'll see about that!' She stormed off down the jetty without waiting for Ezio to put on his shoes and doublet. By the time he caught up with her she had reached the ferry and was already, from what he could gather, giving the quaking man an earful. All he could hear as he arrived was the captain burbling in the most servile way: 'Yes, *Altezza*; of course, *Altezza*; whatever you say, *Altezza*.'

'It had better be as I say! Unless you want your head on a spike! Here he is! Go and fetch his horse and his things yourself! Go on! And treat him well! I'll know about it if you don't!' The captain hurried away. Caterina turned to Ezio. 'There, you see? Settled!'

'Thank you, Madonna.'

'One good turn –' She looked at him. 'But I hope our paths cross again.' She held out her hand. 'I am from Forlì. Come there one day. It would be my pleasure to welcome you.' She gave him her hand, and was about to depart.

'Don't you want to get to Venice too?'

She looked at him again, and at the ferry. 'On this scrapheap? Don't jest with me!' And she was gone, sailing along the quay in the direction of her husband, who was just seeing the last of their luggage loaded.

The captain scuttled up, leading Ezio's horse. 'Here you are sir. My most humble apologies, sir. Had I but known, sir . . .'

'I'll need my horse stabled when we arrive.'

'It'll be my pleasure, sir.'

As the ferry pulled away and set off across the lead-coloured water of the lagoon, Leonardo, who'd watched the whole episode, said wryly, 'You know who that was, don't you?'

'I wouldn't mind if she were my next conquest,' smiled Ezio.

'Then watch your step! That's Caterina Sforza, the

daughter of the Duke of Milan. And her husband's the Duke of Forlì, and a nephew of the Pope.'

'What's his name?'

'Girolamo Riario.'

Ezio was silent. The surname rang a bell. Then he said, 'Well, he married a fireball.'

'As I say,' replied Leonardo. 'Watch your step.'

Venice in 1481, under the steady rule of Doge Giovanni Mocenigo, was, on the whole, a good place to be. There was peace with the Turks, the city prospered, the trade routes by sea and land were secure, interest rates were admittedly high, but investors were bullish, and savers content. The Church was wealthy too, and artists flourished under the dual patronage of their spiritual and temporal patrons. The city, rich from the wholesale looting of Constantinople after the Fourth Crusade, diverted by Doge Dandolo from its true object, had brought Byzantium to its knees, displayed the booty unashamedly: the four bronze horses ranged along the upper façade of St Mark's Basilica being the most obvious.

But Leonardo and Ezio, arriving at the Molo on that early summer morning, had no idea of the city's debased, treacherous and pilfering past. They only saw the glory of the pink marble and brickwork of the Palazzo Ducale, the broad square reaching forwards and to the left, the brick campanile of astonishing height, and the slightly built Venetians themselves, in their dark clothes, flitting like shadows along the *terra ferma*, or navigating their labyrinthine, malodorous canals in a variety of boats, from elegant gondolas to ungainly barges, the latter laden with all sorts of produce, from fruit to bricks.

The Conte da Pexaro's servants took charge of Leonardo's effects and, at his suggestion, also took charge of Ezio's horse, and further promised to arrange suitable lodgings for the young banker's son from Florence. They then dispersed, leaving one behind, a fat, sallow young man with bulging eyes, whose shirt was damp with sweat, and whose smile would have made syrup hang its head in shame.

'*Altezze*,' he simpered, approaching them. 'Allow me to introduce myself. I am Nero, the Conte's personal *funzionario da accoglienza*. It will be my duty and my pleasure to offer you a short guided introduction to our proud city before the *Conte* receives you . . .' here Nero looked nervously between Leonardo and Ezio, trying to decide which of the two was the commissioned artist, and luckily for him settled on Leonardo, the one who looked less like a man of action, '. . . *Messer* Leonardo, for a glass of Veneto before dinner, which meal *Messer* will be pleased to take in the upper servants' hall.' He bowed and scraped a little more, for good measure. 'Our gondola awaits . . .'

For the next half-hour, Ezio and Leonardo were able – indeed, obliged – to enjoy the beauties of La Serenissima from the best place that it is possible to enjoy them – a gondola, expertly managed by its fore-and-aft gondoliers. But the enjoyment was marred by Nero's oily spiel. Ezio, despite his interest in the unique beauty and architecture of this place, still wet from his rescue of Madonna Caterina, and tired, tried to find refuge in sleep from Nero's dreary monologuing, but suddenly he snapped awake. Something had caught his attention.

From the canal bank, not far from the palace of the Marchese de Ferrara, Ezio heard raised voices. Two armed guards were harassing a businessman.

'You were told to stay at home, sir,' said one of the uniforms.

'But the rent is paid. I have every right to sell my wares here.'

'Sorry, sir, but it's in contravention of *Messer* Emilio's new rules. I'm afraid you're in rather a serious situation, sir.'

'I'll appeal to the Council of Ten!'

'No time for that, sir,' said the second uniform, kicking down the awning of the businessman's stall. The man was selling leather goods, and the uniforms, between them, while pocketing the best, threw most of his wares into the canal.

'Now, let's not have any more of this nonsense, sir,' said one of the uniforms, as they swaggered off, unhurriedly.

'What's going on?' Ezio asked Nero.

'Nothing, *Altezza*. A little local difficulty. I beg you to ignore. And now we are about to pass under the famous wooden bridge of the Rialto, the *only* bridge over the Grand Canal , famed in all history for . . .'

Ezio was happy to let the poor bugger ramble on, but what he had seen had disturbed him, and he had heard the name Emilio. A common enough Christian name – but: Emilio *Barbarigo*?

Not long afterwards, Leonardo insisted that they stop so that he could look at a market with stands selling children's toys. He went up to the one that had caught his eye immediately. 'Look, Ezio,' he cried.

'What have you found?'

'It's a lay figure. A little articulated manikin we artists use as models. I could do with a couple. Would you be so kind – ? I seem to have sent my purse with my bags to my new workshop.'

But as Ezio was reaching for his own purse, a bunch of young people pushed past them, and one of them tried to cut his purse from his belt.

'Hey!' yelled Ezio. '*Coglione!* Stop!' And he raced after them. The one he'd marked as his attacker turned for an instant, pushing a tress of auburn hair clear of the face. A woman's face! But then she was gone, vanishing into the crowd with her companions.

They resumed their tour in silence, Leonardo, however, now contentedly clutching his two lay figures. Ezio was impatient to be rid of the buffoon who was their guide, and even of Leonardo. He needed time alone, time to think.

'And now we approach the famous Palazzo Seta,' Nero droned on. 'Home of *Su Altezza* Emilio Barbarigo. *Messer* Barbarigo is famous at present for his attempts to unify the merchants of the city under his guiding control. A laudable undertaking which has, alas, encountered some resistance from the more radical elements in the city . . .'

A grim fortified building stood back from the canal, allowing for a flagstoned space in front of it, at whose quay three gondolas were moored. As their own gondola passed, Ezio noticed the same businessman he had seen harassed earlier try to enter the building. He was being held back by two more guards, and Ezio noticed on their shoulders a yellow blazon crossed with a red chevron, below it a black horse, above it a dolphin, star and grenade. Barbarigo men, of course!

'My stall has been destroyed, my goods ruined. I demand compensation!' the businessman was saying in an angry tone.

'Sorry sir, we're closed,' said one of the uniforms, poking the poor man with his halberd.

'I haven't finished with you. I'll report you to the Council!'

'Much good may it do you,' snapped the older, second uniform. But now an officer and three more men appeared.

'Causing an affray, are we?' said the officer.

'No, I –'

'Arrest this man!' barked the officer.

'What are you doing?' said the businessman, frightened. Ezio watched powerless and in growing anger, but he had marked the place in his mind. The businessman was dragged off in the direction of the building, where a small ironclad door opened to admit him, and immediately closed behind him.

'You haven't chosen the best of places, though it may be the prettiest,' Ezio told Leonardo.

'I am beginning to wish that I'd plumped for Milan after all,' replied Leonardo. 'But a job is a job.'

13

After Ezio had taken leave of Leonardo and settled into his own lodgings, he wasted no time in making his way back to the Palazzo Seta, not an easy task in this city of alleyways, twisting canals, low arches, little squares and dead-ends. But everyone knew the palazzo, and locals willingly gave him directions when he got lost – though they all seemed at a loss as to why anybody should wish to go there of their own free will. One or two suggested that it would be simplest for him to take a gondola, but Ezio wanted to familiarize himself with the city, as well as to arrive at his goal unnoticed.

It was late afternoon as he approached the palazzo, though it was less of a palace than a fortress, or a prison, since the main building complex had been erected within the battlemented walls. On either side it was hemmed in by other buildings which were separated from it by narrow streets, but to its rear was what looked like a sizeable garden surrounded by another high wall, and at the front, facing the canal, was the wide, open area Ezio had seen earlier. Here now, though, a pitched battle seemed to be taking place between a bunch of Barbarigo guardsmen and a motley group of young people who were taunting them and then skipping lightly out of reach of their swinging halberds and stabbing pikes, throwing bricks, stones, and rotten eggs and fruit at the infuriated uniforms. Perhaps they were just creating a diversion, for Ezio, looking beyond them, could see a figure scaling the wall of the palazzo beyond the scene of the mêlée. Ezio was impressed – the wall was so sheer that even he would have thought twice about tackling it. But whoever it was reached the battlements without detection or difficulty, and then, astoundingly, leapt up from them to land on the roof of one of the watchtowers. Ezio could see that the person was planning to jump again from there to the roof of the palace itself and try to gain access to the interior from there, and he made a note of the tactic should he ever need – or be able – to use it himself. But the guards in the watchtower had heard the person land, and called a warning to their fellows on guard in the palace proper. A bowman appeared at a window in the eaves of the palace roof and fired. The figure jumped gracefully and the arrow went wide, clattering off the tiles, but the second time the archer fired his aim was true, and, with a faint cry, the figure staggered, clutching a wounded thigh.

The bowman fired again, but missed, since the figure had retraced its steps, skipping from the tower roof back down to the battlements, along which other guardsmen were already running, then leapt back over the wall and half-slid, half-fell down it to the ground.

On the other side of the open space in front of the palazzo, the Barbarigo guards were pushing their attackers back into the alleyways beyond, down which they were beginning to pursue them. Ezio took this opportunity to catch up with the figure, which was beginning to limp away to safety in the opposite direction.

When he caught up, he was struck by the person's light, boy-like, but athletic shape. As he was about to offer his assistance, the person turned towards him and he recognized the face of the girl who'd tried to cut his purse in the market earlier.

He found himself surprised, confused, and – curiously – smitten.

'Give me your arm,' said the girl, urgently.

'Don't you remember me?'

'Should I?'

'I'm the one you tried to rob in the market today.'

'I'm sorry but this is no time for comfortable reminiscences. If we don't get out of sight fast we'll be dead meat.'

As if to illustrate her point, an arrow whizzed past between them. Ezio put her arm round his shoulders, and his round her waist, supporting her as he had once supported Lorenzo. 'Where to?'

'The canal.'

'Of course,' he said sarcastically. 'There's only one in Venice, isn't there?'

'You're damned cocky for a newcomer. This way – I'll

show you – but be quick! Look – they're after us already.'
And it was true that a small detachment of men had
started across the cobblestones towards them.

One hand gripping her wounded thigh, and tense
with pain, she guided Ezio down an alley, which led to
another, and another, and another, until Ezio had lost
all sense of the compass points. Behind them, the voices
of the men pursuing them gradually receded and then
were lost.

'Hirelings brought in from the mainland,' said the girl
in tones of great contempt. 'Don't stand a chance in this
city against us locals. Get lost too easily. Come *on*!'

They had arrived at a jetty on the Canale della Miser-
icordia. A nondescript boat was tied up there with two
men in it. On seeing Ezio and the girl, one immediately
started to unloop the mooring-rope, while the other
helped them in.

'Who's he?' the second man asked the girl.

'No idea, but he was in the right place at the right
time and apparently he's no friend of Emilio's.'

But she was close to fainting now.

'Wounded in the thigh,' said Ezio.

'I can't take that out now,' said the man, looking at
the bolt where it had lodged. 'I haven't got any balsam
or bandages here. We must get her back fast, and before
those sewer-rats of Emilio's catch up with us.' He
looked at Ezio. 'Who are you anyway?'

'My name is Auditore, Ezio. From Florence.'

'Hmmn. Mine's Ugo. She's Rosa, and the guy up there with the paddle is Paganino. We don't like strangers much.'

'Who are you?' Ezio replied, ignoring the last remark.

'Professional liberators of other people's property,' said Ugo.

'Thieves,' explained Paganino with a laugh.

'You take the poetry out of everything,' said Ugo, sadly. The he suddenly became alert. 'Watch out!' he yelled as one arrow, then another, thudded into the hull of the boat from somewhere above. Looking up, they could see two Barbarigo bowmen on a nearby rooftop, fitting fresh arrows to their longbows. Ugo scrabbled in the well of the boat and came up with a businesslike, stubby crossbow, which he quickly loaded, aimed and fired, while at the same time Ezio flung two throwing-knives in quick succession at the other archer. Both bowmen plunged screaming into the canal below.

'That bastard's got goons everywhere,' said Ugo to Paganino in a conversational tone.

They were both short, broad-shouldered, tough-looking men in their twenties. They handled the boat skilfully and evidently knew the canal system like the backs of their hands, for more than once Ezio was convinced they had turned into the aquatic version of a blind alley only to find that it ended not in a brick wall but a low arch under which the boat could just pass, if they all bent low.

'What were you doing attacking the Palazzo Seta?' Ezio asked.

'What's it to you?' answered Ugo.

'Emilio Barbarigo is no friend of mine. Perhaps we can help each other.'

'What makes you think we need your help?' retorted Ugo.

'Come on, Ugo,' said Rosa. 'Look what he's just done. And you're also overlooking the fact that he saved my life. I'm the best climber of the lot of us. Without me, we'll never get inside that viper's nest.' She turned her face to Ezio. 'Emilio is trying to get a monopoly on trade within the city. He's a powerful man, and he has several councillors in his pocket. It's getting to the stage when any businessman who defies him and tries to maintain his independence is simply silenced.'

'But you aren't merchants – you're thieves.'

'*Professional* thieves,' she corrected him. 'Individual businesses, individual shops, individual people – they all make for easier pickings than any corporate monopoly. Anyway, they have insurance, and the insurance companies pay up after fleecing their customers of giant premiums. So everyone's happy. Emilio would turn Venice into a desert for the likes of us.'

'Not to mention that he's a piece of shit who wants to take over not just local business, but the city itself,' put in Ugo. 'But Antonio will explain.'

'Antonio? Who's he?'

'You'll find out soon enough, Mr Florentine.'

At last they reached another jetty and tied up, moving quickly, since Rosa's wound needed to be cleaned and treated if she were not to die. Leaving Paganino with the boat, Ugo and Ezio between them half-dragged, half-carried Rosa, who had by now all but lost consciousness from loss of blood, the short distance down yet another twisting lane of dark-red brick and wood to a small square, a well and a tree at its centre, and surrounded by dirty-looking buildings from which the stucco had long since peeled.

They made their way to the dirty-crimson door of one of the buildings and Ugo rapped a complex pattern of knocks on it. A peephole opened and shut, and the door was swiftly opened and as swiftly closed. Whatever else had been neglected, Ezio noticed, hinges and locks and bolts were well oiled and free of rust.

He found himself in a shabby courtyard surrounded by high, streaky grey walls, which were punctuated by windows. Two wooden staircases ran up on either side to join wooden galleries that ran all round the walls at first- and second-floor level, and from which a number of doorways led.

A handful of people, some of whom Ezio recognized from the mêlée outside the Palazzo Seta earlier, gathered round. Ugo was already issuing orders. 'Where's Antonio? Go get him! – And clear some space for Rosa, get a blanket, some balsam, hot water, a sharp knife, bandages . . .'

A man raced up one of the staircases and vanished through a first-floor doorway. Two women unrolled a very nearly clean mat and laid Rosa tenderly down on it. A third disappeared to return with the medical kit Ugo had requested. Rosa recovered consciousness, saw Ezio, and reached a hand out to him. He took her hand and knelt down by her.

'Where are we?'

'I think this must be your people's headquarters. In any case, you're safe.'

She squeezed his hand. 'I'm sorry I tried to rob you.'

'Think nothing of it.'

'Thank you for saving my life.'

Ezio looked anxious. She was very pale. They would have to work fast if they were indeed going to save her.

'Don't worry, Antonio will know what to do,' Ugo told him as he stood up again.

Hurrying down one of the staircases came a well-dressed man in his late thirties, a large gold earring in his left earlobe and a scarf on his head. He made straight for Rosa and knelt by her, snapping his fingers for the medical kit.

'Antonio!' she said.

'What's happened to you, my little darling?' he said in the harsh accent of the born Venetian.

'Just get this thing out of me!' snarled Rosa.

'Let me take a look first,' said Antonio, his voice suddenly more serious. He examined the wound carefully.

'Clean entry and exit through your thigh, missed the bone. Lucky it wasn't a crossbow bolt.'

Rosa gritted her teeth. 'Just. Get it. Out.'

'Give her something to bite on,' said Antonio. He snapped off the arrow's fletching, wrapped a cloth round the head, soaked the points of entry and exit with balsam, and pulled.

Rosa spat out the wadding they'd placed between her teeth and screamed.

'I am sorry, *piccola*,' said Antonio, keeping his hands pressed on both points of the wound.

'Go fuck yourself with your apologies, Antonio!' yelped Rosa, as the women held her down.

Antonio looked up to one of his entourage. 'Michiel! Go and fetch Bianca!' He cast a sharp eye on Ezio. 'And you! Help me with this! Take those compresses and hold them on the wounds as soon as I remove my hands. Then we can bandage her properly.'

Ezio hastened to obey. He felt the warmth of Rosa's upper thigh under his hands, felt the reaction of her body to them, and tried not to meet her eyes. Meanwhile Antonio worked quickly, elbowing Ezio aside at last, and finally gently articulating Rosa's immaculately bandaged leg. 'Good,' he said. 'It'll be a while before we have you scaling any battlements again, but I think you'll make a full recovery. Just be patient. I know you!'

'Did you have to hurt me so much, you clumsy *idiota*?'

she flared at him. 'I hope you catch the plague, you bastard! You and your whore of a mother!'

'Take her inside,' said Antonio, smiling. 'Ugo, go with her. Make sure she gets some rest.'

Four of the women picked up the corners of the mat and carried the still-protesting Rosa through one of the ground-floor doors. Antonio watched them go, then turned again to Ezio. 'Thank you,' he said. 'That little bitch is most dear to me. If I had lost her –'

Ezio shrugged. 'I've always had a soft spot for damsels in distress.'

'I'm glad Rosa didn't hear you say that, Ezio Auditore. But your reputation goes before you.'

'I didn't hear Ugo tell you my name,' said Ezio, on his guard.

'He didn't. But we know all about your work in Florence and San Gimignano. Good work too, if a little unrefined.'

'Who are you people?'

Antonio spread his hands. 'Welcome to the headquarters of the Guild of Professional Thieves and Whoremongers of Venice,' he said. 'I am de Magianis, Antonio – the *amministratore*.' He gave an ironic bow. 'But of course we only steal from the rich to give to the poor, and of course our whores prefer to call themselves courtesans.'

'And you know why I am here?'

Antonio smiled. 'I have an idea – but it's not one I've

shared with any of my ... employees. Come! We should go to my office and talk.'

The office reminded Ezio so vividly of Uncle Mario's study that at first he was taken aback. He didn't know what he had expected exactly, but here he was confronted by a book-lined room, expensive books in good bindings, fine Ottoman carpets, walnut and boxwood furniture, and silver-gilt sconces and candelabras.

The room was dominated by a table at its centre, on which sat a large-scale model of the Palazzo Seta and its immediate environs. Innumerable tiny wooden manikins were distributed around and within it. Antonio waved Ezio to a chair and busied himself over a comfortable-looking stove in one corner, from which a curiously attractive but unfamiliar smell wafted.

'Can I offer you something?' Antonio said. He reminded Ezio so much of Uncle Mario that it was uncanny. '*Biscotti*? *Un caffè*?'

'Excuse me – a what?'

'A coffee.' Antonio straightened himself. 'It's an interesting concoction, brought to me by a Turkish merchant. Here, try some.' And he passed Ezio a tiny white porcelain cup filled with a hot black liquid from which the pungent aroma came.

Ezio tasted it. It burned his lips, but it wasn't bad, and he said so, but added, injudiciously, 'It might be better with cream and sugar.'

'The most certain way to ruin it,' snapped Antonio,

offended. They finished their coffees, however, and Ezio soon felt a certain nervous energetic buzz that was new to him. He would have to tell Leonardo about this drink when he next saw him. As for now, Antonio was pointing at the model of the Palazzo Seta.

'These were the positions we had planned if Rosa had succeeded in getting in and opening one of the postern-gates. But as you know, she was seen and shot and we had to withdraw. Now we will have to regroup, and in the meantime Emilio will have time to strengthen his defences. Worse than that, this operation was costly. I am almost down to my last *sòldo*.'

'Emilio must be loaded,' said Ezio. 'Why not attack again now and relieve him of his money?'

'Don't you listen? Our resources are under strain and he is on the alert. We could never overcome him without the element of surprise. Besides, he has two powerful cousins, the brothers Marco and Agostino, to back him up, though I believe Agostino at least to be a good man. As for Mocenigo, well, the Doge is a good man, but he is unworldly, and leaves matters of business to others – others who are already in Emilio's pocket.' He looked hard at Ezio. 'We need help to fill our coffers again. I think you may be able to provide that help. If you do, it will demonstrate to me that you are an ally worth helping. Might you undertake such a mission, Mr Cream-and-Sugar?'

Ezio smiled. 'Try me,' he said.

14

It took a long time, and Ezio's interview with the sceptical Chief Treasurer of the Thieves' Guild had been uncomfortable, but Ezio was able to use the skills he'd learned from Paola to cut purses with the best of them, and to rob the rich burghers of Venice allied with Emilio of as much as he could get. A few months later, in the company of other thieves – for he was now an Honorary Member of the Guild – he had brought in the two thousand *ducati* Antonio needed to relaunch his operation against Emilio. But there was a cost. Not all the Guild members had escaped capture and arrest by the Barbarigo Guards. So that, while the Thieves now had the funds they needed, their manpower had been depleted.

But Emilio Barbarigo made an arrogant mistake. To make an example of them, he placed the captured thieves on public display in cramped iron cages around the district he controlled. If he'd kept them in the dungeons of his palazzo, God himself would not have been able to get them out, but Emilio preferred to show them off, deprived of food and water, prodded with sticks by his guards whenever they sought sleep, and meant to starve them to death in full public view.

'They won't last six days without water, let alone food,' Ugo said to Ezio.

'What does Antonio say?'

'That it's up to you to plan a rescue.'

How much more proof of my loyalty does the man need, thought Ezio, before he realized that he already had Antonio's confidence, to the extent that the Prince of Thieves was entrusting to him this most crucial mission. He hadn't much time.

Carefully, Ugo and he observed in secret the comings and goings of the Watch. It appeared that one group of guards continuously passed from one cage to the next. Though each cage was constantly surrounded by a clutch of curious rubberneckers, among whom there may well have been Barbarigo spies, Ezio and Ugo decided to take the risk. On the night shift, when there were far fewer observers about, they made their way to the first cage when the Guard was just about to leave for the second. Once the Guard had departed and were out of sight and earshot, they managed to spring the locks, their spirits raised by a desultory cheer from the handful of bystanders, who couldn't care less one way or the other who had the upper hand so long as they were entertained, and some of whom followed them to the second cage, and even to the third. The men and women they liberated, twenty-seven in number, were already, after two and a half days, in a sorry plight, but at least they had not been individually manacled, and

Ezio led them to the wells that could be found in the centre of almost every frequent square, so that their first and most important need – thirst – was satisfied.

At the end of the mission, which took from candlelight until cock-crow, Ugo and his liberated associates looked at Ezio with deep respect. 'Rescuing my brothers and sisters was more than just an act of charity, Ezio,' said Ugo. 'These . . . colleagues will play a vital role in the weeks to come. And –' his tone became solemn, '– our Guild owes you an undying debt of gratitude.'

The group had arrived back at the Guild's headquarters. Antonio embraced Ezio, but his face was grave.

'How is Rosa?' asked Ezio.

'Better, but she was hurt worse than we thought, and she tries to run before she can walk!'

'Sounds like her.'

'It's typical.' Antonio paused. 'She wants to see you.'

'I'm flattered.'

'Why be? You are the hero of the hour!'

Some days later, Ezio was summoned to Antonio's office and found him poring over his model of the Palazzo Seta. The little wooden manikins had been redeployed around it, and there was a pile of papers covered in calculations and notes on the table by its side.

'Ah! Ezio!'

'*Signore.*'

'I have just returned from a little foray of my own into

enemy territory. We managed to liberate three boatloads of armoury destined for dear Emilio's little palazzo. So we thought we might organize a little fancy-dress party, with us dressed in the uniforms of Barbarigo archers.'

'Brilliant. That should get us into his fortress without any problem. When do we start?'

Antonio held up a hand. 'Not so fast, my dear. There is a problem, and I'd like to ask your advice.'

'You honour me.'

'No, I just value your judgement. The fact is, I have it on the best authority that some of my people have been suborned by Emilio and are now his agents.' He paused. 'We cannot strike until the traitors are dealt with. Look, I know I can depend on you, and your face is not well known within the Guild. If I were able to give you certain pointers about the whereabouts of these traitors, do you think you could deal with them? You can take Ugo with you as back-up, and whatever task-force you may require.'

'*Messer* Antonio, the fall of Emilio is as important to me as it is to you. Let us join hands in this.'

Antonio smiled. 'The very answer I expected from you!' He gestured Ezio to join him at a map table which had been set up near the window. 'Here is a plan of the city. The men of mine who have defected meet, as my own loyal spies tell me, in a taverna here. It's called Il Vecchio Specchio. There they make contact with Emilio's agents, exchange information, and take their orders.'

'How many?'

'Five.'

'What do you want me to do with them?'

Antonio looked at him. 'Why, kill them, my friend.'

Ezio summoned the group he had hand-picked for the mission the following day at sunset. He had laid his plans. He dressed them all in Barbarigo uniforms from the boats Antonio had sequestered. Emilio, he knew from Antonio, believed that the stolen equipment had been lost at sea, so his people would suspect nothing. Together with Ugo and four others, he descended on Il Vecchio Specchio soon after dark. It was a Barbarigo hangout, but at that time of night only a handful of customers were there, apart from the turncoats and their Barbarigo controls. They hardly looked up as they saw a group of Barbarigo guards enter the inn, and it was only when they were surrounded that their attention turned to the newcomers. Ugo pulled back his hood, revealing himself in the half-light of the taverna. The conspirators made to rise, astonishment and fear written in their faces. Ezio placed a firm hand on the shoulder of the nearest traitor, then with a detached economy of effort thrust his now-released Codex blade between the man's eyes. Ugo and the others followed suit and dispatched their traitorous brethren.

In the meantime, Rosa had continued to make a gradual and ever-impatient recovery. She was up and about, but she depended on a cane to get around, and her damaged leg was still swathed in bandages. Ezio, despite himself, and constantly making mental apologies to Cristina Calfucci, spent as much of his time as he could in her company.

'*Salute*, Rosa,' he said on a typical morning. 'How are things? I see your leg is healing.'

Rosa shrugged. 'It's taking for ever, but I'm getting there. And you? How are you finding our little town?'

'It is a great city. But how do you cope with the smell of the canals?'

'We're used to it. We wouldn't like the dust and filth of Florence.' She paused. 'So, what brings you to me this time?'

Ezio smiled. 'What you think and also *not* what you think.' He hesitated. 'I was hoping you could teach me how to climb like you do.'

She tapped her leg. 'Time was,' she said. 'But if you are in a hurry, my friend Franco can do almost as well as me.' She raised her voice. '*Franco!*'

A lissom, dark-haired youth appeared almost instantly in the doorway, and Ezio, to his private mortification, felt a pang of jealousy that was apparent enough for Rosa to notice. She smiled. 'Don't worry, *tesoro*, he's as gay as Santo Sebastiano. But he's also as tough as old boots. Franco! I want you to show Ezio some of our tricks.' She looked out of the window. An unoccupied building opposite was covered with bamboo scaffolding tied together with leather thongs. She pointed. 'Take him up that for a start.'

Ezio spent the rest of the morning – three hours – chasing after Franco, under Rosa's strident direction. At the end of it, he could clamber up to a giddying height with almost all the speed and address of his mentor, and had learned how to jump *upwards* from one handhold to the next, though he doubted if he'd ever reach Rosa's own standard.

'Lunch lightly,' Rosa said, sparing him any praise. 'We haven't finished for the day.'

In the afternoon, in the hours of the siesta, she took him to the square of the massive redbrick Frari church. Together they looked up at its bulk. 'Climb that,' Rosa said. 'Up to the very top. And I want you back down here before I have counted three hundred.'

Ezio sweated and strained, his head swimming with the effort.

'Four hundred and thirty-nine,' announced Rosa when he rejoined her. 'Again!'

At the end of the fifth attempt an exhausted and sweating Ezio felt that all he wanted to do now was smash Rosa in the face, but that desire melted when she smiled at him and said, 'Two hundred and ninety-three. You'll just about do.'

The small crowd that had gathered applauded.

15

Over the following months the Thieves' Guild tackled
the tasks of reorganizing and refitting. Then, one morning, Ugo arrived at Ezio's lodgings to invite him to a
meeting. Ezio packed his Codex weapons in a satchel
and followed Ugo to the headquarters, where they
found Antonio, in an ebullient mood, once again
moving the little wooden manikins around the model
of the Palazzo Seta. Ezio wondered if the man wasn't
a little obsessed. Rosa, Franco and two or three of the
other senior members of the Guild were also present.

'Ah, Ezio!' he smiled. 'Thanks to your recent successes
we are now in a position to counter-attack. Our target
is Emilio's warehouse, not far from his palazzo. This is
the plan. Look!' He tapped the model and indicated lines
of little blue wooden soldiers ranged around the perimeters of the warehouse. 'These are Emilio's archers. They
represent our greatest danger. Under cover of night, I
intend to send you and a couple of others up to the
roofs of the buildings adjoining the warehouse – and I
know that you are up to this task, thanks to Rosa's recent
training – to drop down on the archers and dispose of
them. Quietly. As you do so, our men, dressed in the

Barbarigo uniforms we have captured, will move in from the alleyways around and take their places.'

Ezio pointed to the red manikins within the warehouse walls. 'What about the guards inside?'

'When you've dealt with the archers we'll gather here . . .' Antonio pointed to a piazza nearby which Ezio recognized as the one where Leonardo had his new workshop – he wondered briefly how his friend was progressing with his commissions, '. . . and discuss the next steps.'

'When do we make our move?' asked Ezio.

'Tonight!'

'Excellent! Let me have a couple of good men. Ugo, Franco, are you with me?' The two nodded, grinning. 'We'll take care of the archers and meet you as you suggest.'

'With our men in place of their archers, they won't suspect a thing.'

'And the next move?'

'Once we've secured the warehouse, we'll launch an attack on the palazzo itself. But remember! Be stealthy! They must not suspect a thing!' Antonio grinned, and spat. 'Good luck, my friends – *in bocca al lupo*!' He patted Ezio's shoulder.

'*Crepi il lupo*,' Ezio replied, spitting too.

The operation passed off that night without a hitch. The Barbarigo archers didn't know what had hit them, and so subtly were they replaced with Antonio's men that the guards inside the warehouse fell quietly and without much resistance to the thieves' onslaught, having been unaware that their comrades outside had been neutralized.

The attack on the palazzo was next on Antonio's agenda, but Ezio insisted that he went ahead first to assess the lie of the land. Rosa, the last stages of whose recovery had been remarkable thanks to the combined skills of Antonio and Bianca, and who could now climb and leap almost as well as if she had been back to her full fitness, wanted to accompany him, but Antonio, to her anger, vetoed this. It crossed Ezio's mind that Antonio, in the end, considered him more expendable than her, but he brushed off the thought and prepared himself for the reconnaissance mission, strapping on his left arm the Codex guard-brace with its double-dagger, and, on his right, the original spring-blade. He had a lot of difficult climbing to do, and he didn't want to risk the poison-blade since in any circumstances it was a truly lethal weapon and he was keen to avoid any accident with it that might prove fatal to himself.

Pulling his hood up over his head and using the new techniques of upward leaping which Rosa and Franco had taught him, he stormed up the outer walls of the palazzo, silent as a shadow and drawing less attention, until he was on its roof and looking down into its garden. There he noticed two men in deep conversation. They were making for a side gate leading to a narrow, private canal which led round the back of the palazzo. Following their progress from the roof, Ezio could see that a gondola was moored at a little jetty there, its two gondoliers clad in black and its lanterns doused. Sure-footed as a gecko on the roofs and walls, he hastened down and sheltered himself in the branches of a tree from which he could hear their conversation. The two men were Emilio Barbarigo and, as Ezio recognized with a shock, none other than Carlo Grimaldi, one of Doge Mocenigo's entourage. They were accompanied by Emilio's secretary, a spindly man dressed in grey, whose heavy reading glasses kept slipping down his nose.

'. . . Your little house of cards is crumbling, Emilio,' Grimaldi was saying.

'It's a minor setback, nothing more. The merchants who defy me, and that piece of shit Antonio de Magianis will soon be dead or in chains, or working the oars of a Turkish galley.'

'I'm talking about the *Assassin*. He's here, you know. That's what's made Antonio so bold. Look, we've all been robbed or burgled, and our guardsmen have been outsmarted; it's as much as I've been able to do to keep the Doge from poking his nose in.'

'The Assassin? Here?'

'You numbskull, Emilio! If the Master knew how stupid you are, you'd be dead meat. You know the damage he's already done to our cause in Florence and San Gimignano.'

Emilio made a fist of his right hand. 'I'll crush him like the bedbug he is!' he snarled.

'Well, he's certainly sucking the blood out of you. Who knows if he's not here now, listening to us as we speak?'

'Now, Carlo – you'll be telling me next you believe in ghosts.'

Grimaldi fixed him with his eyes. 'Arrogance has made you stupid, Emilio. You do not see the whole picture. You are nothing but a big fish in a small pond.'

Emilio grabbed him by the tunic, and pulled him close, angrily. 'Venice will be mine, Grimaldi! I provided all the armaments to Florence! Not my fault if that idiot Jacopo didn't use them wisely. And don't try to make things bad for me with the Master. If I wanted to, I could tell him some things about you which would –'

'Save your breath! I must go now. Remember! The meeting is set ten days from now at San Stefano, outside Fiorella's.'

'I'll remember,' said Emilio sourly. 'The Master will hear then how –'

'The Master will speak, and you will listen,' retorted Grimaldi. 'Farewell!'

He stepped into the darkened gondola as Ezio watched, and it glided off into the night.

'*Cazzo!*' muttered Emilio to his secretary as he watched the gondola disappear in the direction of the Grand Canal. 'What if he's right? What if that damned

Ezio Auditore *is* here?' He brooded for a moment. 'Look, get the boatmen ready, now. Wake the bastards up if you have to. I want those crates loaded now and I want the boat ready in half an hour by your water-clock. If Grimaldi *is* speaking the truth, I must find a place to hide, at least until the meeting. The Master will find a way of dealing with the Assassin . . .'

'He must be working with Antonio de Magianis,' put in the secretary.

'I know that, you idiot!' hissed Emilio. 'Now come, and help me pack the documents we spoke of before our dear friend Grimaldi came calling.'

They moved back towards the interior of the palazzo, and Ezio followed, giving away no more sense of his presence than if he had been a spirit. He blended into the shadows and his footfall was no more noticeable than a cat's. He knew Antonio would hold off the attack on the palazzo until he gave the signal, and first he wanted to get to the bottom of what Emilio was up to – what were these documents of which he had spoken?

'Why won't people listen to sense?' Emilio was saying to his secretary as Ezio continued to tail them. 'All this freedom of opportunity, it just leads to more crime! We must ensure that the State has control of all aspects of the people's lives, and at the same time gives free rein to the bankers and the private financiers. That way, society flourishes. And if those who object have to be silenced, then that is the price of progress. The

Assassins belong to a bygone age. They don't realize that it's the State that matters, not the individual.' He shook his head. 'Just like Giovanni Auditore, and he was a banker himself! You'd have thought he'd have shown more integrity!'

Ezio drew in his breath sharply at the mention of his father's name, but continued to pursue his quarry as Emilio and his secretary made their way to his office, selected papers, packed them, and returned to the little jetty by the garden gate where another, larger gondola was now awaiting its master.

Emilio, taking his satchel of papers from his secretary, snapped a last order. 'Send some overnight clothes after me. You know the address.'

The secretary bowed and disappeared. There was no one else about. The gondoliers prepared to cast off, fore and aft.

Ezio sprang from his vantage-point on to the gondola, which rocked alarmingly. With two swift elbow movements, he knocked the boatmen into the water, and then had Emilio by the throat.

'Guards! Guards!' gurgled Emilio, groping for the dagger at his belt. Ezio seized his wrist just as he was about to plunge the weapon into Ezio's belly.

'Not so fast,' said Ezio.

'Assassin! You!' growled Emilio.

'Yes.'

'I killed your enemy!'

'That does not make you my friend.'

'Killing me will solve nothing for you, Ezio.'

'I think it will rid Venice of a troublesome . . . bedbug,' said Ezio, releasing his spring-blade. '*Requiescat in pace.*' With barely a pause, Ezio eased the deadly steel between Emilio's shoulder blades – death came quickly and silently. Ezio's proficiency in killing was matched only by the cold metallic resolve with which he fulfilled the duty of his calling.

Bundling Emilio's body over the gondola's side, Ezio set to rifling through the papers in his satchel. There was much to interest Antonio, he thought, as he swiftly sifted through them, for there was no time now to examine them thoroughly; but there was one parchment which caught his own attention – a rolled and sealed page of vellum. Surely another Codex page!

As he was about to break the seal – *shoof!* – an arrow rattled and clanged into the baseboard of the gondola between his legs. Instantly alert, Ezio crouched, peering up in the direction the missile had come from. High above him on the ramparts of the palazzo a vast number of Barbarigo archers was ranged.

Then one of them waved. And acrobatically tumbled down from the high walls. In another second she was in his arms.

'Sorry, Ezio – foolish prank! But we couldn't resist.'

'Rosa!'

She snuggled. 'Back in the fray and ready for action!'

She looked at him with shining eyes. 'And the Palazzo Seta is taken! We have freed the merchants who opposed Emilio, and we now control the district. Now, come! Antonio is planning a celebration, and Emilio's wine cellars are legendary!'

Time passed, and Venice seemed to be at peace. No one mourned Emilio's disappearance; indeed, many believed him still to be alive, and some assumed he had just gone on a journey abroad to look after his business interests in the Kingdom of Naples. Antonio made sure that the Palazzo Seta still ran like clockwork, and as long as the mercantile interests of Venice as a whole were not affected, nobody really cared about the fate of one businessman, however ambitious or successful he may have been.

Ezio and Rosa had grown closer, but a fierce rivalry still existed between them. Now she was healed, she wanted to prove herself, and one morning she came to his rooms and said, 'Listen Ezio, I think you need a re-tune. I want to see if you're still as good as you became when Franco and I first trained you. So – how about a race?'

'A race?'

'Yes!'

'Where?'

'From here to the Punta della Dogana. Starting *now*!' And she leapt out of the window before Ezio could react. He watched her as she scampered over the red rooftops and seemed almost to dance across the canals that separated the buildings. Throwing off his tunic, he raced after her.

At last they arrived, neck-and-neck, on the rooftop of the wooden building that stood on the spit of land at the end of the Dorsoduro, overlooking St Mark's Canal and the lagoon. Across the water stood the low buildings of the monastery of San Giorgio Maggiore, and opposite, the shimmering pink stone edifice which was the Palazzo Ducale.

'Looks like I won,' said Ezio.

She frowned. 'Nonsense. Anyway, even by saying that, you show yourself to be no gentleman and certainly no Venetian. But what can one expect of a Florentine?' She paused. 'In any case you are a liar. *I* won.'

Ezio shrugged and smiled. 'Whatever you say, *carissima*.'

'Then, to the victor, the spoils,' she said, pulling his head down to hers and kissing him passionately upon the lips. Her body, now, was soft and warm, and infinitely yielding.

16

Emilio Barbarigo may not have been able to make the appointment in the Campo San Stefano himself, but Ezio was certainly not going to miss it. He positioned himself in the already bustling square at dawn on that bright morning late in 1485. The battle for ascendancy over the Templars was hard and long. Ezio began to believe that, as it had been for his father and was for his uncle, it would turn out to be *his* life's work too.

His hood pulled up over his head, he melted into the crowd but stayed close as he saw the figure of Carlo Grimaldi approaching with another man, ascetic-looking, whose bushy auburn hair and beard were ill-sorted with his bluish, pallid skin, and who wore the red robes of a State Inquisitor. This, Ezio knew, was Silvio Barbarigo, Emilio's cousin, whose soubriquet was '*Il Rosso*'. He did not look in a particularly good mood.

'Where *is* Emilio?' he asked impatiently.

Grimaldi shrugged. 'I told him to be here.'

'You told him yourself? In person?'

'Yes,' Grimaldi snapped back. 'Myself! In person! I'm concerned that you don't trust me.'

'As am I,' muttered Silvio. Grimaldi gritted his teeth

at that, but Silvio merely looked around, abstractedly. 'Well, perhaps he'll arrive with the others. Let's walk a while.'

They proceeded to stroll around the large, rectangular *campo*, past the church of San Vidal and the palaces at the Grand Canal end, up to San Stefano at the other, pausing from time to time to look at the wares the stallholders were setting out at the beginning of the day's trading. Ezio shadowed them, but it was difficult. Grimaldi was on edge, and kept turning round suspiciously. At times it was all Ezio could do to keep his quarry within earshot.

'While we're waiting, you can bring me up to date with how things are at the Doge's Palace,' said Silvio.

Grimaldi spread his hands. 'Well, to be honest with you, it's not easy. Mocenigo keeps his circle close. I have tried to lay the groundwork, as you asked, making suggestions in the interest of our Cause, but of course I am not the only one vying for his attention, and old though he is, he's a canny bugger.'

Silvio picked up a complicated-looking glass figurine from a stall, inspected it, and put it back. 'Then you must work harder, Grimaldi. You must become part of his inner circle.'

'I am already one of his closest and most trusted associates. It has taken me years to establish myself. Years of patient planning, of waiting, of accepting humiliations.'

'Yes, yes,' said Silvio impatiently. 'But what have you to show for it?'

'It's harder than I expected.'

'And why is that?'

Grimaldi made a gesture of frustration. 'I don't know. I do my utmost for the State, I work hard . . . But the fact is, Mocenigo doesn't like me.'

'I wonder why not,' said Silvio coolly.

Grimaldi was too absorbed in his thoughts to notice the snub. 'It's not my fault! I keep trying to please the bastard! I find out what he most desires and lay it on for him – the finest jams from Sardinia, the latest fashions from Milan –'

'Maybe the Doge just doesn't like sycophants.'

'Do you think that's what I am?'

'Yes. A doormat, flatterer, a bootlicker – need I go on?'

Grimaldi looked at him. 'Don't you insult me, *Inquisitore*. You haven't a clue what it's like. You don't understand the pressure in the –'

'Oh, *I* don't understand *pressure*?'

'No! You have no idea. You may be a state official but I am two steps from the Doge almost every waking hour of the day. You wish you could be in my shoes, because you think you could do better, but –'

'Have you finished?'

'No! Just listen. I am close to the man. I have dedicated my life to establishing myself in this position, and

I tell you I am convinced I can recruit Mocenigo to our Cause.' Grimaldi paused. 'I just need a little more time.'

'It seems to me that you've had more than enough time already.' Silvio broke off, and Ezio watched as he raised a hand to attract the attention of an expensively dressed elderly man with a flowing white beard, accompanied by a bodyguard who was the largest person Ezio had ever seen.

'Good morning, Cousin,' the newcomer greeted Silvio. 'Grimaldi.'

'Greetings, Cousin Marco,' replied Silvio. He looked around. 'Where is Emilio? Did he not come with you?'

Marco Barbarigo looked surprised, then grave. 'Ah. Then you have not yet heard the news.'

'What news?'

'Emilio is dead!'

'What?' Silvio, as always, was irritated that his older and more powerful cousin should be better informed than he was. 'How?'

'I can guess,' said Grimaldi, bitterly. 'The *Assassino*.'

Marco looked at him sharply. 'It is so. They pulled his body out of one of the canals late last night. It must have been in there for – well, for long enough. They say he'd swollen up to twice his usual size. That's why he floated to the surface.'

'Where can the Assassin be hiding?' Grimaldi said. 'We must find him and kill him before he does any more damage.'

'He could be anywhere,' said Marco. 'That is why I take Dante here everywhere with me. I wouldn't feel safe without him.' He broke off. 'Why, he could be here, even now, for all we know.'

'We must act fast,' said Silvio.

'You're right,' said Marco.

'But Marco, I'm so close. I feel it. Just give me a few more days,' Grimaldi pleaded.

'No, Carlo, you've had quite enough time. We no longer have the leisure for subtlety. If Mocenigo will not join us, we must remove him and replace him with one of our own, and we must do it this very week!'

The giant bodyguard, Dante, whose eyes had not ceased to scan the crowd from the moment he and Marco Barbarigo had arrived, now spoke. 'We should keep moving, *signori*.'

'Yes,' agreed Marco. 'And the Master will be waiting. Come!'

Ezio moved like a shade among the crowds and the stalls, striving to keep the men within earshot as they crossed the square and made off down the street which led in the general direction of Saint Mark's Square.

'Will the Master agree to our new strategy?' asked Silvio.

'He'd be a fool not to.'

'You're right, we have no choice,' Silvio agreed, then looked at Grimaldi. 'Which kind of makes you redundant,' he added unpleasantly.

'That is a matter for the Master to decide,' retorted Grimaldi. 'Just as he will decide whom to place in Mocenigo's shoes – you, or your cousin Marco here. And the best person to advise him on that is me!'

'I wasn't aware that there was a decision to be made,' said Marco. 'Surely the choice is obvious to all.'

'I agree,' said Silvio, edgily. 'The choice should fall on the person who organized the entire operation, the one who came up with the idea of how to save this city!'

Marco was quick to reply. 'I would be the last to undervalue tactical intelligence, my good Silvio; but in the end it is wisdom which one needs in order to rule. Do not think otherwise.'

'Gentlemen, please,' said Grimaldi. 'The Master may be able to advise the Committee of Forty-One when they meet to elect the new Doge, but he cannot sway them. And for all we know, the Master may be thinking of someone quite other than either of you . . .'

'You mean yourself?' said Silvio incredulously, while Marco merely gave vent to a sneering laugh.

'And why not? I'm the one who's put in all the real graft!'

'*Signori*, please, keep moving,' put in Dante. 'It'll be safer for you all when we get back inside.'

'Of course,' agreed Marco, quickening his pace. The others followed suit.

'He's a good man, your Dante,' said Silvio. 'How much did you pay for him?'

'Less than he is worth,' replied Marco. 'He's loyal and he's trustworthy – he's saved my life on two occasions. But I wouldn't say he was exactly loquacious.'

'Who needs conversation from a bodyguard?'

'We're here,' said Grimaldi, as they arrived at a discreet door in the side of a building off the Campo Santa Maria Zobenigo. Ezio, keeping a safe distance between them and himself, aware as he was of Dante's extreme vigilance, rounded the corner of the square just in time to see them enter. Looking round to ensure that the coast was clear, he climbed the side of the building and positioned himself on the balcony above the door. The windows to the room beyond were open, and within it, seated in a heavy oak chair behind a refectory table covered with papers, and dressed in purple velvet, sat the Spaniard. Ezio dissolved into the shadows, and waited, ready to listen to all that transpired.

Rodrigo Borgia was in a filthy mood. Already the Assassin had frustrated him in several major enterprises and escaped every attempt to kill him. Now he was in Venice and had eliminated one of the cardinal's principal allies there. And as if that wasn't enough, Rodrigo had had to spend the first fifteen minutes of this meeting listening to the parcel of fools left in his service bickering about which of them should be the next Doge. The fact that he had already made his choice and greased the palms of all the key members of the Council of

Forty-One seemed to have passed these idiots by. And his choice had fallen on the oldest, vainest and most pliable of the three.

'Shut up, the lot of you,' he finally spat out. 'What I need from you is discipline and unwavering dedication to the Cause, not this pusillanimous quest for self-advancement. *This* is my decision and it *will* be carried out. Marco Barbarigo will be the next Doge and he will be elected next week following the death of Giovanni Mocenigo, which, given that the man is seventy-six years old, will hardly raise an eyebrow but which nevertheless must look natural. Do you think you are capable of arranging that, Grimaldi?'

Grimaldi cast a glance at the Barbarigo cousins. Marco was preening and Silvio was trying to look dignified in his disappointment. What fools they were, he thought. Doge or no Doge, they were still the puppets of the Master, and the Master was now conferring the real responsibility on him. Grimaldi allowed himself to dream of better things as he replied, 'Of course, Master.'

'When are you closest to him?'

Grimaldi reflected. 'I have the run of the Palazzo Ducale. Mocenigo may not like me much but I do have his full confidence, and I'm at his beck and call most of the time.'

'Good. Poison him. At the first opportunity.'

'He has food tasters.'

'Good God, man, do you think I don't know that?

You Venetians are supposed to be good at poisoning. Get something into his meat *after* they've tasted it. Or stick something into that Sardinian jam they tell me he's so fond of. But think of something or it'll be the worse for you!'

'Leave it to me, *su altezza*.'

Rodrigo turned his irritable gaze on Marco. 'I take it you can lay your hands on a suitable product for our purpose?'

Marco smiled deprecatingly. 'That is rather my cousin's area of expertise.'

'I should be able to lay my hands on enough *cantarella* for our purposes,' said Silvio.

'And what is that?'

'It's a most effective form of arsenic and it is very difficult to trace.'

'Good! See to it!'

'I must say, Maestro,' said Marco, 'we are lost in admiration that you should associate yourself personally so closely with this enterprise. Is that not dangerous for you?'

'The Assassin will not dare come after me. He is clever, but he will never outwit me. In any case, I feel inclined to involve myself more directly. The Pazzi disappointed us in Florence. I hope sincerely that the Barbarigi will not do the same . . .' He glowered at them.

Silvio snickered. 'The Pazzi were a bunch of amateur –'

'The Pazzi,' Rodrigo interrupted him, 'were a potent

and venerable family, and they were brought to their knees by one young Assassin. Do not underestimate this troublesome foe, or he will bring the Barbarigi down too.' He paused to let that sink in. 'Now go, and get this done. We cannot afford another failure!'

'What are your own plans, Master?'

'I return to Rome. Time is of the essence!'

Rodrigo rose abruptly and left the room. From his vantage-point hidden on the balcony, Ezio watched him leave alone and cross the square, causing a flock of pigeons to scatter as he strode in the direction of the Molo. The other men soon followed him, separating and taking their own paths out of the square. When all was silent, he leapt down to the flagstones beneath and hurried off in the direction of Antonio's headquarters.

Once there, he was met by Rosa, who greeted him with a lingering kiss. 'Put your dagger back in its sheath,' she smiled as their bodies pressed together.

'You're the one who made me draw it. And you're the one,' he added knowingly, 'with its sheath.'

She took his hand. 'Come on, then.'

'No, Rosa, *mi dispiace veramente* but I can't.'

'So – you tire of me already!'

'You know it isn't that! But I have to see Antonio. It's urgent.'

Rosa looked at him and saw the intense expression on his face, in his cold blue-grey eyes. 'OK. For this once I forgive you. He's in his office. I think he misses that model of the Palazzo Seta now that he's got the real thing! Come!'

'Ezio!' said Antonio as soon as he saw him. 'I don't like that look. Is everything all right?'

'I wish it was. I've just discovered that Carlo Grimaldi and the two Barbarigi cousins Silvio and Marco are in league with . . . a man I know too well, whom people call the Spaniard. They plan to murder Doge Mocenigo and replace him with one of their own.'

'That is terrible news. With their own man as Doge they'll have the entire Venetian fleet and trade empire in their grasp.' He paused. 'And they call *me* a criminal!'

'So – you'll help me stop them?'

Antonio extended his hand. 'You have my word, little brother. And the support of all my men.'

'And women,' put in Rosa.

Ezio smiled. '*Grazie, amici.*'

Antonio looked thoughtful. 'But Ezio, this will take some planning. The Palazzo Ducale is so strongly defended that it makes the Palazzo Seta look like an open park. And we don't have time for me to have a scale model built so we can plan –'

Ezio held up his hand and said firmly, 'Nothing is impenetrable.'

The two of them looked at him. Then Antonio laughed, and Rosa smiled naughtily. 'Nothing is impenetrable! – No wonder we like you, Ezio!'

*

Late in the day, when there were fewer people about, Antonio and Ezio made their way to the Doge's Palace. 'Treachery like this no longer surprises me,' Antonio was saying as they went. 'Doge Mocenigo is a good man and I'm surprised he's lasted so long. As for me, when I was a child, we were taught that the nobles were just and kind. I believed it, too. And though my father was a cobbler and my mother a scullery-maid, I aspired to be much more. I studied hard, I persevered, but I could never make myself one of the ruling class. If you aren't born into it, acceptance is impossible. So – I ask you, Ezio, who are the true nobles of Venice? Men like Grimaldi or Marco and Silvio Barbarigo? No! We are! The thieves and the mercenaries and the whores. We keep this place going and each one of us has more honour in his little finger than the whole pack of our so-called rulers! We love Venice. The others merely see it as a means of enriching themselves.'

Ezio kept his counsel, for he could not see Antonio, good as the man was, ever wearing the *corno ducale*. In due course they arrived at St Mark's Square, making their way round it to the pink palace. It was quite clearly heavily guarded, and although the two of them managed to clamber undetected up scaffolding which had been erected on the side wall of the cathedral which adjoined the palace, when they looked over from their vantage-point they could see that even though they could – and did – leap across on to the palace roof, access to the courtyard, even from there, was barred by a high grille whose spiked top curved outwards and downwards. Below them in the courtyard they could see the Doge himself, Giovanni Mocenigo, a dignified old man who nevertheless seemed like a shrivelled husk inhabiting the gorgeous robes and *corno* of the leader of the city and the state, in conversation with his appointed murderer, Carlo Grimaldi.

Ezio listened intently.

'Don't you understand what I'm offering you, *Altezza*?' Carlo was saying. 'Listen to me, please, for this is your last chance!'

'How dare you speak to me like that? How dare you threaten me!' retorted the Doge.

Carlo was immediately apologetic. 'Forgive me, sir. I meant nothing by it. But please believe that your safety is my principal concern . . .'

With that, the pair moved into the building and out of sight.

'We have very little time,' said Antonio, reading Ezio's thoughts. 'And there's no way through this grille. Even if there were, look at the number of guards around. *Diavolo!*' He swiped the air in frustration, causing a cluster of pigeons to take to the air. 'Look at them! The birds! How easy it might be for us if we could only fly!'

Suddenly, Ezio grinned to himself. It was high time he looked up his friend Leonardo da Vinci.

17

'Ezio! How long has it been?' Leonardo greeted him like a long-lost brother. His workshop in Venice had taken on all the look of his workshop in Florence, but dominating it was a full-scale version of the bat-like machine whose purpose, Ezio now knew, was one which he had to take seriously. But first things first, for Leonardo.

'Listen, Ezio, you sent me via a very nice man called Ugo another Codex page, but you never followed up on it. Have you been that busy?'

'I have rather had my hands full,' replied Ezio, remembering the page he had taken from Emilio Barbarigo's effects.

'Well, here it is.' Leonardo rummaged in the apparent chaos of his room, but quickly came up with the neatly rolled Codex page, its seal restored. 'There's no new weapon-design on this one, but from the look of the symbols and the manuscript writing on it, which I believe to be Aramaic or even Babylonian, it will be a significant page in whatever jigsaw puzzle you are assembling. I think I recognize traces of a map.' He held up his hand. 'But tell me nothing! I am only interested in the *inventions* these pages you bring me reveal. More than that, I do not care to know. A man like me is only immune from danger according to his usefulness; but if it were discovered that he knew too much –' And Leonardo expressively slit his throat with his finger. 'Well, that's that,' he continued. 'I know you by now, Ezio, your visits are never simply social. Have a glass of this rather awful Veneto – give me Chianti any day – and there are some fishcakes somewhere or other, if you're hungry.'

'Have you completed your commission?'

'The *Conte* is a patient man. *Salute!*' Leonardo raised his glass.

'Leo – does this machine of yours actually *work*?' asked Ezio.

'You mean, does it fly?'

'Yes.'

Leonardo rubbed his chin. 'Well, it's still in the early stages. I mean, it's nowhere near ready yet – but I think, in all modesty, that – yes! Of course it will work. God knows I've spent enough time on it! It's an idea that just won't let go of me!'

'Leo – can I try it?'

Leonardo looked shocked. 'Of course you can't! Are you mad? It's far too dangerous. For a start, we'd have to get it to the top of a tower to launch you . . .'

The following day, before dawn, but just as the first streaks of greyish pink were colouring the eastern horizon, Leonardo and his assistants, having dismantled the flying-machine in order to transport it, had reconstructed it on the flat high roof of the Ca' Pexaro, the family mansion of Leonardo's unsuspecting employer. Ezio was with them. Beneath them, the city slept. There were not even any guards on the roofs of the Palazzo Ducale, for this was the Hour of the Wolf, when vampires and spectres were most powerful. No one but madmen and scientists would venture forth at such a time.

'It's ready,' said Leonardo. 'And thank God the coast is clear. If anyone saw this thing they'd never believe their eyes – and if they knew it was my invention I'd be finished in this town.'

'I'll be quick,' said Ezio.

'Try not to break it,' said Leonardo.

'This is a test flight,' said Ezio. 'I'll go easy. Just tell me again how this *bambina* works.'

'Have you ever watched a bird in flight?' asked Leonardo. 'It's not about being lighter than air, it's about grace and balance! You must simply use your body-weight to control your elevation and direction, and the wings will carry you.' Leonardo's face was very serious. He squeezed Ezio's arm. '*Buona fortuna*, my friend. You are – I hope – about to make history.'

Leonardo's assistants strapped Ezio carefully into position below the machine. The bat-like wings stretched out above him. He was secured face forwards in a tight leather cradle, though his arms and legs were free, and before him was a horizontal crossbar of wood, attached to the main wooden frame which held the wings aloft. 'Remember what I told you! Side-to-side controls the rudder. To-and-fro controls the angle of the wings,' Leonardo explained earnestly.

'Thank you,' said Ezio, breathing hard. He knew that if this didn't work, in a moment he'd be taking the last leap of his life.

'Go with God,' said Leonardo.

'See you later,' said Ezio with a confidence he didn't really feel. He balanced the contraption over him, settled, and took a run off the edge of the roof.

His stomach left him first, and then there was a feeling of wonderful exhilaration. Venice reeled beneath him as he tumbled and rolled, but then the machine started to tremble, and fall down the sky. It was only by keeping his head, and remembering Leonardo's instructions regarding the use of the joystick, that Ezio was able to right the craft and guide it back – just – to the Pexaro palace roof. He landed the strange craft at a running pace – using all his strength and agility to keep it stable.

'Christ Almighty, it *worked*!' yelled Leonardo, careless of security for a moment, unravelling Ezio from the machine and hugging him frantically. 'You wonderful man! You *flew*!'

'Yes, by God, so I did,' said Ezio, breathless. 'But not as far as I need to go.' And his eyes sought out the

Doge's Palace and the courtyard that was his goal. He was also thinking of how little time he had, if the murder of Mocenigo was to be averted.

Later, back in Leonardo's workshop, Ezio and the artist-inventor gave the machine a careful overhaul. Leonardo had his blueprints laid out on a large trestle table.

'Let me look over my plans here. Maybe I can find something, some way to extend the duration of the flight.'

They were interrupted by the hasty arrival of Antonio. 'Ezio! I am so sorry to disturb you but this is important! My spies tell me that Silvio has obtained the poison they need, and he's handed it over to Grimaldi.'

But just then Leonardo shouted in despair. 'It's no good! I've been over it and over it and it just won't work! I don't know how to extend the flight. Oh, bugger it!' He swept papers angrily off the table. Some of them wafted into the large fireplace nearby, and as they burned, rose. Leonardo watched, his expression clearing, and at last a broad smile cleared the anger from his face. 'My God!' he cried, '*Eureka!* Of course! Genius!'

He snatched the papers that weren't already burnt out of the fire and stamped the flames out. 'Never give in to your temper,' he advised them. 'It can be terribly counter-productive.'

'So what's cured yours?' asked Antonio.

'Look!' Leonardo said. 'Did you not see the ashes

rise? Heat lifts things up! How often have I seen eagles high in the air, not flapping their wings at all, and yet staying aloft! The principle is simple! All we have to do is apply it!'

He reached for a map of Venice and spread it out on the table. Leaning over it with a pencil, he marked out the distance between the Palazzo Pexaro and the Palazzo Ducale, putting crosses at key points between the two buildings. 'Antonio!' he cried. 'Can you get your people to build bonfires at each of the places I've marked, and light them in a close sequence?'

Antonio studied the map. 'I think we could arrange that – but why?'

'Do you not see? This is Ezio's flight path! The fires will carry my flying machine and him all the way to his target! Heat rises!'

'What about the guards?' said Ezio.

Antonio looked at him. 'You'll be flying that thing. For once, leave the guards to us. In any case,' he added, 'some of them at least will be busy elsewhere. My spies tell me there's a curious shipment of coloured powder in little tubes which has just arrived from a country far away to the east called China. God knows what it is but it must be valuable, they're taking such good care of it.'

'Fireworks,' said Leonardo to himself.

'What?'

'Nothing!'

*

Antonio's men had the fires Leonardo had ordered built and ready by dusk. They had also cleared the areas around them of any watchmen or idle bystanders who might be inclined to warn the authorities of what was afoot. Leonardo's assistants had meanwhile transported the flying-machine to the Pexaro roof once more, and Ezio, armed with his spring-blade and arm-guard, had taken up his position in it. Antonio stood nearby.

'Rather you than me,' he said.

'It's the only way to get into the palace. You said so yourself.'

'I never dreamed this could actually happen, though. I still find it almost impossible to believe. If God had meant us to fly —'

'Are you ready to give the signal to your men, Antonio?' asked Leonardo.

'Absolutely.'

'Then do so now, and we'll get Ezio airborne.'

Antonio walked to the edge of the roof and looked down. Then he took out a large red handkerchief and waved it. Far below they could see first one, then two, three, four and five huge bonfires leap into flame.

'Excellent, Antonio. My congratulations.' Leonardo turned to Ezio. 'Now, remember what I told you. You must fly from fire to fire. The heat of each one as you pass over it should keep you in the air all the way to the Ducal Palace.'

'And be careful,' said Antonio. 'There are archers

posted on the roofs and they'll certainly shoot as soon as they see you. They'll think you're some demon from hell.'

'I wish there was some way I could use my sword at the same time as flying this thing.'

'Your feet are free,' said Leonardo thoughtfully. 'If you manage to steer close enough to the archers and avoid their arrows, you might be able to kick them off the rooftops.'

'I'll bear that in mind.'

'And now you must go. Good luck!'

Ezio sailed off the roof into the night sky, setting a course for the first fire. He was beginning to lose height as he approached, but then, as he reached it, he felt the machine lift again. Leonardo's theory worked! On he flew, and he could see the thieves tending the bonfires look up and cheer. But the thieves were not the only ones aware of him. Ezio could see Barbarigo archers posted on the cathedral roof and on the other buildings near the Doge's Palace. He managed to manoeuvre the flying-machine out of the way of most of the arrows, though one or two thudded into its wooden frame, and he also managed to swoop low enough to knock a handful of bowmen off their perches. But as he approached the Palace itself, the Doge's own guards opened fire and they were using fire-arrows. One caught in the starboard wing of the machine and it immediately burst into flames. It was all Ezio could do to keep on course, and he was losing height fast. He saw a pretty young noble-woman looking up and screaming something about the devil having come to claim her, but then he was past. He let go of the controls and fumbled with the harness buckles which held him in. At the last moment he wrenched himself free and leapt forwards and outwards, to land in a perfect crouch on an inner courtyard roof, past the grille which guarded the palace interior from all but the birds. Looking up, he saw the flying-machine crash into the campanile of St Mark's and its wreckage fall to the square below, causing panic and pandemonium among the people there. Even the ducal archers' attention was diverted, and Ezio took advantage of that to climb swiftly down and out of sight. As he did so, he saw Doge Mocenigo appear at a second-storey window.

'*Ma che cazzo?*' said the Doge. 'What was that?'

Carlo Grimaldi appeared at his elbow. 'Probably just some youths with firecrackers. Come, finish your wine.'

Hearing that, Ezio made his way via roofs and walls and, taking care to keep out of sight of the archers, to a spot just outside the open window. Looking in, he saw the Doge draining a goblet. He threw himself over the sill and into the room, exclaiming, 'Stop, *Altezza*! Don't drink – !'

The Doge looked at him in astonishment as Ezio realized he had arrived a moment too late. Grimaldi smiled wanly. 'Not quite your usual accursed good timing, young Assassin! *Messer* Mocenigo will be leaving us shortly. He's drunk enough poison to fell a bull.'

Mocenigo rounded on him. 'What? What have you done?'

Grimaldi made a gesture of regret. 'You should have listened to me.'

The Doge staggered and would have fallen if Ezio had not rushed forward to support him and guide him to a chair, where he sat down heavily.

'Feel tired . . .' said the Doge. '. . . Going dark . . .'

'I am so sorry, *Altezza*,' said Ezio helplessly.

'About time you tasted failure,' snarled Grimaldi at Ezio, before flinging open the door of the room and bellowing, 'Guards! Guards! The Doge has been poisoned! I have the killer here!'

Ezio sprang across the room and grabbed Grimaldi by the collar, dragging him back into the room, banging the door shut and locking it. Seconds later he heard the guards running up and hammering on it. He turned to Grimaldi. 'Failure, eh? Then I'd better do something to make up for it.' He released his spring-blade.

Grimaldi smiled. 'You can kill me,' he said, 'But you can never defeat the Templars.'

Ezio plunged the dagger into Grimaldi's heart. 'Peace be with you,' he said, coldly.

'Good,' said a feeble voice behind him. Looking round, Ezio saw that the Doge, though deadly pale, was still alive.

'I'll fetch help – a doctor,' he said.

'No – it's too late for that. But I shall die happier for seeing my assassin go before me into the dark. Thank you.' Mocenigo was struggling for breath. 'I'd long suspected he was a Templar but I was too weak, too trusting . . . But look in his wallet. Take his papers. I don't doubt that you'll find something among them to help your own cause, and avenge my death.'

Mocenigo was smiling as he spoke. Ezio watched as the smile froze on his lips, his eyes glazed, and his head lolled sideways. Ezio put a hand on the side of the Doge's neck to ascertain that he was dead, that there was no pulse. Ezio drew his fingers over the dead man's face to close his eyelids, muttered a few words of blessing, and hastily took and opened Grimaldi's wallet. There, among a small sheaf of other documents, was another Codex page.

The guards continued to hammer at the door, and now it was beginning to give. Ezio ran to the window and looked down. The courtyard was alive with guards. He'd have to take his chances on the roof. Climbing out of the window, he started to scale the wall above him as arrows hissed around his head, clattering against the stonework on either side of him. When he reached the roof he had to contend with more archers, but they were off guard and he was able to use the element of surprise to dispense with them. But he was confronted with another difficulty. The grille which had kept him out before now trapped him within! He ran up to it, and realized that it was designed only to keep people out – its spiked top curved *outwards* and downwards. If he could climb to the top, he could leap clear. Already he could hear the footfalls of many guards thundering up the stairs to the roof. Summoning all the strength his desperation could give him, he took a running jump and clambered to the top of the grille. The next moment he was safely on the other side of it and it was the guards who were trapped by it. They were too heavily armed to be able to scale it, and Ezio knew that in any case they lacked his agility. Running to the edge of the roof, he looked down, leapt across to the scaffolding erected along the cathedral wall, and shinned down it. Then he sped into St Mark's Square and lost himself in the crowd.

18

The death of the Doge on the same night that the bizarre bird-demon appeared in the sky caused a great stir in Venice which lasted many weeks. Leonardo's flying-machine had crashed into St Mark's Square, already a conflagration, and had burnt to ashes, as no one would dare approach the strange contraption. In the meantime, the new Doge, Marco Barbarigo, was duly elected and took office. He swore a solemn public oath to track down the young assassin who had avoided capture and arrest by the skin of his teeth, and who had murdered that noble servant of the state, Carlo Grimaldi, and probably the old Doge too. Barbarigo and Ducal guards were to be seen at every street corner and they also patrolled the canals day and night.

Ezio, on Antonio's advice, lay low at his headquarters, but he was boiling with a frustration that wasn't helped by the fact that Leonardo had temporarily left town in the entourage of his patron, the Conte de Pexaro. Even Rosa lacked the means to distract him.

But soon, one day not far into the new year, Antonio called him to his office, greeting him with a broad smile.

'Ezio! I have two pieces of good news for you. First of all, your friend Leonardo has returned. Secondly, it's *Carnevale*! Nearly everyone is wearing a mask and so you –' But Ezio was already halfway out of the room. 'Hey! Where are you off to?'

'To see Leonardo!'

'Well, come back soon – there's someone I want you to meet.'

'Who is it?'

'Her name's Sister Teodora.'

'A nun?'

'You'll see!'

Ezio made his way through the streets with his hood up over his head, making his way unobtrusively between the groups of extravagantly dressed and masked men and women who thronged the streets and the canals. He was keenly aware of the clusters of guards on duty as well. Marco Barbarigo was no more concerned about Grimaldi's death than he was about the death of his predecessor, which he had helped to plan; and now that he had made a pious show of seeking out a culprit, he could let the matter drop with a good public conscience, and appear to scale down the costly public operation. But Ezio also knew that if the Doge could secretly trap and kill him, he would. As long as he was alive and could be a thorn in the Templars' side, they would count him among their bitterest enemies. He would have to remain constantly on the lookout.

He made his way to Leonardo's workshop successfully, however, and entered it unseen.

'It's good to see you again,' Leonardo greeted him.
'This time I thought you were dead for sure. I heard no
more of you, then there was all that business over
Mocenigo and Grimaldi, then my patron took it into
his head to travel and insisted I went with him – to
Milan, as it happens – and I never have the leisure
to rebuild my flying-machine because the Venetian
Navy finally want me to start designing stuff for them
– it's all very vexing!' Then he smiled. 'But the main
thing is, you are alive and well!'

'And the most wanted man in Venice!'

'Yes. A double murderer, and of two of the state's
most prominent citizens.'

'You know better than to believe that.'

'You wouldn't be here if I did. You know you can
trust me, Ezio, as you can everybody here. After all,
we're the ones who flew you into the Palazzo Ducale.'
Leonardo clapped his hands and an assistant appeared
with wine. 'Luca, can you find a carnival mask for our
friend here? Something tells me it might come in handy.'

'*Grazie, amico mio*. And I have something for you.'
Ezio handed over the new Codex page.

'Excellent,' said Leonardo, recognizing it immediately. He cleared some space on the table near him,
unrolled the parchment and started to examine it.

'Hmnn,' he said, frowning in concentration. 'This one

does have the design for a new weapon, and it's quite complex. It looks as if it'll attach to your wrist once again, but this is no dagger.' He pored over the manuscript some more. 'I know what this is! It's a firearm, but on a miniature scale – as small as a humming-bird in fact.'

'That doesn't sound possible,' said Ezio.

'Only one way to find out, and that's to make it,' said Leonardo. 'Luckily these Venetian assistants of mine are expert engineers. We'll get down to it straight away.'

'What about your other work?'

'Oh, that'll keep,' said Leonardo airily. 'They all think I'm a genius and it does no harm to let them – in fact, it means they tend to leave me in peace!'

In a matter of days the gun was ready for Ezio to test. For its size, its range and power turned out to be quite extraordinary. Like the blades, it was designed to attach to the spring-mechanism which strapped to Ezio's arm, and could be pushed back to conceal it, shooting out in an instant when required for use.

'How can it be that I never thought of something like this myself?' Leonardo said.

'The bigger question,' Ezio replied wonderingly, 'is how the idea could have come to a man who lived hundreds of years ago.'

'Well, however it came about, it's a magnificent piece of machinery, and I hope it serves you well.'

'I think this new toy comes at a most timely moment,' said Ezio, earnestly.

'I see,' said Leonardo. 'Well, the less I know about it the better, though I can hazard a guess that it may have something to do with the new Doge. I'm not much of a politician, but sometimes even I can smell skulduggery.'

Ezio nodded meaningfully.

'Well, that's something you'd better talk to Antonio about. And you'd better hang on to that mask – as long as it's *Carnevale*, you should be safe on the streets. But remember – no weapons out there! Just keep it up your sleeve.'

'I'm going to see Antonio now,' Ezio told him. 'There's someone he wants me to meet – some nun called Sister Teodora, over in Dorsoduro.'

'Ah! Sister Teodora!' smiled Leonardo.

'Do you know her?'

'She's a mutual friend of Antonio's and mine. You'll like her.'

'Who is she, exactly?'

'You'll find out,' grinned Leonardo.

Ezio made his way to the address Antonio had given him. The building certainly didn't look like a convent. Once he'd knocked and been admitted, he was convinced that he'd come to the wrong place, for the room he found himself in reminded him more than anything of Paola's salon in Florence. And the elegant young women who came and went were certainly no nuns. He was about to put his mask back on and go when he heard Antonio's voice, and moments later the man himself appeared, leading on his arm an elegant and beautiful woman with full lips and sultry eyes, who was, indeed, dressed as a nun.

'Ezio! There you are,' said Antonio. He was slightly drunk. 'Allow me to introduce . . . Sister Teodora. Teodora, meet the – how shall I put this? – most talented man in all Venice!'

'Sister,' said Ezio bowing. Then he looked at Antonio. 'Am I missing something here? I've never really seen you as the religious type.'

Antonio laughed, but Sister Teodora, when she spoke, was surprisingly serious. 'It all depends on how you view religion, Ezio. It's not men's souls alone that require solace.'

'Have a drink, Ezio!' said Antonio. 'We must talk, but first, relax! You're perfectly safe here. Have you met the girls yet? Anyone take your fancy? Don't worry, I won't tell Rosa. And you must tell me –'

Antonio was interrupted by a scream from one of the rooms that surrounded the salon. The door flew open to reveal a wild-eyed man wielding a knife. Behind him on the blood-soaked bed, a girl writhed in agony. 'Stop him,' she screamed. 'He's cut me and he's stolen my money!'

With a furious roar the maniac grabbed another girl before she could react and held her close, his knife at her throat. 'Let me out of here or I'll carve this one up too,' he bawled, pressing the tip of the knife so that a little bead of blood appeared on the girl's neck. 'I mean it!'

Antonio, instantly sober, stared from Teodora to Ezio. Teodora herself was looking at Ezio. 'Well, Ezio,' she said with a coolness that took him aback, 'now's the chance to impress me.'

The maniac was making his way across the salon to the door, where a small knot of girls was standing. As he reached it, he growled at them, 'Open it!' But they seemed rooted to the spot with fear. 'Open the sodding door or she gets it!' He dug the knife a little further into the girl's throat. Blood began to flood from her neck.

'Let her go!' commanded Ezio.

The man swung round to face him, an ugly expression on his face. 'And who are you? Some kind of *benefattore del cazzo*? Don't make me finish her off!'

Ezio looked from the man to the door. The girl in his arms had fainted, a dead weight. Ezio could see the man hesitate, but any moment now he would have to let her go. He readied himself. It would be hard, the other women were close; he'd have to pick the precise moment and then act fast, and he knew he had very little experience of his new weapon. 'Open the door,' he said firmly to one of the terrified prostitutes in the group.

As she turned to do so, the madman let the bleeding girl fall to the ground. As he prepared to rush out into the street, he took his attention off Ezio for a second, and in that second Ezio released his little pistol and fired.

There was a snapping report and a burst of flame followed by a puff of smoke seemed to shoot out from between the fingers of Ezio's right hand. The maniac, a surprised expression still on his face, fell to his knees, a neat little hole in the middle of his forehead and some of his brains spattered on the doorpost behind him. The girls screamed and moved hastily away from him as he slowly toppled forward. Teodora shouted orders, and attendants hurried to succour the two wounded girls, but they were too late for the one in the bedroom, as she had bled to death.

'You have our gratitude, Ezio,' said Teodora, once order had been restored.

'I was too late to save her.'

'You saved the others. He might have slaughtered more if you hadn't been here to stop him.'

'What sorcery did you use to bring him down?' asked an awe-struck Antonio.

'No sorcery. Just a secret. A grown-up cousin of the throwing-knife.'

'Well, I can see that it's going to come in handy. Our new Doge is scared stiff. He surrounds himself with guards and he never leaves the palazzo.' Antonio paused. 'I imagine that Marco Barbarigo is next on your list?'

'He is as big an enemy as his cousin Emilio was.'

'We will help you,' said Teodora, joining them. 'And

our chance presents itself soon. The Doge is throwing a massive party for *Carnevale* and he will have to leave the palazzo for that. No expense has been spared, as he wants to buy the people's favour even if he cannot earn it. According to my spies, he has even ordered fireworks from China!'

'This is why I asked you here today,' Antonio explained to Ezio. 'Sister Teodora is one of us, and she has her finger on the very pulse of Venice.'

'How do I get invited to this party?' Ezio asked her.

'It isn't easy,' she replied. 'You need a golden mask to get you in.'

'Well, it can't be so hard to lay hands on one of those.'

'Not so fast – each mask *is* an invitation, and each is numbered.' But then Teodora smiled. 'Never mind, I have an idea. I think it's possible that we might *win* you a mask. Come, walk with me.' She led him away from the others to a quiet little courtyard at the rear of the building, where a fountain played in an ornamental pool.

'They are holding some special carnival games which are open to all tomorrow. There are four events, and the winner will be awarded a golden mask and will be an honorary guest at the party. You must win it, Ezio, for access to the party gives you access to Marco Barbarigo.' She looked at him. 'When you go, I advise you to take that little spitfire of yours with you, for you won't get close enough to knife him.'

324

'May I ask you a question?'

'You can try. I cannot guarantee an answer.'

'I am curious. You wear the habit of a nun, and yet clearly you are no such thing.'

'How do you know that? I assure you, my son, that I am married to the Lord.'

'But I don't understand. You are also a courtesan. Indeed, you run a bordello.'

Teodora smiled. 'I see no contradiction. How I choose to practise my faith, what I choose to do with my body – these are my choices and I am free to make them.' She paused in thought for a moment. 'Look,' she continued. 'Like so many young women, I was drawn to the Church, but gradually I became disillusioned with the so-called believers in this city. Men only hold God as an idea in their heads, and not in the depths of their hearts and their bodies. Do you see what I am getting at, Ezio? Men must know how to love in order to attain salvation. My girls and I provide that knowledge to our congregation. Of course, no imaginable sect of the Church would agree with me, so I was obliged to create my own. It may not be traditional, but it works, and men's hearts grow firmer in my care.'

'Among other things, I imagine.'

'You are cynical, Ezio.' She extended her hand to him. 'Come back tomorrow and we will see about these games. Take care of yourself in the meantime and don't forget your mask. I know you can take care of yourself, but our enemies are still out to get you.'

There were some small adjustments Ezio wanted on his new gun, so he returned to Leonardo's workshop on his way back to the Thieves' Guild headquarters.

'I am glad to see you again, Ezio.'

'You were right about Sister Teodora, Leonardo. Truly a Freethinker.'

'She would get into trouble with the Church if she weren't so well protected; but she has some powerful admirers.'

'I can imagine.' But Ezio noticed that Leonardo was slightly abstracted, and looking at him strangely. 'What is it, Leo?'

'Perhaps it would be better not to tell you, but if you found out by accident it would be worse. Look, Ezio, Cristina Calfucci is in Venice with her husband for *Carnevale*. Of course she's Cristina d'Arzenta now.'

'Where is she staying?'

'She and Manfredo are the guests of my patron. That is how I know.'

'I must see her!'

'Ezio – are you sure that's such a good idea?'

'I'll collect the gun in the morning. I'll need it by then, I'm afraid – I have some urgent business to attend to.'

'Ezio, I wouldn't go out unarmed.'

'I still have my Codex blades.'

Heart pumping, Ezio made his way to the Palazzo Pexaro, via the office of a public scribe whom he paid to write a short note, which read:

Cristina my darling
I must meet you alone and away from our hosts this evening at
the nineteenth hour. I will await you at the Sign of the
Sundial in the Rio Terra degli Ognisanti –

– and he had it signed, 'Manfredo'. Then he delivered it to the *Conte*'s palazzo, and waited.

It had been a long shot, but it worked. She soon emerged with only a maidservant to chaperone her, and hurried in the direction of Dorsoduro. He followed her. When she arrived at the appointed spot and her chaperone had retired to a discreet distance, he stepped forward. Both of them were wearing their carnival masks, but he could tell that she was as beautiful as ever. He could not help himself. He took her in his arms and kissed her long and tenderly.

Finally she broke free and, taking off her mask, she looked at him uncomprehendingly. Then, before he could stop her, she had reached up and removed his own mask.

'Ezio!'

'Forgive me, Cristina, I –' He noticed she no longer wore his pendant. Of course not.

'What the hell are you doing here? How dare you kiss me like that?'

'Cristina, it's all right . . .'

'All *right*? I haven't seen or heard from you in eight *years*!'

'I was just afraid you wouldn't come at all if I didn't use a little subterfuge.'

'You're quite right – of course I wouldn't have come! I seem to remember that the last time we met you kissed me in the street and then, as cool as a cucumber, saved my fiancé's life and left me to marry him.'

'It was the right thing to do. He loved you, and I –'

'Who cares what he wanted? I loved *you*!'

Ezio didn't know what to say. He felt as if the world had fallen away from him.

'Don't seek me out again, Ezio,' continued Cristina, tears in her eyes. 'I can't bear it, and you clearly have another life now.'

'Cristina –'

'There was a time when you would only have had to crook your finger, and I –' She interrupted herself. 'Goodbye, Ezio.'

He watched helplessly as she walked away, rejoined her companion, and disappeared round a corner of the street. She had not looked back.

Cursing himself and his fate, Ezio made his way back to the Thieves' headquarters.

The following day found him in a mood of grim determination. He collected his gun from Leonardo, thanked him, and retrieved the Codex page, hoping that in time he would be able to get it and the other, taken from Emilio, back to his uncle Mario. Then he made his way back to Teodora's house. From there, she conducted him to the Campo di San Polo, where the games were to take place. In the centre of the square a rostrum had been erected, and on it two or three officials sat at a desk, taking the competitors' names. Among the people around, Ezio noticed the unhealthy, gaunt figure of Silvio Barbarigo. With him he was surprised to see the enormous bodyguard, Dante.

'You'll be up against him,' Teodora was saying. 'Think you can take him on?'

'If I have to.'

Finally, when all the competitors' names had been taken (Ezio gave a false one), a tall man in a bright red cloak took his place on the rostrum. He was the Master of Ceremonies.

There were four games in all. The contestants would vie with one another in each, and at the end an overall winner would be decided on by a panel of judges. Luckily for Ezio, many of the competitors, in the spirit of Carnival, elected to keep their masks on.

The first game was a foot-race, which Ezio won easily, to the intense chagrin of Silvio and Dante. The second, more complicated, involved a tactical battle of wills in which the contestants had to vie with each other as they tried to capture from one another emblematic flags which each had been provided with.

In this game, too, Ezio was pronounced the winner, but he felt uneasy as he saw the expressions on the faces of Dante and Silvio.

'The third contest,' announced the Master of Ceremonies, 'combines elements of the first two and adds new ones of its own. This time, you will have to use speed and skill, but also charisma and charm!' He spread his arms wide, to indicate a number of fashionably dressed women about the square, who giggled prettily as he did so. 'A number of our ladies have volunteered to help us with this one,' continued the Master of Ceremonies. 'Some are here in the square. Others are walking in the streets around. You may even find some in gondolas. Now, you will recognize these ladies by the ribbons they wear in their hair. Your job, honoured competitors, is to collect as many ribbons as you can by the time my hour-glass runs out. We'll ring the church bell when your time is up, but I think I can safely say that however fortune favours you, this will be the most enjoyable event of the day! The man who returns with the most ribbons will be the winner, and one step closer to gaining the Golden Mask. But remember, if there is no outright victor in these games, the judges will decide which lucky one of you will attend the Doge's party! And now – Begin!'

The time passed, as the Master of Ceremonies had

promised, quickly and enjoyably. The bell of San Polo rang out at a sign from him as the last sands trickled from the upper to the lower chamber of the glass, and the competitors took up their positions back in the square, handing their ribbons over to the adjudicators, some smiling, others blushing. Only Dante remained stony-faced, though his face grew red with anger when the count had been made and it was – once again – Ezio's arm that the Master of Ceremonies held high.

'Well, my mysterious young man, you are in luck today,' the Master of Ceremonies said. 'Let's hope your good fortune doesn't desert you at the last hurdle.' He turned to address the crowd in general, while the rostrum was cleared and ropes set up round it to convert it into a boxing ring. 'The last contest, ladies and gentle-men, is a complete contrast. It concerns itself only with brute strength. The competitors will fight each other, until all but the last two are eliminated. The last two will fight until one of them is knocked out. And then comes the moment you've all been waiting for! The *overall* winner of the Golden Mask will be announced, but be careful how you place your bets – there's plenty of time for upsets and surprises yet!'

It was in this last game that Dante excelled, but Ezio, using different skills and light on his feet, managed to make the final pair, confronting the giant bodyguard. The man swung at Ezio with fists like piledrivers, but Ezio was agile enough to ensure that no seriously heavy punches landed and he was able to get some meaning-ful left uppercuts and right hooks in himself.

There were no breaks between rounds in this last bout, and after a time Ezio could see that Dante was tiring. But he also, out of the corner of his eye, noticed that Silvio Barbarigo was speaking urgently to the Master of Ceremonies and the panel of judges who had gathered at a table under a canopy not far from the ring. He thought he saw a fat leather purse change hands, which the Master of Ceremonies quickly pock-eted, but he couldn't be sure, as he had to return his attention to his opponent, who, angry now, was coming at him with flailing arms. Ezio ducked and landed two quick jabs to Dante's chin and body, and at last the big man went over. Ezio stood over him and Dante glow-ered up. 'This isn't over yet,' he growled, but he was finding it hard to get up.

Ezio looked over at the Master of Ceremonies, lifting his arm in appeal, but the man's face was stony. 'Are we sure all the competitors have been eliminated?' the Master of Ceremonies called. '*All* of them? We cannot announce a winner until we are *sure*!'

There was a murmur in the crowd as two grim-looking men detached themselves from it and clambered into the ring. Ezio looked towards the judges but they had averted their gaze. The men were closing in on him and Ezio now saw that each had a stubby little knife, almost invisible, clutched in his paw.

'So that's how it's going to be, eh?' he said to them. 'No holds barred, then.'

He danced out of the way as the fallen Dante tried to pull him off balance by grabbing his ankles, then leapt in the air to kick one of his new opponents in the face. The man spat out teeth and reeled away. Ezio came down and stamped hard on the second man's left foot, crushing the instep. Then he punched him viciously in the stomach and, as he doubled up, brought his knee into hard contact with the man's descending chin. Howling with pain, the man went over. He had bitten through his tongue, and blood gushed through his lips.

Without looking back, Ezio vaulted out of the ring and confronted the Master of Ceremonies and the sheepish-looking judges. The crowd behind him cheered.

'I think we have a winner,' Ezio told the Master of Ceremonies. The man exchanged glances with the judges and with Silvio Barbarigo, who was standing close by. The Master of Ceremonies climbed into the ring, avoiding the blood as best he could, and addressed the crowd.

'Ladies and gentlemen!' he announced after clearing his throat a little nervously. 'I think you'll all agree that we've enjoyed a hard and fairly fought battle today.'

The crowd cheered.

'And on such an occasion it's hard to choose a real winner –'

The crowd looked puzzled. Ezio exchanged glances with Teodora, who was standing on its fringe.

'It's been a hard job for the judges and myself,' continued the Master of Ceremonies, sweating slightly and mopping his brow, but a winner there has to be, and, on aggregate, mind, we have picked one.' Here he stooped and with difficulty raised Dante to a sitting position. 'Ladies and gentlemen – I give you the winner of the Golden Mask – Signore Dante Moro!'

The crowd hissed and booed, yelling their disapproval, and the Master of Ceremonies, together with the judges, had to beat a hasty retreat as the bystanders began to pelt them with any rubbish they could lay their hands on. Ezio hurried across to Teodora and the two of them watched as Silvio, a twisted smile on his livid face, helped Dante off the rostrum and bundled him away down a side-alley.

19

Back at Teodora's 'convent', Ezio struggled to contain himself as Teodora herself and Antonio watched him with concern.

'I saw Silvio bribe the Master of Ceremonies,' said Teodora. 'And no doubt he lined the judges' pockets too. There was nothing I could do.'

Antonio laughed derisively and Ezio cast him an irritable look.

'It's easy to see why Silvio was so determined to get their man to win the Golden Mask,' Teodora went on. 'They're still on the alert and they don't want to take any chances with Doge Marco.' She looked at Ezio. 'They won't rest until you are dead.'

'Then they'll have a lot of sleepless nights.'

'We must think. The party's tomorrow.'

'I'll find a way of shadowing Dante to the party,' decided Ezio. 'I'll get the mask off him somehow, and —'

'How?' Antonio wanted to know. 'By killing the poor *stronzo*?'

Ezio turned on him angrily. 'Do you have a better idea? You know what's at stake!'

Antonio held up his hands, deprecatingly. 'Look, Ezio – if you kill him, they'll cancel the party, and Marco will retreat back into the palazzo. We'll have wasted our time – again! No, the thing to do is steal the mask, quietly.'

'My girls can help,' put in Teodora. 'Plenty of them will be going to the party themselves – as entertainers! They can distract Dante while you acquire the mask. And once you're there, have no fear. I will be there too.'

Ezio nodded reluctantly. He didn't like being told what to do, but in this instance he knew that Antonio and Teodora were right. '*Va bene*,' he said.

The following day, as the sun was setting, Ezio made sure he was in place near where Dante would pass by on the way to the party. Several of Teodora's girls loitered nearby. At last the big man appeared. He'd gone to some lengths with his clothes, which were expensive but flashy. The Golden Mask hung at his belt. As soon as they saw him the girls cooed and waved, moving up to either side of him, two of them linking arms with him, making sure the mask swung behind him, and walking him to the large, cordoned-off area by the Molo where the party was taking place, and had, indeed, already begun. Timing his action precisely, Ezio chose the last possible minute to cut the mask free of Dante's belt. He snatched it away and ducked ahead of Dante, to appear with it before the guardsmen who were controlling entrance to the party. Seeing it, they let Ezio in, but when, a few moments later, Dante appeared, and reached behind him to put the mask on, he found that it had gone. The girls who'd escorted him had melted into the crowd and put on their own masks, so he would not recognize them.

Dante was still arguing with the guards at the gate, who had their inflexible orders, as Ezio made his way through the revellers to make contact with Teodora. She greeted him warmly. 'You made it! Congratulations! Now, listen. Marco remains very cautious indeed. He's staying on his boat, the Ducal Bucintoro, on the water just off the Molo. You won't be able to get all that close to him, but you should find the best vantage-point for your attack.' She turned to summon three or four of her courtesans. 'These girls will help cover your movements as you make your way through the party.'

Ezio set off, but as the girls, radiant in shimmering silver and red satins and silks, moved through the sea of guests, his attention was taken by a tall, dignified man in his mid-sixties, with clear, intelligent eyes and a white spade beard, who was talking to a Venetian noble of similar age. Both wore small masks which covered little of the face, and Ezio recognized the first of them as Agostino Barbarigo, the younger brother of Marco. Agostino might have a lot to do with the fate of Venice if anything untoward should happen to his brother, and Ezio thought it expedient to manoeuvre himself into

337

a position from which he could overhear the man's conversation.

As Ezio edged up, Agostino was laughing gently. 'Honestly, my brother embarrasses himself with this display.'

'You have no right to speak of him that way,' replied the noble. 'He is the Doge!'

'Yes, yes. He is the Doge,' replied Agostino, stroking his beard.

'This is his Party. His *Carnevale*, and he'll spend his money as he sees fit.'

'He's the Doge in name only,' Agostino said rather more sharply. 'And it's Venetian money that he's spending, not his own.' He lowered his voice. 'There are larger things at stake, and you know it.'

'Marco was the man chosen to lead. It's true your father may have thought that he'd never amount to much, and so transferred his political ambitions to you, but that hardly matters now, does it, given how things stand?'

'I never *wanted* to be Doge –'

'Then I congratulate you on your success,' said the nobleman, coldly.

'Look,' said Agostino, keeping his temper. 'Power is more than wealth. Does my brother truly believe he was chosen for any other reason than his riches?'

'He was chosen for his wisdom and his leadership!'

They were interrupted by the beginning of the firework display. Agostino watched it for a moment, then said, 'And this is what he does with such wisdom? Offer a light show? He hides away in the Ducal Palace while the city comes apart at the seams, and then thinks some expensive explosions will make people forget all their problems.'

The noble made a dismissive gesture. 'The people love the spectacle. It's human nature. You'll see . . .'

But at that moment Ezio spotted the burly figure of Dante, in the company of a posse of guards, barging through the party, doubtless looking for him. He continued to make his way to an unexposed spot from where he might gain access to the Doge if ever he left the Bucintoro, moored a few yards out from the quay.

There was a fanfare and for now the fireworks ceased. The people fell silent, then broke into applause as Marco came to the portside of his state barge to address them, and a page introduced him: '*Signore e signori!* I present to you the beloved Doge of *Venezia!*'

Marco began his address: '*Benvenuti!* Welcome, my friends, to the grandest social event of the season! In peace or at war, in times of prosperity or paucity, *Venezia* will always have *Carnevale!* . . .'

As the Doge continued to speak, Teodora rejoined Ezio.

'It's too far,' Ezio told her. 'And he's not going to leave the boat. So I'll have to swim out there. *Merda!*'

'I wouldn't try it,' said Teodora in hushed tones. 'You'd be spotted right away.'

'Then I'll have to fight my way out th—'

'Wait!'

The Doge was continuing. 'Tonight, we celebrate what makes us great. How brightly our lights shine over the world!' He spread his arms, and there was another short firework display. The crowd cheered and roared their approval.

'That's it!' said Teodora. 'Use your *pistola*! The one you stopped the murderer with in my bordello. Use the sound of the fireworks when they start again to cover the noise of your gunshot. Time it right, and you'll walk out of here unnoticed.'

Ezio looked at her. 'I like the way you think, Sister.'

'You'll just have to be very careful how you aim. You'll only get one chance.' She squeezed his arm. '*Buona fortuna*, my son. I'll be waiting for you back at the bordello.'

She vanished among the partygoers, among whom Ezio could also see Dante and his goons still searching for him. Silent as a wraith, he made his way to a point on the quay as close as he dared get to the spot where Marco was standing on the barge. Fortunately, his resplendent robes, bathed in the lights of the party, made him an excellent target.

The Doge's speech continued, and Ezio used it to prepare himself, listening carefully for the resumption of the fireworks. His timing would have to be accurate if he was to get his shot off undetected.

'We all know we have come through troubled times,' Marco was saying. 'But we have come through them together, and *Venezia* stands a stronger city for it . . . Transitions of power are difficult for all, but we have weathered the shift with grace and tranquillity. It is no easy thing to lose a Doge in the prime of life – and it is frustrating to see our dear brother Mocenigo's assassin still roam free and unpunished. However, we may comfort ourselves with the thought that many of us were beginning to grow uncomfortable with my predecessor's policies, to feel unsafe, and to doubt the road he was guiding us down.' Several voices in the crowd were raised in agreement, and Marco, smiling, held up his hands for silence. 'Well, my friends, I can tell you that I have found the right road for us again! I can see down it, and I know where we are going! It's a beautiful place, and we are going there together! The future I see for *Venezia* is a future of strength, a future of wealth. We will build a fleet so strong that our enemies will fear us as never before! And we will expand our trade routes across the seas and bring home spices and treasures undreamed of since Marco Polo's time!' Marco's eyes glittered as his voice took on a minatory tone. 'And I say this to those who stand against us: be careful which side of the line you choose, because either you are with us or you are on the side of evil. And we will harbour no enemies here! We will hunt you down, we will root you out, we will destroy you!' He raised his hands again and declaimed: 'And *Venezia* shall always stand – the brightest jewel in all civilization!'

As he let his arms fall in triumph, a mighty display of fireworks went up – a grand finale which turned night into day. The noise of the explosions was deafening – Ezio's little lethal gunshot was quite lost in it. And he was well on his way out through the crowd before the people in it had had time to react to the sight of Marco Barbarigo, one of the shortest-reigning doges in Venetian history, stagger, clutching at his heart, and falling dead on the deck of the Ducal Barge. '*Requiescat in pace*,' Ezio muttered to himself as he went.

But once the news was out, it travelled fast, and reached the brothel before Ezio did. He was greeted with cries of admiration from Teodora and her courtesans.

'You must be exhausted,' said Teodora, taking his arm and leading him away from the others towards an inner room. 'Come, relax!'

But first Antonio offered his congratulations. 'The saviour of Venice!' he exclaimed. 'What can I say? Perhaps it was wrong of me to doubt so readily. Now at least we'll have a chance to see where the pieces fall . . .'

'Enough of that now,' said Teodora. 'Come, Ezio. You've worked hard, my son. I feel your tired body is in need of comfort and succour.'

Ezio was quick to catch her meaning, and played along. 'It is true, Sister. I have such aches and pains that

I may need a great deal of comfort and succour. I hope you are up to it.'

'Oh,' grinned Teodora, 'I don't intend to ease your pain single-handed! Girls!'

A gaggle of courtesans slipped smilingly past Ezio into the inner room, at the centre of which he could see a truly massive bed, by whose side was a singular contraption like a couch, but with pulleys and belts, and chains. It reminded him of something out of Leonardo's workshop, but he couldn't imagine what possible use it might be put to.

He exchanged a long look with Teodora and followed her into the bedroom, closing the door firmly behind him.

A couple of days later Ezio was standing on the Rialto Bridge, relaxed and refreshed, and watching the crowds go by. He was just considering leaving to go and drink a couple of glasses of Veneto before the *ora di pranzo*, when he saw a man he recognized hurrying towards him – one of Antonio's messengers.

'Ezio, Ezio,' the man said as he came up. '*Ser* Antonio wishes to see you – it's a matter of importance.'

'Then we'll go immediately,' said Ezio, following him off the bridge.

They found Antonio in his office in the company – to Ezio's surprise – of Agostino Barbarigo. Antonio made the introductions.

'It is an honour to meet you, sir. I am sorry for the loss of your brother.'

Agostino waved a hand. 'I appreciate your sympathy, but to be frank my brother was a fool and completely under the control of the Borgia faction in Rome – something I would not wish on Venice ever. Luckily, some public-spirited person has averted that danger by assassinating him. In a curiously original way . . . There will be inquiries, of course, but I am at a loss personally to see where they will lead . . .'

'*Messer* Agostino is shortly to be elected Doge,' put in Antonio. 'It is good news for Venice.'

'The Council of Forty-One has worked fast this time,' said Ezio, drily.

'I think they have learnt the error of their ways,' replied Agostino with a wry smile. 'But I do not wish to be Doge in name only, as my brother was. Which brings us to the business in hand. Our ghastly cousin Silvio has occupied the Arsenal – the military quarter of town – and garrisoned it with two hundred mercenaries!'

'But when you are Doge, can't you command them to stand down?' asked Ezio.

'It would be nice to think so,' said Agostino, 'but my brother's extravagances have depleted the city's resources, and we will be hard put to it to withstand a determined force who have control of the Arsenal. And without the Arsenal, I have no real control of Venice, Doge or no Doge!'

'Then,' said Ezio. 'We must raise a determined force of our own.'

'Well said!' Antonio beamed. 'And I think I have just the man for the job. Have you heard of Bartolomeo d'Alviano?'

'Of course. The *condottiero* who used to serve the Papal States! He's turned against them, I know.'

'And just now he's based here. He has little love for Silvio, who, as you know, is also in Cardinal Borgia's pocket,' said Agostino. 'Bartolomeo's based on San Pietro, east of the Arsenal.'

'I'll go and see him.'

'Before you do that, Ezio,' said Antonio, '*Messer* Agostino has something for you.'

From his robes Agostino withdrew a rolled, ancient vellum scroll, with a heavy black seal, broken, hanging from a tattered red ribbon. 'My brother had it among his papers. Antonio thought it might interest you. Consider it a payment for . . . services rendered.'

Ezio took it. He knew immediately what it was. 'Thank you, Signore. I am sure this will be of great help in the battle which will surely come.'

Pausing only to arm himself, Ezio wasted no time in making his way to Leonardo's workshop, where he was surprised to find his friend in the process of packing up.

'Where are you off to now?' asked Ezio.

'Back to Milan. I was going to send you a message

345

before I left, of course. And to send you a packet of bullets for your little gun.'

'Well, I am very glad I've caught you. Look, I have another Codex page!'

'Excellent. I am most interested in seeing those. Come in. My servant Luca and the others can carry on with this. I've got them quite well trained by now. Pity I can't take them all with me.'

'What are you going to do in Milan?'

'Lodovico Sforza made me an offer I couldn't refuse.'

'But what about your projects here?'

'The navy's had to cancel. No money for new projects. Apparently the last Doge ran through most of it. I could have done him fireworks, no need to have gone to all the expense of sending off to China for them. Never mind, Venice is still at peace with the Turks, and they've told me I'm welcome to come back – in fact, I think they'd like me to. Meanwhile I'm leaving Luca behind – he'd be a fish out of water away from Venice – with a few basic designs to get them started. And as for the Conte, he's happy with his family portraits – though personally I think they could do with more work.' Leonardo started to unroll the vellum sheet. 'Now, let's have a look at this.'

'Promise you'll let me know when you return here.'

'I promise, my friend. And you – keep me posted on your movements if you can.'

'I will.'

'Now . . .' Leonardo spread the Codex page out and examined it. 'There's something here that looks like a blueprint for the double-bladed knife that went with your metal guard-bracer, but it's incomplete and may be an earlier draft of the design. The rest can only be significant in connection with the other pages – look, there are more map-like markings and some kind of picture that puts me in mind of those complex knot-patterns I used to doodle when I had any time to think for myself!' Leonardo rolled up the page again and looked at Ezio. 'I'd put this in a safe place with the other two pages you've shown me here in Venice. They're all clearly of great significance.'

'Actually, Leo, if you're going to Milan I wonder if I might ask you a favour?'

'Fire away.'

'When you get to Padua, would you please organize a trustworthy courier to take these three pages to my Uncle Mario in Monteriggioni? He's an . . . antiquarian . . . and I know he'll find them interesting. But I need someone I can depend on to do this for me.'

Leonardo gave him the ghost of a smile. If Ezio hadn't been so preoccupied, he might almost have thought it *knowing*. 'I'm sending my stuff straight on to Milan, but as for myself I'm paying a flying visit – to coin a phrase – to Florence first to check on Agniolo and Innocento, so I'll be your courier as far as there, and I'll send Agniolo on to Monteriggioni with them, have no fear.'

'That is better than I could have hoped for.' Ezio grasped his hand. 'You are a good and wonderful friend, Leo.'

'I certainly hope so, Ezio. Occasionally I think you could do with someone truly to look out for you.' He paused. 'And I wish you well in your work. I hope one day you will be able to bring it to a conclusion, and find rest.'

A distant look came into Ezio's steel-grey eyes, but he didn't reply except to say, 'You've reminded me – I have another errand to run. I'll send one of my host's men over with the other two Codex pages. And now, for the moment, *addio*!'

20

The quickest way to reach San Pietro from Leonardo's workshop was by taking the ferry or hiring a boat from the Fondamenta Nuova and sailing east from the north shores of the city. To his surprise Ezio found it hard to get anyone to take him there. The regular ferries had been suspended, and it was only by digging deep into his pockets that he managed to persuade a pair of young gondoliers to make the journey.

'What's the problem?' he asked them.

'Word is, there's been some bad fighting down there,' said the aft oarsman, straining against choppy water. 'Seems that it's died down now, just a local feud. But the ferries aren't risking starting up again just yet. We'll drop you on the north foreshore. Just keep an eye out for yourself.'

They did as they had promised. Ezio soon found himself alone, plodding up a muddy bank to the brick retaining wall, from where he could see the spire of the church of San Pietro di Castello a short way off. What he could also see was several plumes of smoke rising from a group of low brick buildings some distance south-east of the church. They were Bartolomeo's barracks. His heart pounding, Ezio hastened in their direction.

The first thing that struck him was the silence. Then, as he drew nearer, he began to see dead bodies strewn around, some of the men wearing the blazon of Silvio Barbarigo, others a device he did not recognize. Finally he came upon a sergeant, badly wounded but still alive, who had managed to prop himself up against a low wall.

'Please . . . help me,' said the sergeant when Ezio approached.

Ezio searched around quickly and located the well, from which he drew water, praying that the attackers had not poisoned it, though it looked clean and clear enough. He poured some into a beaker he'd found and put it gently to the man's lips, then moistened a cloth and wiped the blood from his face.

'Thank you, friend,' said the sergeant. Ezio noticed that he wore the unfamiliar badge, and guessed that it must be Bartolomeo's. Evidently Bartolomeo's troops had been worsted by Silvio's.

'It was a surprise attack,' the sergeant confirmed. 'Some whore of Bartolomeo's betrayed us.'

'Where have they gone now?'

'The Inquisitor's men? Back to the Arsenal. They've established a base there, just before the new Doge could take control. Silvio hates his cousin Agostino because he isn't part of whatever plot the Inquisitor's involved in.' The man coughed blood, but endeavoured to continue. 'Took our Captain prisoner. Carried him off with them. Funny really, *we* were just planning to attack *them*. Bartolomeo was simply waiting for . . . a messenger from the city.'

'Where are the rest of your men now?'

The sergeant tried to look around. 'Those that weren't killed or taken prisoner scattered, tried to save themselves. They'll be lying low in Venice and on the islands in the lagoon. But they'll need someone to unite behind. They'll be waiting for word of the Captain.'

'And he's a prisoner of Silvio?'

'Yes. He . . . ' But the unfortunate sergeant here started to fight for breath. His struggle ended as his mouth opened and a shower of blood streamed from it, drenching the grass for three yards in front of him. But the time the flow had stopped, the man's eyes were staring sightlessly in the direction of the lagoon.

Ezio closed them for him, and crossed his arms on his chest. '*Requiescat in pace,*' he said, solemnly.

Then he hitched his sword-belt tighter – he had also strapped the guard-brace to his left forearm, but had left off the double-bladed dagger attachment. To his right forearm he had attached the poison-blade, always so useful when faced with huge odds. The pistol, most useful when a single, certain target was in view, as it had to be reloaded after each firing, he kept in his belt-pouch with powder and shot, and the original spring-blade as back-up. He pulled up his hood, and headed for the wooden bridge which connected San Pietro to Castello. From there he made his way unobtrusively but quickly down the main street in the direction of the Arsenal. He noticed that the people around him were subdued, though they went about their daily work as usual. It would take more than a local war to stop the business of Venice entirely, though of course few of the ordinary citizens of Castello could know just how important for their city the outcome of this conflict was.

Ezio didn't know then that it would be a conflict which would drag on for many, many months, indeed, into the following year. He thought of Cristina, of his mother Maria and his sister Claudia. And he felt himself to be homeless, and getting older. But there was the Creed to be served and upheld, and that was more important than anything else. No one, perhaps, would ever know that their world had been saved from the dominion of the Templars by the select Order of Assassins, which had pledged itself to opposing their evil hegemony.

His first task was clearly to locate and, if possible, free Bartolomeo d'Alviano, but getting into the Arsenal would be hard. Surrounded by high brick fortified walls, and containing a warren of buildings and shipyards, it stood at the eastern limit of the main city, and it was heavily guarded by Silvio's private army, whose numbers seemed to exceed the two hundred mercenaries Agostino Barbarigo had told him of. Ezio, passing the architect Gamballo's recently built main gate, wandered round the outside perimeters of the buildings as far as they were accessible by land, until he came to a heavy door with a wicket gate built into it, and, observing from a distance, saw that this unobtrusive entry was used by guards on the outside when they changed shift. He had to wait unobtrusively for four hours, but at the next shift change he was ready. It was baking hot in the late afternoon sun, the atmosphere was humid, and everyone except Ezio was torpid. He watched as the relief soldiers marched out through the gate, which had only one guard, and then followed the mercenaries coming off shift, bringing up the rear and blending in as best he could. Once the last soldier was through, he cut the throat of the guard posted at the gate and slipped through it himself before anyone had noticed what was happening. As had happened years ago at San Gimignano, Silvio's force here, big as it was, wasn't sufficient to cover the entire area it guarded. It was, after all, the city's military focal point. No wonder Agostino couldn't wield any real power without control of it.

Once inside, it was relatively easy to move about between the wide open spaces beween the huge buildings – the *Cordelie*, the *Artiglierie*, the shot-towers, and above all, the shipyards. As long as Ezio kept to the dark late-afternoon shadows and took care to avoid the patrols within the vast complex, he knew he would be all right, though naturally he remained extremely vigilant.

Guided at last by the sounds of merriment and mocking laughter, he found his way to the side of one of the main dry-docks, into which a massive galley was drawn. On the side of one of the dock's massive walls, an iron cage had been hung. In it was Bartolomeo, a vigorous bear of a man in his early thirties and so just four or five years' Ezio's senior. Around him was a crowd of Silvio's mercenaries, and Ezio thought how much better employed they'd have been patrolling than triumphing over an enemy they'd already rendered helpless, but he reflected that Silvio Barbarigo, Grand Inquisitor though he was, was not experienced in matters of handling troops.

Ezio didn't know how long Bartolomeo had been chained up in his cage; certainly for many hours. But his anger and energy seemed unaffected by his ordeal. Given that he'd almost certainly been given nothing to eat or drink, this was remarkable.

'*Luridi codardi!* Filthy cowards!' he was shouting at his tormentors, one of whom, Ezio noticed, had dipped a sponge in vinegar and was pushing it up to Bartolomeo's lips on the tip of a lance in the hope that he'd think it was water. Bartolomeo spat it away. 'I'll take you all on! At the same time! With one arm – no, *both* arms – tied behind my back! I'll fucking eat you *alive*!' He laughed. 'You must be wondering how such a thing could be even possible, but just let me out of here and I'll gladly demonstrate! *Miserabili pezzi di merda!*'

The Inquisitor's guards howled in derision, and poked at Bartolomeo with poles, making the cage swing. It had no solid bottom, and Bartolomeo had to grip hard with his feet on the bars beneath to keep his balance.

'You have no honour! No valour! No virtue!' He summoned enough saliva into his mouth to spit down at them. 'And people wonder why the star of Venice has begun to wane.' Then his voice took on almost a pleading tone. 'I'll show mercy to whomever here has the courage to release me. All the rest of you are going to die! By my hand! I swear it!'

'Save your fucking breath,' one of the guards called out. 'No one's going to die today but you, you fucking turdbag.'

All this time Ezio, sheltered by the shadow of a brick colonnade that skirted a basin where some of the smaller war-galleys were moored, was working out a way of saving the *condottiero*. There were ten guards around the cage, all with their backs to him, and there was none other in view. What was more, they were off-duty and had no armour on. Ezio checked his poison-dagger. Dispatching the guards should present no difficulty. He'd timed the passing of the on-duty patrols and they came by every time the shadow of the dock wall lengthened by three inches. But there was the additional problem of releasing Bartolomeo, keeping him quiet while doing so, and making quick work of it. He thought hard. He knew there wasn't much time.

'What sort of man sells his honour and dignity for a few pieces of silver?' Bartolomeo was bellowing, but his throat was getting dry and he was running out of steam despite his iron will.

'Isn't that what you do, fuckwit? Aren't you a mercenary like us?'

'I have never been in the service of a traitor and a coward, as you are!' Bartolomeo's eyes glittered. The men standing beneath him were momentarily cowed. 'Do you think I don't know why you've chained me up? Do you think I don't know who your boss Silvio's puppet-master is? I've been fighting the weasel who controls him since most of you boys were puppies suckling your mothers' teats!'

Ezio was now listening with interest. One of the soldiers picked up a half-brick and threw it angrily. It bounced harmlessly off the bars of the cage.

'That's right, you fuckers!' Bartolomeo yelled hoarsely. 'You just try it on with me! I swear, once I'm free of this cage I'm going to make it my mission to sever each and every one of your fucking heads and shove them up your fucking girlie arses! And I'll mix and match the heads too, because you little tykes clearly don't know your heads from your arses anyway!'

The men below were getting seriously angry now. It was clear that only orders prevented them from stabbing the man to death with their pikes, or shooting arrows at him, as he hung defencelessly above them in his cage.

But by now Ezio had seen that the padlock which secured the door of the cage was relatively small. Bartolomeo's captors relied on the fact that the cage was hung high. No doubt they intended that the harsh sun of the day, and chill of the night, coupled with dehydration and starvation, would finish him off, unless he broke down and agreed to talk. But from the look of him, that was something Bartolomeo would never do.

Ezio knew he had to act fast. An on-duty patrol would pass by very shortly. Releasing the spring on his poison-blade, he moved forward with the speed and grace of a wolf, covering the distance in a matter of seconds. He scythed through the group and had sliced death into the bodies of five men before the others knew what was happening. Drawing his sword, he savagely killed the rest, their vain blows glancing off the metal guard on his left forearm, while Bartolomeo watched open-mouthed. At last, silent, Ezio turned and looked up.

'Can you jump from there?' he asked.

'If you can get me out, I'll jump like a fucking flea.'

Ezio grabbed one of the dead soldiers' pikes. Its point was iron, not steel, and cast, not forged. It would do. Balancing it in his left hand, he prepared himself, crouched, and sprang into the air, at last clinging to the outer bars of the cage.

Bartolomeo looked at him pop-eyed. 'How in buggery did you do that?' he asked.

'Training,' said Ezio, smiling tightly. He forced the point of the pike through the hasp of the lock and twisted. It resisted at first, then broke. Ezio pulled the door open, free-falling to the ground as he did so, and landing with the grace of a cat. 'Now you jump,' he ordered. 'Be quick.'

'Who are you?'

'Get on with it!'

Nervously, Bartolomeo braced himself against the open door of the cage and then flung himself forwards. He landed heavily, the breath knocked out of him, but when Ezio helped him to his feet, he shook his rescuer off proudly. 'I'm all right,' he huffed. 'I'm just not used to doing fucking circus tricks.'

'No bones broken, then?'

'Fuck you, whoever you are,' said Bartolomeo, beaming. 'But you have my thanks!' And to Ezio's surprise, he gave him a bear-hug. 'Who are you anyway? The Arch-fucking-angel Gabriel or what?'

'My name is Auditore, Ezio.'

'Bartolomeo d'Alviani. Delighted.'

'We haven't got time for this,' Ezio snapped. 'As you well know.'

'Don't try to teach me my job, acrobat,' said Bartolomeo, still quite genially. 'Anyway, I owe you one for this!'

But they had already wasted too much time. Someone must have noticed from the ramparts what was going on, for now alarm bells started to ring and patrols emerged from the buildings nearby to close on them.

'Come on, you bastards!' bellowed Bartolomeo, swinging fists that made Dante Moro's look like panelling hammers. It was Ezio's turn to look on admiringly, as Bartolomeo ploughed into the oncoming soldiers. Together, they beat their way back to the wicket gate, and at last were clear.

'Let's get out of here!' Ezio exclaimed.

'Shouldn't we break a few more heads?'

'Perhaps we should try to avoid conflict for now?'

'Are you afraid?'

'Just practical. I know your blood's up, but they do outnumber us by one hundred to one.'

Bartolomeo considered. 'You have a point. And after all, I'm a commander. I ought to think like one, not leave it to some whippersnapper like you to make me see sense.' And then he lowered his voice and said in a concerned tone, 'I just hope my little Bianca is safe.'

Ezio didn't have time to question or even wonder about Bartolomeo's aside. They had to make tracks, and they did, racing through the town back towards Bartolomeo's headquarters on San Pietro. But not before Bartolomeo had made two important diversions, to the Riva San Basio and the Corte Nuova, to alert his agents in those places that he was alive and free, and to summon his scattered forces – those who had not been taken prisoner – to regroup.

Back at San Pietro at dusk, they found that a handful of Bartolomeo's *condottieri* had survived the attack and had now emerged from their hiding-places, moving among the already fly-blown dead and attempting to bury them and put matters in order. They were elated to see their Captain again, but he was distracted, running here and there in his encampment, calling mournfully, 'Bianca! Bianca! Where are you?'

'Who's he after?' Ezio asked a sergeant-at-arms. 'She must be worth a lot to him.'

'She is, *Signore*,' grinned the sergeant. 'And far more reliable than most of her sex.'

Ezio ran to catch up with his new ally. 'Is everything all right?'

'What do you think? Look at the state of this place! And poor Bianca! If something's happened to her . . .'

The big man shouldered a door, already half off its hinges, on to the ground and entered a bunker which, from the look of it, must have been a map-room before the attack. The valuable maps had been mutilated or stolen, but Bartolomeo sifted through the wreckage until, with a cry of triumph –

'Bianca! Oh, my darling! Thank God you're all right!'

He had pulled a massive greatsword clear of the rubble and brandished it, roaring, 'Aha! You are safe! I never doubted it! Bianca! Meet . . . What's your name again?'

'Auditore, Ezio.'

Bartolomeo looked thoughtful. 'Of course. Your reputation goes before you, Ezio.'

'I am glad of it.'

'What brings you here?'

'I too have business with Silvio Barbarigo. I think he's outstayed his welcome in Venice.'

'Silvio! That turd! He needs flushing down a fucking latrine!'

'I thought I might be able to rely on your help.'

'After that rescue? I owe you my life, let alone my help.'

'How many men do you have?'

'How many survivors here, Sergeant-at-Arms?'

The sergeant-at-arms Ezio had spoken to earlier came running up and saluted. 'Twelve, *Capitano*, including you and me, and this gentleman here.'

'Thirteen!' shouted Bartolomeo, waving Bianca.

'Against a good two hundred,' said Ezio. He turned to the sergeant-at-arms. 'And how many of your men did they take prisoner?'

'Most of them,' the man replied. 'The attack took us completely by surprise. Some fled, but Silvio's men took far more away with them in chains.'

'Look, Ezio,' said Bartolomeo. 'I'm going to supervise rounding up the rest of my men who are at liberty. I'll get this place cleaned up and bury my dead and we'll regroup here. Do you think in the meantime you can see to the business of liberating the men Silvio's taken prisoner? Since that's a thing you seem to be very good at?'

'*Intensi.*'

'Get back here with them as soon as you can. Good luck!'

Ezio, his Codex weapons buckled on, headed west-ward again towards the Arsenal but wondered if Silvio would have kept all Bartolomeo's men prisoner there. He hadn't seen any of them when he had gone to rescue their Captain. At the Arsenal itself he stuck to the shadows of the falling night and tried to listen to the conversations of the guards stationed along the perimeter walls.

'Have you ever seen bigger cages?' said one.

'No. And the poor bastards are crammed into them like sardines. I don't think Captain Barto would have treated *us* like that, if *he'd* been the victor,' said his comrade.

'Of course he would. And keep your noble thoughts to yourself, if you want to keep your head on your shoulders. I say finish them off. Why don't we just lower the cages into the basins, and drown the lot of them?'

At that, Ezio tensed. There were three huge rectan-gular basins inside the Arsenal, each designed to hold thirty galleys. They were on the north side of the complex, surrounded by thick brick walls and covered by heavy wooden roofs. Doubtless the cages – larger versions of the one which had imprisoned Bartolomeo

– were suspended by chains over the water in one or more of the *bacini*.

'One hundred and fifty trained men? That'd be a waste. For my money, Silvio's hoping to turn them to our cause,' said the second uniform.

'Well, they're mercenaries like us. So why not?'

'Right! They just need to be softened up a little first. Show them who's boss.'

'*Spero di sì.*'

'Thank God they don't know their boss has escaped.'

The first guard spat. 'He won't last long.'

Ezio left them and made his way to the wicket gate he'd discovered earlier. There was no time to wait for any changing of the guard, but he could judge the time by the distance of the moon from the horizon and he knew he had a couple of hours. He flicked the spring-blade out – his original Codex weapon and still his favourite – and slashed open the throat of the fat old guard Silvio had seen fit to put on duty alone there, pushing him clear before any of the man's blood could get on to his clothes. Quickly he wiped the blade clean on the grass and exchanged it for his poison-blade. He made the sign of the Cross over the body.

The compound within the walls of the Arsenal looked different by the light of a sickle moon and a few stars, but Ezio knew where the basins were located and went, skirting the walls and keeping an ever-watchful eye out for Silvio's men, to the first one. He peered through the great open arches into the watery gloom beyond, but could see nothing but galleys bobbing gently in the half-light of the stars. The second bore the same fruit, but as he approached the third he heard voices.

'It's not too late for you to pledge yourselves to our cause. Only say the word and you'll be spared,' one of the Inquisitor's sergeants was calling in a mocking tone.

Ezio, pressing himself against the wall, saw a dozen troops, weapons laid down, bottles in their hands, gazing up into the gloom of the roof, where three massive iron cages were suspended. He saw that an invisible mechanism was slowly lowering the cages towards the water beneath. And there were no galleys in this basin. Only black, oily water, in which something unseen but frightful teemed.

The Inquisitor's guards included one man who wasn't drinking, a man who seemed constantly on the alert, a huge, terrible man. Ezio instantly recognized Dante Moro! So, with the death of his master Marco, the man-mountain had transferred his allegiance to the cousin, Silvio, the Inquisitor, who had already professed his admiration for the massive bodyguard.

Ezio made his way cautiously round the walls until he came to a large open-frame box containing an arrangement of cog-wheels, pulleys and ropes that might have been designed by Leonardo. This was the mechanism, driven by a water-clock, which was lowering the cages. Ezio drew his ordinary dagger from its sheath on the left-hand side of his belt and jammed it between two of the cogwheels. The mechanism stopped, and not before time, for the cages were now inches from the water's surface. But the guards instantly noticed that the cages' descent had ceased, and some came running towards the machinery that controlled it. Ezio sprang out his poison-blade and hacked at them as they came. Two fell into the water from the jetty and screamed, briefly, sinking into the oily black water. Meanwhile, Ezio raced along the perimeter of the basin towards the others, all of whom fled in alarm save Dante, who stood his ground and loomed like a tower over Ezio.

'Silvio's dog now, are you?' said Ezio.

'Better a live dog than a dead lion,' said Dante, reaching out to cuff Ezio into the water.

'Stand down!' said Ezio, ducking the blow. 'I have no quarrel with you!'

'Oh, shut your face,' said Dante, picking Ezio up by the scruff of the neck and bashing him against the wall of the basin. 'I have no serious quarrel with you, either.' He could see that Ezio was stunned. 'Just stay there. I must go and warn my master, but I'll be back to feed you to the fishes if you give me any more trouble!'

And he was gone. Ezio shook his head to clear it,

and stood up, groggily. The men in the cages were shouting and Ezio saw that one of Silvio's guards had crept back in and was about to dislodge the dagger he'd jammed in the cage-lowering mechanism. He thanked God he had not forgotten his old knife-throwing skills learned at Monteriggioni, produced a knife from his belt, and hurled it with deadly accuracy. The guard stumbled over, groaning, snatching helplessly at the blade which was buried between his eyes.

Ezio snatched a gaff from a rack on the wall behind him, and, leaning over the water dangerously, deftly hauled the nearest cage towards him. Its door was closed by a simple bolt and he shot it back, releasing the men inside, who tumbled out on to the wharf. With their help, he was able to haul in the remaining cages and release their prisoners in turn.

Exhausted though they were by their ordeal, they cheered him.

'Come on!' he cried. 'I've got to get you back to your Captain!'

Once they had overwhelmed the men guarding the basins, they returned unopposed to San Pietro, where Bartolomeo and his men had an emotional reunion. In Ezio's absence all the mercenaries who'd escaped Silvio's initial onslaught had returned, and the encampment was once again *in perfetto ordine*.

'*Salute*, Ezio!' said Bartolomeo. 'Welcome back! And well done, by God! I knew I could depend on you!' He took Ezio's hands between his. 'You are indeed the mightiest of allies. One might almost think –' but then he stopped himself, and said instead, 'Thanks to you my army is restored to its former glory. Now our friend Silvio will see just how grave a mistake he's made!'

'So, what should we do? Make a direct assault on the Arsenal?'

'No. A head-on assault would mean we'd be massacred at the gates. I think we should plant my men throughout the district and get them to cause enough trouble locally to tie most of Silvio's men up.'

'So – if the Arsenal is almost empty –'

'You can take it with a hand-picked team.'

'Let's hope he takes the bait.'

'He's an Inquisitor. He knows how to bully people who are already at his mercy. He's not a soldier. Hell, he doesn't even have the wit to be a halfway decent chess-player!'

It took a few days to deploy Bartolomeo's *condottieri* about Castello and the Arsenal district. When all was ready, Bartolomeo and Ezio gathered the small group of hand-picked mercenaries they'd kept back for the assault on Silvio's bastion. Ezio himself had selected the men for their agility and skill at arms.

They'd planned the assault on the Arsenal with care. The following Friday night, all was in readiness. A mercenary was sent to the top of the tower of San Martino and, when the moon was at its height, he set off a massive Roman candle designed and provided by Leonardo's workshop. This was the signal for the attack. Dressed in dark leather gear, the *condottieri* of the task-force scaled the walls of the Arsenal on all four sides. Once over the battlements, the men moved like spectres through the quiet and undermanned fortress and quickly contained the skeleton guard within. It wasn't long before Ezio and Bartolomeo found themselves confronting their deadliest foes – Silvio and Dante.

Dante, wearing iron knuckle-dusters, was swinging a massive chain-mace around, protecting his master. It was hard for either Ezio or Bartolomeo to come within range, as their own men engaged the enemy.

'A fine specimen, isn't he?' crowed Silvio from the safety of the ramparts. 'You should be honoured to die by his hand!'

'Suck my balls, you fuck!' Bartolomeo yelled back. He'd managed to snag the mace in his battle-staff, and Dante, his weapon torn from his hand, retreated. 'Come on, Ezio! We need to catch that *grassone bastardo*!'

Dante turned, having reached his objective, an iron club pierced with twisted nails, and faced them again. He swung it at Bartolomeo and one of the nails tore a furrow in his shoulder.

'I'll have you for that, you pig-eyed sack of shit!' bellowed Bartolomeo.

Meanwhile Ezio had loaded and fired his pistol at

Silvio, and missed. His shot ricocheted off the brick walls in a shower of sparks and splinters.

'Do you think I don't know why you're really here, Auditore?' Silvio barked, though clearly frightened by the gunshot. 'But you're too late! There's nothing you can do to stop us now!'

Ezio had reloaded, and fired again. But he was angry, and confused at Silvio's words, and once again the shot went wide.

'Hah!' spat Silvio from the ramparts as Dante and Bartolomeo slogged it out. 'You pretend you don't know! Though once Dante's done with you and your muscle-bound friend, it'll hardly matter either way. You'll just follow your fool of a father! Do you know what my greatest regret is? That I couldn't have been Giovanni's hangman myself. How I would have loved to pull that lever and watch your miserable dad kick and gasp and dangle! And then of course there would have been plenty of time for that winesack of an uncle of yours, *ciccione* Mario, and your not-quite-past-it mother, droopy-dugs Maria, and that luscious little strawberry Claudia, your sister. How long it's been since I fucked anything under twenty-five! Mind you, I'd keep the last two for the voyage – it can get quite lonely out at sea!'

Through the red mist of his fury, Ezio concentrated on the information the spittle-strewn lips of the Inquisitor were madly spewing forth along with the insults.

By now, Silvio's guards, at superior odds, were

beginning to rally against Bartolomeo's commandos. Dante dealt another swingeing blow at Bartolomeo, thumping him in the ribcage with his knuckle-dusters and causing him to falter. Ezio fired a third bullet at Silvio and this time it ripped through the Inquisitor's robes close to his neck, but though the man staggered, and Ezio saw a thin line of blood, he did not fall. He shouted a command to Dante, who fell back, swarming up to the rampart to join his master, and with him disappearing over the other side of the wall. Ezio knew there'd be a ladder on the other side to take them down to the jetty, and, yelling to Bartolomeo to follow him, he dashed out of the arena of battle to cut his foes off.

He saw them clambering into a large boat, but noticed the anger and despair on their faces. Following their gaze, he saw a huge black galley disappearing across the lagoon southwards.

'We've been betrayed!' Ezio heard Silvio say to Dante. 'The ship has sailed without us! God damn them! I've been nothing but loyal and yet this – *this!* – is how they repay me!'

'Let's use this boat to catch them up,' said Dante.

'It's too late for that – and we'd never get to the Island in a craft this size; but at least we can use it to get away from this catastrophe!'

'Then let us cast off, *Altezza.*'

'Indeed.'

Dante turned to the trembling crew. 'Cast off! Raise the sails! Look lively!'

At that moment Ezio sprang from the shadows across the wharf and on to the boat. The frightened sailors made themselves scarce, diving into the murky lagoon.

'Get away from me, murderer!' shrieked Silvio.

'You've delivered your last insult,' said Ezio, stabbing him in the gut and drawing the blades of his double-dagger slowly across his belly. 'And for what you said about my kinswomen I'd cut your balls off with this if I thought it was worth it.'

Dante stood rooted to the spot. Ezio fixed him with his eye. The big man looked tired.

'It's over,' Ezio told him. 'You backed the wrong horse.'

'Maybe I did,' said Dante. 'I'm going to kill you anyway. You filthy assassin. You make me tired.'

Ezio snapped out his *pistola* and fired. The slug hit Dante full in the face. He fell.

Ezio knelt by Silvio to give him absolution. He was nothing if not conscientious, and always remembered that killing should only happen if there were no alternative; and that the dying, who very soon would have no rights at all, should at least be accorded the last rites.

'Where were you going, Silvio? What is that galley? I thought you sought the Doge's seat?'

Silvio smiled thinly. 'That was just a distraction . . . We were meant to sail . . .'

'Where?'

'Too late,' smiled Silvio, and died.

Ezio turned to Dante and cradled the massive leonine head in the crook of his arm.

'Cyprus is their destination, Auditore,' croaked Dante. 'I can perhaps redeem my soul at the last by telling you the truth. They want ... They want ...' But choking on his own blood, the big man passed on.

Ezio searched both men's wallets but found nothing except a letter to Dante from his wife. Shamefacedly, he read it.

Amore mio

I wonder if ever the day will come when these words might make sense to you once more. I am sorry for what I have done – for allowing Marco to take me from you, divorce you, and make me his wife. But now that he has died, I may yet find a way for us to be joined again. I wonder, though, if you will even remember me? Or were the wounds you suffered in battle too grave? Do my words stir, if not your memory, then your heart? But perhaps it doesn't matter what they say, because I know you're still in my heart, somewhere. I will find a way, my love. To remind you. To restore you ...

Forever yours

Gloria

There was no address. Ezio folded the letter carefully and put it in his wallet. He would ask Teodora if she knew of this strange history, and if she could return the letter to its sender, with news of the death of this faithless creature's true husband.

He looked at the corpses and made the sign of the Cross over them '*Requiescant in pace*,' he said, sadly.

Ezio was still standing over the dead men when Bartolomeo came up, panting. 'See you didn't need my help, as usual,' he said.

'Have you taken back the Arsenal?'

'Do you think I'd be here if we hadn't?'

'Congratulations!'

'*Evviva!*'

But Ezio was watching the sea. 'We've got Venice back, my friend,' he said. 'And Agostino can rule it without further fear of the Templars. But I think there'll be little rest for me. Do you see that galley on the horizon?'

'Yes.'

'Dante told me with his dying breath that it is bound for Cyprus.'

'To what end?'

'That, *amico*, is what I need to find out.'

Ezio could not believe it was Midsummer's Day, in the Year of Christ 1487. His twenty-eighth birthday. He was by himself on the Bridge of the Fistfighters, leaning on the balustrade and gloomily looking at the dank water of the canal beneath him. As he watched, a rat swam by, pushing a cargo of cabbage leaves filched from the nearby greengrocer's barge towards a hole in the black brick of the canal's bank.

'There you are, Ezio!' said a cheery voice, and he could smell Rosa's musky scent before he turned to greet her. 'It's been too long! I might almost think you've been avoiding me!'

'I've been . . . busy.'

'Of course you have. What would Venice do without you!'

Ezio shook his head sadly, as Rosa leant comfortably on the balustrade beside him.

'Why so serious, *bello*?' she asked.

Ezio gave her a deadpan look and shrugged. 'Happy Birthday to Me.'

'It's your birthday? You serious? Wow! *Rallegramenti!* That's wonderful!'

'I wouldn't go that far,' sighed Ezio. 'It's been over ten years since I watched my father and brothers die. And I have spent ten years hunting down the men responsible, the men on my father's list, and those added to it since his death. And I know I am close to the end now – but I am no closer to understanding what any of it has really been *for*.'

'Ezio, you've dedicated your life to a good cause. It has made you lonely, isolated, but in one sense it has been your vocation. And though the instrument you have used to further your cause is death, you have never been unjust. Venice is a far better place now than it ever was, because of you. So cheer up. Anyway, seeing as it's your birthday, here's a present. Very good timing, as it happens!' She took out an official-looking logbook.

'Thank you, Rosa. Not quite what I'd imagined you'd give me for my birthday. What is it?'

'Just something I happened to . . . pick up. It's the shipping manifest from the Arsenal. The date your black galley sailed for Cyprus late last year is entered in it –'

'Seriously?' Ezio reached for the book but Rosa teasingly held it away from him. 'Give it to me, Rosa. This isn't a joke.'

'Everything has its price . . .' she whispered.

'If you say so.'

He held her in his arms for a long, lingering moment. She melted against him and he quickly snatched the book away.

'Hey! That isn't fair!' she laughed. 'Anyway, just to spare you the suspense, that galley of yours is scheduled to return to Venice – tomorrow!'

'What, I wonder, can they have on board?'

'Why am I not surprised that someone not a million miles from here is going to find out?'

Ezio beamed. 'Let's go and celebrate first!'

But at that moment a familiar figure bustled up.

'Leonardo!' said Ezio, greatly surprised. 'I thought you were in Milan!'

'Just got back,' replied Leonardo. 'They told me where to find you. Hello, Rosa. Sorry, Ezio, but we really need to talk.'

'Now? This minute?'

'Sorry.'

Rosa laughed. 'Go on boys, have fun, I'll keep!'

Leonardo ushered a reluctant Ezio away.

'This had better be good,' muttered Ezio.

'Oh, it is, it is,' said Leonardo placatingly. He led Ezio along several narrow alleys until they arrived back at his workshop. Leonardo busied about, producing some warm wine and stale cakes, and a pile of documents which he dumped on a large trestle table in the middle of his study.

'I had your Codex pages delivered to Monteriggioni as promised, but I couldn't resist studying them some more myself and I've copied out my findings. I don't know why I'd never made the connection before, but

376

when I put them together I realized the markings and symbols and ancient alphabets can be decoded and we seem to have struck gold – for all these pages are contiguous!' He interrupted himself. 'This wine is too warm! Mind you, I've got used to San Colombano; this Veneto stuff is like gnat's piss by comparison.'

'Go on,' said Ezio patiently.

'Listen to this.' Leonardo produced a pair of eyeglasses and perched them on his nose. He shuffled through his papers and read: 'The Prophet . . . will appear . . . when the Second Piece is brought to the Floating City . . .'

Ezio drew in his breath sharply at the words. 'Prophet?' he repeated. ' "Only the Prophet may open it . . ." "Two Pieces of Eden . . ."'

'Ezio?' Leonardo looked quizzical, doffing his eyeglasses. 'What is it? Does this ring some kind of bell with you?'

Ezio looked at him. He appeared to be coming to some kind of decision. 'We've known each other a long time, Leonardo. If I can't trust you, there's nobody . . . Listen! My Uncle Mario spoke of it, long ago. He's already deciphered other pages of this Codex, as had my father, Giovanni. There's a prophecy hidden in it, a prophecy about a secret, ancient vault, which holds something – something very powerful!'

'Really? That's amazing!' But then a thought struck Leonardo. 'Look, Ezio, if we've found all this out from the Codex, how much do the Barbarigi and the others you've been pitched against know about it? Maybe they know about the existence of this vault you mention too. And if so, that's not good.'

'Wait!' said Ezio, his brain racing. 'What if that's why they sent the galley to Cyprus? To *find* this "Piece of Eden"! And *bring it back to Venice*!'

' "When the Second Piece is brought to the Floating City" – of course!'

'It's coming back to me! "The Prophet will appear ..." "... Only the Prophet can open the Vault!" ... My God, Leo, when my Uncle told me about the Codex, I was too young, too brash, to imagine that it was anything but an old man's fantasy. But now I see it plain! The murder of Giovanni Mocenigo, the killing of my kinsmen, the attempt on the life of Duke Lorenzo and the horrible death of his brother – it's all been part of *his* plan – to find the Vault – the first name on my *List*! The one I have yet to strike a line through – *The Spaniard*!'

Leonardo breathed deeply. He knew whom Ezio was talking about. 'Rodrigo Borgia.' His voice was a whisper.

'The same!' Ezio paused. 'The Cyprus galley arrives tomorrow. I plan to be there to meet it.'

Leonardo embraced him. 'Good luck, my dear friend,' he said.

The following dawn found Ezio, armed with his Codex weapons and a bandolier of throwing-knives, standing in the shadows of the colonnade near the docks, watching closely as a group of men, dressed in plain uniforms to avoid attracting undue attention but discreetly displaying the crest of Cardinal Rodrigo Borgia, unloaded a plain-looking, smallish crate from a black galley which had recently put in from Cyprus. They handled the crate with kid gloves, and one of their number, under guard, hoisted it on to his shoulder and prepared to set off with it. But then Ezio noticed that several other guards were hoisting similar crates on to their shoulders, five of them in all. Did each crate contain some precious artefact, the second piece, or were all but one of them decoys? And the guards all looked the same, certainly from the distance at which Ezio would be obliged to shadow them.

Just as Ezio prepared to break cover and follow, he noticed another man watching what was going on from a similar vantage-point to his own. He suppressed an involuntary gasp as he recognized this second man as his uncle, Mario Auditore; but there was no time to hail or challenge him, as the Borgia-trooper carrying the crate had already moved off with his guard. Ezio pursued them at a safe distance. However, a question nagged him – had the other man really been his uncle? And if so, how had he got to Venice, and why, at this precise moment?

But he had to put the notion away as he tailed the Borgia guards, concentrating hard to keep the one with the original crate in his line of sight — if that indeed were the one that contained — whatever it was. One of the 'Pieces of Eden'?

The guards arrived at a square which had five streets leading off it. Each crate-carrying guard, with his escort, here set off in a different direction. Ezio swarmed up the side of a nearby building so that he could follow the course of each guard from the rooftops. Watching them keenly, he saw one of them leave his escort and turn into the courtyard of a solid-looking brick building, place his crate on the ground there, and open it. He was quickly joined by a Borgia sergeant. Ezio bounded over the roofs to hear what was being said between them.

'The Master awaits,' the sergeant was saying. 'Repackage it with care. Now!'

Ezio watched as the guard transferred an object wrapped carefully in straw from the crate to a teak box brought to him from the building by a servant. Ezio thought fast. The Master! In his experience, when Templar minions mentioned that title it could only refer to one man — Rodrigo Borgia! They were clearly repacking the true artefact in an attempt to double their security. But now Ezio knew exactly which guard to target.

He slipped down to street level again and cornered the trooper carrying the teak box. The sergeant had left to rejoin the escort of Cardinal's guards, waiting outside the courtyard. Ezio had a minute to slit the throat of the trooper, pull the body out of sight, and don his outer uniform, cape and helmet.

He was about to shoulder the box when the temptation to have a quick glance inside it overwhelmed him and he lifted the lid. But at that moment the sergeant re-appeared at the gateway of the courtyard.

'Get a move on!'

'Yessir!' said Ezio.

'Just look fucking lively. This is probably the most important thing you'll do in your life. Do you get me?'

'Yessir.'

Ezio took his place at the centre of his escort and the detail set off.

They made their way through the city north from the Molo to the Campo dei Santi Giovanni e Paolo, where Messer Verrocchio's recent and massive equestrian statue of the *condottiero* Colleone dominated the square. Following the Fondamenta dei Mendicanti north again, they arrived at last at a dull-looking house in a terrace overlooking the canal. The sergeant knocked on the door with the pommel of his sword, and it immediately swung open. The group of guards hustled Ezio in first, and followed, and the door closed behind them. Heavy bolts were shot across it.

They were facing an ivy-festooned loggia, in which a beak-nosed man in his mid to late fifties sat, dressed in robes of dusty purple velvet. The men saluted. Ezio did so too, trying not to meet the icy cobalt eyes he knew too well. The Spaniard!

Rodrigo Borgia spoke to the sergeant. 'Is it really here? You were not followed?'

'No, *Altezza*. Everything went perfectly –'

'Go on!'

The sergeant cleared his throat. 'We followed your orders exactly as specified. The mission to Cyprus was more difficult than we had anticipated. There were . . . complications at the outset. Certain adherents to the Cause . . . had to be abandoned in the interests of our success. But we have returned with the artefact. And have transported it to you with all due care, as *Su Altezza* instructed. And according to our agreement, *Altezza*, we now look forward to being generously recompensed.'

Ezio knew that he could not allow the teak box and its contents to fall into the hands of the Cardinal. At that moment, when the unpleasant but necessary subject of payment for services rendered had come up, and as usual the supplier had to nudge the client for the cash due for the special duties undertaken, Ezio grasped his opportunity. Like so many rich people, the Cardinal could be miserly when the time came for handing over money. Unspringing the poison-blade on his right forearm and the double-bladed dagger on his left, Ezio cut down the sergeant, a single stab to the man's exposed neck enough to deliver the deadly venom to his bloodstream. Ezio quickly turned on the five guards of the escort with his double-dagger in one hand, and the poison-blade under his right wrist, spinning like a dervish, using quick, clinical movements to deliver single lethal blows. Moments later, all the guards lay dead at his feet.

Rodrigo Borgia looked down at him, sighing heavily. 'Ezio Auditore. Well, well. It's been some time.' The Cardinal seemed completely unruffled.

'*Cardinale.*' Ezio gave an ironic bow.

'Give it to me,' said Rodrigo, indicating the box.

'Tell me first where he is.'

'Where who is?'

'Your Prophet!' Ezio looked around. 'It doesn't look as if anyone's shown up.' He paused. More seriously, he continued: 'How many people have died for this? For what's in this box? And look! There's *nobody* here!'

Rodrigo chuckled. A sound like bones rattling. 'You claim not to be a Believer,' he said. 'And yet here you are. Do you not see the Prophet? He is already present! *I am the Prophet!*'

Ezio's grey eyes widened. The man was possessed! But what curious madness was this, which seemed to transcend the rational and the natural courses of life itself? Alas, Ezio's pondering left him momentarily off-guard. The Spaniard drew a *schiavona*, a light but deadly-looking sword, with a cat's-head pommel, from his robes and leapt from the loggia, aiming the thin sword at Ezio's throat. 'Give me the Apple,' he snarled.

'That's what's in this box? An *apple*? It must be a pretty special one,' said Ezio, while in his mind his uncle's voice reverberated: *a piece of Eden.* 'Come and take it from me!'

Rodrigo sliced at Ezio with his blade, slashing his tunic and drawing blood at the first pass.

'Are you alone, Ezio? Where are your Assassin friends now?'

'I don't need their help to deal with you!'

Ezio used his daggers to cut and slash, and his left-forearm guard-brace to parry Rodrigo's blows. But, though he landed no cut with the poison-blade, his double-blade stabbed through the velvet robe of the Cardinal and he saw it stained with the man's blood.

'You little shit,' bellowed Rodrigo, in pain. 'I can see that I'll need help to master you! Guards! Guards!'

Suddenly, a dozen armed men bearing the Borgia crest on their tunics stormed into the courtyard where Ezio and the Cardinal were confronting one another. Ezio knew there was precious little poison left in the hilt of his right-hand dagger. He leapt back, the better to defend himself against Rodrigo's reinforcements, and at that moment one of the new guards stooped to sweep the teak box off the ground and hand it to his Master.

'Thank you, *uomo coraggioso*!'

Ezio, meanwhile, was seriously outmatched, but he fought with a strategic coldness born of an absolute desire to recapture the box and its contents. Sheathing his Codex blades, he reached for his bandolier of throwing-knives and shot them from his hands with deadly accuracy, first bringing down the *uomo coraggioso* and then, with a second knife, knocking the box from Rodrigo's gnarled hands.

The Spaniard bent to pick it up again and make his retreat, when – *shoof!* – another throwing-knife hurtled through the air to clatter against a stone column inches from the Cardinal's face. But this knife had not been thrown by Ezio.

Ezio whirled round to see a familiar, jovial, bearded figure behind him. Older, perhaps, and greyer, and heavier, but no less deft. 'Uncle Mario!' he exclaimed. 'I knew I'd seen you earlier!'

'Can't let you have all the fun,' said Mario. 'And don't worry, *nipote*. You are not alone!'

But a Borgia guard was bearing down on Ezio, halberd raised. The moment before he could deliver the crushing blow which would have sent Ezio into an endless night, a crossbow bolt appeared as if by magic, buried in the man's forehead. He dropped his weapon and fell forwards, a look of disbelief etched on his face. Ezio looked round again and saw – *La Volpe*!

'What are you doing here, Fox?'

'We heard you might need some back-up,' said the Fox, reloading quickly as more guards began to pour out of the building. It was as well that more reinforcements, in the shape of Antonio and Bartolomeo, appeared on Ezio's side.

'Don't let Borgia get away with that box!' yelled Antonio.

Bartolomeo was using his greatsword Bianca like a scythe, cutting a swathe through the ranks of guards as they tried to overpower him by sheer force of numbers. And gradually the tide of battle turned back in favour of the Assassins and their allies.

'We've got them covered now, *nipote*,' called Mario. 'Look to the Spaniard!'

Ezio turned to see Rodrigo making for a doorway at the rear of the loggia and hastened to cut him off, but the Cardinal, sword in hand, was ready for him. 'This is a losing battle for you, my boy,' he snarled. 'You cannot stop what is written! You'll die by my hand like your father and your brothers —for death is the fate that awaits all who attempt to defy the Templars.'

Nevertheless, Rodrigo's voice lacked conviction and, looking round, Ezio saw that the last of his guards had fallen. He blocked Rodrigo's retreat at the threshold of the doorway, raising his own sword and preparing to strike, saying, 'This is for my father!' But the Cardinal ducked the blow, knocking Ezio off balance, yet dropping the precious box as he darted through the doorway to save his skin.

'Make no mistake,' he said balefully as he left. 'I live

to fight another day! And then I'll make sure your death is as painful as it will be slow.'

And he was gone.

Ezio, winded, was trying to catch his breath and struggle to his feet when a woman's hand reached down to help him. Looking up, he saw that the owner of the hand was – Paola!

'He's gone,' she said, smiling. 'But it doesn't matter. We have what we came for.'

'No! Did you hear what he said? I must get after him and finish this!'

'Calm yourself,' said another woman, coming up. It was Teodora. Looking round the assembled company, Ezio could see all his allies, Mario, the Fox, Antonio, Bartolomeo, Paola and Teodora. And there was someone else. A pale, dark-haired young man with a thoughtful, humorous face.

'What are you all doing here?' asked Ezio, sensing a tension among them.

'Perhaps the same thing as you, Ezio,' said the young stranger. 'Hoping to see the Prophet appear.'

Ezio was confused and irritated. 'No! I came here to kill the Spaniard! I couldn't care less about your Prophet – if he exists at all. He certainly isn't here.'

'Isn't he?' The young man paused, looking steadily at Ezio. '*You* are.'

'What?'

'A prophet's arrival was foretold. And here you have

been among us for so long without our guessing the truth. All along you were the One we sought.'

'I don't understand. Who are you, anyway?'

The young man sketched a bow. 'My name is Niccolò di Bernardo dei Machiavelli. I am a member of the Order of the Assassins, trained in the ancient ways, to safeguard the future of mankind. Just like you, just like every man and woman here.'

Ezio was astounded, looking from one face to the next. 'Is this true, Uncle Mario?' he said at last.

'Yes, my boy,' said Mario, stepping forward. 'We have all been guiding you, for years, teaching you all the skills you'd need to join our ranks.'

Ezio's head filled with questions. He did not know where to begin. 'I must ask you for news of my family,' he said to Mario. 'My mother, my sister . . .'

Mario smiled. 'You are right to do so. They are safe and well. And they are no longer at the convent but at home with me at Monteriggioni. Maria will always be touched by the sadness of her loss, but she has much to console herself with now as she devotes herself to charitable work alongside the abbess. As for Claudia, the abbess could see, long before she could herself, that the life of a nun was not ideal for one of her temperament, and that there were other ways in which she might seek to serve Our Lord. She was released from her vows. She married my senior captain and soon, Ezio, she will present you with a nephew or niece of your own.'

'Excellent news, Uncle. I never quite liked the idea of Claudia spending her life in a convent. But I have so many more questions to ask you.'

'There will be a time for questions soon,' said Machiavelli.

'Much remains to be done before we can see our loved ones again, and celebrate,' said Mario. 'And it may be that we never will. We made Rodrigo abandon his box but he will not rest until it is back in his possession, so we must guard it with our lives.'

Ezio looked around the circle of Assassins, and noticed for the first time that each of them had a brand around the base of his or her left ring finger. But there was clearly no time for further questions now. Mario said to his associates, 'I think it is time . . .' Gravely, they nodded their assent, and Antonio took out a map and unfolded it, showing Ezio a point marked on it.

'Meet us here at sunset,' he said, in a tone of solemn command.

'Come,' said Mario to the others.

Machiavelli took charge of the box with its precious, mysterious contents, and the Assassins filed silently out into the street and departed, leaving Ezio alone.

Venice was eerily empty that evening and the great square in front of the basilica was silent and unoccupied save for the pigeons which were its permanent denizens. The bell tower rose to a giddying height above Ezio's head as he began to climb it, but he did not hesitate. The meeting to which he'd been summoned would surely provide him with the answers to some of his questions, and though he knew in his heart of hearts that he would find some of the answers frightening, he also knew that he could not turn his back on them.

As he approached the top he could hear muted voices. At last he reached the stonework at the very top of the tower and swung himself into the bell-loft. A circular space had been cleared and the seven Assassins, all wearing cowls, were ranged around its perimeter, while a fire in a small brazier burned at its centre.

Paola took him by the hand and led him to the centre as Mario began to utter an incantation:

'*Laa shay'a waqi'un moutlaq bale koulon moumkine* . . . These are the words, spoken by our ancestors, that lie at the heart of our Creed . . .'

Machiavelli stepped forward and looked hard at Ezio. 'Where other men blindly follow the truth, remember –'

And Ezio picked up the rest of the words as if he had known them all his life: '– Nothing is true.'

'Where other men are limited by morality or law,' continued Machiavelli, 'remember –'

'– Everything is permitted.'

Machiavelli said, 'We work in the dark, to serve the light. We are Assassins.'

And the others joined in, intoning in unison: 'Nothing is true, everything is permitted. Nothing is true, everything is permitted. Nothing is true, everything is permitted . . .'

When they had finished, Mario took Ezio's left hand. 'It is time,' he told him. 'In this modern age, we are not so literal as our ancestors. We do not demand the sacrifice of a finger. But the seal we mark ourselves with is permanent.' He drew in his breath. 'Are you ready to join us?'

Ezio, as if in a dream, but somehow knowing what to do and what was to come, extended his hand unhesitatingly. 'I am,' he said.

Antonio moved to the brazier and from it drew a red-hot branding-iron ending in two small semi-circles which could be brought together by means of a lever in the handle. Then he took Ezio's hand and isolated the ring finger. 'This only hurts for a while, brother,' he said. 'Like so many things.'

He inserted the branding-iron over the finger and squeezed the red-hot metal semi-circles together around its base. It seared the flesh and there was a burning smell but Ezio did not flinch. Antonio quickly removed the branding-iron and put it safely to one side. Then the Assassins removed their hoods and gathered round him. Uncle Mario clapped him proudly on the back. Teodora produced a little glass phial containing a clear, thick liquid, which she delicately rubbed on the ring burnt for ever on to Ezio's finger. 'This will soothe it,' she said. 'We are proud of you.'

Then Machiavelli stood in front of him and gave him a meaningful nod. '*Benvenuto*, Ezio. You are one of us now. It only remains to conclude your initiation ceremony, and then – then, my friend, we have serious work to do!'

With that, he glanced over the edge of the bell-tower. Far below, a number of bales of hay had been stacked a short distance away in various locations around the campanile – horse-fodder destined for the Ducal Palace. It seemed impossible to Ezio that from this height anyone could direct their fall accurately enough to land on one of those tiny targets, but that is what Machiavelli now did, his cloak flying in the wind as he leapt. His companions followed suit, and Ezio watched with a mixture of horror and admiration as each made perfect landings and then gathered, looking up at him with what he hoped were encouraging expressions on their faces.

Used as he was to bounding over rooftops, he had never faced a leap of faith from such a height as this. The hay-bales seemed the size of slices of polenta, but he knew that there was no other way for him to reach the ground again but this; and that the longer he hesitated, the harder it would be. He took two or three deep breaths and then cast himself outwards and downwards into the night, arms aloft in a perfect swallow dive.

The fall seemed to take hours and the wind whistled past his ears, ruffling and shaking his clothing and his hair. Then the hay-bales rushed up to meet him. At the last moment, he shut his eyes . . .

. . . And crashed down into the hay! All the breath was knocked from his body, but as he got shakily to his feet he found that nothing was broken, and that he was, in fact, elated.

Mario came up to him, Teodora at his side. 'I think he'll do, don't you?' Mario asked Teodora.

The middle of that evening found Mario, Machiavelli and Ezio sitting around the big trestle table in Leonardo's workshop. The peculiar artefact which Rodrigo Borgia had set so much store by lay before them, and they all regarded it with curiosity and awe.

'It's fascinating,' Leonardo was saying. 'Absolutely fascinating.'

'What is it, Leonardo?' asked Ezio. 'What does it do?'

Leonardo said, 'Well, so far, I'm stumped. It contains dark secrets, and its design is unlike anything, I would guess, ever seen on earth before – I've certainly never seen such sophisticated design . . . And I could no more *explain* this than explain to you why the earth goes round the sun.'

'Surely you mean, "the sun goes round the earth"?' said Mario, giving Leonardo an odd look. But Leonardo continued to examine the machine, carefully turning it in his hands, and as he did so, it started to glow in response, with a ghostly, inner, self-generated light.

'It's made of materials that really shouldn't, in all logic, exist,' Leonardo went on, wonderingly. 'And yet this is clearly a very ancient device.'

'It's certainly referred to in the Codex pages we have,' put in Mario. 'I recognize it from its description there. The Codex calls it "a Piece of Eden".'

'And Rodrigo called it "the Apple",' added Ezio.

Leonardo looked at him sharply. 'As in the apple from the Tree of Knowledge? The apple Eve gave to Adam?'

They all turned to look at the object again. It had begun to glow more brightly, and with a hypnotic effect. Ezio felt increasingly impelled, for reasons which he couldn't fathom, to reach out and touch it. He could feel no heat coming from it, and yet along with the fascination there came a sense of inherent danger, as if to touch it might send bolts of lightning through him. He was unaware of the others; it seemed as if the world around him had grown dark and cold, and nothing existed any more outside himself and this . . . thing.

He watched as his hand moved forwards, as if it were no longer a part of him, as if he had no control over it, and at last it placed itself firmly on the artefact's smooth side.

The first reaction he had was one of shock. The Apple looked metallic, but to the touch it was warm and soft, like a woman's skin, as if it were *alive*! But there was no time to ponder that, for his hand was thrown free, and the following instant the glow from within the device, which had been steadily getting brighter, suddenly burst into a blinding kaleidoscope of light and colour, within whose whirling chaos Ezio could make out forms. For a moment he wrenched his eyes from it to look at his companions. Mario and Machiavelli had turned away, their eyes screwed up, their hands covering their heads in fear or pain. Leonardo stood transfixed, eyes wide, mouth open in awe. Looking back, Ezio saw the forms begin to coalesce. A great garden appeared, filled with monstrous creatures; there was a dark city on fire, huge clouds in the shape of mushrooms and bigger than cathedrals or palaces; an army on the march, but an army unlike any Ezio had ever seen or even imagined could exist; starving people in striped uniforms driven into brick buildings by men with whips and dogs; tall chimneys belching smoke; spiralling stars and planets; men in weird armour rolling in the blackness of space – and there, too, was another Ezio, another Leonardo, and Mario and Machiavelli, and more and more of them, the dupes of Time itself, tumbling helplessly over and over in the air, the playthings of a mighty wind, which now indeed seemed to roar around the room they were in.

'Make it stop!' someone bellowed.

Ezio gritted his teeth, and, without precisely knowing why, holding his right wrist in his left hand, forced his right hand back into contact with the thing.

Instantly, it ceased. The room resumed its normal

features and proportions. The men looked at each other. Not a hair was out of place. Leonardo's eyeglasses were still on his nose. The Apple sat on the table inert, a plain little object that few would have given a second glance to.

Leonardo was the first to speak. 'This must *never* fall into the wrong hands,' he said. 'It would drive weaker minds insane . . .'

'I agree,' said Machiavelli. 'I could hardly stand it, hardly believe its power. Carefully, after putting on gloves, he picked up the Apple and repacked it in its box, sealing the lid securely.

'Do you think the Spaniard knows what this thing does? Do you think he can control it?'

'He must *never* have it,' said Machiavelli in a voice of granite. He handed the box to Ezio. 'You must take charge of this and protect it with all the skills we have taught you.'

Ezio took the box carefully from him and nodded.

'Take it to Forlì,' Mario said. 'The citadel there is walled, protected by cannon, and it is in the hands of one of our greatest allies.'

'And who is that?' asked Ezio.

'Her name is Caterina Sforza.'

Ezio smiled. 'I remember now . . . an old acquaintance, and one which I shall be happy to renew.'

'Then make your preparations to leave.'

'I will accompany you,' said Machiavelli.

'I shall be grateful for that,' Ezio smiled. He turned to Leonardo. 'And what about you, *amico mio*?'

'Me? When my work here is done I'll return to Milan. The Duke there is good to me.'

'You must come to Monteriggioni too, when you're next in Florence and have time,' said Mario.

Ezio looked at his best friend. 'Goodbye, Leonardo. I hope our paths cross again one day.'

'I am sure they will,' said Leonardo. 'And if you need me, Agniolo in Florence will always know where to find me.'

Ezio embraced him. 'Farewell.'

'A parting gift,' said Leonardo, handing him a bag. 'Bullets and powder for your little *pistola*, and a nice big phial of poison for that useful dagger of yours. I hope you won't need them, but it's important to me to know that you're as well protected as possible.

Ezio looked at him with emotion. 'Thank you – thank you for everything, my oldest friend.'

22

After a long, uneventful journey by galley from Venice, Ezio and Machiavelli arrived at the wetlands port near Ravenna, where they were met by Caterina herself and some of her entourage.

'They sent me word by courier that you were on your way, so I thought I'd come down and accompany you back to Forlì myself,' she said. 'You were wise, I think, to make the journey in one of Doge Agostino's galleys, for the roads are often unsafe and we have trouble with brigands. Not, I think,' she added, casting an appreciative eye over Ezio, 'that they would have given *you* much trouble.'

'I am honoured that you remember me, *Signora.*'

'Well, it has been a long time, but you certainly make an impression.' She turned to Machiavelli. 'It's good to see you again too, Niccolò.'

'You two know each other?' asked Ezio.

'Niccolò's been able to advise me . . . on certain matters of state.' She changed the subject. 'And now I hear that you've become a fully fledged Assassin. Congratulations.'

They'd arrived at Caterina's carriage but she told her

servants that she preferred to ride, it being a delightful day and the distance not great. The horses were duly saddled and after they had mounted Caterina bade Ezio ride beside her.

'You're going to love Forlì. And you will be safe there. Our cannon have protected the city well for over a century and the citadel is all but impregnable.'

'Forgive me, *Signora*, but there is one thing which intrigues me –'

'Please tell me what it is.'

'I've never heard of a woman ruling a city-state before. I am impressed.'

Caterina smiled. 'Well, it was in my husband's hands before, of course. Do you remember him? A little? Girolamo.' She paused. 'Well, he died –'

'I am so sorry.'

'Don't be,' she said simply. 'I had him assassinated.'

Ezio tried to conceal his amazement.

'It was like this,' put in Machiavelli. 'We found out that Girolamo Riario was working for the Templars. He was in the process of completing a map which shows the locations of the remaining unretrieved Codex pages –'

'I never liked the goddamned son-of-a-bitch, anyway,' said Caterina flatly. 'He was a lousy father, boring in bed, and a general all-round pain in the arse.' She paused reflectively. 'Mind you, I've had a couple of other husbands since – rather overrated, if you ask me.'

They were interrupted by the sight of a riderless

horse coming towards them at the gallop. Caterina dispatched one of her outriders to go after it, and the rest of the party carried on towards Forlì, but now the Sforza retainers had their swords drawn. Soon they came upon an overturned wagon, its wheels still spinning in the air, surrounded by dead bodies.

Caterina's brow darkened, and she spurred her horse on, closely followed by Ezio and Machiavelli.

A little further down the road, they encountered a group of local peasants, some wounded, making their way towards them.

'What's going on?' Caterina accosted a woman at the head of the group.

'*Altezza*,' said the woman, tears pouring down her face. 'They came almost as soon as you had left. They're preparing to lay siege to the city!'

'Who are?'

'The Orsi brothers, *Madonna*!'

'*Sangue di Giuda!*'

'Who are the Orsi?' asked Ezio.

'The same bastards I hired to kill Girolamo,' spat Caterina.

'The Orsi work for anyone who'll pay them,' observed Machiavelli. 'They're not very bright, but unfortunately they have a reputation for getting a job done.' He paused in thought. 'The Spaniard'll be behind this.'

'But how could he possibly know where we were taking the Apple?'

'They're not looking for the Apple, Ezio; they're after Riario's Map. The Map is still in Forlì. Rodrigo needs to know where the other Codex pages are concealed, and we cannot afford to let him get his hands on the Map!'

'Never mind the Map,' cried Caterina. 'My children are in the city. Ah, *porco demonio!*'

They kicked their horses into a gallop until they came within sight of the town. Smoke was rising from within the walls and they could see the city gates were closed. Men stood along the outer ramparts under the bear-and-bush crest of the Orsi family. But inside the town, the citadel on its hill still flew the flag of the Sforza.

'It looks as if they've gained control of at least part of Forlì, but not the citadel,' said Machiavelli.

'Double-crossing bastards!' spat Caterina.

'Is there a way I can get into the city without their seeing me?' asked Ezio, gathering up his Codex weapons and strapping them on in readiness, keeping the gun and the spring-blade in his satchel.

'There's a possibility, *caro*,' said Caterina. 'But it'll be hard. There's an old tunnel that leads under the western wall from the canal.'

'Then I'll try,' said Ezio. 'Be ready. If I can get the city gates open from the inside, be prepared to ride like hell. If we can reach the citadel and your people there see your crest and let you in, we'll be safe enough to plan the next move.'

'Which will be to string these cretins up and watch them dangle in the wind,' growled Caterina. 'But go on, Ezio, and good luck! I'll think of something to distract the Orsi troops' attention.'

Ezio dismounted and ran round to the western walls, keeping low and taking cover behind hillocks and bushes. Meanwhile Caterina stood up in her stirrups and bawled at the enemy within the city walls: 'Hey, you! I'm talking to *you*, you spineless *dogs*. You occupy *my* city? *My* home? And you really think I'm going to do nothing about it? Why, I'm coming up there to rip off your *coglioni* – if you've got any, that is!'

Groups of soldiers had appeared on the ramparts now, looking across at Caterina, half-amused, half-intimidated as she kept it up: 'What kind of men are you? Doing the bidding of your paymasters for handfuls of loose change! I wonder if you'll think it was worth it after I've come up there, cut your heads off, pissed down your necks and shoved your faces up my *figa*! I'll stick your balls on a fork and roast them over my kitchen fire! How does *that* sound?'

By now there were no men on watch along the western ramparts. Ezio found the canal unguarded, and, swimming down it, he located the overgrown entrance of the tunnel. Slipping out of the water, he plunged into the tunnel's black depths.

It was well maintained inside, and dry, and all he had to do was follow it until he saw light at its other end.

He approached it cautiously, and as he did so Caterina's voice came to him again. The tunnel ended in a short flight of stone steps which led up into a back room on the ground floor of one of the western towers of Forlì. It was deserted, Caterina had collected quite a crowd. Through a window he could see most of the Orsi troops' backs, as they watched, and even occasionally applauded, Caterina's performance.

'. . . if I were a man I'd wipe those grins off your faces! But don't think I won't give it my best shot anyway. Don't be misled by the fact that I've got tits –' A thought struck her. 'I bet you'd like to see them, wouldn't you? I bet you wish you could touch them, lick them, give 'em a squeeze! Well, why don't you come down here and try? I'd kick your balls so hard they'd fly out through your nostrils! *Luridi branco di cani bastardi!* You'd better pack up and go home while you still can – if you don't want to be impaled and stuck up all along my citadel walls! Ah! But maybe I'm wrong! Maybe you'd actually *enjoy* having a long oaken pole up your arses! You disgust me – I even begin to wonder if you're worth the bother. I've never seen such a piss-poor shower of shite. *Che vista penosa!* I can't see that it'd make much difference to you as *men* even if I had you castrated.'

By now Ezio was in the street. He could see the gate closest to where Caterina and Machiavelli were located. At the top of its arch a bowman stood by the heavy lever which operated it. Moving as silently and as quickly as he could, he shinned up to the top of the arch and stabbed the soldier once in the neck, dispatching him instantly. Then he threw all his weight on to the lever, and the gates below swung open with a mighty groan.

Machiavelli had been watching carefully all this time, and as soon as he saw the gates opening, he leant over and spoke softly to Caterina, who immediately spurred her horse forward at a frantic gallop, closely followed by Machiavelli and the rest of her entourage. As soon as they saw what was happening, the Orsi troops on the ramparts let out a yell of anger and started to swarm down to intercept, but the Sforza faction was too quick for them. Ezio seized the bow and arrows from the dead guard and used them to fell three Orsi men before he swiftly climbed a nearby wall and started to run over the city's rooftops, keeping pace with Caterina and her group as they rode through the narrow streets towards the citadel.

The deeper they went into the city, the greater was the confusion that reigned. It was clear that the battle for control of Forlì was far from over, as knots of soldiers under the banner of the blue snakes and black eagles of the Sforza fought the Orsi mercenaries, as ordinary citizens rushed for shelter in their houses or simply ran aimlessly hither and yon in the confusion. Market-stalls were overturned, chickens ran squawking underfoot, a small child sat in the mud and bawled for its mother, who ran out and snatched it to safety; and all around the noise of battle roared. Ezio, leaping from roof to roof, could see something of the lie of the land from his vantage-point, and used his arrows with deadly accuracy to protect Caterina and Machiavelli whenever Orsi guards got too close to them.

At last, they arrived in a broad piazza in front of the citadel. It was empty, and the streets leading off it appeared deserted. Ezio descended and rejoined his people. There was nobody on the citadel's battlements, and its massive gate was firmly closed. It looked every bit as impregnable as Caterina had said it was.

She looked up, and cried: 'Open up, you bloody parcel of fools! It's me! *La Duchessa!* Get your arses in gear!'

Now some of her men in the citadel did appear above them, among them a captain who said, '*Subito, Altezza!*' and issued orders to three men who disappeared immediately to open the gate. But at that instant, howling for blood, dozens of Orsi troops poured from the surrounding streets into the square, blocking any retreat and pinning Caterina's company between them and the unforgiving wall of the citadel.

'Bloody ambush!' shouted Machiavelli, with Ezio rallying their own handful of men, and keeping between Caterina and their enemies.

'*Aprite la porta! Aprite!*' yelled Caterina. And at last the mighty gates swung open. Sforza guards rushed out to aid them, and, slashing at the Orsi in vicious hand-to-hand

405

fighting, beat a retreat back through the gates, which quickly slammed shut behind them. Ezio and Machiavelli (who had quickly dismounted) both leaned against the wall, side by side and breathing hard. They could scarcely believe that they had made it. Caterina dismounted too, but didn't rest for an instant. Instead she ran across the inner courtyard to a doorway in which two little boys and a wet-nurse holding a baby were waiting fearfully.

The children ran to her and she embraced them, greeting them by name, 'Cesare, Giovanni – *no preoccuparvi.*' She stroked the baby's head, cooing, '*Salute*, Galeazzo.' Then she looked around, and at the wet-nurse.

'Nezetta! Where are Bianca and Ottaviano?'

'Forgive me, my lady. They were playing outside when the attack began and we haven't been able to find them since.'

Caterina, looking frightened, was about to reply when suddenly a huge roar went up from the Orsi troops outside the citadel. The Sforza captain came rushing up to Ezio and Machiavelli. 'They're bringing in reinforcements from the mountains,' he reported. 'I don't know how long we'll be able to hold out.' He turned to a lieutenant. 'To the battlements! Man the cannon!'

The lieutenant rushed off to organize gun-crews, and these were hurrying to their positions when a hail of arrows fired by Orsi archers started to descend on the inner courtyard and the ramparts above. Caterina hustled her younger children to safety, shouting to Ezio at the same time, 'Look after the cannon! They're our only hope! Don't let those bastards breach the citadel!'

'Come!' shouted Machiavelli. Ezio followed him up to where the cannon were ranged.

Several of the gun-crews were dead, along with the captain and the lieutenant. Others were wounded. The survivors were struggling to trim and angle the heavy cannon to bring them to bear on the Orsi men in the square below. Huge numbers of reinforcements had come up, and Ezio could see that they were manhandling siege-engines and catapults through the streets. Meanwhile, directly below, a contingent of Orsi troops were bringing up a battering-ram. If he and Machiavelli didn't think of something quickly there would be no chance of saving the citadel, but to withstand this new assault he would have to fire the cannon at targets within the walls of Forlì itself, and so risk injuring or even killing some of its innocent citizens. Leaving Machiavelli to organize the gunners, he raced down to the courtyard and sought out Caterina.

'They are storming the city. To keep them at bay I must fire the cannon at targets within its walls.'

She looked at him with steely calm. 'Then do what you must do.'

He looked up to the ramparts where Machiavelli stood, waiting for the signal. Ezio raised his arm, and lowered it decisively.

The cannon roared, and even as they did so Ezio was flying back up to the ramparts where they were located. Directing the gunners to fire at will, he watched as first one siege-engine and then another was blown to bits, as well as the catapults. There was little room for the Orsi troops to manoeuvre in the narrow streets and after the cannon had wreaked their havoc, Sforza archers and crossbowmen began to pick off the surviving invaders within the city walls. At last, the remaining Orsi troops had been driven out of Forlì altogether, and those Sforza troops who had survived outside the citadel itself were able to secure the outer curtain walls. But the victory had come at a cost. Several houses within the city were smouldering ruins, and in order to win it back, Caterina's gunners had not been able to avoid killing some of their own people. And there was something else to consider, as Machiavelli was quick to point out. They had flushed the enemy out of the city, but they had not raised the siege. Forlì was still surrounded by Orsi battalions, cut off from supplies of fresh food and water; and Caterina's two older children were still out there somewhere, at risk.

Some little time later, Caterina, Machiavelli and Ezio were standing on the ramparts of the outer walls surveying the host encamped around them. Behind them, the citizens of Forlì were doing their best to put the city back in order, but food and water wouldn't last for ever and everyone knew it. Caterina was haggard, worried to death about her missing children – Bianca, the older, was nine, and Ottaviano a year younger.

They had yet to encounter the Orsi brothers themselves, but that very day a herald appeared at the centre of the enemy army and blew a clarion call. The troops parted like the sea to allow two men riding chestnut horses and dressed in chain-steel hauberks to pass between them, accompanied by pages bearing the crest of the bear-and-bush. They reined in well out of arrow range.

One of the horsemen stood up in his stirrups and raised his voice. 'Caterina! Caterina Sforza! We think you are still cooped up in your dear little city, Caterina – so answer me!'

Caterina leant over the battlements, a wild expression on her face. 'What do you want?'

The man grinned broadly. 'Oh, nothing. I was just wondering if you were missing . . . any children!'

Ezio had taken up a position at Caterina's side. The man who was speaking looked up at him in surprise. 'Well, well,' he said. 'Ezio Auditore, if I am not mistaken. How pleasant to meet you. One has heard so much about you.'

'And you, I take it, are the *fratelli* Orsi,' Ezio said.

The one who had not yet spoken raised a hand. 'The same. Lodovico –'

'– and Checco,' said the other. 'At your service!' He gave a dry laugh.

'*Basta!*' cried Caterina. 'Enough of this! Where are my *children*? Let them *go!*'

Lodovico bowed ironically in the saddle. '*Ma certo, Signora.* We'll happily give them back. In exchange for something of yours. Something, rather, that belonged to your late lamented husband. Something he was working on, on behalf of . . . some friends of ours.' His voice suddenly hardened. 'I mean a certain Map!'

'And a certain Apple, too,' added Checco. 'Oh yes, we know all about that. Do you think we are fools? Do you think our employer doesn't have spies?'

'Yes,' said Lodovico. 'We'll have the Apple too. Or shall I slice your little ones' throats from ear to ear and send them to join their pappa?'

Caterina stood listening. Her mood had changed to one of icy calm. When her turn came to speak, she cried, '*Bastardi!* You think you can intimidate me with your vulgar threats? You scum! I'll give you *nothing!* You want my children? Take them! I have the means to make more!' And she raised her skirts to show them her vagina.

'I'm not interested in your histrionics, Caterina,' said Checco, wheeling his horse around. 'And I'm not interested in staring at your *figa* either. You'll change your mind, but we're only giving you an hour. Your brats will be safe enough until then in that slummy little village of yours just down the road. And don't forget – we *will* kill them and then we *will* come back and smash your city and take what we want by force – so you just take advantage of our generosity and we can all save ourselves a lot of bother.'

And the brothers rode off. Caterina collapsed against the rough wall of the rampart, breathing heavily through her mouth, in shock at what she'd just said and done.

Ezio was by her side. 'You're not going to sacrifice your children, Caterina. No Cause could ever be worth that.'

'To save the world?' She looked at him, lips parted, pale blue eyes wide under her mane of red hair.

'We cannot become people like them,' said Ezio simply. 'There are some compromises which cannot be made.'

'Oh, Ezio! That is what I expected you to say!' She flung her arms round his neck. 'Of course we can't sacrifice them, my darling!' She stood back. 'But I cannot ask you to take the risk of getting them back for me.'

'Try me,' said Ezio. He turned to Machiavelli. 'I won't be gone long – I hope. But whatever happens to me, I know you will guard the Apple with your life. And Caterina –'

'Yes?'

'Do you know where Girolamo hid the Map?'

'I'll find it.'

'Do so, and protect it.'

'And what will you do about the Orsi?' asked Machiavelli.

'They are already added to my list,' said Ezio. 'They belong to the company of men who killed my kinsmen and destroyed my family. But I now see that there is a greater Cause to be served than mere revenge.' The two men shook hands and their eyes locked.

'*Buona fortuna, amico mio*,' said Machiavelli sternly.

'*Buona fortuna anche*.'

It wasn't hard to reach the village whose identity Checco had so carelessly given away, even if his description of it as a slum had been a little ungracious. It was small and poor, like most serf-villages in the Romagna, and it showed signs of having recently been flooded by its nearby river; but on the whole it was neat and clean, the houses roughly whitewashed and the thatch new. Although the water-logged road that divided the dozen or so houses was still mired from the flood, everything suggested order, if not contentment, and industry, if not happiness. The only thing which distinguished Santa Salvaza from a peacetime village was that it was peppered with Orsi men-at-arms. No wonder, mused Ezio, that Checco thought he could afford to mention where he was holding Bianca and Otta-viano. The next question was, where exactly in the village might Caterina's children be located?

Ezio, having armed himself this time with the double-blade on his left forearm with his metal arm-guard, and the *pistola* on his right, as well as a light arming-sword hung from his belt, was dressed simply in a peasant's woollen cloak which hung down below his knees. He pulled his hood up to avoid recognition, and, dismounting some way outside the village and keeping a weather-eye out for Orsi scouts, he slung a fardel of kindling borrowed from an outhouse on to his back. Stooping beneath it, he made his way into Santa Salvaza.

The residents of the village tried to go about their business as they normally did, despite the military presence that had been foisted on to them. Naturally, no one was particularly enamoured of the Orsi mercenaries, and Ezio, unnoticed by the latter but almost instantly recognized as a stranger by the locals, was able to gain their support in his mission. He made his way to a house at the end of the village, larger than the others and set slightly apart. It was there, he'd been told by an old woman carrying water from the river, that one of the children was being held. Ezio was grateful that the Orsi soldiery was pretty thinly spread. Most of the force were busy laying siege to Forlì.

But he knew he had very little time to rescue the children.

The door and windows of the house were firmly shut, but as he made his way round the back, where two wings of the building formed a courtyard, Ezio heard a young, firm voice delivering a severe lecture. He climbed on to the roof and peered down into the courtyard, where

Bianca Sforza, the miniature image of her mother, was giving two surly Orsi guardsmen a dressing-down.

'Are you two sorry-looking specimens all they could rustle up to guard me?' she was saying regally, drawn up to her full height and showing as little fear as her mother would have done. '*Stolti!* It won't be enough! My mamma is fierce and would never let you hurt me. We Sforza women are no shrinking violets, you know! We may look pretty to the eye, but the eyes deceive. As my pappa found out!' She drew breath, and the guards looked at each other nonplussed. 'I hope you don't imagine I'm scared of you either, because if you did you'd be very much mistaken. And if you touch one hair of my little brother's head, my mamma will hunt you down and eat you for breakfast! *Capito?*'

'Just button it, you little fool,' growled the older of the guards. 'Unless you want a clip round the ear!'

'Don't you dare talk to me like that! In any case, it's absurd. You'll never get away with this, and I'll be safe at home within the hour. In fact, I'm getting bored. I'm surprised you don't have anything better to do, while I wait for you to die!'

'All right, that's quite enough,' said the older guard, reaching out to grab her. But at that moment Ezio fired his *pistola* from the rooftop, hitting the soldier squarely in the chest. The man was launched from his feet – crimson blossoming through his tunic even before he hit the ground. Ezio mused for a second that Leonardo's powder mix must be improving. In the flurry of confusion that followed the guard's sudden death, Ezio leapt down from the rooftop, landing with the grace and power of a panther, and with his double-blades quickly rounded on the younger guard, who fumbled in drawing an ugly-looking dagger. Ezio slashed precisely at the man's forearm, shearing through tendons as though they were ribbons. The man's dagger dropped to the ground, sticking point first in the mud – and before he could muster any further defence, Ezio had brought the double-blade under his jaw, stabbing through the soft tissue of the mouth and tongue, into the cavity of the skull. Ezio calmly withdrew the blades, leaving the corpse to slump to the ground.

'Are they the only two?' he asked the undismayed Bianca as he quickly reloaded.

'Yes! And thank you, whoever you are. My mother will see that you are amply rewarded. But they've got my brother Ottaviano too –'

'Do you know where he is?' asked Ezio, swiftly reloading his pistol.

'They've got him in the watchtower – by the ruined bridge! We must hurry!'

'Show me where, and stay very close!'

He followed her out of the house and along the road until they came upon the tower. They were just in time, for there was Lodovico himself, dragging the whimpering Ottaviano along by the scruff of his neck. Ezio could see that the little boy was limping – he must have twisted his ankle.

'You!' shouted Lodovico when he saw Ezio. 'You'd better hand the girl over and go back to your mistress – tell her we'll finish the pair of them if we don't get what we want!'

'I want my mamma,' bawled Ottaviano. 'Let me go you, you big thug!'

'Shut up, *marmocchio*!' Lodovico snarled at him. 'Ezio! Go fetch the Apple and the Map or the kid gets it.'

'I need to pee!' wailed Ottaviano.

'Oh, for God's sake, *chiudi il becco*!'

'Let him go,' said Ezio firmly.

'I'd like to see you make me! You'll never get close enough, you fool! The minute you make a move, I'll slit his throat as easily as winking!'

Lodovico had dragged the little boy in front of him with both hands, but now had to free one hand in order to draw his sword. At that moment Ottaviano tried to break free, but Lodovico grasped him firmly by the wrist. Nevertheless, Ottaviano was no longer between Lodovico and Ezio. Seeing his opportunity, Ezio sprang out his pistol and fired.

Lodovico's enraged expression was transformed to one of disbelief. The ball had hit him in the neck – cutting the jugular. His eyes goggling, he let go of Ottaviano and sank to his knees, clutching his throat

– the blood seeping through his fingers. The boy ran forward to be embraced by his sister.

'Ottaviano! *Stai bene*!' she said, hugging him close.

Ezio moved forward to stand over Lodovico, but not too close. The man hadn't fallen yet and his sword was still in his hand. Blood oozed down on to his jerkin, a trickle becoming a torrent.

'I don't know what Devil's instrument has given you the means to get the better of me, Ezio,' he panted. 'But I am sorry to tell you that you will lose this game whatever you do. We Orsi are not the fools you seem to take us for. If anyone is a fool, you are – you and Caterina!'

'You are the fool,' said Ezio, his voice cold with scorn, 'To die for a bagful of silver. Do you really think it was worth it?'

Lodovico grimaced. 'More than you know, friend. You've been outwitted. And whatever you do now, the Master will gain his prize!' His face contorted in agony at the pain from his wound. The bloodstain had spread. 'You'd better finish me, Ezio, if you have any mercy in you at all.'

'Then die with your pride, Orsi. It means nothing.' Ezio stepped forward and further opened the wound in Lodovico's neck. An instant later, he was no more. Ezio stooped over him and closed his eyes. '*Requiescat in pace*,' he said.

But there was no time to be lost. He returned to the

children, who had been watching wide-eyed. 'Can you walk?' he asked Ottaviano.

'I'll try, but it hurts terribly.'

Ezio knelt and looked. The ankle wasn't twisted, but sprained. He lifted Ottaviano on to his shoulders. 'Courage, little *Duce*,' he said. 'I'll get you both home safe.'

'Can I have a pee first? I really do need to.'

'Be quick.'

Ezio knew it wouldn't be an easy matter to get the children back through the village. It was impossible to disguise them, as they were gorgeously dressed, and in any case by now Bianca's escape would surely have been discovered. He exchanged the gun on his wrist for the poison-blade, putting the wrist mechanism in his pack. Taking Bianca's right hand in his left, he made for the woods that skirted the western side of the village. Climbing a low hill, he was able to look down on Santa Salvaza and saw Orsi troops running in the direction of the watchtower, but none seemed to have deployed in the woods. Grateful for the respite, and after what seemed an age, he arrived with the children back where he had tethered his horse, placed them on its back and got up behind them.

Then he rode back north to Forlì. The city looked quiet. Too quiet. And where were the Orsi forces? Had they raised the siege? It didn't seem possible. He spurred his horse on.

'Take the southern bridge, *Messere*,' said Bianca, in front, holding on to the saddle's pommel. 'It's the most direct way home from here.'

Ottaviano nestled against him.

As they approached the walls of the town, he saw the southern gates open. Out came a small troop of Sforza guards, escorting Caterina and, close behind her, Machiavelli. Ezio could see at once that his fellow Assassin had been wounded. He urged his mount forwards, and when he reached the others, swiftly dismounted and passed the children into Caterina's waiting arms.

'What in the name of the Blessed Virgin is going on?' he asked, looking from Caterina to Machiavelli and back again. 'What are you doing out here?'

'Oh, Ezio,' said Caterina. 'I'm so sorry, so sorry!'

'What's *happened*?'

'The whole thing was a trick. To lower our defences!' Caterina said despairingly. 'Taking the children was a diversion!'

Ezio turned his glance back to Machiavelli. 'But the city is safe?' he said.

Machiavelli sighed. 'Yes, the city is safe. The Orsi no longer have an interest in it.'

'What do you mean?'

'After we'd driven them out, we relaxed – only momentarily, to regroup and see to our wounded. It was then that Checco counter-attacked. They must have planned the whole thing! He stormed the city. I fought him man-to-man and hard, but his soldiers came on me from behind and overwhelmed me. Ezio, now I must ask you to show courage: for Checco has taken the Apple!'

Ezio was stunned for a long moment. Then he said slowly, 'What? No – that cannot be.' He looked around wildly. 'Where has he gone?'

'As soon as he had what he wanted, he beat a retreat with his men, and the army split up. We couldn't see which group had the Apple, and we were too battle-weary to give effective chase anyway. But Checco himself led a company into the mountains to the west –'

'Then all is lost?' Ezio cried, thinking that Lodovico had been right – he had underestimated the Orsi.

'We still have the Map, thank God,' said Caterina. 'He didn't dare spend too much time searching for it.'

'But what if, now he has the Apple, he no longer *needs* the Map?'

'The Templars cannot be allowed to triumph,' said Machiavelli, grimly. 'They cannot! We must go!'

But Ezio could see that his friend had turned grey from his wounds. 'No – you stay here. Caterina! Tend to him. I must leave now! There may yet be time!'

23

It took a long time for Ezio, riding by day and taking what little rest he could when changing his horse, to arrive in the Appenines, and when he did, he knew the search for Checco Orsi would take him even longer. But he also knew that if Checco had returned to his family's seat at Nubilaria, he would be able to cut him off on the road that led from there south on the long, winding route it took to Rome. There was no guarantee that Checco wouldn't have gone directly to the Holy See, but Ezio thought that with such a precious cargo as the Apple, his adversary would first seek safety where he was known, and from there send couriers to establish whether the Spaniard had returned to the Vatican before making contact with him there.

Ezio therefore decided to take the Nubilaria road himself, and, entering the town in secret, set about discovering what he could about Checco's whereabouts. But Checco's own spies were everywhere, and it wasn't long before Ezio learned that Checco was aware that he was closing in, and was planning to take off in a caravan of two carriages with the Apple, in order to escape from him and foil his plans.

On the morning Checco planned to depart, Ezio was ready, keeping a close watch on the southern gates of Nubilaria, and soon the two carriages he'd been expecting rumbled out through them. Ezio mounted his horse to give chase, but at the last moment a third, lighter carriage, driven by an Orsi henchman, came fast out of a side street and deliberately blocked Ezio's path, causing his horse to rear and throw him. With no time to waste, Ezio was obliged to abandon his steed, and, jumping up, clambered on to the Orsi carriage, felling its driver with a single blow and throwing him to the ground. He whipped up the horses and gave chase.

It wasn't long before he had his adversary's vehicles in sight, but they saw him too and increased their speed. As they pelted down the treacherous mountain road, Checco's escort-carriage, filled with Orsi soldiers who were preparing to fire their crossbows at Ezio, took a corner too fast. The horses broke their traces and raced on round the bend ahead, but the carriage, its steering-gear gone and its hafts empty, shot straight on over the edge of the road and crashed hundreds of feet into the valley below. Under his breath, Ezio thanked fate for her kindness. He urged his own horses on, worried that he would drive them too hard and cause their hearts to burst, but they were pulling less weight than the animals pulling Checco's carriage and steadily made up the distance that separated Ezio from his quarry.

As Ezio drew level, the Orsi coachman struck out at

him with his whip, but Ezio caught it in his hand and pulled it free. Then, when the right moment came, he let go of his own reins and leapt from his carriage to the roof of Checco's. In panic, the horses of his carriage, relieved of both the weight and the control of a driver, bolted, and careered out of sight down the road ahead of them.

'Get the hell off!' yelled Checco's driver, alarmed. 'What in God's name do you think you are doing? Are you crazy?' But without his whip, he was finding it harder to control his own team of horses. He had no leisure to fight.

From inside the carriage, Checco himself was shouting, 'Don't be a fool, Ezio! You'll never get out of this!' Leaning half out of the window, he lunged at Ezio with his sword while the coachman frantically tried to control the horses. 'Get off my carriage, *now*!'

The driver tried deliberately swerving the carriage to throw Ezio off, but he clung on for dear life. The carriage veered dangerously and, at last, as they were passing a disused marble quarry, it ran completely out of control, crashing on to its side and throwing the driver heavily on to a pile of slabs of marble of all sizes that had been sawn out by the masons and then abandoned owing to faults that ran through the stone. The horses were pulled down in their traces, pawing the ground in frantic terror. Ezio jumped clear, landed in a crouch, and had his sword out ready for Checco, who, winded but unhurt, was clambering out, fury in his face.

'Give me the Apple, Checco. It's all over.'

'Imbecile! It'll be *over* when you're *dead*!' Checco swung his sword at his opponent, and immediately they were cutting and slashing at each other dangerously close to the edge of the road.

'Give me the Apple, Checco, and I'll let you go. You have no idea of the power of what you have!'

'You'll never have it. And when my Master does, he will have undreamed-of power, and Lodovico and I will be there to enjoy our share of it!'

'Lodovico is dead! And do you really think your Master will let you live, once your usefulness to him is over? You already know too much!'

'You killed my brother? Then *this* is for you, for his sake!' Checco rushed at him.

They closed, blades flashing, and Checco struck at Ezio again, his sword deflected by the metal arm-guard. The fact that his well-aimed blow had not struck home momentarily put Checco off his guard, but he quickly recovered and struck a blow at Ezio's right arm, cutting deeply into his bicep and causing him to let his weapon fall.

Checco gave a hoarse cry of triumph. He held the point of his sword at Ezio's throat. 'Don't beg for mercy,' he said, 'for I'll give you none.' And he drew back his arm to drive in the fatal blow. At that instant, Ezio unleashed the double-bladed dagger from its mechanism on his left forearm and, swinging round with lightning speed, rammed it into Checco's chest.

Checco stood stock still for a long moment, looking down at the blood dripping on to the white roadway. He dropped his sword and fell against Ezio, clutching on to him for support. Their faces were close. Checco smiled. 'So, you have your prize again,' he whispered, as the life-blood pumped out faster from his chest.

'Was it really worth it?' asked Ezio. 'So much carnage!'

The man gave what sounded like a chuckle, or it might have been a cough, as more blood flooded his mouth: 'Look, Ezio, you know how hard it will be for you to hold on to a thing of such value for long.' He fought for breath. 'I am dying today, but it will be *you* who dies tomorrow.' And as the expression faded from his face and his eyes rolled upwards, his body sank to the ground at Ezio's feet.

'We shall see, my friend,' Ezio told him. 'Rest in peace.'

He felt groggy. Blood was pouring from the wound in his arm, but he made himself walk to the carriage and calmed the horses, cutting them free of their traces. Then he searched the interior and quickly located the teak box. Opening it quickly to ensure that its contents were safe, he reclasped it shut again and tucked it firmly under his good arm. He glanced across the quarry, where the driver lay inert. It wasn't necessary to verify that the man was dead, for the broken angle of the body told him everything.

The horses had not moved far, and Ezio went over

to them, wondering if he had the strength to mount one and use it at least to get him part of the way back to Forlì. He hoped he would find everything there as he had left it, for his tracing of Checco had taken far longer than he'd hoped or expected. But he had never pretended that his work would be easy, and the Apple was back in Assassin control. The time he had spent had not been in vain.

He looked at the horses again, deciding that the lead-beast would be his best choice of the four. He went to put his hand on its mane, to pull himself up, for it was not equipped with riding tack, but as he did so he staggered.

He had lost more blood than he'd thought. He would have to bind up his wound somehow before he did anything else. He tethered the horse to a tree, and cut a strip from Checco's shirt to use as a bandage. Then he dragged the body out of sight. If anyone came by, they would assume, if they did not look too carefully, that Ezio and the driver had been the victims of a tragic road accident. But it was getting late, and there would be few travellers abroad at this hour.

However, the effort drained the last of his resources. Even I have to rest, he thought, and the thought was a sweet one. He sat down in the shade of the tree and listened to the sound of the horse as it gently grazed. He placed the teak box on the ground beside him, and took one last cautious look round, for this was the last place he should remain for long; but his eyelids were heavy, and he did not see the silent watcher concealed by a tree on the knoll which rose above the road behind him.

When Ezio awoke, darkness had fallen, but there was just enough moonlight for him to see a figure moving silently near him.

Ezio's right bicep ached dully, but when he tried to raise himself with his good left arm, he found he could not move it. Someone had brought a slab of marble from the quarry and used it to pin the arm down. He struggled, using his legs to try to stand, but he could not. He looked down to where he had left the box containing the Apple.

It was gone.

The figure, who was dressed, Ezio saw, in the black *cappa* and white habit of a Dominican monk, had noticed him wake, and turned to him, adjusting the marble slab so that it held him more securely. Ezio noticed that a finger was missing from one of the monk's hands.

'Wait!' he said. 'Who are you? What are you doing?'

The monk didn't reply. Ezio could see the box as the monk stooped to pick it up again. 'Don't touch that! Whatever you do, don't —'

But the monk opened the box, and a light as bright as the sun shone forth.

Ezio thought he heard the monk give a sigh of satisfaction, before he passed out again.

When he woke again, it was morning. The horses were all gone, but with daylight, some of his strength had returned. He looked at the marble slab. It felt heavy, but it did move slightly when his arm moved under it. He looked around. Just within reach of his right hand he could see a stout branch that must have fallen from the tree at some point in the past but which was still green enough to be strong. Gritting his teeth, he picked it up and manoeuvred it under the slab. His right arm hurt like hell and started to bleed again as he wedged one end of the branch under the slab and heaved. A half-forgotten line from his schooldays had flashed through his mind: *Give me a lever long enough, and I will lift the earth* . . . He pushed hard. The slab started to move, but then his strength failed him and it fell back into place again. He lay back, rested, and tried again.

At the third attempt, screaming inwardly with pain, and thinking the muscles of his wounded right arm would tear through the skin, he pushed again, as if his very life depended on it, and, finally, the slab rolled over on to the ground.

Gingerly, he sat up. His left arm was sore, but nothing was broken.

Why the monk had not killed him as he slept, he had no idea. Perhaps murder was not part of the Man of

God's plan. But one thing was certain – the Dominican, and the Apple, were gone.

Dragging himself to his feet, he found his way to a nearby stream and drank thirstily before bathing his wound and redressing it. Then he set off eastwards, back over the mountains towards Forlì.

At last, after a journey of many days, he saw the towers of the town in the distance. But he was tired, drained by his unremitting task, by his failure, by his loneliness. On the journey back he had had plenty of time to think about Cristina and what might have been, had he not been given this Cross to bear. But since he had, he could not change his life; nor, as he realized, would he.

He had reached the far end of the bridge to the southern gate and was close enough to see people on the battlements when exhaustion finally overcame him, and he passed out.

When he next awoke, it was to find himself lying in a bed, covered in pristine linen sheets, out on a sunny terrace shaded by vines. A cool hand stroked his forehead, and pressed a beaker of water to his lips.

'Ezio! Thank God you are back with us. Are you all right? What happened to you?' The questions flowed from Caterina's mouth with all her usual impetuosity.

'I . . . I don't know . . .'

'They saw you from the ramparts. I came out personally. You had been travelling for I don't know how long, and you have a horrific wound.'

Ezio struggled with his memory. 'Something is coming back to me now . . . I had retrieved the Apple from Checco . . . but there was another man who came soon afterwards – he took the Apple!'

'Who?'

'He wore a black hood, like a monk – and I think . . . had a finger missing!' Ezio struggled to sit up. 'How long have I been lying here? I have to go – right away!' he started to rise, but it was as if his limbs were made of lead, and as he moved, a terrible dizziness overcame him, so he was obliged to lie back again.

'Whoa! What did that monk do to me?'

Caterina leaned over him. 'You can't go anywhere yet, Ezio. Even you need time to recover if you are to fight the battles well which lie ahead; and I can see a long and arduous journey in front of you. But cheer up! Niccolò has returned to Florence. He will look after matters there. And your other fellow Assassins are vigilant. So stay a while . . .' She kissed his forehead, then, tentatively at first, his lips. 'And if there is anything I can do to . . . hasten your recovery, you have only to say the word.' Her hand began very gently to wander downwards beneath the sheets until she found her objective. 'Wow,' she smiled. 'I think I am already succeeding – a little.'

'You are quite a woman, Caterina Sforza.'

She laughed. '*Tesoro*, if ever I were to write the story of my life, I would shock the world.'

*

Ezio was strong and still, at thirty years old, a young man in his prime. Moreover, he had undergone some of the toughest training known to man, so it was really no wonder that he was up and about again sooner than most would have been. But his right arm had been severely weakened by Checco's blow, and he knew he needed to work hard to recover the full strength he required to resume his quest. He made himself be patient, and under Caterina's strict but understanding guidance, spent his enforced time at Forlì in quiet contemplation, when he could often be found sitting under the vines lost in one of Poliziano's books, or, more frequently, in vigorous exercise of every kind.

And then a morning came when Caterina arrived in his chamber to find him dressed for travel, and a page helping him pull on his riding boots. She sat on the bed beside him.

'So the time has come?' she said.

'Yes. I can delay no longer.'

She looked sad and left the room, to return not long afterwards with a scroll. 'Well, the time had to come,' she said, 'and God knows your task is more important than our enjoyment – for which I hope another time will come round again soon!' She showed him the scroll. 'Here – I have brought you a leaving-present.'

'What is it?'

'Something you will need.'

She unrolled it and Ezio saw that it was a map of the

entire peninsula, from Lombardy to Calabria, and all across it, as well as the roads and towns, a number of crosses were marked on it, in red ink.

Ezio looked up at her. 'It's the map Machiavelli spoke of. Your husband's –'

'My *late* husband's, *mio caro*. Niccolò and I made a couple of important discoveries while you were on your travels. The first is that we timed our . . . removal of dear Girolamo rather well, for he'd just about completed his work on this. The second is that it is of inestimable value, for even if the Templars have the Apple, they cannot hope to find the Vault without the Map.'

'You know about the Vault?'

'Darling, you can be just a tad naïve at times. Of course I do.' She became more businesslike. 'But fully to disarm our enemies, you must recover the Apple. This map will help you bring your full great task to an end.'

As she handed him the Map, their fingers touched, lingered and entwined. And their eyes would not leave each other's.

'There is an abbey in the Wetlands near here,' Caterina said at last. 'Dominicans. Their Order wears black hoods. I'd start there.' Her eyes were shining and she looked away. 'Now *go*! Find us that troublesome monk!'

Ezio smiled. 'I think I'm going to miss you, Caterina.'

She smiled back, a bit too brightly. For once in her life she was finding it hard to be brave. 'Oh, I know you will.'

24

The monk who welcomed Ezio at the Wetlands Abbey was as monks should be – plump and rubicund, but he had flaming red hair and puckish, shrewd eyes, and spoke with an accent Ezio recognized from some of the *condottieri* he'd encountered in Mario's service – the man was from Ireland.

'Blessings on you, brother.'

'*Grazie, Padre* –'

'I am Brother O'Callahan –'

'I wonder if you can help me?'

'That's why we are here, brother. Of course, we live in troubled times. It's hard to think straight without something in our stomachs.'

'You mean something in your coin-purse.'

'You take me wrong. I'm not asking you for anything.' The monk spread his hands. 'But the Lord helps the generous.'

Ezio shook out some florins and passed them across. 'If it's not enough . . .'

The monk looked reflective. 'Ah, well, the thought is there. But the truth is that the Lord actually *helps* the slightly more generous.'

Ezio continued shaking out coins until Brother O'Callahan's expression cleared. 'The Order appreciates your open-handedness, brother.' He folded his hands on his belly. 'What do you seek?'

'A black-hooded monk – who lacks one of his ten fingers.'

'Hmmn. Brother Guido has only nine toes. Are you sure it wasn't a toe?'

'Quite sure.'

'And then there's Brother Domenico, but it's his entire left arm he's lacking.'

'No. I'm sorry, but I'm quite sure it was a finger.'

'Hmmn.' The monk paused, deep in thought. 'Now, wait a moment! I do recall a black-cowled monk with only nine fingers . . . Yes! Of course! It was when we had our last San Vicenzo's Feast at our abbey in Tuscany.'

Ezio smiled. 'Yes, I know the place. I'll try there. *Grazie.*'

'Go in peace, brother.'

'I always do.'

Ezio crossed the mountains westwards into Tuscany, and though the journey was a long and difficult one, as autumn approached and the days became unkinder, he felt his greatest trepidation when he approached the abbey – for it was the place where one of those implicated in the plot to assassinate Lorenzo de' Medici – Jacopo de' Pazzi's secretary, Stefano de Bagnone – had met his end at Ezio's hands long ago.

It was unfortunate that the abbot who greeted him here was one who had been a witness to that killing.

'Excuse me,' Ezio said to him first. 'I wonder if you can –'

But the abbot, recognizing him, drew back in horror, and cried, 'May *all* the Archangels – Uriel, Raphael, Michael, Saraquêl, Gabriel, Remiel and Raguel – may they *all* in their Mightiness protect us!' He turned his blazing eyes from heaven to Ezio. 'Unholy Demon! Begone!'

'What's the matter?' said Ezio, in consternation.

'What's the matter? What's the *matter*? You are the one who murdered Brother Stefano. On this Holy Ground!' A nervous group of brothers had gathered at a safe distance, and the abbot now turned to them. 'He has *returned*! The killer of monks and priests has *returned*!' he pronounced in a voice of thunder, and then took flight, followed by his flock.

The man was clearly in a state of high panic. Ezio had no choice but to give chase. The abbey was not as familiar to him as to the Abbot and his troop of monks. At last he tired of hurtling round unfamiliar stone corridors and cloisters, and leapt to the rooftops to get a better view of where the monks were headed, but this only threw them into a greater panic, and they started to scream, 'He's come! He's come! Beëlzebub *is* come!' and so he desisted and stuck to conventional means of pursuit.

Finally, he caught up with them. Panting, the Abbot

rounded on him and croaked: 'Begone, demon! Leave us alone! We have done no sin so great as thine!'

'No, wait, listen,' panted Ezio, almost equally out of breath. 'I just want to ask you a question.'

'We have called down no demons upon us! We seek no journey to the Afterlife just yet!'

Ezio placed his palms downwards. 'Please. *Calma!* I wish you no harm!'

But the Abbot wasn't listening. He rolled his eyes. 'My God, my God, why have You forsaken me? I'm not yet *ready* to join your angels!'

And he took to his heels again.

Ezio was obliged to bring him down in an arms-to-feet tackle. They both got up, dusting themselves down in the middle of a circle of goggling monks.

'Stop running away, please!' pleaded Ezio.

The Abbot cowered. 'No! Have mercy! I don't want to die!' he burbled.

Ezio, conscious that he was sounding prim, said: 'Look, Father Abbot, I only kill those who kill others. And your Brother Stefano was a killer. He tried to murder Duke Lorenzo in 1478.' He paused, breathing heavily. 'Be reassured, *Messer Abate*, I'm certain you are no such thing as a murderer.'

The Abbot's look became a trace calmer, but there was still suspicion in his eyes.

'What do you want, then?' he said.

'All right, now, listen to me. I'm looking for a monk

dressed like you are – a Dominican – who is missing a finger.'

The Abbot looked wary. 'Missing a finger, do you say? Like Fra' Savonarola?'

Ezio seized on the name. '*Savonarola*? Who is he? Do you know him?'

'I did, *Messer*. He was one of us . . . for a time.'

'And then?'

The Abbot shrugged. 'We suggested he take a nice long rest at a hermitage in the mountains. He didn't quite . . . fit in here . . .'

'It seems to me, *Abate*, that his time as a hermit may be over. Do you know where he may have gone now?'

'Oh dear me . . .' The Abbot searched his mind. 'If he's left the hermitage, it may be that he has returned to Santa Maria del Carmine, in Florence. It's where he studied. Perhaps that's where he'd go back to.'

Ezio breathed a sigh of relief. 'Thank you, Abbot. Go with God.'

It was strange for Ezio to be in his home town again, after so long. There were many memories to deal with. But circumstances dictated that he work alone. He could not contact even old friends or allies, lest the enemy were alerted.

It was also clear that even if the city remained stable, the church, at least, which he sought, was in turmoil. A monk came running from it in fear.

He accosted the monk. 'Whoa, there, Brother. It's all right!'

The monk looked at him, wild-eyed. 'Stay away, my friend. If you value your life!'

'What's happened here?'

'Soldiers from Rome have seized our church! They've scattered my brothers, asking questions that make no sense. They keep demanding that we give them *fruit*!'

'What kind of fruit?'

'Apples!'

'Apples? *Diavolo!* Rodrigo has got here before me!' hissed Ezio to himself.

'They've dragged one of my fellow Carmelites behind the church! I'm sure they're going to kill him!'

'Carmelites? You are not *Dominicans*?' Ezio left the man, and made his way carefully round the outer walls of Santa Maria, hugging them. He moved as stealthily as a mongoose confronting a cobra. When he reached the walls of the church's garden, he skimmed to the roof. What he saw below him took even his experienced breath away. Several Borgia guards were beating the shit out of a tall young monk. He looked about thirty-five years old.

'Tell us!' cried the leader of the guards. 'Tell us, or I will make you hurt so badly you'll wish you'd never been born. *Where is the Apple?*'

'Please! I don't know! I don't know what you're talking about!'

The lead guard leaned in close. 'Confess! Your name is Savonarola!'

'Yes! I told you! But you beat the name out of me!'

'Then tell us and your suffering will cease. Where the fuck is *the Apple*?' The interrogator kicked the monk savagely in the crotch. The monk howled in pain. 'Not that *that'll* make much difference to a man in your *missionary* position,' jeered the guard.

Ezio watched, deeply concerned. If this monk was indeed Savonarola, the Borgia thugs might kill him before he himself got the truth out of the man.

'Why do you keep lying to me?' sneered the guard. 'My Master will not be pleased to hear you made me torture you to death! Do you want to get me into *trouble*?'

'I don't have any apple,' sobbed the monk. 'I'm just a simple friar. *Please* let me go!'

'In a pig's eye!'

'I know *nothing*!' the monk cried piteously.

'If you want me to stop,' shouted the guard, kicking him again in the same place, 'then tell me the truth, Brother Girolamo – *Savonarola*!'

The monk bit his lip, but stubbornly replied, 'I've told you everything I know!'

The guard kicked him again, and had his henchmen grab his ankles and drag the man mercilessly along the cobbled ground, his head bouncing painfully on the hard stone. The monk screamed, and struggled in vain.

'Had enough, you *abominato*?' The lead guard held his

face close again. 'Are you so ready to meet your Maker, that you would lie again and again, just to see Him?'

'I am a plain monk,' wept the Carmelite, whose robes were dangerously similar in cut and colour to that of the Dominicans. 'I have no *fruit* of any kind! Please . . .'

The guard kicked him. In the same place. Again. The monk's body twisted in an agony beyond tears.

Ezio had had enough. He sprang down, a phantom of vengeance, slicing for once in pure rage with poison-dagger and double-blade. Within a minute of sheer slaughter, the Borgia thugs, all of them, lay either dead or groaning in the same agony they'd inflicted, on the flagstones of the courtyard.

The monk, weeping, clung to Ezio's knees: '*Grazie, grazie, Salvatore.*'

Ezio stroked his head. '*Calma, calma.* It will be all right now, my Brother.' But Ezio also looked at the monk's fingers.

All ten were intact.

'You have ten fingers,' he murmured, disappointed despite himself.

'Yes,' cried the monk. 'I have ten fingers. And I don't have any other apples than those that come to the monastery from the market every Thursday!' He stood up, shook himself down, tenderly readjusted himself, and swore. 'In the name of God! Has the whole world stopped making *sense*?'

'Who are you? Why did they take you?' asked Ezio.

'Because they found out that indeed my family name is Savonarola! But why should I betray my cousin to those thugs?'

'Do you know what he's done?'

'I know nothing! He is a monk, like me. He chose the harsher Order of the Dominicans, it is true, but –'

'He has lost a finger?'

'Yes, but how could anyone – ?' A kind of light was dawning in the monk's eyes.

'Who is Girolamo Savonarola?' persisted Ezio.

'My cousin, and a devoted man of God. And who, may I ask, are you, though I thank you humbly for my rescue, and owe you whatever favour you may ask?'

'I am . . . nameless,' said Ezio. 'But do me the favour of telling your name.'

'Fra' *Marcello* Savonarola,' the monk replied meekly.

Ezio took that in. His mind raced. 'Where is your cousin Girolamo?'

Fra' Marcello thought, struggling with his conscience. 'It is true that my cousin . . . has a singular view of how to serve God . . . He is spreading a doctrine of his own . . . You may find him now in Venice.'

'And what does he do there?'

Marcello straightened his shoulders. 'I think he has set off on the wrong path. He preaches fire and brimstone. He claims to see the future.' Marcello looked at Ezio through red-rimmed eyes, eyes full of agony. 'If you really want my opinion, he spews *madness*!'

25

Ezio felt that he had spent too long on what seemed to be a fruitless quest. Chasing Savonarola seemed like chasing a will o' the wisp, or a chimera, or your own tail. But the search had to continue, remorselessly, for the nine-fingered man of God held the Apple – the key to more than he could imagine possible, and he was a dangerous religious maniac, a loose cannon potentially less controllable than the Master, Rodrigo Borgia, himself.

It was Teodora who met him as he disembarked from the Ravenna galley at the Venice docks.

Venice in 1492 was still under the relatively honest rule of Doge Agostino Barbarigo. The city was abuzz with talk of how a Genoese seaman called Christoffa Corombo, whose mad plans to sail westwards across the Ocean Sea had been turned down by Venice, had got funding from Spain, and was about to set out. Had Venice itself been mad not to fund the expedition? If Corombo succeeded, a safe sea passage to the Indies might be established, side-stepping the old land route now blocked by the Ottoman Turks. But Ezio's mind was far too full of other matters to pay much attention to these matters of politics and trade.

'We have your news,' Teodora said. 'But are you certain?'

'It's the only lead I've got, and it seems a good one. I am certain that the Apple is here again, in the hands of the monk, Savonarola. I hear he preaches to the masses of the hell and fire to come.'

'I have heard of this man.'

'Do you know where he can be found, Teodora?'

'No. But I've seen a Herald drawing crowds in the industrial district, preaching the kind of fire-and-brimstone stuff-and-nonsense you speak of. Perhaps he is a disciple of your monk. Come with me. You will certainly be my guest while you are here, and once you are settled we will go straight to where this man delivers his sermons.'

Both Ezio and Teodora, and indeed all intelligent and rational people, knew why a kind of blood-and-thunder hysteria was beginning to grip the people. The half-millennium year of 1500 was not far off, and many believed that that year would mark the Second Coming, when the Lord would '*come with clouds, in his own glory, and the glory of his Father, with ten thousand of his saints, even myriads of angels, and shall sit upon the throne of his glory. And before him shall be gathered all nations; and he shall separate them one from another, and shall set the sheep, the Saved, on his right hand, and the goats, the Damned, upon the left*'.

San Matteo's description of the Last Judgement reverberated through the imaginations of many.

'This Herald and his boss are really cashing in on the *febbre di fine secolo*,' said Teodora. 'For all I know, they believe in it themselves.'

'I think they must do,' said Ezio. 'The danger is, that with the Apple in their hands, they may actually bring about a world disaster that has nothing to do with God, and everything to do with the Devil.' He paused. 'But for the moment they have not unleashed the power they have, and thank God for that, for I doubt if they would know how to control it. For the moment at least they seem content to foretell the Apocalypse – and that –' he laughed bitterly, '– has always been an easy sell.'

'But it gets worse,' said Teodora. 'Indeed, you might almost believe that the Apocalypse were really at hand. Have you heard the bad news?'

'I have heard none since I left Forlì.'

'Lorenzo de' Medici has died at his villa in Careggi.'

Ezio looked grim. 'That is indeed a tragedy. Lorenzo was a true friend to my family and without his protecting hand I fear I may never recover the Palazzo Auditore. But that is as nothing compared with what his death may mean to the peace he maintained between the city-states. It was always fragile at the best of times.'

'There is more,' said Teodora, 'And it is, if anything, worse news even than Lorenzo's death.' She paused. 'You must brace yourself for this, Ezio. The Spaniard, Rodrigo Borgia, has been elected Pope. He rules the

Vatican and Rome as the Supreme Pontiff, Alexander VI!'

'*What!* By what devilry – ?'

'The Conclave of Rome has only just ended – this month. The rumour is that Rodrigo simply bought most of the votes. Even Ascanio Sforza, who was the most likely candidate standing against him, voted for him! Four mule-loads of silver was his bribe, they say.'

'What profits him to be Pope? What is it he seeks?'

'Is such great influence not enough?' Teodora looked at him. 'Now we are in the power of a wolf, Ezio. The most rapacious, perhaps, the world has ever seen.'

'What you say is true, Teodora. But the power he seeks is even greater than that which the Papacy will give him. If he controls the Vatican, he is that much closer to gaining access to the Vault; and he is still on the trail of the Apple, the "Piece of Eden" he needs to give him – the power of God Himself!'

'Let us pray that you get it back into the hands of the Assassins – Rodrigo as Pope and Master of the Templars is dangerous enough. Once he has the Apple as well . . .' She broke off. 'As you say, he will be indestructible.'

'It's odd,' said Ezio.

'What is?'

'Our friend Savonarola doesn't know it, but he has two huntsmen chasing him.'

*

Teodora conducted Ezio to the large open square in the industrial quarter of Venice where the Herald was wont to conduct his sermons, and left him there. Ezio, his hood up and his face lowered but watchful, blended in with the crowd that was already gathering. It wasn't long before the square was packed, the mob thronging around a small wooden stage on to which a man now stepped, an ascetic-looking man with cold blue eyes and hollow cheeks, iron-grey hair and gnarled hands, dressed in a plain grey woollen robe. He started to speak, pausing only when the mad cheers of the crowd obliged him to. Ezio saw how skilfully one man could work hundreds into a state of blind hysteria.

'Gather, children, and hear my cry! For the End of Days draws nigh. Are you ready for what is to come? Are you ready to see the Light my brother Savonarola has blessed us with?' He raised his hands, and Ezio, who knew exactly what light the Herald was referring to, listened soberly. 'Dark days are upon us,' continued the Herald, 'But my brother has shown me the path forward unto salvation, unto the heavenly light that awaits us. But only if we are ready, only if we embrace him. Let Savonarola be our guide, for he alone knows what is to come. He shall not lead us astray.' Now the Herald leant forward earnestly on the lectern before him. 'Are you ready for the final reckoning, brothers and sisters? Whom shall you follow when the time comes?' He paused again for effect. 'There are many in the churches who claim to offer salvation, the summoners, the pardoners, the scatterbrained slaves of superstition . . . But nay, my children! They are all in thrall to the Borgia pope, all in thrall to "Pope" Alexander, the sixth and most mortgaged of that name!'

The crowd screamed. Ezio, inwardly, winced. He remembered the apparent prophecies he had seen the Apple project in Leonardo's workshop. Somewhere in the distant future: a time when hell would *truly* be unleashed upon the earth – unless he could stop it.

'Our new Pope Alexander is not a spiritual man; he is not a man of the soul. Men like him buy your prayers and sell your benefices for profit. All the priests of our churches are ecclesiastical merchants! Only one among us is a true man of the spirit, only one among us has seen the future, and spoken with the Lord! My brother, Savonarola! He shall lead us!'

Ezio thought: had that mad monk *opened* the Apple, as he had himself? Had he unleashed the same visions? What was it Leonardo had said about the Apple – *unsafe for weaker brains?*

'Savonarola shall lead us to the light,' the Herald was concluding. 'Savonarola shall tell us what is to come! Savonarola shall carry us to the front door of heaven itself! We shall not want in the new world that Savonarola has borne witness to. Brother Savonarola walks the very path to God we have been seeking!'

He raised his hands again, as the mob yelled and cheered.

Ezio knew that the only way to find the monk was through this acolyte. But he had to find a way to reach the man without arousing the suspicions of the devoted crowd. He made his way forward cautiously, acting the role of the meek man seeking conversion to the Herald's flock.

It wasn't easy. He was jostled aggressively by people who could see he was a stranger, a newcomer, a person to be regarded with reserve. But he smiled, bowed, and even, as a last resort, threw money down, saying, 'I want to give alms to the cause of Savonarola and those who support him and believe in him.' And money worked its usual charm. In fact, Ezio thought, money is the greatest converter of them all.

At last the Herald, who'd observed Ezio's progress with a mixture of amusement and contempt, bade his minders step aside and beckoned to him, leading him to a quiet place, a little piazzetta off the main square, where they could have a private conversation. Ezio was pleased to see that the Herald clearly thought he'd made an important and wealthy new addition to his flock.

'Where is Savonarola himself?' he asked.

'He is everywhere, brother,' replied the Herald. 'He is at one with all of us, and all of us are at one with him.'

'Listen, friend,' said Ezio, urgently. 'I seek the man, not the myth. Please tell me where he is.'

The Herald looked at him askance, and Ezio clearly saw the madness in his eyes. 'I have told you where he is. Look, Savonarola loves you just as you are. He will show you the Light. He will show you the *future*!'

'But I must talk to him myself. I must see the great leader! And I have great riches to bring to his mighty crusade!'

The Herald looked cunning at that. 'I see,' he said. 'Be patient. The hour is not yet come. But you *shall* join us in our pilgrimage, brother.'

And Ezio was patient. He was patient for a long time. Then, one day, he received a summons from the Herald to meet him at the Venice dockyards at dusk. He arrived early and waited impatiently and nervously, until finally he saw a shadowy figure approaching through the evening mists.

'I was not sure you would come,' he greeted the Herald.

The Herald looked pleased. 'The quest for Truth is passionate in you, brother. And it has withstood the test of time. But now we are ready, and our great leader has assumed the mantle of command he was born to. Come!'

He motioned ahead of him, and led Ezio to the quayside where a large galley waited. Near it, a crowd of the Faithful waited. The Herald addressed them:

'My children! It is time at last for us to depart. Our

449

brother and spiritual leader Girolamo Savonarola awaits us in the city he has at last made his own!'

'Yes, he has! The son-of-a-bitch bastard has brought my town and my home to its knees – to the brink of insanity!'

The crowd and Ezio turned to look at the person who had spoken, a long-haired young man in a black cap, with full lips and a weak face, now contorted in anger.

'I have just escaped from there,' he continued. 'Thrown out of my dukedom by that prick King Charles of France, whose meddling has caused me to be replaced by that Dog of God, Savonarola!'

The crowd's mood turned ugly, and they would surely have seized the young man and thrown him into the lagoon if the Herald had not stayed them.

'Let the man speak his mind,' ordered the Herald, and, turning to the stranger, asked: 'Why do you take Savonarola's name in vain, brother?'

'Why? *Why?* Because of what he's done to Florence! He controls the city! The Signoria are either behind him, or powerless against him. He whips up the mob, and even people who should know better, like *Maestro* Botticelli, follow him slavishly. They burn books, works of art, anything which that madman deems immoral!'

'Savonarola is in Florence now?' asked Ezio intently. 'You're sure?'

'Would it were otherwise! Would he were on the

moon or in hell's mouth! I barely got away with my life!'

'And who might you be exactly, brother?' asked the Herald, impatient now and showing it.

The young man drew himself up. 'I am Piero de' Medici. Son of Lorenzo, *Il Magnifico*, and rightful ruler of Florence!'

Ezio clasped his hand. 'Well met, Piero. Your father was my staunch friend.'

Piero looked at him. 'Thank you for that, whoever you may be. As for my father, he was lucky to die before all this madness broke like a giant wave over our city.' He turned heedlessly to the angry crowd. 'Do not support that wretched monk! He is a dangerous fool with an ego the size of the Duomo! He should be put down like the mad dog that he is!'

Now, as one, the crowd growled in righteous fury. The Herald turned to Piero and yelled, 'Heretic! Seeder of evil thoughts!' To the crowd he cried, 'This is the man who must be *put down*! Be *silenced*! He must *burn*!'

Both Piero and Ezio, by his side, had their swords out by now, and faced the menacing mob.

'Who are you?' asked Piero.

'Auditore, Ezio,' he replied.

'Ah! *Sono grato del tuo aiuto*. My father spoke of you often.' His eyes flickered over their adversaries. 'Are we going to get out of this?'

'I hope so. But you weren't exactly tactful.'

'How was I to know?'

'You've just destroyed untold effort and preparation; but never mind. Look to your sword!'

The fight was hard but short. The two men let the mob beat them back to an abandoned warehouse, and it was there that they took their stand. Luckily, though enraged, the crowd of pilgrims were far from being seasoned fighters, and once the boldest of them had retreated nursing deep cuts and slashes from Ezio's and Piero's longswords, the rest of them fell back, and fled. Only the Herald, grim and grey, stood his ground.

'Impostor!' he said to Ezio. 'You shall freeze for ever in the ice of the Fourth Ring of the Ninth Circle. And it is I who will send you there.' From his robes he produced a keen-edged basilard and ran at Ezio holding it above his head, ready to strike. Ezio, backing, almost fell and was at the Herald's mercy, but Piero sliced at the man's legs and Ezio, having regained his feet, unleashed his double-blade – punching the sharp points deep into the man's abdomen. The herald's whole frame shuddered with the impact; he gasped, and fell, writhing and twitching, clawing the ground, until at last he was still.

'Hope that pays you back for the bad turn I've done you,' said Piero, with a rueful smile. 'Come on! Let's get to the Doge's Palace and tell Agostino to send the Watch out to make sure that bunch of lunatics has split up, and that they've all gone back to their kennels.'

'*Grazie*,' said Ezio. 'But I go the other way. I go to Florence.'

Piero looked at him incredulously. 'What? Into the mouth of hell itself?'

'I have my own reasons for seeking out Savonarola. But perhaps it's not too late to undo the damage he's done to our native city as well.'

'Then I wish you luck,' said Piero. 'Whatever end you seek.'

26

Fra' Girolamo Savonarola took over the effective government of Florence in 1494, aged forty-two. He was a tormented man, a twisted genius, and the worst kind of fanatical believer; but the most frightening thing about him was that people allowed him not only to lead them, but to incite them to commit the most ludicrous and destructive acts of folly. All based on a terror of hell-fire, and on a doctrine which taught that all pleasure, all worldly goods, and all the works of man, were despicable, and that only by complete self-abnegation could a person find the true light of faith.

No wonder, thought Ezio, pondering these things as he rode towards his home town, that Leonardo stayed put in Milan – apart from anything else, from his friend's point of view, Ezio had learned that homosexuality, hitherto winked at or punishable by an affordable fine, was once again a capital offence in Florence. And no wonder, too, that the great materialist and humanist school of thinkers and poets who had gathered around the nurturing and enlightened spirit of Lorenzo had broken up, and sought less barren soil than the intellectual desert which Florence was fast becoming.

As he approached the city, Ezio became aware of large groups of black-robed monks and soberly attired laymen heading in the same direction. All looked solemn but righteous. All walked with their heads bent.

'Where are you bound?' he asked one of these passers-by.

'To Florence. To sit at the feet of the great leader,' said a pasty-faced merchant, before continuing on his way.

The road was broad, and approaching him from the city Ezio saw another mass of people, evidently leaving town. They also walked with their heads bent, and their expressions were serious and depressed. As they passed him, Ezio heard snatches of their conversations, and realized that these people were going into voluntary exile. They pushed carts piled high, or carried sacks, or bundles of possessions. They were refugees, banished from their home either by edict of the Monk, or by choice, since they could bear to live under his rule no longer.

'If Piero had had only a tenth of his father's talent, we'd have somewhere to call home . . .' said one.

'We never should have let that madman gain a foothold in our city,' muttered another. 'Look at all the misery he's wrought . . .'

'What I don't understand is why so many of us are willing to accept his oppression,' said a woman.

'Well, anywhere's better than Florence now,' another woman said. 'We were just thrown out when we refused to hand over everything we own to his precious Church of San Marco!'

'It's sorcery, that's the only way I can explain it. Even *Maestro* Botticelli is under Savonarola's spell . . . Mind you, the man's getting old, he must be damned near fifty, maybe he's hedging his bets with heaven.'

'Book burnings, arrests, all those endless bloody sermons! And to think what Florence was just two short years ago . . . a beacon against ignorance! And now here we are again, back mired in the Dark Ages.'

And then a woman said something which made Ezio prick up his ears. 'Sometimes I wish the Assassin would return to Florence, that we might be free of this tyranny.'

'In your dreams!' replied her friend. 'The Assassin's a myth! A bogey-man parents tell their children about.'

'You're wrong – my father saw him in San Gimignano,' the first woman sighed. 'But it *was* years ago.'

'Yeah, yeah – *se lo tu dici*.'

Ezio rode on past them, his heart heavy. But his spirits rose when he saw a familiar figure coming along the road to meet him.

'*Salute*, Ezio,' said Machiavelli, his serious-humorous face older now, but more interesting for the etching of the years.

'*Salute*, Niccolò.'

'You've picked a fine time for a homecoming.'

'You know me. Where there's sickness, I like to try to cure it.'

'We could certainly use your help now,' Machiavelli sighed. 'There's no doubt Savonarola couldn't have got where he is now without the use of that powerful artefact, the Apple.' He held up his hand. 'I know all about what has happened to you since last we met. Caterina sent a courier from Forlì two years ago, and more recently one arrived with a letter from Piero in Venice.'

'I am here for the Apple. It has been out of our hands far too long.'

'I suppose in a sense we should be grateful to the ghastly Girolamo,' said Machiavelli. 'At least he kept it out of the new Pope's hands.'

'Has he tried anything?'

'He keeps trying. There's a rumour that Alexander's planning to excommunicate our dear Dominican. Not that that'll change much around here.'

Ezio said, 'We should get to work on retrieving it without delay.'

'The Apple? Of course – though it'll be more complicated than you might think.'

'Hah! When isn't it?' Ezio looked at him. 'Why don't you fill me in on things?'

'Come, let's go back to the city. I'll tell you everything I know. There's little to relate. In a nutshell, King Charles VIII of France finally managed to bring Florence to its knees. Piero fled. Charles, land-hungry as ever – why the hell they call him "the Affable" is beyond me – marched on to Naples, and Savonarola, the Ugly Duckling, suddenly saw his chance and filled the power-vacuum. He's like any dictator anywhere, tinpot or grand. Totally humourless, totally convinced, and filled with an unshakeable sense of his own importance. The most effective and the nastiest kind of Prince you could wish for.' He paused. 'One day I'll write a book about it.'

'And the Apple was the means to his end?'

Machiavelli spread his hands. 'Only in part. A lot of it, I hate to say, is down to his own charisma. It isn't the city itself he's enthralled, but its leaders, men possessed of influence and power. Of course some of the Signoria opposed him at first, but now –' Machiavelli looked worried. 'Now they're all in his pocket. The man everyone once reviled suddenly became the one they worshipped. If people didn't agree, they were obliged to leave. It's still happening, as you've seen today. And now the Florentine council oppress the citizens and ensure that the mad Monk's will is done.'.

'But what of decent ordinary people? Do they really act as if they had no say at all in the matter?'

Machiavelli smiled sadly. 'You know the answer to that as well as I do, Ezio. Rare is the man willing to oppose the status quo. And so – it falls to us to help them see their way through this.'

By now the two Assassins had reached the city gates. The armed guards of the city, like all police, serving the interest of the state without reference to its morality, scrutinized their papers and waved them through, though not before Ezio had noticed another pack of them busy piling up the corpses of some other uniforms who carried the Borgia crest. He pointed this out to Niccolò.

'Oh yes,' said Machiavelli. As I said, friend Rodrigo – I'll never get used to calling the bastard Alexander – keeps trying. He sends his soldiers into Florence, and Florence sends them back, usually in pieces.'

'So he does know the Apple's here?'

'Of course he does! And I must admit, it's an unfortunate complication.'

'And where is Savonarola?'

'He rules the city from the Convento di San Marco. Almost never leaves it. Thank God *Fra'* Angelico didn't live to see the day Brother Girolamo moved in!'

They dismounted, stabled their horses, and Machiavelli arranged lodgings for Ezio. Paola's old house of pleasure was shut down, along with all the others, as Machiavelli explained. Sex and gambling, dancing and pageantry, were all high on the list of Savonarola's no-nos. Righteous killing, and oppression, on the other hand, were fine.

After Ezio was settled, Machiavelli walked with him towards the great religious complex of Saint Mark. Ezio's eyes ranged the buildings appraisingly. 'A direct assault against Savonarola would be dangerous,' he decided. 'Especially with the Apple in his possession.'

'True,' agreed Machiavelli. 'But what other option is there?'

459

'Aside from the city leaders, who doubtless have vested interests, are you convinced that the people's minds are fundamentally their own?'

'An optimist might be inclined to take a bet on it,' said Machiavelli.

'My point is, they follow the Monk not by choice, but by dint of force and fear?'

'No one apart from a Dominican or a politician would argue with that.'

'Then I propose we use this to our advantage. If we can silence his lieutenants and stir up discontent, Savonarola will be distracted, and we'll have a chance to strike.'

Machiavelli smiled. 'That's clever. There ought to be an adjective to describe people like you. I'll speak with La Volpe and Paola – yes, they're still here, though they've had to go underground. They can help us organize an uprising as you free the districts.'

'Then it's settled.' Ezio was troubled, though, and Machiavelli could see it. He led him to the quiet cloister of a little church nearby, and sat him down.

'What is it, friend?' he asked.

'Two things, but they are personal.'

'Tell me.'

'My old family palazzo – what's become of it? I hardly dare go to look.'

A shadow passed across Machiavelli's face. 'My dear Ezio, be strong. Your palazzo stands, but Lorenzo's ability to protect it lasted only as long as his own power, his own life. Piero tried to follow his father's example but after he was kicked out by the French the Palazzo Auditore was requisitioned and used as a billet for Charles's Swiss mercenaries. After they had moved south, Savonarola's men stripped it of everything that was left in it, and closed the place down. Have courage. One day you will restore it.'

'And Annetta?'

'She escaped, thank God, and joined your mother at Monteriggioni.'

'That at least is something.'

After a silence, Machiavelli asked, 'And what is the second thing?'

Ezio whispered, 'Cristina –'

'You ask me to tell you hard things, *amico mio.*' Machiavelli frowned. 'But you must know the truth.' He paused. 'My friend, she is dead. Manfredo would not leave, as many of their friends left after the twin plagues of the French and Savonarola. He was convinced that Piero would organize a counter-offensive and get the city back. But there was an horrific night, soon after the Monk came to power, when all those who would not voluntarily commit their belongings to the bonfires of the vanities which the Monk organized to burn and destroy all luxurious and worldly things, had their houses ransacked and put to the torch.'

Ezio listened, making himself stay calm, though his heart was bursting.

'Savonarola's fanatics,' Machiavelli went on, 'forced their way into the Palazzo d'Arzenta. Manfredo tried to defend himself, but there were too many pitted against him and his own men . . . And Cristina would not leave him.' Machiavelli paused for a long moment, fighting back tears himself. 'In their frenzy, those religious maniacs cut her down too.'

Ezio stared at the whitewashed wall in front of him. Every last detail, every last crack, even the ants moving across it, all were thrown into dreadful focus.

27

How every hope of ours is raised in vain,
How spoiled the plans we laid so fair and well,
How ignorance throughout the earth doth reign,
Death, who is mistress of us all, can tell.
In song and dance and jousts some pass their days,
Some vow their talents unto gentle arts,
Some hold the world in scorn and all its ways,
Some hide the impulses that move their hearts.
Vain thoughts and wishes, cares of every kind
Greatly upon this erring earth prevail
In various presence after nature's lore;
Fortune doth fashion with inconstant mind,
All things are transient here below and frail,
Death only standeth fast for evermore.

Ezio let the book of Lorenzo's sonnets fall from his hand. The death of Cristina made him all the more determined to remove its cause. His city had suffered long enough under the rule of Savonarola, too many of his fellow citizens, from every conceivable walk of life, had fallen under his spell, and those who disagreed were either discriminated against, driven underground, or forced into exile. It was time to act.

'We have lost to exile many people who might have helped us,' Machiavelli explained to him. But even Savonarola's chief enemies outside the city-state, I mean the Duke of Milan and our old friend Rodrigo, Pope Alexander VI, haven't been able to dislodge him.'

'And what of these bonfires?'

'The most insane thing of all. Savonarola and his close associates organize groups of their followers to go from door to door, demanding the surrender of any and all objects they deem to be morally questionable, even cosmetics and mirrors, let alone paintings, books considered to be immoral, all sorts of games including chess, for God's sake, musical instruments – you name it; if the Monk and his followers think they distract from their take on religion, they've been brought to the Piazza della Signoria, placed on huge bonfires, and burned.' Machiavelli shook his head. 'Florence has lost much of value and much of beauty in this way.'

'But surely the city must be getting weary of this kind of behaviour?'

Machiavelli brightened. 'That is true, and that feeling is our best ally. I think Savonarola genuinely believes that the Day of Judgement is at hand – the only trouble is, it shows no sign of coming, and even some who started out believing in him fervently are beginning to falter in their faith. Unfortunately there are many of influence and power here who still support him without question. If they could be removed . . .'

So began for Ezio a frenetic period of hunting down and dispatching a series of such supporters, and they did indeed come from all walks of life – there were an artist of note, an old soldier, a merchant, several priests, a doctor, a farmer, and one or two aristocrats, all of whom clung fanatically to the ideas imbued in them by the Monk. Some saw the folly of their ways before they died; others remained unshaken in their conviction. Ezio, as he carried out this unpleasant task, was more often than not threatened with death himself. But soon the rumours began to filter through the city – talk heard in the late hours, mutterings in illicit tavernas and back alleys. The Assassin is back. The Assassin has come to save Florence . . .

It saddened Ezio to the core to see the city of his birth, his family, his heritage so abused by the hatred and insanity of religious fervour. It was with a hardened heart that he plied his trade of death – a cold icy wind cleansing the bastardized city of those who had pulled *Firenze* from her glory. As ever, he killed with compassion, knowing that no other way was possible for those who had fallen so far from God. Through these hours of darkness, he never once swerved from his duty to the Creed of the Assassin.

Gradually the general mood of the city wavered, and

Savonarola saw his support ebbing, as Machiavelli, La Volpe and Paola worked in tandem with Ezio to organize an uprising, an uprising guided by a slow but forceful process of enlightenment of the people.

The last of the 'targets' for Ezio was a beguiled preacher, who at the time Ezio tracked him down was preaching to a crowd in front of the church of Santo Spirito.

'People of Florence! Come! Gather round. Listen well to what I say! The end approaches! Now is the time to repent! To beg God's forgiveness. Listen to me, if you cannot see what is happening for yourselves. The *signs* are all around us: Unrest! Famine! Disease! Corruption! These are the harbingers of *darkness*! We must stand firm in our devotion lest they *consume us all*!' He scanned them with his fiery eyes. 'I see you doubt, that you think me mad. Ahhhh . . . but did the Romans not say the same of Jesus? Know that I, too, once shared your uncertainty, your fear. But that was before Savonarola came to me. He showed me the *truth*! At last, my eyes were *opened*. And so I stand before you today in the hope that I might open yours as well!' The preacher paused for breath. 'Understand that we stand upon a precipice. On one side, the shining, glorious *Kingdom of God*. On the other – a bottomless pit of *despair*! Already you teeter precariously on the edge. Men like the Medici and the other families you once called masters sought earthly goods and gain. The abandoned their beliefs in favour of material pleasures, and they would have seen you all do the same.' He paused again, this time for effect, and continued: 'Our wise prophet once said, "The only good thing that we owe Plato and Aristotle is that they brought forward many arguments which we can use against the heretics. Yet they and other philosophers are now in hell." If you value your immortal souls you'll turn back from this unholy course and embrace the teachings of our prophet, Savonarola. Then you will sanctify your bodies and spirits – you will discover the Glory of God! You will, at last, become what our Creator intended: loyal and obedient servants!'

But the crowd, already thinning out, was losing interest, and the last few people were now moving away. Ezio stepped forward and addressed the beguiled preacher. 'Your mind,' he said. 'I sense it is your own.'

The preacher laughed. 'Not all of us required persuasion or coercion to be convinced. I already believed. All I have said is true!'

'Nothing is true,' replied Ezio. 'And what I do now is no easy thing.' He unsprung his wrist-blade and ran the preacher through. '*Requiescat in pace*,' he said. Turning away from the kill, he pulled his cowl close over his head.

It was a long, hard road, but towards the end Savonarola himself became the Assassins' unwitting ally, because Florence's financial power waned: the Monk detested both commerce and making money, the two things which had made the city great. And still the Day of Judgement did not come. Instead, a liberal Franciscan friar challenged the Monk to an ordeal by fire. The Monk refused to accept, and his authority took another knock. By the beginning of May 1497, many of the city's young men marched in protest, and the protest became a riot. After that, taverns started to reopen, people went back to singing and dancing and gambling and whoring – enjoying themselves, in fact. And businesses and banks reopened as, slowly at first, exiles returned to the city quarters now liberated from the Monk's regime. It didn't happen overnight, but finally, a year almost to the day after the riot, for the man clung doggedly to power, the moment of Savonarola's fall seemed imminent.

'You've done well, Ezio,' Paola told him, as they waited with La Volpe and Machiavelli before the gates of the San Marco complex, together with a large, expectant and unruly crowd gathered from the free districts.

'Thank you. But what happens now?'

'Watch,' said Machiavelli.

With a loud crash a door opened above their heads and a lean figure swathed in black appeared on a balcony. The Monk glowered at the assembled populace. 'Silence!' he commanded. 'I demand silence!'

Awed despite themselves, the crowd quietened.

'Why are you here?' demanded Savonarola. 'Why do you disturb me? You should be cleansing your homes!'

But the crowd roared its disapproval. 'Of what?' one man yelled. 'You've already taken everything!'

'I have held my hand!' Savonarola shouted back. 'But now you will do as I command! You will *submit*!'

And from his robes he produced the Apple and raised it high. Ezio saw that the hand which held it lacked a finger. Instantly, the Apple started to glow, and the crowd fell back, gasping. But Machiavelli, remaining calm, steadied himself and unhesitatingly threw a knife which pierced the Monk's forearm. With a cry of pain and rage, Savonarola let go of the Apple, which fell from the balcony into the throng below.

'*Nooooo!*' he screamed. But all of a sudden he seemed diminished, his demeanour both embarrassing and pathetic. That was enough for the mob. It rallied, and stormed the gates of San Marco.

'Quick, Ezio,' said La Volpe. 'Find the Apple. It can't be far away.'

Ezio could see it, rolling unheeded between the feet of the crowd. He dived in among them, getting badly knocked about, but at last it was within his grasp. Quickly he transferred it to the safety of his belt-pouch. The gates of San Marco were open now – probably some of the brethren within considered that discretion was the better part of valour and wanted to save their church and monastery as well as their own skins by bowing to the inevitable. There were not a few among them too who had had enough of the Monk's tiresome despotism. The crowd surged through the gates, to re-emerge, some minutes later, bearing Savonarola, kicking and screaming, on their shoulders.

'Take him to the Palazzo della Signoria,' commanded Machiavelli. 'Let him be tried there!'

'Idiots! Blasphemers!' yelled Savonarola. 'God bears witness to this sacrilege! How dare you handle His prophet in this way!' He was partly drowned out by the angry shouts of the crowd, but he was as livid as he was frightened, and he kept it up – for the Monk knew (not that he thought in quite these terms) that this was his last roll of the dice. 'Heretics! You'll all burn in hell for this! *Do you hear me? Burn!*'

Ezio and his fellow Assassins followed as the mob bore the Monk away, still crying out his mixture of pleas and threats: 'The sword of God will fall upon the Earth swiftly and suddenly. Release me, for only I can save you from His wrath! My children, heed me before it is too late! There is but one true salvation, and you forsake the path to it for mere material gain! If you do not bow again to me, all Florence shall know the anger of the Lord – and this city will fall like Sodom and Gomorrah, for He will know the depth of your betrayal. *Aiutami, Dio!* I am brought down by ten thousand Judases!'

Ezio was close enough to hear one of the citizens carrying the Monk say, 'Oh, enough of your lies. You've been pouring out nothing but misery and hatred since you first walked among us!'

'God may be in your head, Monk,' said another, 'but he is far from your heart.'

They were approached the Piazza della Signoria now, and others in the crowd took up the triumphant cry.

'We have suffered enough! We shall be free people once more!'

'Soon, the light of life will return to our city!'

'We must punish the traitor! *He* is the true heretic! He twisted the Word of God to suit himself!' a woman shouted.

'The yoke of religious tyranny is broken at last,' another exclaimed. 'Savonarola will at last be punished.'

'The truth illuminates us and fear has fled!' yelled a third. 'Your words hold sway here no more, Monk!'

'You claimed to be His prophet, but your words were dark and cruel. You called us puppets of the devil – I think, perhaps, the true puppet was *you*!'

Ezio and his friends had no need to intercede further – the machinery they had set in motion would do the rest of their work for them. The leaders of the city, as eager to save their own skins as to claw back power for themselves, streamed out of the Signoria to show their support. A stage was erected and on it a huge stack of kindling and wood was raised around three stakes, while Savonarola and his two most ardent lieutenants were dragged into the Signoria for a brief and savage trial.

As he had shown no mercy, no mercy would be shown to him. Soon they reappeared in shackles, were led to the stakes, and bound to them.

'Oh Lord my God, pity me,' Savonarola was heard to plead. 'Deliver me from evil's embrace! Surrounded as I am by sin, I cry out to you for salvation!'

'*You* wanted to burn *me*,' a man jeered. 'Now the tables are turned!'

The executioners put torches into the wood around the stakes. Ezio watched, his mind on his kinsmen who had met their ends so many years ago at this selfsame place.

'*Infelix ego*,' prayed Savonarola in a loud voice filled with pain as the fire began to take. '*Omnium auxilio destitutus* . . . I have broken the laws of heaven and earth. Which way can I turn? Whom can I run to? Who will take pity on me? I dare not look up to Heaven as I have sinned grievously against it. I can find no refuge on Earth as I have been a scandal to it also . . .'

Ezio approached, getting as close as he could. Despite the grief he has occasioned me, no man, even this one, deserves to die in such pain, he thought. He extracted his loaded *pistola* from his satchel and attached it to his right-arm mechanism. At that moment, Savonarola noticed him and stared, half in fear and half in hope.

'It's you,' he said, raising his voice above the roar of the fire, but in essence the two communicated by an interconnection of their minds. 'I knew this day would come. Brother, please show me the pity I did not show you. I left *you* to the mercy of wolves and dogs.'

Ezio raised his arm. 'Fare well, *padre*,' he said, and fired. In the pandemonium around the blaze his movement and the noise the gun made went unnoticed. Savonarola's head sank on to his chest. 'Go now in peace, that you may be judged by your God,' said Ezio quietly. '*Requiescat in pace*.' He glanced at the two lieutenant monks, Domenico and Silvestro, but they were already dead, their burst guts spewed out on the hissing fire. The stench of burnt meat was heavy in everyone's nostrils. The crowd was beginning to calm down. Soon, there was little noise other than the crackling of the flames as they finished their work.

Ezio stepped away from the pyres. Standing at a short distance, he saw Machiavelli, Paola and La Volpe watching him. Machiavelli caught his eye and made a small gesture of encouragement. Ezio knew what he had to do. He mounted the stage at the far end from the bonfires and all eyes turned to him.

'Citizens of Florence!' he said in a clarion voice. 'Twenty-two years ago, I stood where I stand now, and watched my loved ones die, betrayed by those I had counted friends. Vengeance clouded my mind. It would have consumed me, had it not been for the wisdom of a few strangers, who taught me to look beyond my instincts. They never preached answers, but guided me to learn from myself.' Ezio saw that his fellow Assassins had now been joined by Uncle Mario, who smiled and raised a hand in salute. 'My friends,' he continued, 'we don't need anyone to tell us what to do. Not Savonarola, not the Pazzi, not even the Medici. We are free to follow our own path.' He paused. 'There are those who would take that freedom from us, and too many of you – too many of us – alas – gladly give it. But we have it within our power to *choose* – to choose whatever we deem *true* – and it is the exercise of that power which makes us human. There is no book or teacher to give us the answers, to show us a path. So – choose your *own* way! Do not follow me, or anyone else!'

With an inward smile he noticed how disquieted some of the members of the Signoria were looking. Perhaps mankind would never change, but it didn't hurt to give it a nudge. He jumped down, pulled his hood over his head, and walked out of the square, down the street running along the north wall of the Signoria which he had memorably walked down twice before, and vanished from sight.

And there then began for Ezio the last long hard quest of his life before the final confrontation he knew was inevitable. With Machiavelli at his side, he organized his fellows of the Order of the Assassins from Florence and Venice to roam throughout the Italian peninsula, travelling far and wide, armed with copies of Girolamo's map, painstakingly gathering the remaining missing pages of the Great Codex; scouring the provinces of Piedmont, of Trent, of Liguria, Umbria, Veneto, Friuli, Lombardy; of Emilia-Romagna, the Marche, Tuscany, Lazio, Abruzzo; of Molise, Apulia, Campania and Basilicata; and of dangerous Calabria. They spent perhaps too much time in Capri, and crossed the Tyrrhenian Sea to the land of kidnappers, Sardinia, and wicked, gangsterized Sicily. They visited kings and courted dukes, they battled those Templars they encountered on the same mission; but in the end they triumphed.

They reassembled at Monteriggioni. It had taken five long years, and Alexander VI, Rodrigo Borgia, old now, but still strong, remained Pope in Rome. The power of the Templars, though diminished, still posed a grave threat.

Much remained to be done.

28

One morning early in August 1503, Ezio, a man now of forty-four, his temples streaked with grey but his beard still dark chestnut, was bidden by his uncle to join him and the rest of the Company of Assassins there assembled, in his study at his castle of Monteriggioni. Paola, Machiavelli and La Volpe had been joined by Teodora, Antonio and Bartolomeo.

'It is time, Ezio,' said Mario solemnly. 'We hold the Apple and now all the missing Codex pages are collected here together. Let us now finish what you and my brother, your father, started so long ago . . . Perhaps we can at long last make sense of the prophecy buried within the Codex, and finally break the inexorable power of the Templars for ever.'

'Then, Uncle, we should begin by locating the Vault. The Codex pages you have reassembled should lead us to it.'

Mario swung back the bookcase to reveal the wall on which the Codex – now in its entirety – hung. Near it, on a pedestal, stood the Apple.

'This is how the pages relate to one another,' said Mario as they all took in the complex design. 'It appears to show a map of the world, but a world bigger than we know, with continents to the west and south which we are unaware of. Yet I am convinced they exist.'

'There are other elements,' said Machiavelli. 'Here, on the left, you can see the traced outline of what can only be a crozier, indeed what may be a Papal staff. On the right is clearly a depiction of the Apple. In the middle of the pages we can now see a dozen dots marked in a pattern whose significance is as yet mysterious.'

As he spoke, the Apple began to glow of its own accord, and finally flashed blindingly, illuminating the Codex pages and seeming to embrace them. Then it resumed its dull, neutral state.

'Why did it do that – at that precise moment?' asked Ezio, wishing Leonardo had been there to explain, or at least deduce. He was trying to remember what his friend had said about the singular properties of this curious machine, though Ezio didn't know what it was – it seemed to be as much living thing as mechanism. But some instinct told him to trust in it.

'Another mystery to unravel,' said La Volpe.

'How can this map be possible?' asked Paola. 'Undiscovered continents . . . !'

'Perhaps continents waiting to be rediscovered,' suggested Ezio, but his tone was one of awe.

'How can this be?' said Teodora.

Machiavelli replied, 'Perhaps the Vault holds the answer.'

'Can we see where it is located, now?' asked the ever-practical Antonio.

'Let's look . . .' said Ezio, examining the Codex. 'If we trace lines between these dots . . .' He did so. 'They converge, see! On a single location.' He stepped back. 'No! It cannot be! The Vault! It looks as if the Vault is in Rome!' He looked round the assembled company, and they read his next thought.

'It explains why Rodrigo was so anxious to become Pope,' said Mario. 'Eleven years he's ruled the Holy See, but he still lacks the means to crack its darkest secret, though he clearly must know he's at the spot itself.'

'Of course!' said Machiavelli. 'In a sense you have to admire him. He's not only managed to locate the Vault, but by becoming Pope he has control of the Staff!'

'The Staff?' said Teodora.

Mario spoke: 'The Codex always mentioned two "Pieces of Eden" – that is, two *keys* – it can mean nothing else. One –' he turned his eyes to it, '– is the Apple.'

'And the other is the Papal staff!' cried Ezio, in realization. '*The Papal staff is the second "Piece of Eden"!*'

'Precisely,' said Machiavelli.

'My God, you are right!' Uncle Mario barked. He suddenly became grave. 'For years, for decades, we have sought these answers.'

'And now we have them,' added Paola.

'But so, too, might the Spaniard,' put in Antonio. 'We don't know that there aren't copies of the Codex – we don't know that, even if his own collection is incomplete, he nevertheless has enough information to . . .' He broke off. 'And if he does, if he finds a way into the Vault . . .' He dropped his voice. 'Its contents will make the Apple seem a trifling thing.'

'Two keys,' Mario reminded them. 'The Vault needs two keys to open it.'

'But we can't take any risks,' said Ezio urgently. 'I must ride now to Rome and find the Vault!' No one disagreed. Ezio looked at each of their faces in turn. 'And what of the rest of you?'

Bartolomeo, who had hitherto remained silent, now spoke, with less than his usual bluffness: 'I'll do what I do best – cause some trouble in the Eternal City, some uproar – cause a diversion so you can get on undisturbed.'

'We'll all help make the way as clear as possible for you, friend,' said Machiavelli.

'Just let me know when you're ready, *nipote*, and we'll all be behind you,' said Mario. '*Tutti per uno e uno per tutti!*'

'*Grazie, amici,*' said Ezio. 'I know you'll be there when I need you. But let me carry the burden of this last quest – a lone fish can slip through a net that catches a shoal, and the Templars will be on their guard.'

They made their preparations fast, and soon after halfway through the month, Ezio, the precious Apple in his custody, arrived by boat on the Tiber at the wharfs near the Castel Sant'Angelo in Rome. He had taken every precaution, but by some devilry or the astuteness of Rodrigo's ubiquitous spies, his arrival did not pass unnoticed, and he was challenged by a squad of Borgia guards at the gates to the wharfs. He would have to fight his way to the Passetto di Borgo, the half-mile-long elevated passage that linked the Castel with the Vatican. Knowing that time was against them, now that Rodrigo must know of his arrival, Ezio decided that a quick, precise attack was his only option. He sprang like a lynx on to the mantle of an ox-drawn cart that was taking barrels from the docks, and skipping on to the higher-most barrel he leapt up to an overhanging gantry. The guards watched open-mouthed as the Assassin launched himself from the gantry – cloak billowing out behind him. Dagger drawn, he slew the Borgia sergeant atop his horse, and relieved him of his mount. The whole manoeuvre had unfolded in less time than it had taken for the remaining guards to draw their swords. Ezio, without looking back, rode off down the Passetto far faster than the Borgia uniforms could pursue him.

As he arrived at his destination, Ezio found that the gate through which he had to enter was too low and narrow for a horseman, so he dismounted and continued through it on foot, dispatching the two men who guarded it with a single deft movement of his blades. Despite his gathering years, Ezio had intensified his training, and was now at the peak of his powers – the pinnacle of his Order, the supreme Assassin.

Beyond the gate he found himself in a narrow court-yard, at the other side of which was yet another gate. It seemed to be unguarded, but as he approached the lever at its side which he assumed would open it, a cry went up from the ramparts above: '*Stop the intruder!*' Glancing behind him, he saw the gate through which he had entered slamming shut. He was caught in that cramped enclave!

He threw himself on the lever controlling the second gate as the archers ranging themselves above him prepared to fire, and just managed to dash through it as the arrows clattered to the ground behind him.

Now he was inside the Vatican. Moving catlike through its labyrinthine corridors, and melting into the shadows at the merest hint of now alerted guards passing, for he could not afford confrontation which might give his position away, he found himself at last in the vast cave of the Sistine Chapel.

Baccio Pontelli's masterpiece, built for the Assassins' old enemy Pope Sixtus IV and completed twenty years earlier, loomed around and above him, the many candles lit at this time just penetrating the gloom. Ezio could make out wall paintings by Ghirlandaio, Botticelli, Perugino and Rosselli, but the great vault of the ceiling had as yet to be decorated.

He had entered by a stained-glass window which was

undergoing repair, and he balanced on an interior embrasure overlooking the vast hall. Below him, Alexander VI, in full golden regalia, was conducting the Mass, reading from the Gospel of San Giovanni.

'*In principio erat Verbum, et Verbum erat apud Deum, et Deus erat Verbum. Hoc erat in pricipio apud Deum. Omnia per ipsum fact sunt, et sine ipso factum est nihil quid factum est* . . . In him was life; and the life was the light of men. And the light shineth in the darkness; and the darkness comprehendeth it not. There was a man sent from God, whose name was John. The same came for a witness, to bear witness of the Light, that all men through him might believe. He was not that Light, but was sent to bear witness of that Light. That was the true Light, which lighteth every man that cometh into the world. He was in the world, and the world was made by him, and the world knew him not. He came unto his own, and his own received him not. But as many as received him, to them gave he power to become the sons of God, even to them that believe on his name: Which were born, not of blood, nor of the will of the flesh, nor of the will of man, but of God. And the Word was made flesh, and dwelt among us (and we beheld his glory, the glory as of the only begotten of the Father,) full of grace and truth . . .'

Ezio watched until the service came to its conclusion and the congregation began filing out, leaving the Pope alone with his cardinals and attendant priests. Did the

Spaniard know Ezio was there? Did he plan some kind of confrontation? Ezio did not know, but he could see that here was a golden opportunity to rid the world of this most menacing Templar. Bracing himself, he threw himself outwards and downwards off the embrasure to land close to the Pope in a perfect crouch, springing up immediately, before the man or his attendants could have time to react or call out, and driving his spring-blade hard and deep into Alexander's swollen body. The Pope sank soundlessly to the ground at Ezio's feet and lay still.

Ezio stood over him, breathing hard. 'I thought . . . I thought I was beyond this. I thought I could rise above vengeance. But I can't. I'm just a man. I've waited too long, lost too much . . . and you are a canker in the world that should be cut out for everyone's good – *Requiescat in pace, sfortunato.*'

He turned to go, but then a peculiar thing happened. The Spaniard's hand curled round the Staff he had been holding. Immediately, it began to glow with a brilliant white light, and as it did so the whole great cavern of a chapel seem to whirl round and round. And the Spaniard's cold cobalt eyes snapped open.

'I'm not quite ready to rest in peace, you pitiful wretch,' said the Spaniard. There was a mighty flash of light and the attendant priests and cardinals, together with those members of the congregation who were still inside the chapel, collapsed, crying out in pain, as curious thin beams of translucent light, smoke-like in the way they curled, emerged from their bodies and travelled into the glowing Staff which the Pope, now standing, held in a grip of steel.

Ezio ran at him, but the Spaniard shouted, 'No you don't, Assassin!' and swung the Staff at him. It crackled in a strange way, like lightning, and Ezio felt himself thrown across the chapel, over the bodies of the moaning and writhing priests and people. Rodrigo Borgia rapped his Staff briskly on the floor by the altar and more smoke-like energy flowed into it – and him – from their hapless bodies.

Ezio picked himself up and confronted his archenemy once more.

'You are a demon!' cried Rodrigo. 'How is it that you can resist?' Then he lowered his eyes and saw that the pouch at Ezio's side, which still contained the Apple, was glowing brightly.

'I see!' said Rodrigo, his eyes glowing like coals. 'You have the Apple! How convenient! Give it to me *now*!'

'*Vai a farti fottere!*'

Rodrigo laughed. 'Such vulgarity! But always the fighter! Just like your father. Well, rejoice, my child, for you will see him again *soon*!'

He swung his Staff again and the crozier's hook smashed against the scar on the back of Ezio's left hand. A shock thrilled through Ezio's veins and he staggered back, but did not fall.

'You *will* give it me,' snarled Rodrigo, closing in.

Ezio thought fast. He knew what the Apple was capable of and he had to take a risk now or die in the attempt. 'As you wish,' he replied. He withdrew the Apple from his pouch and held it aloft. It flashed so powerfully that the entire lofty chapel seemed for a moment to be illuminated by bright sunlight, and when the gloom of the candlelight returned, Rodrigo saw eight Ezios ranged before him.

But he remained unruffled. 'It can make copies of you!' he said. 'How impressive. Hard to tell which is the real you, and which a chimera – but that'd be hard at the best of times, and if you think such a cheap conjuring trick is going to save you, think again!'

Rodrigo swung out at the clones, and each time he hit one, it vanished in a puff of smoke. The ghost-Ezios pranced and feinted, lunging at the now worried-looking Rodrigo, but they could do no harm to the Spaniard other than to distract him. Only the real Ezio was able to land any blows – but they were minor glances, such was the power of the Staff, that he was unable to get close enough to the vile Pope. But Ezio quickly realized that the fight was sapping Rodrigo's strength. By the time the seven ghosts were gone, the repulsive pontiff was tired and out of breath. Madness imparts an energy to the body that few other things can, but despite the powers the Staff imbued in him, Rodrigo was after all a fat old man of seventy-two, and suffering from syphilis. Ezio put the Apple back in its pouch.

Breathless after the fight with the phantoms, the Pope sank to his knees. Ezio, almost equally breathless because his phantoms had necessarily used his energy to disport themselves, stood over him. Looking up, Rodrigo clutched his Staff. 'You will not take this from me,' he said.

'It's all over, Rodrigo. Put the Staff down and I will grant you a swift and merciful death.'

'How generous,' sneered Rodgrio. 'I wonder if you'd give up in such a supine way if things were the other way round?'

Summoning his strength, the Pope rose abruptly to his feet, at the same time slamming the foot of his Staff against the ground. In the dimness beyond them, the priests and people groaned again and new energy whipped from the staff against Ezio, hitting him like a sledgehammer and sending him flying.

'How's that for starters?' said the Pope, with an evil grin. He walked over to where Ezio lay winded. Ezio started to take the Apple out again but too late, for Rodrigo crushed his hand with his boot and the Apple rolled away. The Borgia stooped to pick it up.

'At last!' he said, smiling. 'And now . . . to deal with you!'

He held the Apple up and it glowed banefully. Ezio seemed as if frozen, trapped, for he was unable to move. The Pope leaned over him in fury, but then his expression calmed, seeing his adversary completely in his power. From his robes he drew a short-sword, and, looking at his prostrate foe, stabbed him deliberately in the side, with a look of pity mingled with disdain.

But the pain of the wound seemed to weaken the power of the Apple. Ezio lay prone, but watched through a haze of pain as Rodrigo, thinking himself secure, turned and faced Botticelli's fresco of *The Temptation of Christ*. Standing close to it, he raised the Staff. Cosmic energy arced out of it to embrace the fresco, a part of which swivelled opened to reveal a secret door, through which Rodrigo passed after casting one last triumphant look back at his fallen enemy. Ezio watched helplessly as the door closed behind the Pope, and only had time to fix the location of the door before he passed out.

He came to, he knew not how much later, but the candles were burnt low and the priests and people had vanished. He found that although he was lying in a pool of his own blood, the wound Rodrigo had delivered had cut into his side and touched no fatal organ. He got up shakily, leaning against a wall for support and breathing deeply and regularly until his head cleared. He was able to staunch his wound with strips torn from his shirt. He prepared his Codex weapons – the double-blade on the left forearm, the poison-blade on the right – and approached the Botticelli fresco.

He remembered that the door was concealed in the figure, on the right-hand side, of a woman bearing a fardel of wood to the sacrifice. Stepping close, he examined the painting minutely until he had traced the barely visible outline. Then he looked carefully at the details of the painting both to the right and left of the woman. Near her feet was the figure of a child with an upraised right hand, and it was in the tips of the fingers of this hand that Ezio found the button that triggered the door. As it opened, he slipped through it, and wasn't surprised that it snapped shut behind him immediately. He would not think of retreating now in any case.

He found himself in what looked like a catacomb corridor, but, as he cautiously advanced, the rough walls and dirt floor gave way to smoothly dressed stone and a marble floor that would not have disgraced a palace. And the walls glowed with a pale, supernatural light.

He was weak from his wound but he forced himself onwards, fascinated, and more awed than scared, though he was still on his guard, for he knew the Borgia had passed this way.

At last the passageway opened into a large room. The walls were smooth as glass and glowed with the same blue iridescence he'd seen earlier, only here it was more intense. In the centre of the room was a pedestal, and on it rested, in holders clearly designed for them, the Apple and the Staff.

The rear wall of the room was punctuated with

hundreds of evenly spaced holes, and before it stood the Spaniard, desperately pushing and poking at the wall, oblivious of Ezio's arrival.

'Open, damn you, *open*!' he cried in frustration and rage.

Ezio came forward. 'It's over, Rodrigo,' he said. 'Give it up. It doesn't make sense any more.'

Rodrigo spun round to face him.

'No more tricks,' said Ezio, releasing his own daggers and throwing them down. 'No more ancient artefacts. No more weapons. Now . . . let's see what you're made of, *Vecchio*.'

A smile slowly suffused Rodrigo's debauched and broken face. 'All right – if that's how you want to play it.'

He shook off his heavy outer robe and stood in his tunic and hose. A fat, but compact and powerful body, over which little bolts of lightning raced – gained from the power of the Staff. And he stepped forward and landed the first blow – a vicious uppercut to Ezio's jaw that sent him reeling. 'Why couldn't your father leave well enough alone?' asked Rodrigo sorrowfully as he raised his boot to kick Ezio hard in the gut. 'He just had to keep pursuing it, though . . . And you're just like him. All you Assassins are like mosquitoes to be swatted. I wish to God that idiot Alberti had been able to hang you along with your kinsmen twenty-seven years ago.'

'The evil resides not with us but with *you*, the

Templars,' rejoined Ezio, spitting out a tooth. You thought the people – ordinary, decent folk – were yours to play with, to do with as you pleased.'

'But my dear fellow,' said Rodrigo, getting a body-blow in under Ezio's ribs, 'that is what they are there for. Scum to be ruled and used. Always were, always will be.'

'Stand off,' panted Ezio. 'This fight is immaterial. A more vital one awaits us. But tell me first, what do you even want with the Vault that lies beyond that wall? Don't you already have all the power you could possibly need?'

Rodrigo looked surprised. 'Don't you know what lies within? Hasn't the great and powerful Order of the Assassins figured it out?'

His torvid tone stopped Ezio in his tracks. 'What are you talking about?'

Rodrigo's eyes glittered. 'It's God! It's *God* who dwells within the Vault!'

Ezio was too astonished to reply immediately. He knew that he was dealing with a dangerous madman. 'Listen, do you really expect me to believe that *God* lives beneath the Vatican?'

'Well, isn't that a slightly more logical location than a kingdom on a cloud? – Surrounded by singing angels and cherubim? All that makes for a lovely image, but the *truth* is far more interesting.'

'And what does God do down here?'

'He waits to be set free.'

Ezio took a breath. 'Let's say I believe you – what do you think He'll do if you manage to open that door?'

Rodrigo smiled. 'I don't care. It certainly isn't His approval I'm after – just His power!'

'And do you think He'll give it up?'

'Whatever lies behind that wall won't be able to resist the combined strength of the Staff and the Apple.' Rodrigo paused. 'They were made for felling gods – whatever religion they belong to.'

'But the Lord our God is meant to be all-knowing. All-powerful. Do you really think a couple of ancient relics can harm him?'

Rodrigo gave a superior smile. 'You know nothing, boy. You take your image of the Creator from an old book – a book, mark you, written by *men*.'

'But you are the Pope! How can you dismiss Christianity's central text?'

Rodrigo laughed. 'Are you really so naïve? I became Pope because the position gave me *access*. It gave me *power*! Do you think I believed a single goddamned word of that ridiculous Book? It's all lies and superstition. Just like every other religious tract that's been written since people learned how to put pen to paper!'

'There are those who would kill you for saying that.'

'Perhaps. But the thought wouldn't disturb my sleep.' He paused. 'Ezio, we Templars *understand* humanity, and that is why we hold it in such contempt!'

Ezio was speechless, but he continued to listen to the Pope's ranting.

'When my work here is finished,' Rodrigo went on, 'I think my first order of business will be dismantling the Church, so that men and women may finally be forced to assume responsibility for their actions, and at last be properly *judged*!' His face became beatific. 'It will be a thing of beauty, the new Templar world – governed by Reason and Order . . .'

'How can you speak of reason and order,' interrupted Ezio, 'when your entire life has been governed by violence and immorality?'

'Oh, I know I am an imperfect being, Ezio,' simpered the Pope. 'And I do not pretend otherwise. But, you see, there is no *prize* awarded for morality. You take what you can get and hold on tight to it – by any means necessary. After all,' he spread his hands, 'you only live once!'

'If everyone lived by your Code,' said Ezio, aghast, 'the entire world would be consumed by madness.'

'Exactly! And as if it hadn't been already!' Rodrigo jabbed a finger at him. 'Did you sleep through your history lessons? Only a few hundred years ago or so our ancestors lived in muck and mire, consumed with ignorance and religious fervour – jumping at shadows, afraid of everything.'

'But we have long since emerged from that and become both wiser and stronger.'

Rodrigo laughed again. 'What a pleasant dream you have! But look around you. You have lived the reality yourself. The bloodshed. The violence. The gulf between the rich and the poor – and that is only growing wider.' He fixed his eyes on Ezio's. 'There will *never* be parity. I've made my peace with that. You should, too.'

'Never! The Assassins will always fight for the betterment of humanity. It may ultimately be unattainable, a Utopia, a heaven on earth, but with every day that the fight for it continues, we move forwards out of the swamp.'

Rodrigo sighed. '*Sancta simplicitas!* You'll forgive me if I've grown tired of waiting for humanity to wake up. I am old, I've seen a lot, and now I've only so many years to live.' A thought struck him and he cackled evilly. 'Though who knows? Perhaps the Vault will change that, eh?'

But suddenly the Apple began to glow, brighter and brighter, until its light filled the room, blinding them. The Pope fell to his knees. Shielding his eyes, Ezio saw that the image of the map from the Codex was being projected on the wall which was dotted with holes. He stepped forward and grasped the Papal Staff.

'*No!*' cried Rodrigo, his claw-like hands futilely gripping the air. 'You can't! You *can't*! It is *my* destiny. *Mine! I* am the Prophet!'

In a terrifying moment of clear truth, Ezio realized that his fellow Assassins, so long ago in Venice, had seen what he himself had rejected. The Prophet was indeed there, in that room, and about to fulfil *his* destiny. He looked at Rodrigo, almost in pity. 'You never were the Prophet,' he said. 'You poor, deluded soul.'

The Pope sank back, old and gross and pathetic. Then he spoke with resignation. 'The price of failure is death. Give me at least that dignity.'

Ezio looked at him and shook his head. 'No, old fool. Killing you won't bring my father back. Or Federico. Or Petruccio. Or any of the others who have died, either opposing you, or in your impotent service. And for myself, I am done with killing.' He gazed into the Pope's eyes, and they seemed milky now, and afraid, and ancient; no longer the glittering gimlets of his foe. 'Nothing is true,' said Ezio. 'Everything is permitted. It is time for you to find your own peace.'

He turned from Rodrigo and held the Staff up to the wall, pressing its tip into a sequence of the holes spread across it, as the projected map showed him.

And, as he did so, the outline of a great door appeared.

Which, as Ezio touched the final hole, opened.

It revealed a broad passageway, with glass walls, inset with ancient sculptures in stone, marble and bronze, and many chambers filled with sarcophagi, each marked with Runic letters, which Ezio found himself able to read – they were the names of the ancient gods of Rome, but they were all firmly sealed.

As he passed along the passageway, Ezio was struck

by the unfamiliarity of the architecture and the decoration, which seemed to be a strange mixture of the very ancient, of the style of his own time, and of shapes and forms he did not recognize, but which his instinct suggested might belong to a distant future. Along the walls there were carved reliefs of ancient events, seeming not only to show the evolution of Man, but the Force which guided it.

Many of the shapes depicted seemed human to Ezio, though in forms and clothing he could not recognize. And he saw other forms, and did not know if they were sculpted, or painted, or part of the ether through which he passed – a forest falling into the sea, apes, apples, croziers, men and women, a shroud, a sword, pyramids and colossi, ziggurats and juggernauts, ships that swam underwater, weird shining screens which seemed to convey all knowledge, all communication . . .

Ezio also recognized not only the Apple and the Staff, but also a great sword, and the Shroud of Christ, all carried by figures who were human in shape, but somehow not human. He discerned a depiction of the First Civilizations.

And at last, in the depths of the Vault, he encountered a huge granite sarcophagus. As Ezio approached it began to glow, a welcoming light. He touched its huge lid and it lifted with an audible hiss, though featherlight as if glued to his fingers, and slid back. From the stone tomb a wonderful yellow light shone – warm and nurturing as the sun. Ezio shielded his eyes with his hand.

Then, from the sarcophagus, rose a figure whose features Ezio could not make out, though he knew he was looking at a woman. She looked at Ezio with changing, fiery eyes, and a voice came from her too – a voice at first like the warbling of birds, which finally settled into his own language.

Ezio saw a helmet on her head. An owl on her shoulder. He bent his head.

'Greetings, Prophet,' said the goddess. 'I have been waiting for you for ten thousand thousand seasons.'

Ezio dared not look up.

'It is good that you have come,' the Vision continued. 'And you have the Apple by you. Let me see.'

Humbly, Ezio proffered it.

'Ah.' Her hand caressed the air over it but she did not touch it. It glowed and pulsated. Her eyes bore into him. 'We must speak.' She tilted her head, as if considering something, and Ezio thought he could see the trace of a smile on the iridescent face.

'Who are you?' he dared ask.

She sighed. 'Oh – many names . . . When I died, it was Minerva. Before that, Merva and Mera . . . and back again and again through time . . . Look!' She pointed to the row of sarcophagi which Ezio had passed. Now, as she pointed at them in turn, each glowed with the pale sheen of moonlight. 'And my family . . . Juno, who was before called Uni . . . Jupiter, who before was named Tinia . . .'

Ezio was transfixed. 'You are the ancient gods . . .'

There was a noise like glass breaking in the distance, or the sound a falling star might make – it was her laughter. 'No – not gods. We simply came . . . before. Even when we walked the world, your kind struggled to understand our existence. We were more . . . advanced in time . . . Your minds were not yet ready for us . . .' She paused. 'And perhaps they *still* are not . . . Maybe they never will be. But it is no matter.' Her voice hardened a fraction. 'But although you may not comprehend us, you must comprehend our warning . . .'

She drifted into silence. Into that silence, Ezio said, 'None of what you are saying makes sense to me.'

'My child, these words are not meant for you . . . They are meant for . . .' And she looked into the darkness beyond the Vault, a darkness unbounded by walls or time itself.

'What is it?' asked Ezio, humbled and frightened. 'What are you talking about? There's no one else here!'

Minerva bowed down to him, close to him, and he felt a mother's warmth embrace all his weariness, all his pain. 'I do not wish to speak with you but *through* you. You are the Prophet.' She raised her arms above her and the roof of the Vault became the Firmament. Minerva's glittering and insubstantial face bore an

expression of infinite sadness. 'You've played your part
. . . You anchor Him . . . But please be silent now . . .
that we may commune.' She looked sad. 'Listen!'

Ezio could see all the sky and the stars, and hear their
music. He could see the Earth spinning, as if he were
looking down from Space. He could make out continents, even, on them, a city or two.

'When we were still flesh, and our home still whole,
your kind betrayed us. We who made you. We who gave
you life!' She paused, and if a goddess can shed tears,
she shed them. A vision of war appeared, and savage
humans fought with handmade weapons against their
former masters.

'We were strong. But you were many. And both of
us craved war.'

A new image of the Earth appeared now, close by,
but still seen as from Space. Then it receded, becoming
smaller, and Ezio could see it now as just one of several
planets at the centre of whose orbits stood a great star
– the Sun.

'So busy were we with earthly concerns, we failed to
notice the heavens. And by the time we did . . .'

As Minerva spoke, Ezio saw the Sun flare into a vast
corona, shedding unbearable light, light which licked
the Earth.

'We gave you Eden. But we had between us created
war and death and turned Eden into hell. The world
burned until naught remained but ash. It should have

ended then and there. But we built you in our image. We built you *to survive!*'

Ezio watched as from the total devastation that seemed to have been wrought upon the Earth by the Sun, a single ash-covered arm thrust skyward from the debris. Great visions of a windswept plain swept across the sky, which was the Roof of the Vault. Across it marched people – broken, ephemeral, but brave.

'And we rebuilt.' Minerva continued. 'It took strength and sacrifice and compassion, but we rebuilt! And as the Earth slowly healed, as life returned to the world, as the green shoots thrust up out of the generous earth once more . . . We endeavoured to ensure that such a tragedy would never be repeated.'

Ezio looked at the sky again. A horizon. On it, temples and shapes, carvings in stone like writing, libraries full of scrolls, ships, cities, music and dancing – shapes and forms from ancient times and ancient civilizations he didn't know, but recognized as the work of his fellow beings . . .

'But now we are dying,' Minerva was saying. 'And Time will work against us . . . Truth will be turned into myth and legend. What we built will be misunderstood. But Ezio, let my words preserve the message and make a record of our loss.'

An image arose of the building of the Vault, and others like it.

Ezio watched, as if in a dream.

'But let my words also bring hope. You must find the other temples. Temples like this. Built by those who knew how to turn away from war. They worked to protect us, to save us from the Fire. If you can find them, if their work can be saved, then so, too, might this world.'

Now Ezio saw the Earth again. The skyline of the Roof of the Vault showed a city like a vast San Gimigmano, a city of the future, a city of towers crushed together which made a twilight of the streets below, a city on an island far away. And then all coalesced once more into a vision of the Sun.

'But you must be quick,' said Minerva. 'For time grows short. Guard against the Templar Cross – for there are many who will stand in your way.'

Ezio looked up. He could see the Sun, burning angrily, as if waiting. And then it seemed to explode, though within the explosion he thought he could discern the Templar Cross.

The vision before him was fading. Minerva and Ezio were left all alone, and the voice of the goddess now seemed to be disappearing down a tunnel of infinite length. 'It is done . . . My people must now leave this world . . . All of us . . . But the Message is delivered . . . It is up to you now. We can do no more.'

And then there was darkness and silence, and the Vault became a dark underground room again, with nothing in it at all.

*

Ezio turned back. He re-entered the antechamber and saw Rodrigo lying on a bench, a dribble of green bile oozing from a corner of his mouth.

'I am dying,' said Rodrigo. 'I have taken the poison I kept back for the moment of my defeat, for there is no world for me to live in now. But tell me – tell me before I leave this place of wrath and tears for ever – tell me, in the Vault – what did you see? Whom did you meet?'

Ezio looked at him. 'Nothing. Nobody,' he said.

He walked back out, through the Sistine Chapel and into the sunlight, to find his friends waiting there for him.

There was a new world to be made.

List of Characters

Giovanni Auditore: father
Maria Auditore: mother
Ezio Auditore: second son of Giovanni
Federico Auditore: eldest son of Giovanni
Petruccio Auditore: youngest son of Giovanni
Claudia Auditore: daughter of Giovanni
Mario Auditore: brother of Giovanni
Annetta: Auditore family housekeeper
Paola: sister of Annetta
Orazio: servant of Mario Auditore
Duccio Dovizi: ex-boyfriend of Claudia
Giulio: secretary to Giovanni Auditore
Dottore Ceresa: family doctor
Gambalto: sergeant in command of Mario Auditore's guards

Cristina Calfucci: girlfriend of the young Ezio
Antonio Calfucci: father of Cristina
Manfredo d'Arzenta: son of wealthy family, later married
    to Cristina
Gianetta: friend of Cristina
Sandeo: Cristina's father's clerk

Jacopo de' Pazzi: member of Pazzi family, fifteenth-century Florentine bankers

Francesco de' Pazzi: nephew of Jacopo

Vieri de' Pazzi: son of Francesco

Stefano da Bagnone: priest, secretary to Jacopo

Father Giocondo: priest in San Gimignano

Terzago, Tebaldo, Capitano Roberto, Zohane and Bernardo: soldiers and guards in the service of the Pazzi family

Galeazzo Maria Sforza (Galeazzo): Duke of Milan, 1444–76

Caterina Sforza: daughter of Galeazzo, 1463–1509

Girolamo Riario, Duke of Forlì: Caterina's husband, 1443–88

Bianca Riario: daughter of Caterina, 1478–1522

Ottaviano Riario: son of Caterina, 1479–1523

Cesare Riario: son of Caterina, 1480–1540

Giovanni Riario: son of Caterina, 1484–96

Galeazzo Riario: son of Caterina, 1485–1557

Nezetta: wet-nurse to Caterina's baby

Lodovico Sforza: Duke of Milan, brother of Galeazzo, 1452–1508

Ascanio Sforza: cardinal, brother of Galeazzo and Lodovico, 1455–1505

Lorenzo de' Medici, 'Lorenzo the Magnificent': Italian statesman, 1449–92

Clarice Orsini: wife of Lorenzo de' Medici, 1453–87

Lucrezia de' Medici: daughter of Lorenzo de' Medici,
1470–1553

Piero de' Medici: son of Lorenzo de' Medici, 1471–1503

Maddalena de' Medici: daughter of Lorenzo de' Medici,
1473–1528

Giuliano de' Medici: brother of Lorenzo, 1453–78

Fioretta Gorini: mistress of Giuliano de' Medici

Boetio: servant of Lorenzo de' Medici

Giovanni Lampugnani: conspirator in murder of
Galeazzo, d. 1476

Carlo Visconti: conspirator in murder of Galeazzo, d. 1477

Gerolamo Olgiati: conspirator in murder of Galeazzo,
1453–77

Bernardo Baroncelli: conspirator in murder of Giuliano
de' Medici

Uberto Alberti: Gonfaloniere of Florence (chief official
of the Council of Magistrates)

Rodrigo Borgia: Spaniard, cardinal, later Pope Alexander
VI, 1451–1503

Antonio Maffei: priest, conspirator in murder of Giuliano
de' Medici

Raffaele Riario: Pazzi sympathizer, nephew of the Pope,
1451–1521

Francesco Salviati Riario, Archbishop of Pisa: involved in
Pazzi conspiracy

Lodovico and Checco Orsi: Orsi brothers, mercenaries

Niccolò di Bernardo dei Machiavelli: philosopher and
    writer, 1469–1527
Leonardo da Vinci: artist, scientist, sculptor, etc., 1452–1519
Agniolo and Innocento: assistants to Leonardo da Vinci
Girolamo Savonarola: Dominican priest and political
    leader, 1452–98
Marsilio Ficino: philosopher, 1433–99
Giovanni Pico della Mirandola: philosopher, 1463–94
Poliziano (Angelo Ambrogini): scholar and poet, tutor to
    de' Medici children, 1454–94
Botticelli (Alessandro di Moriano Filipepi): artist,
    1445–1510
Jacopo Saltarelli: artist's model, b. 1459
Fra Domenico da Pescia and Fra Silvestro: monks,
    associates of Savonarola
Brother Girolamo: monk at the abbey of Monteciano,
    cousin of Savonarola

Giovanni Mocenigo: Doge of Venice, 1409–85
Carlo Grimaldi: member of Mocenigo's entourage
Conte de Pexaro: patron of Leonardo in Venice
Nero: official assistant to Conte de Pexaro
Emilio Barbarigo: Venetian merchant, allied to Rodrigo
    Borgia
Silvio Barbarigo ('Il Rosso'): state inquisitor, cousin of
    Emilio Barbarigo
Marco Barbarigo: cousin of Silvio and Emilio
Agostino Barbarigo: younger brother of Marco

Dante Moro: Marco's bodyguard
Carlo Grimaldi: in Doge's entourage
Bartolomeo d'Alviano: mercenary

Gilberto the Fox, la Volpe: member of the Assassins
Corradin: the Fox's assistant
Antonio de Magianis: head of thieves' guild in Venice
Ugo: member of thieves' guild
Rosa: member of thieves' guild
Paganino: member of thieves' guild
Michiel: member of thieves' guild
Bianca: member of thieves' guild
Sister Teodora: brothel owner

Glossary of Italian and Latin terms

abominato filth/wretch
accademico academic
accompagnatrice companions, chaperones
addio goodbye
Ahimè Alas
Aiutami, Dio! Help me, God
Aiuto! Help!
Al ladro! Stop, thief!
Altezza Highness
amici intimi close friends
amico mio my friend
amministratore administrator, manager
amore mio my darling
anche also, too
anch'io me too, same here
Aprite la porta! Open the gate!
Arcivescovo Archbishop
aristocrazia aristocracy
artiglierie artillery
Assassino Assassin

bacino basin (in a dock)
bambina baby
Basta! Enough!
bastardo, bastardi bastard/s
bello handsome
ben fatto well done
benvenuti welcome
Birbante! rascal, rogue
biscotti biscuits
bistecca beefsteak
bordello brothel
buona fortuna good luck
buona sera good evening
buon' giorno good morning, good day
buon viaggio safe journey

caffè coffee
calma calm down
campo area
Cane rognoso! Mangy cur!
capitano captain
Capito? Understand?
cappa cloak, cowl
carcassa carcase
Carnevale Carnival
caro, cara, carissima dearest, darling
casa, dolce casa home, sweet home
castello castle

cazzo! prick/shit
Che vista penosa! What a painful sight!
chiudi il becco shut up
ciao goodbye
ciccione fatty
cimice bedbug
codardo coward
coglioni balls
commandante commander, captain
Commendatore Commander
compagno comrade
condottieri hired soldiers, mercenaries
coniglio! coward, chicken
Cordelie
corno ducale traditional hat worn by the Doges of
    Venice
così like this
Creapa, traditore! Die, traitor!
crepi il lupo may the wolf die
Curia the Roman law courts

diavolo devil
Distinti saluti sincerely, faithfully (in a letter)
dottore doctor
ducati ducats
duce leader
duchessa duchess
Duomo dome (meaning the cathedral in Florence)

Evviva! hurrah

fidanzato fiance
figa vagina (slang)
Figlio d'un cane! Son of a bitch!
finanziatore financier, backer
fiorini florins
fottiti! fuck you!
Fra' Brother
fratelli brothers
fratellino little brother
funzionario da accoglienza reception, welcoming party

grappa Italian alcoholic drink
grassone bastardo fat bastard
Grazie a Dio Thank God
Grazie, amici Thank you, friends
grullo silly

hospitarius guest-master of monastery

idiota idiot
il Magnifico the Magnificent
il Spagnolo the Spaniard
in bocca al lupo! good luck!
Infame Awful, shocking
Infelix ego, omnium auxilio destitutus Unhappy I, bereft of all
    comfort

in perfetto ordine shipshape
inquisitore inquisitor
intensi certainly/understood

liberta liberty
'*Libertà! Libertà! Popolo e libertà!*' Liberty! Liberty! The
    People and Liberty
Luridi branco di cani bastardi! filthy bunch of
    son-of-bitches
luridi codardi filthy cowards
lurido porco filthy pig

Ma certo! But of course
Ma che? But what's this?
Ma che cazzo? What the fuck was that?
madre mother
Maestro Master
maledetto cursed
marmocchio brat
medico doctor
merda! shit!
Messer Sir
mia colomba my dove
mi dispiace veramente I'm truly sorry
miserabili pezzi di merda miserable piece of shit
molto onorato very honoured

nipote nephew
no preoccuparvi not to worry, don't worry
novizia novice nun

ora di pranzo lunchtime
oste innkeeper

palazzo palace
passeggiata evening stroll
Perdonate, Messere Sorry, sir
piccina little one
piccola small, little
pistola pistol
popolo the people
porco pig
porco demonio! spawn of the devil
principessa princess
promesso promise
puttana whore

Rallegramenti! Congratulations!
Requiescat in pace Rest in peace
ribollita Tuscan soup

salute! bless you!
Sancta simplicitas! What Blessed Simplicity
Sangue di Giuda! Christ on a bicycle
scusi excuse me

se lo tu dici if you say so
Ser Sir
sfortunato unlucky
sì yes
signore Mr, gentleman
Signoria governing authority
signorina miss
signorine plural of signorina
soldo penny
Sono grato del tuo aiuto I'm grateful for your help
sorellina little sister
Spero di sì I hope so
Stai bene All right
Stolti! Fools!
stronzo asshole, prick, etc.
su altezza your highness
subito suddenly

tagliagole cut-throat
tartaruga tortoise, slowcoach
terra ferma dry land
tesora, tesoro sweetheart, treasure
Ti arresto! I arrest you!
traditore traitor
Tutti per uno e uno per tutti! All for one and one for all!

ubriacone drunkard
uomo coraggioso brave man

va bene all right
vecchio old

zio uncle

Acknowledgements

Yves Guillemot

Serge Hascoet

Alexis Nolent

Richard Dansky

Olivier Henriot

Sébastien Puel

Patrice Desilets

Corey May

Jade Raymond

Cecile Russeil

Joshua Meyer

Marc Muraccini

The Ubisoft Legal Department

Chris Marcus

Darren Bowen

Amy Jenkins

Caroline Lamache